American Vineyard

A NOVEL

Vincent Lowry

This book is a work of fiction. Names, characters, places and incidents are products of the author's imagination or are used fictitiously. Any resemblance to actual events or locales or persons, living or dead, is entirely coincidental.

Book cover design and layout by Ellie Bockert Augsburger of Creative Digital Studios.
www.CreativeDigitalStudios.com

Cover design features (used per content license agreements):
Friends at Ranch Illustration: © Victorig/istock
Vine Leaves Corner: © by Zdenka/Adobe Stock

Editing services provided by Carl Augsburger of Creative Digital Studios.
www.CreativeDigitalStudios.com

First Printing, 2017

Sandhill Crane Publishing

ISBN: 978-0-692-84584-4

Five Star Reviews

For Vincent Lowry's Books!

★★★★★

(Goodreads.com)

#LucysLetter
The Children of the Greenhouse Age

★★★★★

"Well written. A lovely little story with a big message."
-Doreen Ashbrook

Surfing the Seconds

★★★★★

"I love the way Vincent Lowry writes, each word a picture, each line a memory waiting to be revisited. I have so many bookmarks and underlines in this Kindle edition that I found it hard to pick one line to share."
-Pamela Barrett, Author

Dreams Reign Supreme

★★★★★

"This was a fantastic short read. An excellent balance of short stories and poems."
-Jeanette Glazewski

Constellation Chronicles
The Lost Civilization of Aries

★★★★★

"Vincent Lowry has created a science fiction book that held my attention from the very start."
-Sandra Stiles, Author

For Conner
I love you, son

Let us not become weary in doing good, for at the proper time we will reap a harvest if we do not give up.
— Galatians 6:9

For in every adult there dwells the child that was, and in every child there lies the adult that will be.
— John Connolly

En tiempos de destrucción, crea algo.
— Maxine Hong Kingston

Prologue

It happened in Huckleberry, New Mexico, in May of 1982—the same year John Belushi died of a drug overdose, *ET* topped the box office, *Cheers* aired on TV, and Michael Jackson released the hit album *Thriller*. It had been a long and dry spring. I had spent most of the season out in the Vineyard with five of my closest friends: Tommy, Randy, Jason, Lucy, and Mikey. We were all thirteen at the time, and we were as tight as family. We knew that our friendship would last forever, that we would never grow apart or old, that time would always be on our side.

At least that's what we thought back then, before the lightning split the sky and flooded the desert mesa. An unexpected evil had been lurking at the edge of the horizon, waiting patiently for the perfect opportunity to strike, and when it finally hit it hammered a wedge between us that tested our unity. It was on that violent evening when one of my close friends left our little family.

It was the night of the murder.

Chapter 1

Black Bird

The blazing afternoon sun baked down on a brown, dead field. A crow flew in the scorching sky, and my eyes followed it as it turned and glided in the wind. I caught a whiff of the strong and bitter fertilizer odor behind me and felt the heated breezes of late August. The bird flapped its black wings, uttered a caw, and eventually landed on a barren branch atop a giant oak about fifty yards from where I stood with Tommy.

"It stopped!" Tommy said, and ran off after it.

"That's mine, I saw it first," I replied, chasing after him.

We ran with our pellet guns pointed to the broken ground, feeling the crunch of dry weeds and dirt clods under our feet. It had rained heavily two weeks before, but the unforgiving sun had dried the wet field, leaving it scarred with deep cracks that flowed like jagged canyons.

We stopped in front of the oak with a crescent scar at its base and looked up at its empty limbs. The crow was perched on a stick that jutted out like a bony finger. It moved its head from side to side, swaying gently in the light drafts, and cried another caw. A return call sounded not far from where we stood.

"Okay, you get it," Tommy said. "But hurry up!"

"Don't worry," I replied, pointing my gun at the black beauty.

I looked through the scope of my gun and saw the creature intensified in the lens. Every feature of the bird was now visible: its long sharp beak; its scaly gray feet; its tiny oily eyes; its wind-blown black feathers. I aligned the cross-hairs on the middle of the bird's chest, gripped my gun tightly, and pulled the trigger. A sharp shot rang out over the vacant field, and the bird screamed out. It dropped straight down, hitting several branches as it fell, then made a solid thud on the ground.

"You got it!" Tommy screamed.

We ran over and saw it struggling on the ground. Its black wings were now brown, flapping aimlessly in the dirt. One wing was partially broken, revealing a white hollow bone protruding from its feathers. Dark blood poured from its unnaturally parted beak. The bird's scaly feet clenched the dry earth, and its oily eyes stared at us in pain.

"Shit, it's not dead yet," I said.

"Hurry, shoot again! Put it out of its misery!"

The crow continued to slap the dirt, coughing and wheezing as it circled the scarred ground. I nervously grabbed my rifle and loaded another lead pellet. I cocked the gun quickly, but before I could count to ten, the creature stopped moving.

After a long pause, the words finally crept out of my mouth; my voice was shallow, empty. "Is it dead?"

Tommy poked at it with the greasy black barrel of his gun. The bird rolled eerily from side to side, as if it were sleeping.

"Yeah, it's dead."

I stared at it, catching another whiff of the thick fertilizer. "I didn't want it to die this way."

"Me neither," Tommy replied. "I think we should bury it."

With two digging sticks we made a shallow hole in the cracked earth, gently laid the dusty bird inside, and refilled it. We stood for a moment in silence, blankly looking at the disturbed ground. A vacant, lonely caw sounded in the distance.

"Come on...it's getting late," Tommy finally said, nudging my arm.

We left the unmarked grave and walked away with our heads down, our pellet rifles over our shoulders and our backs facing the indifferent sun. A tumbleweed blew across our barren path.

Tommy and I said nothing more about the black bird.

Not then, not ever.

***

JOURNAL DATE: 8/11/01

Tommy and I buried that crow twenty years ago. Twenty years—damn that's a long time when you write it down like that. It had been the summer before our eighth grade year at Roosevelt, and both Tommy and I were twelve going on thirteen.

I'm thirty-two now. Unlike my colleagues, I'm not afraid to admit my age. I guess I'm still pretty young by some standards and therefore have nothing to hide, but I feel like I've lived a century since the days I hunted with Tommy in the Vineyard. It's funny how time passes so quickly. It creeps up on you after you've woken out of countless sleeps and nips you in the butt just to tell you how many sunsets you've lived through. It's not a pleasant feeling. I'd rather have my teeth drilled than be reminded of my own mortality, but it's part of the way things work. *Older we grow*, as Yoda might say.

So I'm thirty-two, and I've started writing a journal about the year leading up to the murder. For me, that period in time began when I killed that crow. Although we still had two weeks of vacation left before school, that day marked the end of what seemed to be a very short summer. The events that unfolded during the next ten months changed the way I thought about Huckleberry and the world.

But I'll get to all of that in one minute. Right now I should talk a little about how I started writing this journal. It deserves some attention, I think.

I got the idea a week ago, the day I received my high school alumni letter.

***

The knife sliced just above the nail on my thumb and blood seeped out of the opening. "Shit," I yelled and ran to the sink directly behind me.

"What happened?" my wife asked.

I turned the round brass handle and placed my hand under the faucet. Cold water rinsed the blood down the sides of the white porcelain basin and swirled into the silver drain. The cut was small, but the pain was enormous. It felt as if every nerve was located in the tip of my thumb, exploding like miniature lightning bolts. The lipped wound parted under the water's pressure and revealed layers of white skin underneath. I shut the faucet off, grabbed a paper towel, and wrapped my thumb tightly. Susan, my wife, stood beside me, leaning in to get a better look.

"Are you okay?" she asked.

"Yeah," I said, clenching my teeth and swallowing the pain. "It's nothing."

"Let me get a bandage."

"You don't need to."

Susan ignored me and made for the bathroom, walking five paces faster than normal, and I made for the kitchen table, glancing at the dreaded knife and the tomatoes I had cut for the barbecue dinner. The tomatoes were for the six hamburgers grilling outside—one for me, Susan, Nick, and three of Nick's school friends. It was Nick's ninth birthday and he wanted a cheeseburger with extra tomatoes and mustard. Susan is usually the cook in the house, but since August is the sunniest month in San Diego, and since I hadn't cooked on my patio all summer, I'd gladly volunteered for the job. I loved messing with my rusty charcoal grill. It wasn't one of those fancy gas beasts with the extendable metal racks where you could place enough meat patties to feed an army. It was a simple relic from the 70s, a twenty-dollar special that I had picked up at a neighbor's garage sale. It had a single rack, a metal lid with a vent in the center, and a skinny three-legged stand. It was perfect for my limited cooking skills.

I sat at the kitchen table and stared at the smoke curl from three holes in the grill's lid. I heard the meat sizzling.

I then heard the front door open and the bustle of kids storm in. They were laughing about some joke, and Nick's high-pitched cackle stood out above the rest. My wife returned from the bathroom, a roll of white bandage tape in her hand, and sat in a chair beside me. The smell of sweet shampoo from her beautiful crimson hair filled my nose.

"Hey Mom, hey Dad!" Nick said, munching on a cherry licorice stick.

"Hey sport, who are the strangers that followed you in?" I asked, looking at Nick's friends. They were snacking on red sticks of their own.

"You know us, Mr. Blake," said James, the smallest of the kids. At 4'2", James was a good two inches behind the rest of the gang. His thick glasses magnified his bright green eyes.

"Hmmm..." I said and looked closely at them. "Let me see. That's Kevin and Henry and—" Another lightning bolt went off in my thumb. "Ouch!"

"Hold still," Susan insisted, tightly wrapping the tape.

"What happened?" Nick asked, his tongue bright red.

"Your father had a little accident," Susan replied. "What did I tell you about eating candy before dinner?"

"I know, Mom, but Kevin's dad gave 'em to us for my birthday."

Susan looked at the sticks with disdain, and then continued her work. "Well, I guess I can make an exception today, but dinner's almost ready. You and your friends go wash up."

"Okay. I brought the mail in, too."

Nick placed a stack of letters on the table and skipped away happily with Kevin and Henry trailing behind. James continued to stare at my thumb, his huge eyes filled with curiosity, his brown hair blowing from an outside breeze funneling through the wide-open kitchen door.

"Does it hurt, Mr. Blake?" James asked, chomping on his stick.

"Na, I've had worse," I said. "I once had my neck bitten by a tiger at the circus. It was so bad that they had to call an ambulance. The beast almost took my head clean off."

I made a line with my finger across my neck, and James stopped chewing. His eyes opened so wide that I thought they were going to engulf his face. I waited for a minute, then winked at him. He gave a thick, crimson smile and ran after his friends. Susan glanced at me with the same displeased look she had given Nick and the candy and pulled the tape tighter.

"Ouch!"

Nick and his friends had eaten everything on the table, including the strawberry cheesecake that read *Happy 9th*. Susan collected the remains of the torn wrapping paper and stuffed it in the trash with the discarded boxes from the presents. James, Kevin and Henry had gone with Nick into his room to play with his new toys—Power Rangers action figures, Nintendo videogames, and a magic set—and I remained at the kitchen table, opening the day's mail with my white, bandaged thumb. The sun had dipped below the Pacific and now lights from navy ships crept across the black water. The remaining embers in the open grill emitted a deep red glow, like lava inside a black crater. The sour smell of lemon dishwasher detergent had replaced the sweet scent of the barbecue.

Our house stood on a hill that overlooked three sandy volleyball courts on Ocean Beach. My wife and I had picked it out eight years ago, two years after moving to San Diego from Los Angeles. It was the third house that we had seen, and when we found out it was within our budget, we immediately called the real estate agent and told him to put in an offer. It was still expensive—finding cheap beachfront property in Southern California is like finding pennies in a murky pool—but it was well below what we had expected to pay. A low loan interest rate and a new position with a law firm that paid twice as much as the old firm helped me cement the deal for our dream house.

It *was* a dream house by all means—three large bedrooms, a two-car garage, an attic, an eight hundred square foot kitchen with an island stove and hood—but it was a dream from which I swore I'd awaken. I first felt it when Susan and I had moved in. Seeing the emptiness of the polished living room floors, smelling the fresh paint on the glossy walls, hearing the gentle tide of the ocean...it had felt too good to be true, like the brass ring that would be dangled in front of my nose and then taken away after I reached to grab it. I was able to grab it, sure enough, but even after eight years that feeling that I'd somehow lose it never went way. Sometimes I'd have nightmares, waking next to Susan completely drenched with sweat, thinking that what had happened to my parents would soon pay a visit to me. *It's another foolish dream*, Susan would calmly say in bed, telling me not to worry about it. I'd often agree and lie back down on my damp pillow. But in the back of my mind I could still see the remains of that vivid nightmare. I could still picture the jagged tire marks on the intersection and the fragments of broken glass shining like jewels on the black asphalt.

Still seated at the kitchen table, I heard the dishwasher click to a new cycle, producing a low humming noise. Not far from that, the giggling of

Nick and his friends echoed down the length of a long hallway. “Man,” I said, reading a headline.

“What?” my wife asked, cleaning the cutting board counter. She had carefully placed the deadly knife in the sink and out of harm’s way.

On top of the opened envelopes and the countless coupon solicitations on the table was the *St. Joseph Quarterly*. It was my high school alumni paper, and it came like clockwork every three months.

“It’s about Peter Sachs,” I said.

“Who’s that?”

“He was my ninth-grade history teacher.”

Susan placed the cutting board inside a cabinet, wiped her hands, and stared at me. “What about him?” she asked, furrowing her brow.

Peter Donald Sachs, or Mr. S as he was known by most of his students, hadn’t been just my history teacher; he had also been my neighbor. He had lived in a two-bedroom house with his wife and son, just blocks away from the adobe home in which I had grown up. I had known Mr. S years before I went to high school because of his son, Randy, who was a miniature version of his pop with flaming red hair, dark scattered freckles, and skinny legs that looked like stilts. During the weekends, I would spend the night at Randy’s house with a bunch of my friends and we would stay up late in the night talking to Mr. S about things we would never dare discuss in front our own parents. He'd crack open a beer, sit in front of a roaring fire, and reminisce for a good three hours about his days in Vietnam. His most famous story was how he'd saved the captain in his unit from getting his throat cut by two Vietnamese bush crawlers. It was a story he told a thousand times, and it was because of stories like that that he earned our undying gratitude and attention. He was one of the few adults that talked to us like real people instead of rotten kids who would amount to nothing.

We liked him because he understood us. He still remembered what it was like to be twelve.

"He died."

"Is that his picture?" my wife asked.

"Yes," I said, reading the statement beneath his faculty photograph.

In Memory of Peter Donald Sachs, 1943-2001

Peter Sachs passed away last week from heart failure. His dedication to teaching and commitment to student achievement will surely be missed.

"That's awful," Susan said. "Wait, wasn't his son a good friend of yours?"

"Yes...well, at least he used to be."

I looked at Susan and then glanced out the kitchen window, watching the red embers in the grill glow in the ocean breeze. The wind had picked up, and every so often a spark would soar out of the grill and disappear into the night like a firefly.

Behind me the dishwasher clicked again and changed cycles, mixing detergent with the water.

Susan was right; it was awful. Mr. S had died and the only way I had found out was through a damn alumni paper. Not a phone call, not a personalized email. I had gotten the news the same way all distant subscribers had, and I suddenly realized that the friends I had had so long ago, the friends that sat with me around Mr. S's crackling fireplace, telling jokes and listening to stories, were now faded memories. They had become old photographs, forgotten in some deep attic in my head and stored away with the years of my youth. What the hell had happened to them? Had they heard the news the same way I had? Did they think about those many afternoons we had spent out in the Vineyard?

Another spark flew out of the grill and died in the night.

Chapter 2

THE FORT

Jason shouted at Mikey, "Tu turno, estupido!" Mikey stared at his cards in frustration, trying to decide which ones to keep. Jason was directly across from him, glaring angrily at Mikey's Coke-bottle glasses. I was between Jason and Mikey, and Tommy was on the other side of me. We were playing poker on a round green table with a pile of pennies in the middle. Tommy raised the bubble gum cigarette clutched between his fingers and drew a deep hit.

"Hurry the hell up, Mikey!" Tommy said in a cloud of fake smoke.

"All right, all right," Mikey replied, licking his lips. "I'll take two."

Tommy dealt the cards and drew from his candy again. His blue eyes shot around the table, measuring the competition. Beads of sweat rolled from the edge of his blond buzz-cut and ran down his tan face. He was wearing an A-top undershirt, or a wife beater as we learned to call it, with green khaki shorts that were frayed at the knees. He looked at his cards and gave a thick grin.

"Chingada madre, I'm out," Jason said, and threw down his hand. The round, worn bill of his Michigan baseball cap was pulled close to his green eyes. He grabbed an apple from the table and bit into it with a mouth that had more metal than a car engine. The braces tore into the skin of the fruit at jagged angles. He chewed with his lips partly open—ever since the orthodontist had fixed him up he was never able to completely close his mouth.

"Me, too," I said, tossing my cards in and blowing the streaks of black hair from my eyes. I took a swig of my Coke and turned to a seven-inch black-and-white TV we had propped up on an old tire. *Gilligan's Island* was on. It was the episode where the Skipper saves Gilligan from the native headhunters. I had seen it a million times.

"You still in?" Tommy asked.

"Damn betcha," Mikey replied in another one of his annoying Clint Eastwood impressions. He did the voice well, but it was the hardass intimidation that he lacked. It's impossible to imagine a tough gun-slinging cowboy in a four-eyed, flabby twelve-year-old.

We lived in a circular neighborhood named Twin Heights. Nine cul-de-sacs and fifty houses covered the residential area. A three-acre park with a playground, a basketball quad, and a tennis court stood in the middle. The many adobe homes in Twin Heights housed police officers, accountants, teachers, doctors, business owners, and lawyers. It was a peaceful, quaint neighborhood with a spectacular view of the Hillerman Mountains on one side and the western volcanoes on the other. The volcanoes had been extinct for millions of years (the once grand lava peaks had been reduced to hilly stubs after centuries of rain and wind erosion), but the blazing sunsets erupted new life in the barren, bumpy foundations.

Our fort was in Tommy's backyard. The only reason we were able to have it there was because of Mr. and Mrs. Smith—Tommy's parents. Even though the Smiths had the smallest lot in the neighborhood, they didn't care if a bunch of boys built a twenty-foot wooden base in their backyard as long as we followed one simple rule: no digging in the garden. During the wintertime, Mrs. Smith's garden was as dead and barren as the surrounding New Mexican desert mesa, but when spring rolled around and the birds came out from the seasonal freeze, the area exploded into a vegetation madhouse. The change was remarkable. Rows of corn, peas, tomatoes, cucumbers, and other assorted dinner greens covered the fertile ground. Every inch of the garden was utilized, and it had the potential to feed multiple families if the situation called for it. It was Mrs. Smith's pride and joy, not to mention the best escape from her temperamental husband. She cared deeply for that patch of ground in her small backyard, and as long as we kept our space confined to the empty dirt area by the backyard fence, we were allowed to play and build what we wanted. We started construction on the fort in early June, smelling the sweet breeze of the ripening corn behind us, and finished two exhausting weeks later. We placed the fort three feet behind the garden and paid special attention not to lay one finger on Mrs. Smith's sacred soil.

Finding the materials to build the fort hadn't been an easy task. The walls were made out of scavenged boards and nails from Ricky Jay's junkyard about a mile and a half east of Tommy's house. Ricky Jay was a mean bastard. A neighborhood rumor held that he had once shot a limping dog in his front yard because it fell asleep on his doorstep. Whether or not that tale was true was a mystery, but we knew it was out of the question to simply ask Ricky if we could take the wood from his junk pile. After days of talking it out—drinking sodas and playing poker in Tommy's house with our pennies—we decided to take the materials at night.

The operation had been risky. We had to sneak out at midnight, long after our curfews, and walk up Lincoln road—a dark and dangerous stretch that was notorious for drunk driving accidents, especially on Saturday night when patrons at Bob's Long Bar would down one last beer for the road before heading home. In addition to the drunks, we also had to worry about getting caught by some late night neighbor. Most of them would be fast asleep by the time the clock hit twelve, but there was always a chance that someone like Mr. Roseman or Mr. Glendall would wake up and remember that he had forgotten to take out the trash. Any neighbor that found out about our little plan was certain to give our parents a call, and a call, needless to say, was never good.

So we took these risks and braved Lincoln road with giant potato sacks in our hands, an idea that Randy came up with after school, and cautiously avoided all headlights that turned in our direction. We only saw four cars, but that was enough to make our neck hairs stand on end.

The drive-bys were scary, but they paled in comparison to Ricky's dump yard. The moon cast an eerie glow on the mounds of abandoned junk, with broken doors and upturned tables sticking out like headstones on a hilly graveyard. The baying of ferocious dogs sounded in the distance. We entered slowly, smelling the thick odor of rotted furniture and moldy mattresses seep up from the greasy floor. I tried to keep my mind focused on the mission, but I kept eyeing the desolate junk hills, half expecting Ricky to run out from behind one with a double-barreled shotgun in one hand and a dead dog in the other. I think Mikey shared the same feelings, because he had tried to turn tail and run home. Jason's balled up fist convinced him to stay. "You're not going anywhere, amigo," Jason warned Mikey, his metal mouth reflecting the gray of the yard. "We're in this together, entiendo?"

We worked quickly, taking as many items for the fort as we could get our hands on. Our main objective was wood for our walls, but we had found a whole treasure of forgotten goodies that were sure to make excellent decorative items: a rearview mirror, a seventies-style lava lamp, two shiny hubcaps, and a lawn chair with padded arms. Tommy had found the best item—a seven-inch black-and-white TV that looked almost brand new. It had six Duracell batteries in the back. Tommy flipped the switch but it didn't turn on. He bagged it anyway.

We left the yard and dragged our bloated bags home without any trouble from Ricky, the vicious dogs, the drunk drivers, the waking neighbors, or the unsuspecting, sleeping parents. It had been our first mission for the fort, and we had completed it with grand success.

"I'll raise you two," Tommy said, pitching in two coins.

Mikey wrinkled his chubby face and glared at his cards. "I'll see your two and raise you two more, partner."

Mikey skidded his pennies in and Tommy joined him.

"Well?" Tommy asked, a bead of sweat running down the length of his reddish-brown neck. "Whatcha got?"

"Two aces!" Mikey said with an annoying smile.

A cocky twinkle appeared in the corner of Tommy's eyes. It was a look we had seen a million times while playing poker. It meant you were cooked, gone, defeated. Without saying one word you could read Tommy's face and predict who was going to end up with the spoils in the middle.

Mikey's vision was bad, but he would have to be blind not to see what was coming next. The smile faded from his round face, and his lips wrinkled in disgust.

"Let's see 'em," Mikey demanded.

"Full house!" Tommy said, and spread his hand on the table like a professional Vegas dealer.

We looked to verify the cards and sure enough, Tommy had it: two kings and three jacks.

"You're crap out of luck, loco!" Jason said and gave his patented asthma laugh. *Heee, heee, heee!* It wheezed out, sounding just like Ernie's chuckle from Sesame Street.

"There go your pennies, Mikey," I replied, laughing with Jason, clenching my skinny stomach.

"Sometimes you get screwed," Tommy said.

Mikey watched enviously as Tommy scooped the pennies with his arm. Mikey's own pile of copper Lincolns had diminished from thirty to five. He grabbed his remaining coins and stuffed them in his pocket.

"I'm done," Mikey snorted. He joined me at the tube.

Jason moved to the TV and turned the volume up three notches. Gilligan was about to escape from his headhunter cell.

The tire the TV was propped on belonged to an abandoned eighteen-wheeler. It was three feet tall and a foot and a half thick. Jason had found it while riding with his brother, Sam, to visit their mom in Santa Fe. Jason and Sam lived with their divorced father, Adam Sanchez, who was a successful executive for a large shipping company that had offices in thirty-eight states, including Alaska.

"Mikey, move your damned feet," Tommy said. Mikey's stocky legs were propped up on the back of a foldout chair in front of the tube. His ears were glued to the show and he didn't realize what Tommy had said until the foldout was yanked from under his heels.

"Hey!" Mikey said. "Are you feelin' lucky, punk?" Mikey put his hands on his imaginary pistols and made like a gunslinger. Fat Eastwood had returned.

"Go blow yourself," Tommy replied.

A camouflage tarp covered the ceiling of the fort. It was the only item we had paid for, and it had originally belonged to David Calousky, a forty-three-year-old doctor who had lived in a two-story adobe house directly across from Tommy. The tarp had been over his backyard patio; I saw it every time I walked to Tommy's house. It looked like it was straight out of a Vietnam War movie, and I enviously imagined it hanging over our own fort, covering us from the battlefields of our own dangerous jungle. One day I saw Doctor Calousky watering his grass with a hose, and I summoned the courage to ask him if we could have the tarp. He smiled, untied it from four wooden beams, and almost gave it over for free, but then decided that it would be better if we put in a little blood and sweat so we would appreciate it more. He told me to bring my friends. The very next day I rounded up the Gang, then went to his house and negotiated what we thought was a fair price. We all shook on it, feeling like important businessmen closing a multimillion-dollar deal for an international military operation. It took us three exhausting weeks of mowing lawns, trimming hedges, and washing dishes to earn the money, but it was worth every penny. He never asked what we were going to do with it and we never told him. The tarp was now *ours*.

Admiration for adults doesn't come cheap when you're twelve. I thought most of them were dorks. They seemed uptight and grouchy, and they were always willing to spoil your fun for the sake of safety and education. But I honestly admired Doctor Calousky. *We* admired him. The fact that he didn't ask us what our intentions were with the tarp was an example of his relaxed nature. It wasn't that he was a beer-drinking bum that didn't give a shit about a bunch of stupid kids. He just let us do our own thing. Two months after the sale, Doctor Calousky died of a stroke. Out of respect, I drew a small cross on the tarp and Tommy wrote *RIP Doc* in small black letters beneath it.

Jason tossed the brown apple core outside and picked at the chunks of trapped fruit in his braces. "Hey, I've got a new joke," Jason said, smiling wickedly at us. We stared back at him, grinning our own devious smiles. Jason was the undisputed king of telling good dirty jokes. Some were misses, but for the most part, on a scale from 1-5, Jason averaged about a 4.

"Spill it," Tommy said.

Jason rubbed his hands together as if he were getting ready for a grand meal, and turned his hat backwards. "So this blonde walks in this drug store, right. And she goes up to pharmacist behind the counter and screams, 'I want a condom!' The pharmacist puts his finger to his lips and tells her to quiet down, but the blonde doesn't understand him, you know. 'Hey, did ya hear me? I want a condom!' she says. The pharmacist frowns and repeats the gesture with his lips. This blonde just doesn't get it, though, and finally blurts out, 'I need a damn condom!' The other people in the store have now heard her and the pharmacist is pissed. 'We have other customers here! Watch your mouth!' he says. The blonde then thinks about it for a second and looks back at him. 'Yeah,' she says, 'I guess you're right. I'd better take two then."

I snickered and Tommy roared. Mikey looked like he had been hit in the head with a frying pan.

"I don't get it," Mikey said.

Jason's brow furrowed, and he stared at Mikey with impatient, squinted eyes. "Tu estupido. He says 'watch your mouth' and she thinks he means it's for sex."

Suddenly, a light clicked on and Mikey's lips stretched into a smile. "Oh...I see. Yeah, that's real funny, Jason. Hey, I've got one, too."

"Spare us," Tommy replied.

"No way, Mikey. I don't wanna hear it," I groaned.

"Come on, guys. Just listen. There were two farmers and one insurance salesman. They lived in this small town. I forget the name of it. Prairie Falls or Dairy Falls or somethin' like that. Anyway, one day one of the farmers came back from—"

Then, as Mikey was getting started on what was probably destined to be one terrible goose egg (a 0 on the 1-5 joke chart), Randy sprinted into the fort and saved us. He was doubled over and heaving heavily. His red hair was matted to his sweaty, freckled forehead, and his giant ears protruded out like satellite dishes.

"Guys, y'all ga-ga-got to-to," Randy stuttered in his southern accent.

"What?" Tommy asked. "What's wrong?"

We let Randy's lungs get a break for a second. He finally looked up, his blue eyes staring wildly. I had never seen him so afraid.

"There's been an accident," Randy said.

"Hold on, I'm in the middle of a—" Mikey said.

"Shut up, Mikey," Tommy blasted. "Where did you see it?"

"Over by the park," Randy replied. His breath was getting better but he was still halfway hunched over, looking like he was going to puke. Jason offered him a soda, but Randy pushed it away. "It's bad, Tommy. It's your brother."

In an instant, we had all forgotten about the untold joke...including Mikey.

Chapter 3

THE ACCIDENT

A violent thunderstorm rolled in from the western horizon. Lightning flashes exploded chaotically in the darkened sky, silhouetting the black clouds from the deep blue atmosphere. The sun peeked through the billowing darkness and filtered streaks of light across the Rio Grande and into the valley. A cool breeze set in, blowing the fresh scent of afternoon rain to the land.

We sprinted down Tommy's cul-de-sac, crossed Baxter road without looking for oncoming traffic, and cut through Mr. Glendall's front lawn. We stopped abruptly at the park's tennis courts, right next to a bushy willow tree. About fifty feet in front of us, at the edge of the park, a black Buick was turned on its side. The passenger door was completely caved in, facing the air and reflecting the sun in dented angles. The windshield was intact, but fragments of the passenger window were littered all around the vehicle in thin, shiny segments. I couldn't recognize the car at first, but after moving in a little closer, I discovered it was Mrs. Robins's.

A long scar in the grass stretched thirty feet beyond the Buick, right up to Daniel Smith's overturned Jeep. The front of the Jeep was smashed halfway up to the windshield and the roll bars were curved inside the cab from the weight of the car. The rear tires, facing toward the sky, spun aimlessly, and Dan stood beside it, his head buried in his hands.

An officer was scribbling in a yellow pad and taking notes from Mrs. Robins. He stood by her Buick, looking at the caved door and shaking his head.

I couldn't hear what Mrs. Robins was saying but I could understand her body language perfectly. She paced back and forth with one hand on her forehead and the other pointing from the Jeep to the Buick. She looked hysterical, and considering the damages that her car had sustained in less than two seconds, she had a good reason to be.

"Holy shit!" Mikey said. He pushed his glasses up, leaving a small V at the tip of his nose.

"Fuck me!" Jason added, and took a hit of his aspirator. A large whoosh sounded as he inhaled. He had left his Michigan cap at the poker table, but his black hair still took on the hat-like shape.

We stared in disbelief. Dan had turned sixteen two weeks ago and had just received his driver's license after taking a four-month course at Diggen's School of Driving. He'd barely passed the course with a C- average. I was at Tommy's house the day Dan showed up with his new laminated license clenched arrogantly between his teeth. Mrs. Smith snatched the card from his mouth, looked at it with astonishment and threw her arms around her baby boy and told him how proud she was. Mr. Smith, however, remained listless and had a wrinkled expression on his face, like someone had stuck a giant needle in his back. Mr. Smith hated celebrations. While Dan was thinking about all the places he could take his busty girlfriend, Julie Landers, to get inside her pants, Mr. Smith was busy calculating all of the gas he'd have to pay for and insurance money he'd have to shell out. For Mr. Smith, Dan's new right was a burden, not an accomplishment. When Mrs. Smith placed a call for a pizza for Dan, Mr. Smith stormed to the master bedroom, slammed the door, and skipped out on the day's celebration.

But that party had ended, and Dan's great day had passed. Dan was dead meat and we all knew it like we knew our own phone numbers and middle names. The green Jeep—the very one that was flipped upside down like a Tonka toy—belonged to none other than Mr. Smith himself. After major nagging from his wife, Mr. Smith had agreed to loan Dan the car for school and football practice as long as Dan promised that none of his friends would ever drive it. “Remember, if I see a single scratch on my green beauty, I’ll have your head on a platter,” I overheard Mr. Smith tell Dan one day while I was playing with Tommy.

“I’m going over there,” Tommy said.

“Are you kidding?” I replied, grabbing his arm.

Tommy turned and looked at me with piercing green eyes. For a moment, I thought he was going to either punch me in the nose or slug me a solid one in the stomach. He looked scared, yet determined. “I’ve got to, Davy,” Tommy said.

Tommy broke free from my grip and ran toward his brother with the back of his A-top sticking to his sweaty skin. We watched him in disbelief.

“I’d let that bastard sink like the Titanic,” Jason said. “Via con Dios.” The words came out in a thick gurgle, like the apple was coming back up his throat.

“That makes two of us,” Randy said.

“Three,” Mikey said, slapping a mosquito away from his ear.

The accident was bad, needless to say, and as soon as Mr. Smith found out about his green beauty, it would be curtains for old Danny boy. Dan had it coming, and it was about time as far as we were all concerned. Calling Daniel Smith the worst bully on the face of the planet was an understatement. We were convinced he was Satan's personal helper. Every day, Dan and his evil sidekicks—Anthony Sanders, Ricky Adams, and Bruce Brown—terrorized us with atomic wedgies, toilet swirlies, Chinese water tortures, and Indian rug burns. The list of the abominable torments they had put us through went on for miles. It was part of the reason we'd created the fort—to hide from Danny and his twisted buddies.

We had nicknamed Dan's group The Jerks, but I always thought that it was a pansy name. I considered a jerk someone who pulled your leg from time to time, or someone who would kick you in the rear if you weren't looking. Dan's group was much worse than that; The A-holes or The Butt Heads was a more befitting name. Dan's group, in turn, called us The Huckleberry Freaks, but that name wasn't as catchy as the one we had given them, and thus, never really stuck. My friends and I were simply known as The Gang.

"That sucker is going to get it now," Jason said with delight. "It's the last of Captain Shit Head."

"Yeah, and maybe we'll get his Kiss tapes when he goes," Randy said.

"I've got dibs on his Converse sneakers!" Mikey said.

"I get his digital watch," Jason added.

The officer was done with Mrs. Robins and was now making his way to Dan. Tommy had reached his brother and was sitting beside him on a railroad tie—their faces pointed toward the Jeep. It was strange to see Tommy and Dan sitting together; they rarely shared more than two words with each other per day that weren't four letters long, and Tommy hated his brother more than we did. It was bad enough to run from the bully every day when school let out, but living with the bastard was an absolute horror that I could only begin to imagine. Sure, Mrs. Smith could help out from time to time, but when she went out for a grocery run or to drop off a few letters at the post office, it was just Tommy and Dan in the house. And that was never a good combination.

There was a part of me that shared the same twisted pleasure as Mikey, Jason, and Randy, looking at Dan's misfortune, but there was also another part that felt bad for feeling it. It was a soft side; a side that didn't want to think about Danny's face getting turned inside out because of a stupid car. I had never felt it before that day, but watching Tommy and Dan sitting together, staring at the spinning tires of the upside down destroyed machine, there was a wave of regret for hating him. In hate's place was pity.

"No more crap from the asshole," I said at length, shoving the feeling away. "I hope his dad lays him out."

The news had spread like wildfire around the neighborhood. Half the residents filled the streets surrounding the park. It looked like we were watching a concert, waiting anxiously for the fireworks to explode and the rock star to jump on stage with a painted face. Mrs. Neely and Mrs. Wallis, next-door neighbors that lived across the street from the park, stood directly behind us, gossiping animatedly about the scene.

"Isn't that Mr. Smith's boy out there?" Mrs. Neely asked.

"Sure is," Mrs. Wallis replied. "Both boys. Gaawd! Just look at Mr. Robins's car, too. It's ready for the dump. Ain't no fixin' that."

"Oh, that car's done for, let me guarantee you. They were probably drunk as skunks. Wouldn't surprise me, the way those boys act all the damned time...two little hoodlums. Something like this was bound to happen."

Mrs. Wallis wore a blue robe with green iron curlers in her hair. Covering her feet were fluffy, pink, bunny-eared slippers. Mrs. Neely was clad in stonewashed blue jeans, light green tennis shoes, and a white T-shirt that said, *Serve Your Community, Give Blood.*

"Drunk as skunks! I'd sue the pants off the Smith family if I was Mrs. Robins," Mrs. Neely said.

"Gaawd, that's the least I'd do," Mrs. Wallis replied.

A crack of thunder clapped overhead. I looked up at the fast approaching storm; the clouds looked evil, menacing. I could see black billows expanding in all directions, covering the lively blue sky like a spreading disease. The smell of rain was thick and choking.

"I wonder if anyone was hurt?" Mikey asked.

"Na, you'd see ambulances and fire trucks if there was," I said, not really knowing if this was true.

The officer was underneath Dan's car with the lower half of his body hanging out the driver's window. Dan was now obediently looking from three feet behind, squatting on his knees and gesturing information to the cop. Tommy was behind Dan, moving his head from us, to the truck, then to Mrs. Robins.

"What are they doing?" Mikey asked.

"Turnin' it off," Randy replied. "No sense having it run when it's belly up and all."

"I wonder where Mr. and Mrs. Smith are?" Jason asked, and as soon he mentioned it Mrs. Smith came out from a crowd of sightseers. She was without her husband (Dan would later thank God for small favors), and she was running as fast as she could. It was a mother's run. There was an instinctual quickness to it.

She embraced Dan, said something to him, and then turned to the officer.

"I hope those boys get a good whoopin' come tonight," Mrs. Neely said.

"Oh, I'd spank their hides bright red," Mrs. Wallis replied. "They wouldn't be able to walk for weeks without wearing two diapers for padding."

Mrs. Neely nodded earnestly. "I tell ya. Just two hoodlums."

Tommy tried to tell his mother something, but she wouldn't listen to him. She pointed toward their house, Tommy resisted, and she pointed at him. She must have said something threatening because Tommy ceased his protests and turned toward us.

"He's comin' back!" Randy said.

Tommy walked with his head down. His A-top was flapping like a sail against a strong, stormy breeze. A twisted streak of lightning shot behind him, and an earth-shaking boom sounded seconds after. Cold drops of rain tapped my head.

"Let's get inside," Mrs. Wallis said, and turned for her house. Mrs. Neely followed her, clenching the *Serve Your Community, Give Blood* shirt as she went.

The rain fell harder, quickly dispersing the park crowd. Some covered their heads with their shirts, some used their hands, and some just took the beating and ran like crazy. Mrs. Smith and Dan followed the officer to his patrol car and got inside. Mrs. Robins moved underneath a willow tree. It was my guess that she probably didn't want to sit in the same car as the person that had destroyed hers.

"What happened?" Randy asked.

Tommy's flattop had turned into a wet, spiky field. The tiny hairs clung together like magnetized strings, forming clustered locks. Dime sized raindrops hung from his blond eyelashes, and his cheeks were flushed light red.

"He was speeding," Tommy said, wiping the water from his face. "Real fast. He was coming home from football practice when he turned the corner and ran into Mrs. Robins. Didn't see her coming, he said. Just peeled around the turn and then wham, right into her Buick."

"Holy cow!" Mikey said. The rain had fogged his glasses.

"Didn't see her at all?" I asked.

"Nope," Tommy said. "Came right out of the blue. He said the next thing he remembered was lying upside-down, looking up at his feet. He said the seatbelt is what saved him."

It was now pouring. Our clothes were completely soaked, including the insides of our shoes, but we didn't notice. Tommy had captured us with his story, Dan's story, and we were all imagining what it would be like if we had driven that Jeep into the black Buick. Crushing the front hood like a tin can. Flipping over and over. Lying upside-down, looking up at our dangling feet.

"Can I stay with you guys tonight?" Tommy asked. He had to yell over the rain, and the words came from the back of his throat. I thought I had misunderstood him at first, but the frightened look in his blue eyes affirmed the question. It was bizarre to see him look that way—almost as strange as seeing him sitting with his brother on the railroad tie. Tommy had never *asked* to stay with any of us before. He had no need to; we always wanted him to sleep over. He was the first one we'd call to go see a dollar Saturday night movie at the Rio Theater, or the first one we'd bicycle down with to grab a Giant Frosty Bubble at Dave's Ice Cream Palace at the corner of Lincoln and 6th. We called him first because he was cool.

"What about your mom?" Jason asked. His hat head had disappeared and had been replaced by a shaggy mop.

"She wants me to go home, but there's no way I'm gonna go," Tommy replied.

No way I'd go either, I thought. Mr. Smith would see the damage, dish out the punishment on Dan, and if there were any leftovers, he'd finish it on Tommy. Mrs. Smith could save Tommy from his tormenting brother, but when it came to her moody husband, everything was fair game. Dan was peanuts compared to the old man. Dad was the worst bully; there was no escaping his wrath.

"Y'all can sleep over at my place," Randy said. Two small waterfalls were pouring off the base of his giant ears. The rain had blackened his red hair.

We nodded in unison. Instinctively, without saying another word, we sprinted down Baxter road, circled past five cul-de-sacs, cut across a grassy backyard, scaled a chain-link fence, and stopped underneath an enclosed wooden porch. We kicked away our muddy shoes, balancing on one foot at a time as we worked the socks, stripped off our drenched shirts, and walked into Randy's house.

The lightning continued to clap over Huckleberry.

Chapter 4

SUMMER FIRE

Mrs. Sachs almost fainted when she saw us walk into the house like a line of shirtless zombies.

She was frying chicken and sliced potatoes at the stove when we slid in through the kitchen door. A light haze hung over the room like a thin morning fog. The delicious aroma of the fried food filled our noses.

Jason shut the door with a bang that echoed through the house.

"Randy?" Mrs. Sachs said. The overhead stove hood blocked her vision, and we saw her move around to get a better look. She was carrying a metal bowl of crushed crackers and wearing an apron that said *Mama's Good Cookin'*.

"Dear Lord!" she said, dropping the metal bowl on the floor.

The metal struck the lime-green tile with a loud clang, spraying powdered crackers into the air. Randy's dog, Spot, barked from the corner of the kitchen, his tail wagging rapidly.

"What on earth happened to you boys?" she asked, ignoring the crackers and putting her hand on Randy's plastered hair. "For Pete's sake, you're soaking wet!"

"It was raining cats and dogs, ma'am, and we were running like wild outlaws, and—" Mikey started in another Clint Eastwood impression, but was abruptly cut off when Jason elbowed him in the stomach. Mikey's mouth was like an uncontrollable firecracker. He had a horrible sense of timing. If there were a funeral, Mikey would be the jackass in the back telling jokes.

"What were you doing outside?" Mrs. Sachs asked.

We looked at each other for a second, saying nothing. We realized that Mrs. Sachs wasn't going to buy a lie about playing a touch-tag football game in the rain. The look on her face demanded an explanation, and Randy had to be the one to give it to her.

Hesitatingly, Randy told his mom about Dan and Mrs. Robins and the two demolished cars. He told her about the officer and the neighbors that had crowded around the park. She glanced at us from time to time while he told the story, wondering if her son had lost his marbles; we nodded to show that he was indeed telling the truth.

After he finished, she went into the master bedroom and returned with five blue towels. We were worried that she might send us home. Tommy's face suggested that he was more worried than any of us.

"Randy, I want you and your friends to change in your room," she said, her lips pressed tightly together. "Give them some of your clothes. I don't care if it's pants or shorts or swimming trunks, just as long as it's dry. Goodness forbid if any of you get pneumonia."

We obediently agreed and followed Randy out the kitchen, passing Spot, who was now licking the crumbs off the floor. My stomach grumbled as I got a passing whiff of the greasy chicken. Putting on dry clothes was my second priority; my main desire was to sit down at the table and eat as many drumsticks and potato wedges as I could possibly cram into my mouth.

We marched into Randy's room. Before I shut the door, I could hear Mrs. Sachs scolding Spot to get away from the crumbs.

***

The Hawaiian trunks made me look like a dork. Randy had found them in the bottom drawer of his bedside dresser, piled underneath a load of unworn shirts and pants that had collected three years' worth of dust. They were extremely tight around the crotch, feeling like a bad wedgie, and the flower designs looked sissy.

"Aloha, honey," Jason said with a metal grin. He wore a pink flamingo T-shirt with white khaki shorts.

"Screw you," I replied. "You're lookin' pretty cute with that pink flamingo."

Randy's hamper was filled to the rim with smelly clothes. Randy thought about digging into the hamper to let us recycle the dirty laundry, but the stench was unbearable. He told us it was best to use his old clothes in his closet, and we agreed. Now, after seeing the ridiculous forgotten relics, we were beginning to have second thoughts.

Jason and I looked like a couple of screwballs, but Mikey and Tommy put us to shame. They stepped out of Randy's bathroom like they were in some sort of comic skit. Tommy was wearing red and green plaid running shorts with a blue undershirt. Mikey had on a giant-sized Superman T-shirt with the famous *S* painted square in the middle. The sight was too much to handle; Jason and I cracked up.

"Here comes Fat Man to save the day," Jason said, laughing hysterically and pointing at Mikey.

"Yeah, and don't forget his sidekick, Grandpa Jones," I said, looking at Tommy.

Tommy frowned and brandished his fist at me. "Do you want a knuckle sandwich, Davy?"

Jason and I continued to laugh, and Tommy and Mikey eventually joined in. The chuckling escalated into a full roar, and soon we were all doubled over, slapping our legs and grabbing our stomachs.

"What a pretty bird," Tommy said in hysteria, thumbing at Jason.

"Yeah, and Davy's sportin' his Daisy Dukes," Mikey said, looking at my ball-busting shorts.

Tears ran. We had lost control, succumbing to the absurdity of the moment. It felt good to laugh again; too much tension had built up during the last couple of hours. We put the memory of the accident in the back vaults and locked it up for another time.

Randy laughed with us, although he wasn't entirely in on the joke. They were *his* clothes, after all, and he had once worn the Grandpa Jones shorts in third-grade Phys-Ed, and the flamingo shirt in Mrs. Weaver's fourth-grade class. Nobody had thought twice about Randy's wardrobe back then. We were either too busy playing hide-and-go-seek, sneaking around in the mystery maze, or playing marbles at the back of the elementary cafeteria, where all the best marble shooters competed.

But seventh grade was totally different. The marbles had been shelved on the top rack of the closet, the rack that served as the graveyard for all old toys and boring games, and anybody that was caught playing hide-and-go-seek was apt to end up with a sign on their back that read *Freak*, or *Kick Me*. High school was around the corner and the last thing any kid wanted to do was to go in on a bad foot. To go in as a loser.

Jason's laugh grew thin and he made for the aspirator in the seat of his crumpled wet jeans. He found it, inhaled deeply, and gave a comforting smile.

"Gosh Randy, where did you get this stuff?" I asked.

"Different stores," Randy said proudly. "My old man takes me on vacations and he usually lets me pick out a few shirts and souvenirs when we go."

"Why don't you throw them out?" Tommy asked. His flattop was dry again and took on its normal fuzzy look.

"I don't know." Randy shrugged his shoulders. "I was fixin' to, but I guess I just thought I'd wear them again. If they still fit, that is."

I had seen some of Randy's other souvenirs while changing. The memorabilia was scattered all over his room—the floor, the bookshelves, the wall racks, the study desk. He had a visor from Miami, a Lakers jersey from LA, a baseball from Detroit with a signature that I couldn't make out, and a Mickey Mouse hat with giant black ears from Disneyland. He also had state flags, giant coffee mugs, and key chains. Randy's room looked like a regular Mom and Pop tourist shop, complete with all the crap anyone could buy. It was Randy's heap collection, a miniature, fancy version of Ricky Jay's junkyard. The only thing missing from the make-believe store was a cash register and a dusty *WELCOME* sign. Randy Sachs was a born packrat—once he got his hands on something, you'd have to pry his fingers off with a crowbar.

Not all of it was garbage, though. Randy collected one thing that grabbed everybody's attention. He put the collectibles inside a human-sized trunk—about five feet long and three feet wide—and it was the hot spot in his room, the area where everybody flocked to gaze with wonder and awe. He had started filling the trunk just after the summer of 1977, when he had seen the best movie of all time. Every year since then the items kept piling up. He had action figures for Jabba the Hut, Han Solo, Luke Skywalker, and Darth Vader. He had rare posters of X-Wings jumping into hyperdrive, Star Destroyers blasting at Rebel forces, and Obi-Wan Kenobi teaching Luke about the force. He had a gold-plated C-3PO and a silver-coated R2-D2 that had been given to him for his twelfth birthday. Both robots were valued at over fifty dollars apiece. Randy had plastic light-sabers, laser guns, and space boots. He even had a Chewbacca suit he had worn last Halloween.

"Randy, dinner's ready!" Mrs. Sachs yelled from down the hall.

"Okay, ma!" Randy yelled back. He opened the door. "Let's eat."

"Nuh uh," Mikey said, looking down at his Superman shirt. "I'm not going out like this."

"Come on, stop bein' a sissy," Tommy said.

We walked out of Randy's room and made for the fried chicken and potatoes. The delicious greasy smell was taunting my stomach again.

***

My belly felt like it was going to explode. It arched over the waistline of Randy's ridiculously tight shorts, stretching the skin on my torso into a round and tight bulge. In addition to the fried foods I had inhaled, I took on an extra bowl of chocolate pudding with vanilla ice cream. It was yummy, too yummy to pass up, but eating the entire bowl was a costly mistake; the protests in my abdomen proved it.

The guys didn't look much better. Randy had finished more drumsticks than I had, and looked as if he had stuffed a large pot underneath his shirt. Some of the kids at school called him Toothpick because of his skinny arms and gangly legs, but I doubted if any of those kids would call him that name if they saw the way he looked now. Mikey and Jason were still finishing their desserts. Their work was slow, almost standstill, and they both looked as if they might throw in the towel at any moment. Tommy was the only one that passed on the pudding. He told Mrs. Sachs that he was lactose intolerant, and although I didn't quite know what that meant, I knew from hanging out with him that he couldn't drink milk or eat cheese. *Lactose intolerance is a bitch*, Tommy had told me on more than one occasion.

"I'm home," Mr. Sachs yelled from the garage door.

"You're late!" Mrs. Sachs yelled back.

The Sachs' two-car garage was connected to the back of their enormous den. The den had three couches, a giant six-foot theater screen TV, two five-foot speakers that were connected to a record/tape stereo, and one pool table which was usually covered with a tan canvas protector. The den was linked to the living room and the living room led to the kitchen. A long hallway separated the three bedrooms from the rest of the house. The place was spacious, yet comfortable. It wasn't an architectural masterpiece—there was only one house in the neighborhood that earned that status, and that was the seven bedroom Walter mansion on 6th street—but it was stylishly designed. Many neighbors inside the Twin Heights envied Randy's house, including my mother.

"Wow, we've got company!" Mr. Sachs said, strolling in with a briefcase in his hand. His thinning red hair was parted to the side, and his yellow tie was loosened from the collar on his white dress shirt. He dropped the case on the cooking island, gave his wife a kiss, and tousled Randy's hair.

"Hey Dad! Is it okay if my friends stay over tonight?" Randy asked.

"What did your mother say?" Mr. Sachs said, sitting down.

"That it was okay as long as their parents agreed, too."

"I guess it's all right then."

"Have you boys called your parents?" Mrs. Sachs asked us while filling her husband's plate with the leftovers.

We said yes, and we were all telling the truth except for Tommy. I knew that there was only a slight chance that Tommy was going to call home, and there was even a slimmer chance that if he did, his parents would agree to let him stay. Right now, as Tommy crunched on the half-melted ice cubes in his empty glass, Dan was probably getting the business end of Mr. Smith's belt. Mrs. Smith was probably working in her garden, ignoring the slaps echoing inside her house.

"You said seven," Mrs. Sachs said, placing the loaded plate in front of Mr. Sachs.

"I know, sorry Honey," Mr. Sachs replied. "I thought the board would let us out early, but tight-wad George Paka couldn't shut his cheap trap." Mr. Sachs took a heaping bite out of his chicken leg and washed it down with a gulp of water. "Goodness. He kept complaining that the school was wasting its funds on useless programs like the afternoon tutoring sessions and the weekend community service city clean-ups. He thinks the programs are a bunch of bureaucratic bullshit."

"Honey! The kids!" Mrs. Sachs said in disgust.

"Aww, hon. Nothin' to fuss about. They've heard worse at school. I'm sure they could teach me a few four-letter words of their own." Mr. Sachs winked at us with his bright blue eyes. We smiled back in agreement.

"You boys go play now," Mrs. Sachs said. She collected the dishes and made for the sink. Her *Mama's Good Cookin* apron was now folded on the oven stove handle.

"Hey Dad, can we light a fire tonight?" Randy asked. Randy's red bangs brushed the top of his eyebrows.

"In August? Did you hit your head on something hard, son?" Mr. Sachs asked with a raised brow.

"It's stormy, Dad," Randy said, pointing outside. "It's cold enough to pass for October or even November. Can't we build one? Please?"

"Well..." Mr. Sachs stabbed at his potatoes and glanced at Mrs. Sachs. Mrs. Sachs looked displeased with the idea, but she didn't voice her opinion. "I guess it would be okay. No harm in it. But make sure the chimney vent is open and be careful with my lighter."

"Awesome!" Randy said, and jumped out of his chair. "Come on guys!"

***

Randy was Mr. and Mrs. Sachs' only child, and even though he stubbornly denied it, Randy was spoiled. He received more birthday and Christmas gifts than any kid I knew. He got to travel whenever his dad went on trips and he always got his way when he wanted friends to sleep over. He was allowed to drink sodas, eat cookies, and snack on Popsicles as he pleased, even if it was right before dinner. I think he was allowed these goodies because Mr. and Mrs. Sachs had come from poor families that couldn't afford the finer things in life. Randy's father was the son of a shoemaker, and Randy's mother was the daughter of a broke restaurant owner with a drinking problem.

While Randy was given many privileges, he was also put to work. "It's important my boy faces adversity," his dad once said while we were spending the night. "He's got to learn that lesson early on so he can deal with harder things later in life."

I figured that's where Boy Scouts came in. Randy was a First Class Assistant Patrol Leader in his scouts club. He had earned six merit badges, one Huckleberry community strip badge, and an Arrow of Light award for outstanding attendance. Since Randy's dad had served in Vietnam, slaving three years for the army inside the dense and humid Asian jungles, he wanted his son to grow up knowing the value of service and loyalty—two values that Mrs. Jackson, my sixth-grade hippie English teacher, had said never existed throughout the entire war. Randy had made his dad proud and put in two years of service with the scouts; he had learned skills in camping, first aid, mapmaking, outdoor cooking, swimming, and woodcraft. He also found out the importance of obeying the law and keeping all swear words buried behind his lips. He even knew the Scout oath by heart, often reciting it gleefully during lunch at school:

On my honor, I will do my best: To do my duty to God and my country, and to obey the Scout Law. To help other people at all times. To keep myself physically strong, mentally awake, and morally straight.

It would be a fat lie if I told you the other kids wanted to hear Randy's oath. He'd often get many protests in the form of spit wads and paper balls to stop his Scout patriotism. But Randy didn't care. He remained undaunted, speaking with his hand over his heart, his lips to the sky, and his eyes to the flag flapping in his mind.

In addition to the creed, Randy had also learned to create roaring fires. It was an art with him, something that took extreme care and dedication.

The Sachs's fireplace was in the den, sitting in a stone hole that looked like a cave in the center of the back wall. The pre-chopped wood was piled inside a corrugated tin tool shed by their garage. We followed Randy to the wood pile, moving like an army of troops, and helped him collect the fuel for the fire. Randy yelled out orders: "Jason, get the small pieces. Make sure you collect plenty of twigs. Mikey and Tommy, you guys gather the medium pieces. If it looks muddy or wet, don't pick it up. Davy, you and I will take care of the big logs. Grab the chopped ones. The round logs don't burn as well."

We sifted and picked through the timber. I grabbed three giant logs and took them inside Randy's house. The lumber weighed over fifty pounds, and I thought my arms were going to separate from my body while carrying it. A large splinter imbedded itself inside my right palm as I dropped the wood near the fireplace. I quickly removed the nasty needle with my teeth, squinting in pain as a small trickle of blood seeped down my hand.

Randy instructed Jason to put his pieces underneath the iron tray inside the fireplace. Randy then carefully stacked the medium logs atop the tray, forming a small cone. It looked like he was creating a wooden tipi for shop class.

I grabbed my largest log and put it next to Randy.

"No, we don't need that yet," Randy said, pushing it away.

"Why not?" I asked.

"Because, ya need the fire before you can get the big guys burnin'."

Mr. Sachs owned an extended lighter with a six-inch metal igniting shaft. The handle was made out of plastic and it had a trigger switch with an adjustable flame dial. A turn of the dial could make the flame fire like a rocket, or peter out like a struggling candle drowning under the liquid of its own melted wax. Randy turned the meter on high, pointed it at the bottom layer of twigs, and lit the fire.

As the twigs burned, smoke started to build in the fireplace. It got thicker and thicker and then a thin gray cloud escaped from inside and worked its way up the den wall. Randy's blue eyes were as big as melons.

"Crud!" Randy said. "The chimney vent!"

Randy put his face inside the smoke-filled hole and searched frantically for the metal handle. Smoke continued to empty into the den. We moved away from the front of the fireplace, coughing madly and covering our mouths with the ends of our shirts. Our eyes watered and stung. Jason slipped into another asthma attack, his breath whistling in and out.

We heard a loud clang, much like the noise we'd heard when Mrs. Sachs dropped her metal bowl, and Randy withdrew his head from the fireplace. He doubled over and heaved for oxygen.

The smoke stopped pouring into the den, now going up the proper path.

We continued to cough and rub our burning eyes. Jason took a double hit from his aspirator.

“I can’t see,” Tommy said.

“Neither can I,” Mikey replied.

Randy’s entire face was pitch black. He looked as if someone had painted his face for a Halloween school play. His eyes were snow white and looked like glowing marbles inside their sockets. His red hair was now gray, as if he had aged fifty-plus years.

Randy recovered his breath and nervously looked down the hall into the kitchen.

“Did my parents see?” Randy asked.

“No, I don’t think so,” I said.

“Quick! Open the door!” Randy said.

Randy yanked both sliding glass doors open and fanned the smoke out with a nearby newspaper. We helped him with a couple of golf magazines.

The smoke inside wasn’t thick, but it *was* noticeable. If Mr. Sachs were to come into the room, he’d certainly know that something had gone wrong, and that was the last thing that a First Class Boy Scout wanted. All those hours rubbing sticks and covering campfires, and what had his son learned? Nothing except the fact that his face could turn black if stuck inside a smoldering fireplace for an extended period of time.

A piercing ring came from the other side of the den. We turned in fear. *What now?*

"The fire alarm!" Randy said, and sprinted for it.

The round plastic alarm was seven feet above his dad's La-Z-Boy. Randy grabbed a pillow, climbed on the chair, and muffled the screaming pest. I looked down the hallway leading to the kitchen. Mr. and Mrs. Sachs were still eating dinner, talking. *They must be deaf,* I thought. How could they not hear all this racket? The distance between them and us must have been just enough to muffle our noise.

Randy held the pillow tightly, as if his life depended on it, and stared at me with those same frightened eyes.

"Are they coming?" Randy whispered. He coughed and wiped his face against his shoulder.

"Huh uh," Tommy said. "We're okay."

The alarm cut out after a few minutes. We then shut the sliding glass door after fanning out most of the smoke, leaving only a thin haze in the room. Randy, cautiously avoiding his parents, had grabbed a box of tissues to help us clean up. We had little black smudges here and there: cheeks, nose, ears. Randy looked the worst, and we had to help him clear his face.

"Randy, are you sure you're Irish?" I asked, grinning.

"Go do your mother, Davy," Randy said, spitting a mouthful of soot into the fire.

"Look," Mikey giggled. "Even his Dumbo ears are black."

We roared with laughter. Jason was laughing so hard that the pink flamingo on his shirt seemed to dance. Tommy roared with Jason, one hand clutching his bouncing stomach and the other pointing at Randy. Randy, once again, wasn't in on the joke and continued to wipe his face.

"What's so funny?" Mr. Sachs asked.

He was standing in the front of the den, a fresh beer can in his hand. He had removed his tie and loosened the first three buttons of his shirt. The joke ended abruptly and we sat up like army soldiers at attention. Randy hid the tissues behind his back.

"Nothing, we were just goofin' off," Randy said. I couldn't see a trace of soot on his face, but that didn't mean that his dad couldn't.

"Yeah, Tommy told a really good joke," Mikey said. Tommy shot a quick glance at Mikey. He didn't say anything, though the expression on his face said it all: *Shut the hell up, Mikey.*

"Really?" Mr. Sachs asked, surprised. He sat down on his La-Z-Boy, and I looked at the alarm above his head, imagining that high-pitched noise. At any moment it would sing like a canary and sell us out. "Let's hear it."

Tommy's jaw almost dropped to the floor. His right hand nervously rubbed his left elbow.

"It really wasn't that funny, Mr. Sachs," Tommy said. "It was just a stupid joke."

"Humor me, Tommy," Mr. Sachs said with a straight face. He cracked the beer and took three giant gulps. Tommy took a few dry gulps of his own and looked at us. We shrugged our shoulders; the spotlight was on him.

"Well..." Tommy said, scratching his head. "There was this blonde, right. And she walked into this pharmacy..." Tommy told the joke under the watchful eyes of Mr. Sachs. He left a few parts out, but he told it pretty much as Jason had told it to us. It sounded stupid the second time around (don't all jokes?), and I expected it to bomb like a fresh turd.

Mr. Sachs stared at us for a second, then threw back his head and laughed so hard that his beer spilt on his shirt. I could see every line on his aged face and every filling in his cavity-ridden mouth. His tongue flapped in the air like a magic carpet on hyper-drive.

It was actually funny to adults!

Shocked that Tommy had pulled it off, we laughed right along with him. Even Randy joined us. We continued to chuckle into the night as more jokes passed the circle. Jason told another blonde gag he had heard at school, and Mr. Sachs told one about three priests and a rabbi. We roared with the fire at our backs and our flickering shadows on the walls.

The memory of the Jeep accident was stored safely behind closed doors.

***

JOURNAL DATE: 8/29/01

It's late in the afternoon and I'm writing on a cheap rainbow comforter inside a two-bit sweltering motel room with a green neon light flashing *Nice 'n Comfy Inn* outside my clouded window. Nick is sleeping next to me with a new baseball in his hand—one of the many gifts I had given to him on his B-day. The motel was the first I had seen after pulling off the I-40 freeway. I had been driving for an exhausting seven hours, first starting from San Diego, then heading north on I-5 to Los Angles, then from LA to the 210 east where I exited I-15, finally transferring to the I-40 in Barstow. I hit Needles hours later, California's last major rest stop, before braving the blistering desert of Arizona. I thought about driving farther, maybe all the way to Flagstaff where I could cut the distance in half, but my eyes had succumbed to the highway's mesmerizing lines and the afternoon's fading sunlight.

The sign says *Nice 'n Comfy*, but I still haven't found one comforting quality about the motel. The twin bed with the tacky rainbow comforter squeaks like a rusty playground swing, the TV has more snow than a winter blizzard, and the bathroom sink drips water no matter how hard I turn the faucet off. The manager at the front office is a fifty-something smoker with a raspy laugh and crooked yellow teeth. He told me that the place had the bare essentials. "Es got everything you's need," the manager had said, grinning his patented tobacco-stained smile. "Thirty dollars, only price you's pay. Es even got a good bed for some hanky-panky, if you's know what I mean. Got everything, Senor." As soon as I checked into my room, I realized I had received more than I bargained for, like the party of cockroaches I found under the bed, and the nasty brown stain in the toilet I had to flush three times to remove.

The place was cheap, but I'd seen worse. I could care less about the squeaky bed, the annoying sink, and the fuzzy TV. It was the heat that bothered me. A local DJ said that the day's high was ninety-one degrees. Since my window faced west, an obvious flaw any second-rate architect knows to avoid when building in the southwest, my room felt twenty notches hotter than the day's high. The afternoon sun had beamed through the glass and heated my room like a solar oven.

Sitting in my blue jeans with my shirt off, a pen in one thumb, a worn Band-Aid on the other, I'm beginning to wonder why I took this vacation.

It had been my wife's idea. She bumped into my journal two weeks ago while vacuuming in our room and knocked it loose from underneath the mattress. She read my first few entries (I only had about five pages at that point) and cautiously placed it back in its hiding spot. She stayed silent about what she had read until two days later, when the topic came up during dinner.

"It was a complete accident," Susan said, looking at me with guilty blue eyes. "You're not mad, are you, Honey?"

"No," I told her after a small pause. We were eating a late dinner and had decided to reheat the meatloaf from the night before. The meat was rough, but a little ketchup and salt made it bearable. "I don't mind."

"Really?" she said, looking astonished. "It's not some secret?"

I took a sip from my iced tea and picked at the meat. "No. I was thinking about showing you someday anyway. When I finished it, that is."

"Are you just saying that?"

"No, I'm being serious. I've even thought about trying to publish it. As a book or something." I felt like I was twelve again, asking my mom if I could have another cookie before dinner and being promptly denied with a swat on the hand as I reached into the jar. I suddenly felt stupid telling her my premature ambitions.

"That's a great idea," Susan replied.

"You think?"

"Yeah, I really enjoyed what I read. It's a helluva lot better than the romance sap I'm working on now."

Her scarlet hair flamed in the light. She had a slight tan, and it made her look incredibly sexy underneath her tight white T-shirt. It reminded me of the first time I had seen her in college, standing in front of the door for chemistry 101 wearing stone-washed blue jeans, a crop sports shirt, and blue sneakers. I had hated chemistry in high school, ditching a total of six classes with my buddies, but I found a new love for it come freshman year at UCLA. I never thought about skipping that chemistry class. Not once. Not with that hot-looking redhead sitting next to me.

"I'm a little thin on the books where the abusive ex-husband hits the road and leaves the sexually deprived woman to find a beautiful, sensitive man who whisks her away to a fantasy island of luxury and happiness," Susan continued. "The handsome man and the lucky lady live happily ever after. I'm sorry, but that shit never happens."

"It happened with you, didn't it?"

Susan rolled her eyes, and I laughed.

"You should go back to New Mexico."

"Huh?"

"New Mexico. Since you're writing about it, why don't you go back?" I forced down another bite of the meatloaf. She continued, "You're always telling me how you haven't seen you brother in years. Now's your chance to go back and catch up with him, see how he's been holding up. It's not like the firm can't live without you."

"I've got James Walter, though. He's a new client and he needs me to draft his will by next Tuesday."

"That's what interns are for."

"I'm afraid it's not that simple. He owns more land than Rick Shulster. And add in three kids who all get different pieces of the pie."

"What about the other partners? You cover for them all the time."

I grabbed Susan's plate and took it to the sink. She had done a better job of the leftovers than I had.

She had a point about the partners. I had covered for Jay Lewis the last two weeks of June during his messy divorce, an ordeal that had involved four attorneys and two CPAs. I ran close to ninety-five billable hours during that time. And then there was Rick Hemmings. I billed more for his clients than some of my own. Ricky was a senior partner at our firm and he had a bad habit of splitting to Florida or New York at a moment's notice just so he could get in nine holes of golf with a couple of well-to-do clients.

"Like a weekend or something?" I thought aloud.

“Why not take the entire week? Bring Nick with you. You haven’t taken him on vacation in forever. I’ll take care of things while you guys are gone.”

I thought long and hard about the suggestion. Susan often complained that I was a workaholic, and judging from my record, she was right. Spotting for Jay and Ricky was just a small example of my insane work schedule; I often labored six days a week, ten to eleven hours a day.

When I was a teenager, I’d worked at a hamburger restaurant called Ted and Hoppers three streets down from my high school. The job was painfully routine: flipping burgers on a firewood grill, frying potatoes in a boiler, toasting buns in an oven. There were times that I’d completely zone out. During those moments, I’d stare aimlessly at the smoking hamburgers and think about more important things, like whether my old man would let me borrow his new Ford for the next big football game against Huckleberry Academy, or about my big Saturday date with Sara Evans and whether or not she’d let me touch her breasts again. Zoning out was never good, and it caused me to burn more than a dozen hamburgers and vaporize at least two dozen baskets of fries. The manager caught me doing this a few times and gave me the proper scolding, but the repercussions at Ted and Hoppers were far less severe than what could happen to me at the law firm. If an attorney zoned out, he was apt to get sued for malpractice and wind up paying through the nose. Clients had less patience for incompetent lawyers than fast food managers had with pimple-faced hamburger flippers.

So I maintained my focus, billed my hours, and kept my clients happy. I felt bad about not spending enough time with Susan, but I felt awful about Nick. Nick was already nine. He was in the fourth grade, playing sports with his friends. He was a full kid now. My boy had graduated out of his Sesame Street crib, and he would soon be heading off to junior high, telling me how he had scored the final goal in the school's championship soccer game. It was happening much too fast. I wanted to push rewind on the remote and go back to the toddler years where I could still hold the kiddo over my head and tickle his stomach with my mouth. But this wasn't a movie I could plop in the DVD and play again. It ran without pauses, without breaks, and when it finally ended, I wouldn't be around to watch the credits.

I guess it was *that* thought that scared me shitless, the thought of missing more. Susan was right; I needed a break. I hadn't seen my brother in six years, and I knew he'd love to see Nick, too.

So I took her suggestion, and now I've brought my son to a crappy motel in the middle of the desert. Some vacation so far. But I'm hoping our living quarters will improve from here on out on this nostalgia trip; I know it couldn't get much worse.

Chapter 5

Back to School

"Get out of bed, Davy!" my mother screamed, her voice echoing up the staircase.

"I am," I yelled back, reluctantly covering my head with a pillow.

It was seven o'clock, and it was the first day of eighth grade. Three months of summer had somehow flashed by in the blink of an eye, and now all I had left to look forward to was the torturous nine-month stretch of homework assignments, reading projects, and math problems. It was absolutely dreadful, and my mother wasn't going to give me sympathy.

"I said now, Davy!"

I threw the pillow to the floor, rolled out of bed, and stretched in front of my *Jaws* mirror: a skinny white ghost standing half naked in green boxers. *Eighth grade*, I thought, looking at my reflection in the jagged tooth glass, measuring my height for the one-hundredth time against the pencil marks on the wall. It was going to be my last year at Roosevelt Middle School, the last year I would have to deal with Principal Pinner and his stupid detention slips, or Mrs. Peters and her insane algebra problems. After this was high school, where I could leave campus for lunch, drive to school, and play varsity baseball. The thought of finally leaving Roosevelt made me feel better, but I was still bummed that I had another year ahead of me.

"Are you up?"

"Yes, ma," I replied, and moved away from the mirror. Still five foot two. I hadn't grown any since yesterday.

I took a quick shower, brushed my teeth, and combed my hair to the side using a small glob of mousse. The grease plastered my hair so tightly that it resembled the slick 'do atop the Big Boy hamburger statue. I tossed the mousse in a drawer and removed a blue plastic container. I opened the container slowly, like opening a jar full of jumping crickets, and stared at the ugly retainer.

The retainer was Doctor Trueman's doing, and it was a sign of worse things to come. Dr. Trueman was my orthodontist. I had my first checkup with him last week. He'd patiently looked over my jaw x-rays, whistling to a Phil Collins song pouring out of the overhead speakers (from a station entitled EZ Rock), and nodded a few times. After biting my nails for five excruciating minutes, Dr. Trueman finally told us that I had a major overbite that needed correction. "To put it simply, the upper teeth are sticking too far over the lower front teeth, here and here," he said tapping on the display board, pointing to the problem. "We can fix it, but he needs braces."

Braces. It was the dreaded word that I had feared ever since I had laid eyes on Jason's fearsome silver grin. As soon as Dr. Trueman said it, I could hear the echoes of the nicknames that kids at school called Jason: *metal mouth, robot head, Franken face*. The insults were endless. And no more eating candy apples, jawbreakers, or cherry suckers; those candies would shred the wires and waste thousands of dollars of dental work. I'd have to pass up my favorite Halloween goodies when I went trick-or-treating.

"He needs to put it on for three months before we can start," Dr. Trueman had said, handing my mother a blue plastic container. Mom had passed it to me and I opened it. Inside was a skin-colored retainer. "It's only a temporary one until we get his mouth molded," the doctor continued, adjusting the glasses at the edge of his nose. The retainer looked like the thing from the horror movie, *The Blob*. It looked nasty, slimy, and I wanted the throw it to the floor and run out of the office. "Make sure you wear that every day."

Now, after snapping the god-forsaken thing in place while standing in the bathroom, it felt even slimier than it looked—sitting on the roof of my mouth like flattened gum. My tongue moved over the alien object, feeling the slick texture of the plastic, exploring the thin wire around my teeth. I wanted to put it back in its container and lock it away—to stop the Blob before it grew out of control—but I knew my mom would somehow find out if I put it back and coerce me to wear it anyway. I closed the empty container and exited the bathroom with the nasty retainer snugly in place.

Breakfast was bacon, eggs, and orange juice. Mom had scrambled my eggs and poached Lewis's. Lewis, my brother, was sitting opposite from me at the table, stabbing at his plate in chaotic spasms. He was looking outside, smiling at a sparrow taking an early morning birdbath.

"Concentrate on your food, Lewis," Mom said and helped him with his fork.

Although Lewis was a year older than me, we were the same height, and had the same lean build. We had many physical similarities, but there was one major difference between us: Lewis had been born with Mongolism—Down's syndrome. His brain was roughly the equivalent of a 5-year-old's—or at least that's what his IQ test said. My mother, a firm believer that those tests were a bunch of crap, obstinately claimed that Lewis was just a little behind his peers. He wasn't a normal boy, she admitted, but with the right upbringing he could learn to take care of himself. Our family physician, Doctor Cunningham, had his doubts. He told her that there was one in a million chance that Lewis would be able to live independently. That comment alone almost cost him our family business.

"Hand me his juice, Davy," my mother said, reaching for his apple glass.

I gave it to her and then grabbed my retainer by my plate. "I can't believe I have to take this out every time I eat," I said, fidgeting to put it back into my mouth. "This sucks."

"Don't say that word in this house."

Lewis got a laugh out of Mom's outburst and slapped the table, grinning wildly. He wore his favorite fireman T-shirt—a heroic picture of a firefighter speeding in his red truck with his trusty Dalmatian sticking its spotted head out of a window. Lewis had outgrown the shirt years ago, but he refused to retire it. It hugged his body like a glove.

"Not in houfe! Not in houfe!"

"Hush, dear," Mom said, and grabbed Lewis's fork again. "You better leave Davy. The bus is on its way, and I don't want you late for the first day."

The clock on the wall said 7:55. I gave up on the retainer, pocketed it, and grabbed my backpack.

"See ya, Ma," I said, kissing her on the cheek. "Later Lewis." I gave Lewis a hug and ran out the door. I could still hear Lewis' faint voice as I reached the street curb.

"Not in houfe!"

The bus arrived five minutes late. Patrick O'Brian, or Pat'O as all the kids called him, pulled the lever for the sliding door and waved me in.

"Well, it be the luck of the draw," Pat'O said. He had a bowl of bushy red hair that wobbled when he spoke. "How did your summer go?"

"Too short," I replied, fishing the retainer from my pocket and putting it in my mouth. "I wi-sh I coold stey hom."

"Somethin' wrong with ye?" Pat'O said, furrowing his thick brow.

"Nuh, I'm a-kay," I mumbled, trying to snap the dreaded device in place.

Pat'O shut the door and shifted the bus into first. I sat down in the fourth row, in an aisle seat next to Timothy Brown—the brother of the notorious Bruce Brown, the second commander of The Jerks. Timmy wasn't big like his brother, but that didn't stop him from shooting his mouth off like the rat that he was. He'd say things like *kiss my ass* or *eat shit* to bigger kids that could easily pound him into hamburger meat. If trouble came, Timmy would hide in his brother's shadow and let Bruce take care of the dirty work. Jack Thompson, an eighth-grade wrestler, once gave Timmy a black eye at lunch one day when Timmy told him that wrestlers were a bunch of queers. Timmy, the baby that he was, cried home to his big bro and the very next day, right after school was out, Bruce jumped Jack by the basketball courts and gave him two black eyes, a broken nose, and a fat lip the size of Texas. After that, Jack never hit Timmy again, and neither did anyone else.

Timmy was smacking on a sucker, looking at me with a condescending little grin. A ratty Cubs baseball cap was turned backwards on his head.

"What's wrong with you?" Timmy asked, his warm breath smelling like cherries.

"Nothing," I replied, looking away.

Timmy leaned in to get a better look. I tried to hide it from him, covering my mouth as I worked to snap the retainer in place with my tongue, but it was useless. He had seen something and was now curious, and when Timmy Brown got curious, he was determined to weasel his way in to find out what the big secret was all about. I closed my eyes and cursed at myself.

Why didn't I keep the damned thing in my pocket?

"You've got braces!" Timmy squealed, smiling a fat red grin.

"They're not braces," I said, pushing him away.

"Oh yeah? Then why are you covering your mouth like that? If you have nothin' there, then show me."

Hiding it now was impossible. The cat was out of the bag and Timmy, the annoying cuss, wanted to see its yellow eyes. “It’s a retainer,” I said and took it out. A long saliva string followed it and Timmy’s cherry lips shriveled in disgust.

“Ewwwwww, that’s nasty.”

“Like your face,” I said, looking away from him again.

“Davy’s got braces. Davy’s got braces.”

“Shut up.”

“Davy’s got—”

“Listen here,” I said, grabbing his shirt. “If you don’t shut up right now I’m going to—”

“What?” Timmy’s thick incarnadine lips said. “What ya gonna do?”

Punch your face in and throw you through that window, you little rat. That’s what. You and that stupid Blow Pop, and if your bother comes along I’ll throw him out, too–two birds with one stone.

Nothing, I thought again. *I’ll do absolutely nothing, just like Jack the wrestler*. I let go of his shirt.

Timmy smiled, plopped the sucker back in and leaned back in his seat. He had weaseled out of another jam.

Just as I was putting my retainer back in, I heard someone whispering behind me.

“Pssst, Davy!” the voice said.

I looked back and saw Mikey sitting in an aisle seat in the last row. His silver-dollar glasses reflected the landscape outside, casting a bright glare that hid his eyes.

"Hey," I said. I hadn't seen him when I first boarded the bus.

"Sit back here."

"Are there any seats?"

"Yeah, lots of 'em," Mikey replied, pointing the spaces next to him.

I grabbed my book bag and quickly fled pesky Timmy and his baby lollypop. Pat'O glared at me in his giant rearview mirror as I sat in a rear window seat, one space away from Mikey. Mikey had a *Mad* magazine on his lap with the familiar cover of Alfred E. Newman, the kid with freckles, buckteeth, and big ears. The worn, dog-eared magazine read: *Americans gunnin' down the Commies, one bullet at a time*.

"You're taking the bus now?" I asked Mikey, kicking my backpack underneath the seat in front.

"Yep, have to," Mike said. "My dad can't drive me anymore. He's got to work at six every day he said. That's two hours earlier than it was last year. He said something about cutbacks and needing to put in more hours than usual. I guess this is my new ride."

"All year?"

"It looks like it."

Mikey didn't look happy about the new arrangement, but he didn't look completely upset either. He almost looked relieved. It was my guess that it had something to do with his Dad's BMW and Mikey's snobby image at school.

Mikey McNeil was one of the richest kids I knew. Mr. and Mrs. McNeil were lawyers, his dad specializing in immigration law and his mother in real estate. They both worked in the same law firm downtown. Separately, Mr. and Mrs. McNeil earned enough money to keep any respectable attorney satisfied. Combined, their incomes amounted to more in a year than some families made in a decade.

They were rich, but it was impossible to tell from the outside. Their three-bedroom adobe house was nice, but not ostentatious; they shopped at K-mart and Sears, buying more during the sales and less during the markups; they didn't own fancy jewelry or clothes; and they frequently gave to charity. There was only one sign that the McNeil's were better off than the rest of the pack, and that was Mr. McNeil's BMW.

The car was a 1980 model 320i, 4-cylinder stick shift. It was bright blue and had power windows and a large sunroof. We called it the Blue Streak because Mikey's dad loved to race it around Huckleberry, driving ten to twenty miles faster than the posted speed limit. There was a radar detector attached to the dash, a silver square box with a green and a red blinking light (green meant the coast was clear; red meant cop), and a glove box full of crumpled speeding tickets. Mikey told me that his dad liked to keep them in there so he could pay them all at once, like it was a monthly bill. That radar detector, needless to say, didn't work worth a damn. Everyone knew about the tickets and Mr. McNeil's reckless driving, including my mother, to whom it was a great mystery how Mr. McNeil never lost his license.

Blue Streak was amazing, but all good things have a price. It's the inevitable tradeoff. The speeding tickets were one example; the snobby image was another. Middle-income families couldn't afford to throw down forty thousand dollars just to show their neighbors their new sporty toy. Since we lived in a modest neighborhood, I was certain that Mrs. McNeil wasn't the only person giving her husband static about his gift to himself. Envious neighbors scoffed and whispered behind Mr. McNeil's back about what a rich prick he was. I had heard a few complaints from my own parents. My mother often wished he'd take that blue thing back to the dealership and trade it in for a station wagon.

Mr. McNeil had to pay an extra tax on his investment...but I truly believed that Mikey was the one that got the butt end of the snobby stick. Roosevelt was a public school. Many of the kids had fathers that worked in blue-collar jobs, sweating long hours and living paycheck to paycheck. They owned pickups, beat-up used sedans, and old vans.

Everything changed for Mikey at Roosevelt the day his dad pulled the shiny Beemer to the front of the school and told his son goodbye. I wasn't there to see it, but Tommy told me that most kids looked as if they had seen Santa Claus. This Santa, however, had a blue sleigh that could do 0-60 in twelve seconds. From that day forward, Mr. McNeil dropped his son off at the school's front lot, and what was once amazement soon turned into jealousy. Kids started to tease Mikey, calling him rich boy, or money bags, or daddy's golden child. Mikey ignored the insults at first, but it got to be unbearable after a few months, when the threats started to roll in. I had heard some of them firsthand: statements like, *golden child's gonna get his ass kicked*, or *the rich boy has two black eyes coming*, or the notorious note on the bathroom wall that read: *Mikees days are numbared*. The threats never materialized, although it was my guess that Mikey would have gotten his teeth rearranged if it wasn't for Principal Pinner's intervention. Pinner was tough on school violence. He once slapped a four-week suspension on a boy named Luke Plummer because Luke had socked Cris Keller in the stomach for stealing his lunch. Everyone knew that Cris was an ass and that Luke was in the right for hitting him, but Pinner didn't care. *Strict Discipline Makes An A Student* was Pinner's sacred motto (he had it displayed in giant brass letters on the cafeteria wall), and as far as he was concerned, kids like Luke Plummer should guard their lunches better from thieves like Cris Keller. When Pinner heard about the threats against Mikey, he made a special announcement that any school fights would result in an automatic six-week suspension and two months of community service. Most kids could care less about staying home from school for six weeks, since suspension was like a vacation, but the two months of community service—raking leaves and picking up trash—was a major drag. Raking Mikey wasn't worth raking the entire school lot. So the threats stopped and the little friendly note on the bathroom wall was painted over with a blotch of white plaster. Mikey was relieved to know that the death warrants had been remanded.

Now, sitting in the bus, the relief was back in Mikey's eyes. There were worse things than taking the bus, and I had my bets that Mikey would rather choose the smelly back seat he was currently sitting in over the fresh leather passenger chair of a BMW. The damage was done, true enough, and any kid that saw him in Santa's Beemer certainly wouldn't forget about it after the three months of summer break, as if afflicted with a rare case of amnesia, but it was better not to pick at the scabs.

The golden child could take the bus like everybody else. That was acceptable.

Mikey's rich image was ridiculous, especially considering his thriftiness. Mikey might have had more money in his wallet than some teachers had in their checking accounts, but he spent it like he was on his last dime. At lunch, he'd buy water instead of milk because it saved him twenty cents, and he'd order fish sticks in place of pizza pockets, saving another four nickels. One time, while we were buying candy in a gas station, Mikey asked the clerk if he could take ten pennies out of the change tray to buy a pack of grape licorice sticks. He claimed that he didn't have enough money and the clerk let him do it, but an hour later, while we were playing video games at Jason's house, Mikey's wallet accidentally dropped to the floor, spilling three crisp twenty-dollar bills. Mikey quickly stuffed the money back inside, but not fast enough to save his cheap hide. We all had seen his dirty secret.

"Did you hear about Tommy?" Mikey asked, looking at me with a bright glare on his glasses.

"No, what?" I asked, quickly glancing at the Mad magazine in his lap.

"You remember the accident, right?"

"Yeah, of course."

"Well, his dad really let Dan have it the night Tommy slept over with us at Randy's house."

"How bad?"

"Bad. Dan locked himself in his room and piled some furniture against the door. He hoped that it would keep the old man out. When Mr. Smith got home from work and found out about the Jeep, he blew his top and started breaking things. Pissed as hell, you know. Anyway, he got his nine-iron out of his golf bag and smashed that Indian vase in the den into a thousand pieces. You know the one, right? It sits on that small pine table." I nodded; I had seen it every time I walked in through their front door. "Well, Mrs. Smith tried to calm him, but he was out of control. He pushed her away and stormed over to Dan's room. He was crazy, Davy. When he found out that the door was locked he took the club and bashed the door in like he was chopping wood with an ax. As soon as he got inside he found Dan balled up in the corner with a baseball bat in his hands."

"How did you find all this out?" I asked, completely transfixed.

"Tommy told me, a week after it happened. He found out from his mom. You know what the crazy part of the story is?"

"What?"

"Dan *actually* tried to fight his old man back. He gave Mr. Smith two hard hits in the stomach and one knee in the thigh. It didn't faze Mr. Smith, though. He weighs at least fifty pounds more than Dan. I heard Mr. Smith threw the bat aside and tossed Dan around the room like a rag doll, breaking furniture. He pounded on him for almost ten minutes. The only reason he quit was because Mrs. Smith threatened to call the cops. I guess the thought of the police showing up and seeing a bloody sixteen-year-old boy scared the shit out of 'im. Got the old man thinkin' again, you know." Mikey adjusted his glasses and licked his lips. "Tommy managed to get away clean from his dad, but he wasn't so lucky with Dan. Tommy told me that one day, while he was watching TV, Dan snuck up behind him and nailed him in his right eye. Pow! I saw it two days after it happened. He had a black crater the size of an apple. It's healed a little since, but you can still see the bruise if you look close enough."

"Why'd Dan do it?" I asked, but I already knew the answer before I said the words. Why the hell did Mr. Smith or Dan do any of the things they did? Why did Mrs. Smith retreat to her garden every time her husband whaled on her kids? The answer was simple: there wasn't one. Psychologically, there was probably some complex explanation for it—emotional dependency, or maybe subconscious rage due to parental neglect. A shrink could probably pick apart the mess, sink the family into hypnosis and make sense of it, but as far as I was concerned, I had no clue why it happened.

Mikey shrugged his shoulders. "I guess he had it comin' for something else."

"He always does," I replied, looking at passing buildings on Jefferson Boulevard—double story adobe houses, apartment complexes, small ranches. They flew by one after the other, blending together like a long line of freight cars.

The bus turned down Lamont Street and screeched to a stop. Pat'O swung the door open, waved outside, and bellowed, "Come on aboard me ship, ye little Lucy." His red afro bobbed like a giant bowl of jello.

I stared blankly at the bus door, imagining the chain of command at the Smith household—Mr. Smith beating Dan, Dan pounding Tommy, Tommy kicking Lucky. Lucky was Tommy's black Labrador. Tommy absolutely loved Lucky and would sooner hit himself than lay a finger on the poor dog, but I imagined him kicking her anyway. It seemed to complete the pyramid of power, the big fish ruling the smaller ones. I thought about Lucky getting his revenge on some alley cat, and the alley cat, in turn, finding an unfortunate mouse to pick on. Before I could conjure the mouse's victim, I saw Lucy Graham step onto the bus. The image of the mouse puffed away like a cloud of smoke.

"A new year of school, eh Lucy?" Pat'O said.

"Yeah, it really sucks," Lucy said, shifting the weight of her backpack.

"It ain't that bad, ye ought to look at the bright side."

"What's that?"

"Ye get to ditch more days."

Lucy covered her mouth and giggled. She delicately grabbed the strap of her backpack and shifted the weight again.

I had known Lucy Graham since fourth grade. We'd had the same teachers every year, save the sixth grade, and we usually sat next to each other in class. She'd pass me funny notes when the teachers weren't looking, like *Mr. Perry has bad breath*, or Kevin Ball eats his own boogers. She was the only girl that would hang out with my friends during lunch. She didn't have many girlfriends, at least not that I knew of, and we treated her like she was a boy. She might have had pigtails, a round bubblegum face, and girly pink fingernails, but she could play first base better than Mikey and chug Cokes faster than Randy. Lucy was one of us, a part of the Gang, and she'd raise hell with anyone that claimed differently. One time, during an intramural basketball game not far from where Dan jumped Jack the wrestler, Jason made the mistake of calling her a sissy when she missed a crucial three-pointer that cost us the game. She socked Jason in the gut so hard that it took him ten minutes to regain his breath. Lucy later apologized about it and said she was just temperamental, but Tommy, Mikey, Randy and I all agreed that Jason had tripped over his own tongue.

Lucy Graham was one of five kids from a poor family. Her father was a car mechanic that spent more hours at the Angels and Devils bar than at home, and her mother was a chain smoker that never missed an episode of her favorite soap opera, *In this Life*. Lucy had three older brothers that were greasers and drinkers just like their pop, and one two-year-old sister that was in the early stages of talking. Lucy was the shining star of her family. She had straight A's (her brothers had all dropped out by the age of seventeen) and she was on her way to a full scholarship at Huckleberry Academy, one of the finest private high schools in New Mexico. Lucy proved that she could be both smart and tough, a rare combination for a twelve-year-old girl that weighed less than one hundred pounds.

But the Lucy that had socked Jason on that hot afternoon was different from the young woman I was staring at now: the pigtails, the bubblegum face, and the pink fingernails had disappeared. This Lucy had breasts, long tan legs, and radiant brown hair. This Lucy wasn't wearing sneakers and blue jeans like the one that played first base in sixth grade, but rather a reddish-brown flower skirt with matching shoes, a white collared shirt, and a golden crucifix necklace. This Lucy made me feel funny, like the times I looked at the half-naked women in Randy's Peep and Lace magazines in the fort.

During the summer, Lucy had gone into a cocoon and had transformed from a caterpillar into a monarch butterfly.

I stared as she walked down the bus, swaying her slim waist from side to side, one tan leg in front of the other. It was as if she wasn't walking down a cheap, black bus mat but a model runway with dozens of photographers snapping pictures. Lucy was doing her strut, moving in slow motion, and I was snapping my mental photographs.

"Hey Davy! Hey Mikey!" Lucy said, taking the backpack off of her soft shoulders. "Anybody sitting there?"

She pointed at the seat between Mikey and me. I looked at it like I had never seen a seat before. Lucy stared at me for a second, waiting for an answer, and Mikey finally gave her one when he saw the baffled expression on my face.

"Go ahead darlin', I've got a space on my saddle for ya," Mikey said in another Clint Eastwood impression.

Lucy covered her mouth and giggled. She sat between us and kicked her backpack under the seat in front. I felt the blood rushing to my face. I became dizzy, faint. Timmy looked back at us with a prissy smirk, but he might as well have been on another planet as far as I was concerned. It was Lucy's show, Lucy's runway, and all lights and cameras were on her.

"I can't stand that old pack," Lucy said, rubbing her shoulders. "It already weighs a ton and I don't even have my books yet."

"Why don't you get another one?" Mikey asked.

"Yeah, right, like my mom would pay for it," Lucy replied. "She'd never fork the cash out for something as needless as that. 'Just the necessities,' she says. 'A good backpack can last you for years.'" Her backpack had little white and yellow daisies stitched to the front. It was girly, but kind of cool at the same time.

"How was your summer in Santa Fe?" I managed to say, controlling myself. The words felt foreign, like they had come out of someone else's mouth.

"Good," Lucy said, blowing the streaks of brown hair from her face. Lucy had spent the last three months visiting her grandparents. "I wish it were longer."

"Me, too," I said, feeling stupid I had asked the question. I self-consciously tucked my lips over the wire of my retainer.

"I tried calling you guys one day while I was back for a weekend," Lucy said. "I wanted to see if you wanted to get the Baseliners together."

"Really, who'd ya call?" Mikey asked. He rolled up his Mad magazine and stuffed it in his bag.

"You, Tommy, Davy, everybody," Lucy said. "I couldn't get a-hold of you guys."

The Baseliners was the name of our intramural baseball team. Randy came up with it after we had won our first game in sixth grade. He said that it had been the name of his dad's minor league team back in Alabama, and that they had won five consecutive seasons under it. Randy claimed it was a lucky name, and judging from our record he seemed to be right. The Baseliners had gone 14-3 during the last two years. The three losses, we all agreed, were complete gyps.

"You gonna play with us again, darlin'?" Mikey Eastwood said, tipping up his imaginary cowboy hat.

"Damned straight," Lucy replied. "You guys better invite me. When are you gonna start?"

"As soon as possible, right Davy?" Mikey asked, looking at me with his thick glasses.

"Yep, probably in the next couple of weeks," I said. I was regaining the color in my face and the circulation in my veins. Lucy the baseball player was back, and *that* Lucy was much easier to talk to. "Once we find out what our class schedules are."

"My schedule sucks," Lucy said, bending down and unzipping her pack. Her golden crucifix daintily dangled from her neck and winked the sun in brilliant little flashes. She removed a small folded paper. "I've got nasty Mrs. Perkens for English and old fart Mr. Opela for Algebra."

"I've got him, too," Mikey said, gunning for his schedule in the seat of his blue jeans.

"I wish I did," I replied, removing my paper from my right front pocket. "I've got Mrs. Williams for Algebra. I heard she flunked five students last year and gave out seven D minuses."

"Really?" Lucy said, unfolding her paper and putting it in her lap.

Mikey and I lined our schedules next to hers. I had two classes with Mikey (Social Studies at 8:30, and Shop at 1:30) and two classes with Lucy (PE at 9:15 and Typing at 10:30). Mikey pointed at my paper and laughed.

"Ha! You've got Coach Barr for PE," Mikey said, giving a thick grin that reminded me of pesky Timmy.

"Tell me about it," I said. "I'd trade him any day for the girls' coach. You're lucky, Lucy."

"Why? What's wrong with Coach Barr?" Lucy asked.

"Everything," I said. "Before class, he makes you run five laps around the track, do fifty sit-ups, twenty-five pushups, and another twenty-five chin-ups. It's torture. If you're too fat or too weak to make it through, he'll ride your butt and grill you the entire year. I know because Randy had him last year and he was the first to tell me the story about Lucas Foster. Remember Lucas? He's the guy everyone calls Tubby."

Lucy and Mikey nodded. Tubby was well known around the cafeteria snack bars.

"He's kinda big, right?" Lucy said.

"Kinda big?" Mikey said, his head cocked back in surprise. "He's a giant. If he were any bigger we'd have to give him his own zip code."

"Mikey, that's mean," Lucy said, trying to look disgusted but still giggling at the thought.

"Right, well anyway, that's him," I continued. "Lucas always had trouble keeping up with the laps in class. Every day Coach Barr would make him run an extra one around the track with a rope of weights around his neck. They call the rope Big Red because there are three ruby-red five-pound weights tied to it."

"That thing's scary," Mikey said. "I've seen it before. Never worn it, thank God."

"What's it for?" Lucy asked.

"Barr always puts it on the slowest kid in the class. He claims he does it so the slowest man can become the fastest by the end of the year, but Randy said that it was because the coach can't stand fat slobs like Lucas Foster and wants to teach them a lesson for stuffing their chubby faces. Well, one day right after lunch, Lucas stopped in the middle of the first lap, gasping for air. Coach Barr blew his whistle and threatened that if he didn't move his butt he'd end up wearing Big Red and running an extra two laps. Lucas tried to continue, but he had just eaten two greasy burgers and all kinds of candy. The rest of the class was done running, waiting for Lucas on the bleachers."

"You mean they were watching him?" Lucy asked.

"Yep," I replied. "Some of them were even yelling with Coach Barr, telling Tubby to move it."

"Wait, I've heard this story before," Mikey said. "This is the one where—"

"Shhhhh," Lucy replied. "Let Davy tell it."

"Yeah, quiet Mikey. So Tubby tried to run two more laps around the track, but he was sweatin' like a pig. At the end of his first lap, he doubled over and heaved his entire lunch in the middle of the track, right in front of the coach and the class."

"That's gross," Lucy said. Mikey snickered at Lucy's disgust.

"The coach lost it when he saw the mess and put Big Red around Lucas's neck, screaming at him to continue running until the end of the period. Randy told me it was over a hundred degrees out that day and was as humid as a swamp. Tubby ran three more laps with Big Red bouncing off his chest before passing out. Barr and a couple of other volunteers dragged him in the locker shower room and sprayed him with cold water. To wake him up, you know. Randy thought Lucas had died of heat stroke, but after a few minutes and a few slaps in the face, Tubby snapped out of it in a daze and asked the coach if he still had to run. Barr walked him straight to the nurse's office and asked that Lucas be removed from his class."

"Are you kidding?" Lucy asked with wide green eyes.

"Swear my mother's name on it and hope to die," I said, crossing my heart. "Huh, Mikey?"

"Yep," Mikey agreed, nodding his head so hard that his glasses almost fell off.

"They kicked him out of PE and made him take Home Economics instead, baking cakes and mixing brownies. I guess they figured if they couldn't make him lose weight, they might as well make him fatter."

"I heard this story last year," Mikey said. "But I thought he had Twinkies, not candy, that day he barfed up?"

"Maybe," I said. "I've heard a dozen versions around school. All of 'em different. Some said he ate four hotdogs, some say eight. I don't think anyone really knows for sure."

"Gosh, I never knew about that," Lucy said, looking upset. "Poor Lucas, that's just awful. That sort of stuff sticks with you all your life."

"I know," I said. "I feel bad, too. Barr's a real hard-ass. He was in the marines for ten years, you know. Some say it made him crazier than a drunken sailor. I don't think that's far from the truth. Ever since Randy told me that story, I've had nightmares about Big Red. I've never seen that thing and I hope I never have to."

"You'll see it all right," Mikey said, adjusting his glasses. "You might not have to wear it, but someone in that class will. As long as Barr's the boss."

The bus turned down Sherman Street, rolled for a minute longer, and turned again into Roosevelt's front parking lot. Dozens of kids piled out of two buses in front of us, carrying their book bags, backpacks, and lunches. Principal Pinner was standing with his arms crossed underneath the giant *Roosevelt Middle School* sign. He had a thin smile and was wearing a cheap, faded blue suit with black penny loafers. The top of his head was slicker than an oiled bowling ball, reflecting the sun like a mirror. The students kept a safe distance away from him as they funneled under the sign and into the school. Pinner looked like Moses, parting the sea of kids.

"Alas! The ship hath arrived," Pat'O yelled out, punching the parking break, and cranking the door open. "Have a good first day, and watch ye step as ye go down. I don't want'cha suin' me for fallen' on your arsh."

As I was walking out the bus, one step behind Lucy, I saw a kid walk past Principal Pinner with one hand over his face. He walked quickly, as if Pinner were going to give him a detention slip if he saw who it was. It wasn't until I got out of the bus that I realized the kid was Tommy, guarding his faded black eye.

Chapter 6

LUNCH WITH THE GANG

I could tell that Mrs. Williams' Algebra class was going to be a drag. It was only the first day of school, a Monday, and she was already assigning enough homework to last the entire week. We had to read five Chapters by Wednesday and hand in sixty problems by Thursday.

"Make sure you write out the problems and show all your work," Mrs. Williams said, glaring at us with beady blue eyes. Her face had more wrinkles than a prune and had a frown that seemed permanently plastered on even when she smiled—which she did only once, when telling us the story of how she failed Ricky Crass for cheating on a test; Ricky, apparently, had a wandering eye during exams. "If you don't show your work, you'll get a zero for the assignment and a detention slip."

The Algebra textbook was as thick as an unabridged dictionary. It weighed a ton and looked like it could kill a whole family of cockroaches if dropped from the right height. It was the only book in my backpack, save a few notepads and folders that my mom had bought at K-Mart, and it filled up most of the space. *The pack was going to be too small,* I thought, remembering how Lucy said she needed a new backpack. I thought about her soft shoulders and her golden necklace.

"We will have a pop quiz every week," Mrs. Williams continued, writing it out on the blackboard, the chalk chipping with a tap-tap-tap sound as she moved quickly. "The quizzes will make up fifty percent of your grade."

The class was going to suck, but at least Randy was in there with me. His red hair was neatly parted to the side and his white collared shirt was starched like a stiff board. He sat directly behind me with his sneakers on top of the metal book basket beneath my chair. He slipped me a note as Mrs. Williams wrote with her back turned:

Is everyone going to meet us at the table for lunch?

I scribbled yes on the other side of the torn paper and passed it back. Mrs. Williams almost caught me doing it when she snapped back around, and for a moment I thought I was going to be the first kid to end up in detention, the first name on her crap list, but she grabbed her teacher's edition textbook and continued to write on the board. I heard Randy giggling about the close call behind me.

Mrs. Williams was scary, but she was nowhere near as freaky as Coach Barr had been. Hours before Algebra class, I was sitting with thirty other kids in a dark, cold, and musty locker room, freezing my backside on one of three long metal benches and waiting for Barr to step out of his office to start our first PE class. The office—a small square island with the shades drawn and a poster of a bum on the door that read: *If smoking ruined my life, it can ruin yours, too*—was set in the middle of the locker room with Barr's bright orange door directly in front of us, as glaring as a neon light.

The overhead air conditioning was cranked on high, blowing from three main vents directly above our heads, numbing our faces. It was as if Barr had designed the building himself, making the place as uncomfortable as possible for his unfortunate students. The rattling from the vents was the only thing I could hear in the silent room except for a few whispers and mumbles from unknown shadows. We all knew about Barr's reputation, and we were waiting for the inevitable. Barr would soon storm out of the room, the silver whistle hanging from his muscular neck and the infamous Big Red slung over his shoulders, and drill us around the track until we puked our guts out like Tubby.

But it didn't turn out that way. After what seemed to be an eternity, Barr finally came out dressed in a tight red-and-white striped shirt and green running shorts. He didn't have the whistle or Big Red. He was skinnier and shorter than I had imagined him. I had never seen Barr in person or pictures, but I had formed my own image from the many rumors—painting a six-foot, seven-inch giant with Popeye arms and Paul Bunyan legs; his teeth as sharp as knives; his fingers as thick as sausages. The real Barr was no Paul Bunyan. He looked more like an overgrown kid on his first paper route rather than a ten-year, hardcore marine veteran. Seeing him after what we had pictured was a joke, and we might have busted out laughing when he stepped out of the orange door had it not been for one thing. It's what held our laughter at bay, warning us to shut up and keep quiet or suffer the consequences. As far as I was concerned, that one thing made him creepier than all the images I had painted. It was his eyes.

They were small and set deep in their sockets. I couldn't tell if they were green, blue, brown, or red like the devil. From the side, it looked as if he had two holes in his skull, two deep sockets that disappeared into a black abyss. I wanted to look away from them, but I was somehow curiously drawn to the chilling quarter-sized orbs, catching a glimpse of the twitching irises inside. They were dark. They looked like two round black beetles scurrying in their shadowy nests.

"I have ten golden rules," Coach Barr bellowed while holding up nine fingers, his voice echoing down the locker room halls. "The first three are simple: nobody quits, nobody drinks, and nobody smokes. The other seven you'll learn in due time. If anybody here deviates from the golden rules, I will punish them accordingly. I have never put up with slackers in the past and I will not put up with slackers today. I can be your friend or your enemy. Got me?"

We stared at him blankly.

"Got me!"

"Yes, sir," we said in unison, as if in boot camp.

Barr stopped for a second and looked around. It was impossible to see whom he was looking at or if he was looking at anyone at all. The beetles were hidden in the hollows of his skull. Simply looking at them gave me goose bumps.

"Today is your lucky day; it's the only day that you'll get off." A few cheers broke out when he said this, but they were quickly squelched by Barr's booming voice. "Tomorrow is the start of your physical education. Rule number seven: everyone needs to bring clothes to change into before class starts. You'll need a plain white T-shirt, running shorts, and tennis shoes. If you show up with sweat pants, pullover hoods, long-sleeved shirts, cowboy boots, leather jackets, rings, bracelets, necklaces, or anything other than what I just described, I'll send you directly to the principal's office. These changing clothes are to be taken home once a week and washed. I don't want you smelling like a bunch of sewer rats in my gym. Do you see those lockers behind you?"

Barr pointed behind us and we stared at them.

"Everyone is assigned one locker," Barr said, holding up two thumbs.

Jimmy Kurtis, a tall African American kid with thick curly hair, shot his hand up. The class looked at him like he had lost his mind. *Nobody interrupted Barr.*

"What's your name?" Barr asked.

"Ji-ji-jim," Jimmy said, spitting everywhere.

"Jim what?"

"Ji-ji-ji-mmy K-k-k-kurtis."

"Jimmy Kurtis what?"

"Wha-wha-what d-do ya-ya-you m-mean?"

Jimmy frowned in confusion and Barr slapped his forehead. Barr raised five fingers.

"Rule number four: always call me sir," Barr said, facing Jimmy.

"Oh, s-sorry, J-jimmy K-kurtis, s-sir," Jimmy said, rubbing his black hands together. I wanted to tell Jimmy to shut his mouth, to save himself while he still had a chance, but doing that would land me in the quicksand with him. It was cover-your-own-ass time.

"You've got a stuttering problem, Jimbo?"

"Ye-ye-yes, sir."

"I thought so. I had one once when I was a girl your age. You'll eventually grow out of it like I did. If you're strong, that is. Are you strong, Jimbo?"

"I ho-ho-hope so, s-sir."

"Well...we'll find out about that. So Jimmy, what do you want?"

"We-well, sir," Jimmy said, clearing his throat, "you s-said that the-there we-were t-ten ra-rules, but you held up na-nine fa-fa-fingers. You also sa-said that everyone wa-wa-would be assigned one lo-locker, but you ga-ga-gave us t-two thumbs."

"That's right," Barr said calmly.

Jimmy looked at Barr like he had just seen a dog with five heads. Jimmy opened his mouth for a short second, as if he was going to say something more—or at least try to say something—but closed it again. Barr gave him a giant, clown-like grin, showing the pretty whites of his teeth. Barr's teeth were flat, I noticed, not pointy knives.

"Jimmy, you'll get used to the way I do things around here soon enough," Barr said. "By the end the year, all of you will get used to me. You'll know my rules like the back of your hand. Once you leave Roosevelt, you'll be able to say 'em in your sleep. Most of you will never want to see my face again after you go. There are a lot of students that come out hating my guts. It happens every year, but I guess that's just tough shit."

A few muffled laughs broke out at the word *shit* and Barr silenced them with a quick glance.

He looked, or so I thought he looked, back at Jimmy.

"Any more questions, Jimbo?"

"Na-na-no, s-sir," Jimmy said, now rubbing his hands furiously. I was surprised that Barr hadn't busted out Big Red and tied it around Jimbo's neck. The stuttering boy had made it out of the quicksand without running a marathon around the track.

"Good. Now, as I was saying, everyone will get one locker. I'll give the combinations out after class. I will only give them out *once*. If you lose your number, or if you forget it, or if you get amnesia from falling off your bike, you'll end up running all period while the rest of the class works with me. At the end of the class, after your laps, I'll give the number again *if* I'm in a good mood."

The overhead A/C clicked off and gave us a moment of relief. Coach Barr paced back and forth down the length of the metal benches, looking us over like a line of shaggy army soldiers getting drilled for the first time. I was certain he'd scream at us to cut our hair or shave the peach fuzz off our cheeks.

"I hope you learn something here," Barr continued. "If you do just as I tell you, we won't have any problems. If you open your fat traps to your poor mothers and fathers, complaining about how hard PE is or how mean I am, you'll get the bright side of my sneaker in your a-a-ass. Two kicks from each shoe."

Stuttering the word *ass* was a funny joke, but nobody laughed, and nobody raised their hand when Barr held up three fingers when he said two, not even Jimmy. Jimmy's lips, I noticed, were tightly zipped shut, hiding his tangled tongue. Jimbo might have had trouble talking, but his mind worked just fine. I had had Jimmy in two of my seventh-grade classes and he wasn't one of those kids who needed a second slap on the hand to learn his lesson.

"You've got five minutes to change after the bell rings," Barr said, slowing his pace. "Anyone that doesn't have his clothes on by that time will do an extra twenty pushups. Your grade in this class depends on how much sweat you put in, so I don't care how many baskets you can make, goals you can score, or touchdowns you can run. I'm looking for effort. If you put in a half-ass attempt, you'll get a half-ass grade. Got me?"

"Yes, sir," we said.

Barr stopped his pacing and looked at his watch. The round clock on his office wall read 9:35.

"Okay, you can go to the gym for the remainder of class. You can play basketball if you want, or sit on the bleachers. I don't care how you spend your time as long as you don't ditch, smoke, or do something else stupid. I want everybody changed and ready to go tomorrow. Got me?"

"Yes, sir."

Barr opened the door for us and we filed out. As I passed Barr, I stole a glance at his face. I had never seen eyes so black in my life. It was as if Barr had two mini eight balls in his head, spinning aimlessly in their fleshly pockets. He gave me a giant grin as I passed by. I shivered at the ghoulish smile and quickly ran to the gym.

Once PE let out at 10:20, I sat through a quick hour of Typing with Quin Tabby. Quin was a skinny toothpick that had a deep monotone voice that could put even a hyperactive kid to sleep. Quin started us with the alphabet. We spent five minutes typing A-B-C, five minutes punching D-E-F, and so on until we reached the end where we'd start all over again. It was so repetitive and dull that I might have fallen asleep had it not been for Lucy sitting at the computer next to me.

She somehow made the class seem interesting. It had something to do with the delicate way she typed, one soft letter at a time, her fingers falling soft as snow (next to her I looked like an oversized gorilla, stupidly banging away at the foreign keys with my clumsy fingers). It had something to do with her flowery smell, so sweet and fragile, reminding me of the roses I would sometimes come across on the eastern barbwire fence of the Vineyard while hunting with Tommy. It had something to do with her flowing brown hair and bright green eyes and how they made my heart race like a sprinting jackrabbit. Whatever it was, it made me forget about skinny Quin Tabby and his robot voice. Before I knew it, the bell sounded the end of class. An hour had passed in a minute.

"I'll see you at lunch, Davy," Lucy said, walking out the door.

"Yeah, at lunch," I replied, feeling the colors redden in my cheeks. I tried to say something more, but she was off before I could get the words out.

I was walking with Randy when I suddenly felt my backpack rip off my shoulders and fall to the floor. I would have fallen with it if Randy's hand hadn't caught my shirt. Behind me, laughing like an ogre, stood Miles Quincy, arguably the meanest kid at school. Miles was six foot two and weighed over a hundred and seventy pounds. He had a round face and a flat nose that looked like a thick button. The long black hair on his forehead twisted and tangled its way through his bushy eyebrows, falling into his blue eyes. He was wearing a baggy red lumberjack plaid shirt, frayed blue jeans, and steel-toed, mud covered boots. He was a giant, but what he had in size he lacked in brains: he had been held back in the third and fourth grades and had flunked nearly every math and English class since the day he stepped foot in Roosevelt. As far as I knew, and as far as the Gang told me, his highest grade was a C and that was in Mr. Poya's art class, a class that was impossible to fail if you knew how to spell your name right and mold a clay lump into a ball.

Standing next to Miles like Santa's little elf was pesky Timmy Brown, smiling his annoying baby grin. The sucker was gone, but there was still evidence of the red candy stain on his lips.

"Hi-dee-ho!" Timmy said, snickering and pointing at the ground. "Looks like you dropped your bag, metal mouth."

"Ooops, did I do that?" Miles asked, putting his hand over his fat lips.

"What's your problem?" I asked, picking up my backpack. It had fallen on its front; brown streaks covered the green canvas.

"That's your payback for ditching me on the bus," Timmy said.

"Yeah, his payback," Miles replied, stupidly laughing at Timmy's remark.

"Go screw yourself, Timmy," Randy said, giving him the finger.

Timmy's face flushed bright red. He charged in front of Randy and looked him square in the eyes. Randy wasn't as tall as Miles, but he still towered over Timmy by a good five inches.

"What'd you say?" Timmy asked, his voice squeaking like a mouse.

"You heard us," I said, joining Randy. I clenched my fist.

Don't forget about Bruce, I thought.

Miles walked up alongside Timmy. I squeezed my fists harder, making them into two rocks, and stared into Timmy's hazel eyes, feeling the heat of his breath on my neck, smelling the salty sweat of his skin. Timmy's face looked like a miniature version of Miles' with the exception of Timmy's pointy nose. The bottom of the nose was angled in the air, as if pressed up by his thumb, revealing long black hairs inside two large nostrils. A tiny booger dangled out of one of the holes.

"You're askin' for it, Davy," Miles said, punching his fist in his hand. As he moved his arms, a rancid smell shot out of his armpits that reeked like a bag of rotting potatoes. It was so thick and terrible that I had to hold my breath to keep from gagging.

I continued to stare at Timmy's brownish-green eyes, expecting him to flinch, but he just stood perfectly still, waiting for us to throw the first punch. *That's how Timmy wants it,* I thought, biting down on my retainer. *That's how he plays his games and how he suckered Jack in.*

I was about to say heck with it and flatten his face, knowing very well that Miles would soon land a solid one on me, but I heard Mrs. Williams yelling at us from down the hall.

"What are you boys doing down there?" she asked with her hands on her waist and one foot jammed under the class door.

"Uh, nothing, Mrs. Williams, just playin' around," Timmy said in his best *I'm a good kid* voice. Timmy was a master at playing the honorable choirboy.

"Yeah, nothin'," Miles said, stuffing his hands into his pants pockets.

"Get going then, I don't want to see any trouble," Mrs. Willams replied.

Timmy gave us the finger as he withdrew, hiding it from Mrs. Williams. He spat on the floor and nudged Miles on the arm.

"Let's go, Miles," Timmy said, walking off. Miles stood blankly for a second, waiting for the words to sink in, then made after Timmy.

Mrs. Williams gave us a distasteful glare, removed her foot from the door and walked back inside the classroom. Randy grabbed my backpack and looked it over.

"Did they rip it?" Randy asked, dusting it off.

"Na," I replied, reshouldering the pack. "Just dirtied it up a little."

"Man, did you smell the B.O. on Miles?" Randy asked, holding his fingers to his nose.

"Heck yeah. He stunk worse than a block of moldy cheese."

"I wonder if he uses deodorant?"

"Are you kidding?" I laughed. "Those pits haven't seen the light of day for years. I bet there's a dead rat curled up in there."

Randy and I giggled at the gross thought, feeling the cool outside breeze funnel into the hall. A loose sheet of paper blew down the length of the hallway, twisting and turning in small coils. Scattered clouds passed over the sun in thin clusters, brightening and fading the shadows.

"Let's find the Gang," I said, lightly elbowing Randy in the side. "I'm starving."

***

Roosevelt had two lunch hours. One was for the sixth and seventh graders; the other was for the eighth graders and the administrative staff. The faculty rotated the periods each year, depending on the grades they were teaching. Roosevelt used to have three lunch periods, but they changed it the year I arrived because of scheduling conflicts. That was the year Principal Pinner took over for Principal Ridley. Pinner made it his goal to streamline the schedules and crack down on disobedient students—his campaign promise for the school presidency, one could say. Principal Ridley, I heard, had been a real pushover and most students took advantage of him every chance they could get. Pinner was at the opposite end of the spectrum, standing in line with bulls like Coach Barr. If someone so much as sneezed in the wrong direction, Pinner would slap him a detention slip and two weeks of community service. Pinner would sooner jump off a bridge than let himself be reduced to the likes of Ridley.

Strict Discipline Makes An A Student.

The cafeteria was always packed to the gills. If you wanted to beat the crowd and get a good table you had to run from your class, sprint into the dining room, and claim the first seat you could get your hands on. It was much easier for the ones that brought their lunches because once they staked out a spot, they could sit down and enjoy their food right away. The ones that bought their lunches at the cafeteria had to mark their table with a notebook, book bag, or a jacket, and then wait in a long line with their food trays. Ten minutes later, after paying at the register, they were lucky if their stuff was still in the same spot. Sometimes, as I found out during the sixth grade, the big kids with the sacked lunches would just toss the jacket on the floor or scoot the notebooks to the end of the table, and sit down like it was their place to begin with. If you were a seventh grader buying your food, it was a little easier to claim a space because no sixth grader was brave enough to try a stunt like that. But if someone like Miles Quincy stole your seat, there was little you could do about it except tell the teachers on him. And no one would ever do that...that would make you a crybaby.

The Gang and I generally avoided the cafeteria chaos. We ate at a small wooden table in front of the cafeteria, in the middle of what was called the Recess Square (I had no idea where the name came from, since recess ended in the fifth grade). Buildings surrounded all four sides of the Square. In the western wing, five rectangular redbrick structures stood side by side, all of them classrooms. In the eastern wing, looking like two small stadiums, were the gyms. They were painted white and had a picture of a giant pirate on the front, our school mascot. The administrative offices were located to the north, and south of that was the cafeteria. The Recess Square looked like a giant parking lot with four pine trees for shade, three splintery wooden picnic tables, and one drinking fountain that barely spurted out water.

The boards on our lunch table were dark brown and warped. Several inscriptions had been etched into the worn planks, but most of the letters had faded so badly that I couldn't make out what they said. The few that I could read were just sappy love lines engraved by some unknown author: *Al luvs Tina*, *Pete & Kel 4 ever*, and *I♥U*. I had joked to Jason and Mikey about carving their names in the wood, but they promised to return the favor if I dared it.

Our table could seat six to eight people depending on the size of the kids sitting at it. The benches had several jagged knots protruding upward, the surviving remains of the severed branches. We'd learned to adapt to the stumps, eating with them between our legs or at the edge of our thighs, but if we weren't careful and sat down without looking, we were apt to end up with the uncomfortable devils digging in our cracks.

We started eating at the table in the spring of our seventh grade year, the day after Miles Quincy and Sean Haggard had stolen our cafeteria table—Sean was another bully almost as big and mean as Miles; he was forced to transfer schools when Pinner found a bag of weed and a bottle of bourbon in his locker. The day of the incident had been a hot and unlucky one for our Gang. Right after the bell rang for lunch, we grabbed a table, placed our belongings on top of it, and stepped in the cafeteria food line. When we got back roughly fifteen minutes later, we found our stuff sprawled out on the floor with Miles and Sean eating in our spots...grinning like two ogres. We told them to leave and not surprisingly they said no. Tommy lost it and demanded they get lost. They said piss off. Tommy was about to smash his tray on Sean's head when Lucy managed to calm him down and drag him over to a smaller table at the back of the dining room. Tommy later thanked Lucy for stepping in and avoiding a fight, but the look in his eyes suggested he had still wanted to turn Sean's face into a heaping mess of mashed potatoes and brown gravy. The day after that incident, Lucy suggested we eat at a small table outside the cafeteria. Mikey and Randy protested, but since

Tommy, Jason and I agreed, and since majority vote rules in our group, we ended up eating outside until the end of the school year.

And that's where Randy and I found Jason right after my brush up with Timmy and Miles—exactly at that same table.

"Hey amigos," Jason said, removing the food from his lunch bag: a can of Coke, a peanut butter sandwich, and a chocolate chip cookie.

"What's up, Jason," I answered, fishing for the lunch money in my pocket. "Is everybody else already in line?"

"Yeah, what took you guys so long?" Jason asked.

"Got a little occupied," Randy said, looking at me. Telling the story about Miles and Timmy would eat up five more minutes, and that was something that neither Randy nor I wanted...not with our stomachs rumbling.

"You locos better get in line," Jason said, popping his soda with a fizz. "You're going to miss the first lunch of the year."

Tommy, Lucy, and Mikey were paying for their food by the time Randy and I grabbed our trays. Lucy gave us a warm wave from behind the register and I felt my heart skip a beat. Her hair was pulled back in a tight bun with a pencil stabbed through the center. Her golden crucifix sparkled from her soft, tan neck. Tommy and

Mikey stood behind her, thumbing through their wallets.

"Crap," Randy said, throwing his tray on the metal rack with a clang. "They're servin' veggie burgers."

I looked down the length of the long food window and saw a bucket of steaming vegetable patties topped with ketchup. The bucket next to it was filled with broccoli heads, sliced carrots, and green peas, and next to that was a basket of small rolls. None of it looked appetizing. The vegetables were soggy and the rolls looked burnt, but I could care less given my hunger.

"I reckon they'll serve the dreaded fish sticks tomorrow," Randy added and asked the server for two rolls.

Lucy and Mikey sat opposite each other at the far corner of the table. Jason and Tommy, respectively, sat in the middle, with Randy and me on the end. I was halfway relieved that Lucy wasn't sitting next to me for fear that my face might turn redder than Randy's hair had she been so close. Jason was picking some food out of his braces. He had finished half his sandwich and a couple bites of his cookie.

"I say we get him back," Randy said, chomping on his brownish-black roll.

Tommy had shown us his bruised eye and had told us the story about how he had gotten it: starting with the broken vase, then moving on to the shattered door, then to Dan's fractured arm, and finally finishing at his silver dollar black souvenir on his right eye. Tommy's story had been just as Mikey had told it on the bus. It was almost impossible to tell that Tommy's eye was injured without looking at it from close up, and even then it wasn't nearly as bad as we had been expecting. Tommy let out a long sigh of relief when we explained that no one would ask questions about something they couldn't see in the first place.

"Get Dan back?" Tommy asked. "Why waste our time?"

Randy stared at Tommy like Jimmy Kurtis had stared at Coach Barr when asking about his rules. He looked absolutely stunned that Tommy could be defending Dan after the story he had told.

"Are you kidding?" Randy asked.

"I'd like to get them all back," Mikey added. "Every one of the Jerks. Dan, Bruce, Tony, *and* Ricky. With all the crap that we've put up with the last few years, it's about time we strike back. I hate those bastards."

"We all do, loco, but what do you have planned?" Jason asked, taking another bite of his cookie.

"I don't know," Mikey admitted. "Maybe we could lock them in a basement and throw M-80s and stink balls down on them. It'll be just like the movie Revenge of the POWs, where the prisoners lock the guards in their own cells and torture them for all the evil things that they had done."

"Revenge of what?" Lucy asked.

"Revenge of the POWs, it's an oldie," Mikey explained. "It was on TV a few weeks ago."

"And how do you expect to lock them up?" Jason asked. "Tell 'em you're going to play good cop bad cop and slap the cuffs on? They'll beat your face worse than Tommy's if you try something stupid like that."

"We can overpower 'em. There's six of us and only four of them."

"Five of us," Randy said, looking at Lucy. Lucy's face lit up like a terrifying jack-o-lantern. I saw Jason lean back from the table, moving away from Lucy and the wrath that would follow. Randy had slipped in the same mud Jason had on the basketball courts.

"What do you mean five?!" Lucy bellowed across the table. "You don't think I can handle my own weight in a fight?"

"No, I what I meant was—" Randy hesitated.

"Don't give me that boy crap! You think that just because I'm a girl that I'm weaker than you. Well, you're damned wrong! I can run faster, jump higher, and think quicker than most boys my age. Remember when I kicked your butt chugging Cokes? I beat you by a landslide. And what about the time I killed you in chess? You remember that, don't you, Randy?"

"Lucy—"

"I'll fight you after school, if you want. I'll kick your butt from here to China."

Lucy was breathing like a raging bull. She glared directly at Randy's red face. Her fists were balled up and her knuckles were white. It amazed me how she looked both like a fighter that could rip Randy's head off and like a princess that could skip across a field of flowers with a picnic basket in her hand. It was almost frightening to see her so mean and attractive.

"Gee whiz, Lucy, I just meant that I wasn't sure if you could join us, that's all," Randy said, his lips quivering. "It's harder for you to hang out since you don't live in the same neighborhood."

"Oh..." Lucy said, and dropped her eyes to her food. She bit her lip and blushed. "Sorry, Randy."

The table was quiet for a moment. Jason's laughter eventually broke the silence and was soon joined by Tommy, Mikey, and myself. Lucy couldn't hold it in either and spit up a high-pitched giggle, covering her mouth as she laughed. Everyone was roaring except for Randy, caught in the middle of the joke once again.

We continued to laugh while Randy ignored us in frustration and went back to work on his food. After a couple of minutes, when the chuckles died down, Tommy looked up.

"Can you guys promise me something?"

We stared at Tommy and nodded. He was fiddling with his soda, making rings on the table with the condensation on the bottom of the can. I noticed that everyone at the table had taken advantage of the dollar chocolate milk special except for Jason and Tommy. Four white and brown cartons and two Cokes were scattered on the table. Jason had brought his own soda, and Tommy, I imagined, had reluctantly bought his.

Lactose intolerance is a bitch.

"Promise you won't tell anyone else about what I told you. Not anyone, especially adults." We nodded again. The sun crept behind a black cloud. "I just don't want any trouble, you know?"

"Sure Tommy, you've got our word," I said.

"Yeah, Scout's honor," Randy added, holding his fist to his chest.

Tommy smiled at us and for a moment it looked like he had something more to say, something he had left out of the story. "I also don't want anyone getting Dan back for what he did," Tommy said, clicking the aluminum opener on his can. "He's my brother and I can handle my own. I'll get him back in my own way. Besides, the last thing I want is for you guys to end up with a shiner, too. Dan and the Jerks are a lot stronger than you think. We may outnumber them, but it doesn't take much to push the odds against us."

I thought about Dan's sidekick, Tony Sanders, and his long switchblade. We all knew him as

Loony Tony because he had strangled a stray cat in Bruce's driveway with his bare hands. I had first seen the knife while playing catch in Tommy's backyard. Tony had pulled it out of his leather jacket pocket and had bragged to Dan that he had bought it in a pawnshop for forty bucks. The blade was a mirror stainless steel and the handle was made out of yellow ivory and brass links. I remembered jumping in fright after seeing the five-inch blade shoot out of the ivory with one click of a black button. I cringed at Tony's stretched, crazy grin as he admired the deadly way the sun reflected off its shiny blade. Dan, to my surprise, had looked frightened at Tony's look, too. I remembered thinking that Tony probably wouldn't think twice about stabbing that blade inside one of us if he got the chance. He'd watch us bleed with that same greasy smile. It would maybe bring back the joyful memories of the poor cat he had killed at Bruce's house.

"Hey, you guys wanna get the Baseliners together again?" Tommy asked, changing the subject. He took a sip from his soda.

"Damn straight!" Randy said, almost jumping out of his seat. "We've got another winning season ahead of us."

"Another season with the Babe," Mikey added, thumbing at himself, smiling gleefully.

"Babe? What are you smoking, pinche gordo?" Jason said. "I don't remember you hitting any home runs last year."

"Yeah? What about the game against the Chargers? The one where I nailed it over the fence."

"That was a foul, dipstick. It went left of the pole."

"No it wasn't; it was a homer. I saw it with my own eyes."

"What, through those thick bottles? You couldn't see your own hand in front of your fat face. It was a foul!"

"Homer!"

"Foul!"

"Shut-up you two," Lucy said. "When do you want to get together, Tommy?"

Tommy picked at one of the engravings on the table. The jagged letters read *Skhool Sucks*. "I'm not sure. I was thinking this afternoon, right after we get out. What do you think, Davy?"

"Sounds good to me," I said. The sun reappeared and warmed the table. I could feel the cool September breezes moving in. "But we can't play in the school field until next week. Did you guys see the bulletin on the gym wall? The field's gonna be closed because Hillerman West High is going to scrimmage out here. It sucks, but I guess we still have the Vineyard field, though."

"The Vineyard's cool," Tommy said and looked around. "Is everybody in?"

"Si," Jason said.

"Count me in, partner," Mikey said in a Clint Eastwood voice.

Randy and Lucy nodded.

The lunch bell sounded and kids poured out of the cafeteria. Some ran, some walked, and some strolled and talked like they didn't have a care in the world if they got a tardy slip. We threw our lunch remains in a rusted steel barrel and gathered our trays to return to the kitchen.

"We'll go home and get our stuff and then meet at around four," Tommy said.

Chapter 7

3640 Pinon Street

When I returned home, Lewis was eating chocolates and playing in the den with a toy fire truck in front of our nineteen-inch TV. The tube was turned to the Brady Bunch. It was the episode where Marsha gets hit in the face with a stray football right before her big date. My mother was sleeping on the couch with a cooking magazine in her lap and a glass of diluted iced tea on the corner table beside her.

We lived at 3640 Pinon Street, in a two-story, three-bedroom adobe house with a red brick patio and a pine-decked balcony. The bedrooms were on the second floor and the balcony belonged to the master bedroom. Lewis's room was adjacent to mine, with a connecting bathroom in between. The den, living room, and kitchen were the same sizes, 20' x 20', lined one after the other like a shotgun apartment: the kitchen was at the front, the living room was in the middle, and the den was at the rear. A creaky door led out from the den into our messy two-car garage, a garage that was cluttered with boxes of crap that had gradually built up over the years. There were cartons of used books, packages of old toys, and bags of ancient clothes that hadn't been worn since the seventies. It was so packed that my mom's Volvo was the only car that could fit inside; my father was forced to park his lime green Suburban in the front by the kitchen.

The backyard was a small grass lot with a tall elm to the east and a prickly yucca to the west. A tire swing attached by a frayed rope dangled from a gnarled elm limb. In between the elm and the yucca lay a cheap plastic picnic table with a flower umbrella that my dad had picked up at a Sears clearance sale. The umbrella was caked with dirt that had kicked up during the August monsoons.

My father's name was Seth Blake, and he was a pilot for Skyline Airlines, flying 747 and 767 jumbo jets. He traveled all over the world, sometimes spending weeks at a time away from home. The job was as demanding as it was stressful. He was faithful and loving, but he was also a stranger that passed in and out of our lives, a mystery man that brought Christmas presents and birthday toys. The job paid the bills, and that, more than anything else according to my dad, was the most important priority.

"Hey, Lewis," I said.

"Davy home, Davy home," Lewis shouted, rolling his fire truck madly on the carpet.

Mom woke up and stretched her arms. She looked at me briefly and looked down at the scattered chocolate wrappers that circled Lewis's body.

"Lewis!" she said, jumping up and moving to pick up the mess. "I told you, no chocolates."

"Hey, Mom," I said, tossing my backpack on the den floor.

"Take that bag to your room," she replied, never taking her eyes off the floor.

"Aww, Mom, in a minute."

"Do as I said."

"Don't you want to know about my first day?"

"Not right now."

"But Mom."

"Davy!"

I reluctantly picked up my pack and stormed up to my room. I shut the door, tossed the bag against the closet, and played catch against the wall with a tennis ball. *Not right now? Shoot, it was more like not ever.* Sure, I understood how hard it was taking care of Lewis and dealing with his constant needs. Lewis was a job and a half, and Mom didn't have the time or the energy to deal with me. But it still upset me. It still made me wish for some of her attention. Maybe I was being incredibly selfish, but why couldn't I get a little of what Lewis got?

Because you're the fortunate one, Davy. God gave you the brains so you could make something of your life. Please don't argue with me, you know how hard your father and I work to raise you right. We've got our problems, your dad with his drinking and me with my smoking, but we're still a fortunate family. We've got to take what we've got and make the best of it.

Mom's smoking wasn't anywhere as bad as Dad's drinking. Mom hadn't picked up a cigarette in two years, and that had been the time she found out about the head-on collision that had killed her sister during a skiing trip in the Hillerman Mountains. Dad, on the other hand, had made no effort to curb his addiction. Whenever he was in town, he'd get sloshed with his buddies at Big Time's bar on 8th Street. He rarely came home before two in the morning, and when he did return he was usually drunker than a pirate on a rum ship. And the next day...after his morning coffee to cure his hangover, he'd be off again, bright and early, flying to some other city. He promised he'd quit, but he promised a lot of things. The drinking was like a wedge in a log: each time he'd go out and get hammered, the wedge would sink a little deeper into the wood, driving us farther apart.

For fifteen minutes I bounced the tennis ball off the wall, hearing the hollow echo vibrate down the stairs, until I accidentally threw it against a corner of the doorframe and sent it sailing into my closet. When I went to retrieve it, digging underneath a pile of clothes, I saw my worn leather baseball glove. I had completely forgotten about our game in the Vineyard. I threw on a t-shirt and some playing shorts, grabbed my glove, and ran downstairs.

"I'm going to play baseball," I said.

"Not until you do your chores," Mom replied, scrubbing the chocolate stains off Lewis's face.

"Chores, chores!" Lewis replied gleefully.

"What chores?" I asked.

"The trash needs to be taken out and I need you to unload the dishwasher."

"Ma..."

I was about to complain, but I knew it was useless. I would be wasting my breath, and the sooner I got started on the job, the sooner I would be out in the field.

I moaned a reply that I'd do it.

Chapter 8

THE VINEYARD

Every kid has a special place they hide out, a play spot, a magical area that is as familiar to them as their name. It's the place where you can go to get away from the adults. It's a sanctuary for the underage, a refuge for those wanting to flee from mothers that make them wash dishes, clean rooms, and mow lawns. It's the one place where a kid can run as fast as his sneakers can kick up dirt, scream as loud as his lungs can exhale, laugh as long as his belly can hold out. There are no rules in this sacred place, no laws to be broken, and best of all...no responsibilities.

Our place was a five-minute bike ride south of our circular neighborhood. In this area, more than a hundred acres of land stretched out as far as the eye could see—land so wild and natural it almost seemed like something out of a western romance movie. We called it the Vineyard. The land had once been used to harvest grapes for a local winery, but those fruitful days had long since passed. In 1981, it was dry and barren save for a few scattered ponds where ducks and geese flocked. The only incoming source of water in the field was a muddy irrigation ditch that separated the Vineyard from an elementary school. The ditch flowed from west to east, and the school lay on the northern side of the embankment. The only way to cross the stream was over a bridge comprised of four half-rotted two-by-fours, boards which looked as if they might call it quits at a moment's notice and make a suicidal dive into the clouded water. Several irrigation routes ran out from the ditch and fingered through the Vineyard like veins in a leaf.

During the seventies, the land had been owned by Jack Lopez, a Mexican immigrant that struck it rich while drilling for oil in Roswell. Jack sold it in 1980 to a retired cattle rancher named Benjamin Phillips. Mr. Phillips had a two-story, four-bedroom country house with red shingles on a pitched roof. The house had a spectacular view of the Huckleberry landscape: to the east, it overlooked the Vineyard and the Hillerman Mountains; to the west, the mesa volcanoes and the stunning New Mexican sunsets.

The one feature that will always stand out in my memory (for more reasons than one) was a giant stained-glass window on the second floor. The window was a picture of a human-sized dove flying in a cold gray sky. The glass frame stood at least twenty feet high and fifteen feet wide. The bird's beady eyes faced the east, and it could be seen from any point in the field, even if you were way out in the sticks, five hundred yards past the ditch bridge. I've heard that the dove is supposed to be the bird of peace and love, but that particular dove never gave me that feeling. It looked sinister, wicked, like it was going to fly out of that stained-glass prison and dive ruthlessly at my face like in Hitchcock's classic, *The Birds*. Randy always complained that it gave him the heebie-jeebies whenever he looked at it, and although Tommy and Jason teased him about it, I secretly told Randy I shared the same sentiments.

That bird was the only occupant with Mr. Phillips. He was divorced, and his four grown children had moved to other states to start their own families. We often spotted him in the Vineyard, checking his front yard garden or doing repair work on his house. Randy nicknamed him the Handyman. I wasn't sure how handy Mr. Phillips was, but I was positive that he was strange. Sometimes, while playing baseball or touch football in the Vineyard field, we'd catch him staring at us from inside his house, usually from one of the second-story windows. It was like seeing a ghost in a haunted mansion peering down on you from behind dusty shutters. Unlike the bird, that sight gave everyone the heebie-jeebies.

There were rumors within our group that the house had been built on a graveyard and that a wandering, disturbed spirit possessed Mr. Phillips. Most of the rumors came from Mikey and his wild imagination, and although none of us really believed him, no one wanted to take a trip over to the house with a shovel to find out how many skulls we could dig up in the backyard. The creepiest tale came from Randy, who said that the Vineyard was once a bustling Navajo village that had been burned to the ground by white settlers during the Civil War. Randy claimed that over five hundred Indians had died on the very soil on which we were standing. This tale already had the hairs on the nape of our necks standing on end, but Randy made them fall out when he produced a piece of Indian pottery from his pants pocket, pottery he said he had found while playing out in the field. There were red drops on it...blood stains from a murdered family, Randy had said.

Tales like this passed around the group like breezes through a wind chime. Openly, of course, we all agreed that ghosts weren't real. But deep inside, where the monsters still hid underneath our bed and the boogieman still lurked in our closet, we had the uncertain fear that they *could* be real. Anything was possible, right? And even if the ghosts were a bunch of lame horror stories, Mr. Phillips was certainly real, and at times he seemed scarier than the unknown. It was easy to shove the thoughts of an invisible, disturbed spirit to the back our mind, but when the spirit was flesh and blood, staring down at you from a clouded window like a demented serial killer, it became a little harder to push away that picture. It was real.

Because of these stories, we decided to keep a safe distance away from the house. Our make-believe baseball field was a good fifty yards from it. We thought that distance would keep us out of Mr. Phillips's hair, out of the danger zone.

Had we had the benefit of hindsight, we would have doubled that distance...

"Hey, Davy, hurry the shit up!" Tommy yelled at me from the pitcher's mound.

Riding on my ten-speed mountain bike, my right hand gripping the handle, my left clutching my mitt, I cruised over the ditch and the four creaky two-by-four planks. Dust kicked up from my wheels. I sailed down a bumpy embankment, jumped over an oversized dirt clod and slammed on my brakes at first base. The wheels screeched to halt and my back tire jack knifed to the side.

"What took you so long?" Jason asked, thumping the baseball bat against his dusty sneakers.

"Yeah, Davy, we thought you skipped out," Mikey added.

"Relax, I'm not that late," I said, jumping off my bike and tossing it to the ground next to the other five cycles. My kickstand had broken off in an accident I had outside of Dave's Ice Cream Palace during the first week of summer vacation after the seventh grade.

"Davy, cover second base," Tommy said, snapping the ball off the crook of his elbow and catching it in midair.

"Better get ready to run," Jason said. "This one's goin' to la luna."

"The moon my ass," Mikey said, squatting behind Jason. We made Mikey play catcher for two reasons. The first was because of his eyes and second was because of Tommy's right arm. It was a well-known fact that Mikey couldn't see worth the damn out of his two-inch magnifiers; if he played first or second base, he'd probably get clobbered in the head with the ball or trip over one of the bases and break his leg; pitcher was definitely out of the question and no one played outfield since we didn't have enough people. The second reason was because Tommy had an arm of gold. If Mikey signaled a low fastball, Tommy would deliver a low fastball; if it was a high curveball, Tommy would pitch him one without a hitch. Mikey gave the signals in his glove. Tommy would either nod or shake his head, and the only thing Mikey would have to do next was hold his glove in the exact spot and wait for the ball to come. It was magic. Mikey sometimes complained about his pre-assigned duty, bickering about his right to play first base just like the great Bob Watson for the Yankees

(Mikey was a Yankees diehard—he'd sell his right hand to see Rick Cerone and Willie Randolph put on a show), but he was usually content with his position as long as we let him take turns at bat like the rest of us.

Lucy—now dressed in jeans, a light blue T-shirt, and an orange baseball cap with her brown ponytail pulled through the back—was standing guard at first base. Randy held third base, with his red hair swaying in the cool afternoon breeze. The sun seared down on us from a cloudless western horizon and made our shadows stretch long to the east.

I took my place at second base and nodded at Tommy.

"Okay, Jason, you ready for it?" Tommy asked.

"Bring it on," Jason said, spitting on the ground like he was a Major League pro swinging for the World Series.

Tommy took a step back, nodded at Mikey's signal, lowered his head, clenched the ball in his glove and wound up. He unleashed a high fastball that flew at Jason like a rocket. Jason took the biggest swing of his life and completely whiffed it. The ball slammed into Mikey's glove and exploded in a cloud of brown powder. Jason's aspirator slipped out of his back pocket and hit the ground.

"Strike!" Mikey called out. He was also the designated umpire.

"Ha, ha," Randy yelled.

"Wild swinger," I said.

"Vete a la mierda," Jason replied, flashing his middle finger while picking his aspirator out of a small weed and stuffing it in his back pocket.

Mikey tossed the ball back and Tommy wound up for another big throw. The materials for our game were simple: one bat, one ball, and four rocks for bases. The Major League bat belonged to Tommy and the baseball was Jason's. We had scavenged the four rocks from around the field. We had intentions to spray-paint them white so we could see them better, but they never materialized because we couldn't find the motivation or the time to buy the paint cans.

"I got it," Lucy said and chased down Jason's pop fly. Jason ran as fast as he could around first and second. Before he could reach third, Lucy snatched his ball.

"You're out!" Mikey bellowed.

"Puta madre!" Jason said, his lungs whistling from the exertion. He took a hit from his aspirator.

"You're up, Mikey," Tommy said, casually tossing the ball in the blue September sky.

Tommy was the best athlete out of any kid I knew. He was a natural at every sport. I once asked him to join me in an intramural soccer game at Roosevelt; we were short a man for the game and couldn't find any of the regular players. Tommy shrugged his shoulders, put on some spare cleats, and took center halfback. Tommy ended up scoring more goals than anyone had ever done in a single game—six in total. The record before that was five, and that was set by a kid named Doug Hector who'd had five years of practice. That game was Tommy's first and last. After the soccer match, and after all the praises and hollers from the other players, Tommy told me he didn't want to play again because he disliked the running.

Disliked the running... Truly unbelievable.

"All right, Mikey, how do you want it?" Tommy asked.

"A low fastball, why don't ya," Mikey said, swinging the bat in quick, clumsy strokes.

Jason took Mikey's spot as catcher and squatted behind home base. Tommy nodded at Jason's signal and tossed Mikey a present: a low fastball.

Now, what happened next changed the course of our year forever, and perhaps our entire lives. To this day I'm not sure how Mikey managed to hit the ball as far as he did since he rarely hit one past first base. Maybe it had something to do with luck or maybe it was Mikey putting all his weight into the swing, all one hundred and twenty pounds of his oversized belly. Perhaps it was Tommy's fastball served on a silver platter, a throw as perfect as the morning dew. I think it was probably a combination of the three that sent that ball sailing into the air—over the ditch, over the oak tree where I had shot the crow with Tommy just weeks earlier, over Mr. Phillips's backyard.

We watched in disbelief as the ball continued to soar and shrink. It was a complete foul, but no one cared. All we were concerned about was where that ball was headed.

"Holy shi—" Jason said, and it was all he got to say before the ball smashed right through the stained-glass window, smack in the middle of the dove's black eyes.

CRASH!

The window shattered into a million pieces, the fragments looking like twinkling diamonds as they fell. The entire stained-glass pane was destroyed, gone, obliterated. There was no fixing it. Not now, not ever.

"Oh no!" Mikey said, his mouth agape, his eyes wide.

"Get out of here!" Tommy shouted, but we were already making tracks.

We kicked our heels up, stuck our chests in front of our hips and hauled ass. I could feel my heart in my throat, pumping madly, and I could smell the sweet, delicious aroma of a distant barbecue, a dinner I desperately wished I was digging into at that very moment—having nothing to do with the baseball incident.

Tommy was the first to reach the bikes. He was pedaling before the rest of us caught up. Lucy grabbed her pink ten-speed with her flower basket and hopped on. Randy and Jason tossed their cycles up and were rolling in no time. I would have been riding with them, but the left rubber handle on my bike was caught in Mikey's rear spokes. I frantically twisted and turned the handle.

"Get your piece of crap off mine," Mikey screamed, yanking his bike madly.

"Hold on, quit pulling," I said.

Finally the handle came free and I was able to get on. Tommy and Jason were already across the ditch, and I felt an enormous pit of rage watching them pedal away, knowing that they were practically in the clear while I was still at ground zero. I stood up and kicked as hard as I could, but before I reached the ditch I heard a loud crash behind me.

"Ahhh!" Mikey cried.

I didn't want to look back. I wanted to close my eyes until I was home gulping down a glass of milk and snacking on a candy bar, but something forced me to turn my head. Mikey was on the ground, grabbing his ankle.

"Help," Mikey said.

Despite my urge to keep riding, my instinct to disappear into the warmth and safety of our neighborhood, I slammed on the brakes and skidded to a dusty stop in front of the ditch bridge.

"Come on, Mikey!" I screamed.

"I can't," Mikey replied.

"Come on!" I repeated, almost delirious from the fear.

"It's broken."

I didn't care. *Screw your broken ankle. Pick your lard ass up and get out of here. We'll deal with it later.*

But there wouldn't be a later. Only now. Mikey was injured and there was nothing I could say or do that was going to make him get back on his bike. I looked across the ditch and saw the rest of the Gang disappear behind the neighborhood fence. The hate came back with a vengeance.

Those rotten bastards skinned out on us.

"Damn," I said.

I threw my bike down and ran back. Mikey was holding his ankle and rolling back and forth, as if he was trying to rock-a-bye it back to health.

"Where does it hurt?" I asked, staring at his wound and having no idea what I was supposed to be looking for.

"Right here."

Mikey pointed to the bony side of his foot, the part that sticks out like a knob. A two-inch gash was soaking his sock red. I had never seen a broken ankle, but it was my guess that it would look very similar to what I was looking at. It was already swollen and purple.

"I hit it on that rock," Mikey said, pointing behind him.

I followed his finger and saw a large, jagged concrete block. I had seen a lot of them around the Vineyard, most of them along the irrigation routes.

"Come on," I said, putting one arm around his fleshy waist. "You've got to get up."

"Ahhh!" Mikey screamed, and pushed me away.

This is beyond awful, I thought. *Mikey is going to screw us, and if my parents find out about what happened, they'd whip my backside so hard that I'd have to wear diapers for the next few months just to sit down. And that was only the start of it. TV, radio, movies—my parents would ground me from all of that until my high school graduation.*

There had to be a way out of this. I looked around frantically, but before I could conjure up an answer to our predicament, I heard a deep voice vibrate behind me.

"Well, well."

Mikey and I turned to the dreaded voice and saw a man clad in denim overalls, bulky brown boots, and a straw hat. The man's wrinkled face was baked red, and his black hair was sticking out from under his hat in sweaty clumps. In his thick hands, standing toward the dying afternoon sky, was a rusty pitchfork.

Mr. Phillips! The crazy old man is going to kill us. He'll stab us through the neck with his forked weapon and laugh as blood shoots out of our throats. He's been dreaming of the day he could put an end to us, dreaming behind those murky windows in that psycho house of his with the shattered beady-eyed bird of peace. He'll get revenge for his precious bird. He'll stab us and laugh with the feathered beast as we drift into darkness.

"Where did your friends go?" Mr. Phillips asked, scratching his face with the pitchfork.

"What friends?" I asked. It was probably the biggest lie I had ever told, right up there with the time I told my mother I hadn't broken a three hundred dollar vase she had received for her tenth wedding anniversary.

"Don't give me that crap, son," Mr. Phillips said.

Mikey was stone quiet. The little bastard who loved to shoot his mouth off between classes and at group campfires had somehow lost his tongue.

Mr. Phillips had obviously seen my friends playing baseball a hundred times, but I still couldn't give them away. Telling him about the Gang was almost like telling an enemy general which one of your troops you wanted him to shoot first. It was a complete sellout, and although they had technically sold me out, riding like a pack of dogs with their tails between their legs, that still didn't make it right. If I told Mr. Phillips about them, I'd be a rat.

"I don't know what you're talking about," I said, fearfully glancing at his devilish pitchfork.

Mr. Phillips grunted and knelt next to Mikey. "What happened?"

"It's broken, I think," Mikey said.

Mr. Phillips tossed aside his pronged weapon and delicately grabbed the bloody ankle with his calloused hands. The tips of his fingernails were embedded with dirt. Mikey glanced at me with a concerned and frightened expression.

"It's not broken," Mr. Phillips said in an almost academic voice. "But you'll need a bandage for it."

The barbecue aroma returned, stronger now, and once again I imagined myself sitting outside chowing down on a fatty hamburger, far away from this field, light years from the crazy man that loved to stare at his innocent prey.

"Help me get him up," Mr. Phillips said, putting one arm around Mikey.

"What?" I asked, stepping back a pace.

"We need to get this cleaned off. Pick him up."

Before I could tell him that there was no way on God's green Earth that I would let him take me and Mikey into the spook palace, into the house where he would lock us into some metal cage in a dark and damp basement littered with rats the size of dogs, I found myself grabbing Mikey's arm, tossing it around my neck, and lifting him from his indented dirt mold.

"This way," Mr. Phillips said, walking slowly with Mikey's other arm.

We plodded among weeds and mud clods toward the red-shingled house. Above our heads, forming a large V, a flock of geese made their way south, chanting and squawking as the sun pitched below the orange horizon.

Chapter 9

THE HOUSE

We didn't see any cages or rats, nor did we see a dark basement. Instead, we saw colorful paintings of the Hillerman Mountains, life-size sculptures of unknown ranchers and cowboys, and books about the desert frontier. Each art piece had the initials BJP. The masterful works were located all around the four-bedroom house—kitchen, den, living room—and it made the place bright and warm...almost eerily cozy.

Mr. Phillips had led us to the rear of the house and into a small bedroom. Mikey sat on a pine chair with his leg propped up on a twin bed, and I sat beside him, my hands in my lap.

"That should do it," Mr. Phillips said, taping the white bandage in place on Mikey's injury. He was kneeling on the floor with his straw hat perched atop his head.

Mikey moved his ankle from side to side and investigated the repairs. It had only taken Mr.

Phillips a few minutes to complete the bandaging, but it looked like it had taken hours. It was the work of a man that knew what he was doing.

Mr. Phillips placed the adhesive tape back into a small gray medical kit. "I'd stay off that bike for a while if I were you."

"Thanks," Mikey said, his eyes glued to his foot.

"So," Mr. Phillips said, standing up, "you boys gonna tell me the names of the others, or are ya still holdin' out?"

I looked at Mikey and he glanced at me. We both said nothing and kept our eyes fixed on the hardwood floor.

"Yep, yep," Mr. Phillips said, "just as I figured. I've got two hens in the barn with one snake, and both are pecking away as if they weren't in danger." He took off his straw hat and ran his hand through his sweaty hair. "Just as I figured. But it really doesn't matter to me. It's y'all's loss, really."

I thought about the broken beady-eyed bird and the cage in the basement. The house looked all right, clean of torture devices, but what did I know? My heart raced again.

"You boys have any idea what that window cost me?"

We shook our heads.

"Eight thousand dollars."

Mikey and I must have looked like cartoon characters because our jaws hit the floor in unison.

"I don't suppose you two have that kind of dough in your back pocket, do ya?" Silence followed. "No, I didn't figure so," Mr. Phillips said, moving to the bedroom window, which faced the Vineyard. "You kids are always playing baseball and goofing off out there. You know, back when I was a kiddo, I used to work my tail off. When I wasn't at school, I was busy out in the field, or tendin' the animals. I worked from sunrise to sunset and prayed that I had time to eat in between."

Mr. Phillips scratched his baked face and stuffed his thumbs into his blue overall straps. The house had a thin odor of clay and paint.

"Well, what are your names?"

Mikey's lips, once again, were zipped shut.

"Davy and Mikey, sir," I said, thinking about Tommy, Randy, Lucy, and Jason hauling ass on their bikes...pedaling out of sight...into the safety of the neighborhood.

"How often do you play baseball?"

"Ummm, well sir," I said, wondering if I should keep my fat trap shut–plead the fifth, as they say in those movies on TV. "During school, we play almost every day."

"Every day, eh?" Mr. Phillips repeated, walking back to the bed and staring at us with his aged blue eyes. "I got a little work for ya, then. Whether or not your friends are going to help is your business. Again, if I were you, I'd get their tails out here. It'd make the job a lot easier for you two hens."

"What do you want us to do, sir?" Mikey asked, suddenly able to find his voice again.

"That's not important now," Mr. Phillips replied, idly glancing at his callused hands. "You'll find that out tomorrow, after school gets out and you come back."

"Come back?" Mikey asked.

"You got a hearing problem, son?"

"No, sir."

"That's what I said. I want you to come back to my house right after classes. You're going to pay off your debt. Now don't y'all think about skipping out on me, either. I know where you live and I know you have very worried parents that would love to sting your hide if they found out what happened. If you don't come, I reckon I'll have no choice but to tell them about the window."

"You mean you're not going to tell our parents about this now?" I asked.

"Not as long as you cooperate with me. We can keep this little incident just between us."

Mikey and I looked down at the bandaged ankle. We were stuck. If we decided to bail tomorrow and ditch Mr. Phillips, our parents would surely find out and do more than just sting our hide...they'd brand it for life. We'd get out of one jam and into another. But if we showed up, we'd be in the hands of this strange man. We'd be at his mercy.

"If you two pick up your bikes and bring them back, I'll drive you home and tell your parents about...Mikey was your name, wasn't it?" Mikey nodded. "About Mikey's bike accident. Again, I'll leave the rest of the story out of it."

"How do we know you won't just tell anyway?" I asked.

Mr. Phillips frowned at me. "I reckon you really don't have a choice, boy. But since I don't know if your parents can afford to pay for the damages, and since I know none of you kids can, telling them would hurt me as much as it would hurt you. I would lose out on your services."

Hearing him say the word services made my skin crawl. What exactly did that mean? Chopping wood in his backyard? Chopping murdered corpses? There were a million things he could make us do.

Mr. Phillips checked his watch. "It's getting late. Hurry up and bring your bikes back before your parents call the police. I'll get my truck ready."

Chapter 10

LUNCH THE NEXT DAY

I couldn't sleep a wink that night, and I was spacey in my classes the following day, including PE, where Coach Barr drilled us ruthlessly around the gravel track for ten heart-pounding laps. Yesterday's incident played over and over again in my mind like a broken record: the crack of Mikey's bat, the sailing ball, the shattered fragments, the injured ankle. The images were burned in my mind's eye.

Eight thousand dollars.

Mr. Phillips, as he promised, had told my mother about Mikey's fall but mentioned nothing about the window. My mom thanked him kindly and said she was glad I was all right. She didn't suspect anything unusual about his story.

"Hey," I said, sitting down at the lunch table.

"Hey," Tommy replied.

Tommy, Lucy, Randy, and Jason looked at me briefly, then continued to eat. I hadn't said a word to Lucy and Randy in class, and we didn't get a chance to tell Lucy on the bus since her dad had driven her to school, but I knew they were dying to know the story.

The table was quiet for a few painful minutes before Tommy's curiosity boiled over.

"Did you guys get caught?"

I glanced at Mikey, who looked like a little banker with his glaring glasses—a sandwich in one hand, a soda in the other.

"Yeah," I said. "We tried to get away but Mikey fell off and hurt himself. Mr. Phillips was right behind us. We had nowhere to run."

"Shit," Tommy said, speaking the sentiments of the table.

"What did he do?" Jason asked, picking food out of his braces.

I suddenly remembered I had forgotten my retainer at home; I had more important things to worry about than dental work. "Nothing, yet," I said, looking at the peanut butter and jelly sandwich Mom had packed for me. I felt full even though I had only taken a few bites out of it. "We have to go back this afternoon."

"This afternoon?" Lucy asked with her long brown hair streaming in the light wind. "What for?"

"I'm not sure," I said. "He didn't tell us. The window was eight thousand dollars."

The Gang looked exactly as Mikey and I had looked when we first heard the news: their eyes wide, their jaws comically agape.

"That can't be right," Jason said. "He's loco."

"Maybe," I said, "but what was I going to say about it? I couldn't exactly ask him for a receipt to show proof. Not after what we did." The group stared at me. They were hanging on every word, every syllable. "You guys don't have to come. You're not in this yet and you don't have to be. Mikey and I can take the heat."

Mikey shot me a glance as if I were crazy.

"Bullcrap," Tommy said in a commanding voice. "That's total garbage, Davy. We shouldn't have wussed out on you like that. You or Mikey." Tommy looked at the group; his black eye had completely healed. "It was a weak thing to do, a shitty thing, and I'm sorry for it."

Mikey and I nodded.

"I'm sorry, too," Jason said, and creased his Michigan hat. "Lo ciento, amigos."

"Same here," Randy said. "I was just scared, you know?"

"Yeah, sorry Davy...Mikey," Lucy said, flashing her bright green eyes. "That was pretty girly of me."

"Don't worry about it," I said to the Gang. I was beginning to get my appetite back; I took another bite of my sandwich. "I would have done the same thing you guys did if given another chance."

"Yeah, but you didn't," Tommy said in the same commanding voice, sounding strangely like my father. "You stayed behind for Mikey, and we should have joined you. What time does he want us there?"

"Right after school," Mikey said.

"Oh man..." Randy said, running his hand through his red hair. "I reckon he's gonna let us have it."

"He'll do more than that," Jason said. "Eight thousand big ones! Man, it would take me years to earn that kind of green off the allowance I get."

"Try decades for me," Tommy said.

"What if we don't show up?" Randy asked, looking around timidly.

"No go," I said immediately. "He says he knows where Mikey and I live and he'll tell our parents if we ditch out. He was dead serious when he said it."

"So it's the old man and lady or it's Mr. Phillips," Tommy said, making condensation Coke can rings on the jagged table again.

"I'd rather take my old man than that crazy nut," Randy said.

"Not me," Jason said. "My dad would ream me."

"Me, too," Tommy said.

A good reaming was the least that Tommy's father would do, I thought. Tommy might just end up in the hospital if he added to the Jeep crisis.

"I'd do anything to keep what happened away from my parents," Lucy said. "Well, almost anything."

The sun beamed down on us mercilessly and made the table a hot stove. September had arrived, but August was putting up a stubborn fight. Another flock of geese soared far above our heads; they flew on instinct, ignoring the heat, blindly recognizing that winter was on the edge of the seasonal horizon.

We picked at our food and pondered over what Mr. Phillips had in store for us, and how we were going to lie to our parents. I thought about the broken vase I had lied to my mother about. It had happened one day while I was playfully bouncing a tennis ball in the house. The ball hit a crack in the floor, flew in the wrong direction, smacked the vase off its shelf, and shattered on the tile (the vase, not the ball). Since nobody saw or heard the accident, I decided to throw the evidence in a trash bag and stuff it in the bottom of our outdoor garbage can. Throwing it away in the kitchen wastebasket was too risky since there was still a chance they could stumble upon the broken fragments and bust me. I got rid of the ball, too...just in case Mom put two and two together. Several days and several sleepless nights later, my mother asked me what had happened to her precious Chinese vase and I shrugged my shoulders like a good kid that eats all the veggies on his plate and always says please before borrowing five dollars. She believed me and I never told her the truth. I felt like the world's biggest criminal, not to mention the world's worst son, but I couldn't fess up. The more days that passed, the more serious the lie became. It was like a bad weed in a garden—its roots fingering farther into the soil, its ugly branches choking the life out of the surrounding plants. I was the garden, and there was no way I could pull up the behemoth plant after months of nourishment.

"I heard Principal Pinner slipped on the front sidewalk this morning," Jason said, breaking the stress with another subject.

"Biffed it!" Lucy said, laughing wildly, her hand over her mouth.

"Like a cowboy off his saddle," Mikey Eastwood said. "Dat der poor fella didn't see the puddle of water. He stepped in an' down came the giant. Right flat on der backside."

"No way," Tommy said, chuckling so hard the drink in his hand started to fizz over.

"Swear my life on it," I said. "Mikey and I saw it from the bus. A couple of kids had to help him up."

"Man, he looked pissed," Mikey said.

It really wasn't that funny when we saw it in person, but it was somehow hilarious now. Picturing hard-nosed Pinner landing straight on his flabby butt was too comical to bottle up. Pinner always had his finger on us, in and out of the detention room, and it wasn't often that we got the upper hand.

We laughed under the blistering sun, listening to the geese chant in the blue dome hundreds of feet above. The distant cries of the birds seemed light-years away, calls from a strange and foreign world. We laughed in spite of what was to come that afternoon...whatever crazy Mr. Phillips had planned for our group.

Chapter 11

Back Again

After the previous day's episode, I decided to leave my bike in the garage and walk to the Vineyard. I told my mother I was going to play baseball with the Gang—oh, how those dreaded weeds grow—and she told me to be safe. It was a beautiful afternoon in the Twin Heights neighborhood, with the wind caressing the trees and the sun coloring the freshly mowed grass. It was supposed to be a simple walk: around Baxter road, through the gate in the back fence, across Hillwater road, past Grant elementary school, over the rickety ditch bridge, and into the Vineyard. I thought it best to leave the bike after what had happened to Mikey.

It was a costly mistake.

"Hey shit head!"

The voice came from behind me just as I turned out of our cul-de-sac. The terrifying sound was unmistakable. It belonged to one person: Dan Smith.

I should have dropped my glove and hit the road right there, but, like all stupid mistakes, I turned to see who it was. Strolling behind me, like a pack of greasy thugs from a mob movie, were Dan, Bruce, Ricky, and Tony. The whole damned crew.

"Come over here," Dan said, an evil smile creasing his white face.

I continued to walk, a pace faster now, and was paralyzed with fear. *Can't go back home, too far for that. Can't hide, they'll find me. How about help?* I looked around but didn't see a soul. Where were the adults when I needed them?

"I said get your ass over here!" Dan repeated.

The fear hit me and I booked it. I cut into a backyard filled with bushes and shrubs. My heart pounded in my throat, my fists were clenched into iron balls. Thorns and branches tore at my thighs and face. I weaved in and out of the vegetation, hearing the many footsteps closing in, thumping harder with each beat. I ran into a chain-link fence, monkeyed up, and scaled it in a matter of seconds. I thought the fence would deter the mob, but they climbed up faster than I had. They were determined.

I sprinted into another backyard, this one an open grass lot. Blood poured out of a cut just above my left brow and blinded me. I worked with one eye, looking for a place to hide, but found nothing. I turned sharply to the right, racing as fast as my burning legs would carry me. Another fence blocked my path, this one wooden, and I plunged into it at full speed. The baseball glove was still locked in my left hand in a fierce grip, and it slowed me down as I tried to jump the fence. I felt a hand close around my ankle and slip away as I hurdled over.

"You're gonna get it!" Dan shouted behind the fence.

"Dead meat!" another voice said.

I split across a barren plot of land. It was completely empty, the worst place to run. My only hope was a gate at the far end of the lot, the only chain-link door that led out of the neighborhood and into Hillwater road. Beyond that, the vegetation was thick and it might give me the cover I needed. The veins in my neck stuck out like cables. I could feel the blood pulsing in my temples as I pushed faster.

"Quick little bastard," a voice gasped behind me.

My torso stuck out over my legs, my arms pumped up and down as if pulling the imaginary ropes of a church bell. I was halfway to the gate, halfway to safety, but the footsteps were closing in rapidly. I could hear the others panting as they ran.

"Get him, Danny," Bruce yelled from a distance.

About twenty feet from the gate, a five-second dash, my foot clipped the edge of a rotted log. I went down hard, face first, right into the solid dirt. My body skidded over rocks, stickers, and leaves. It was over.

"You little shit," Dan said, doubled over above me, gasping for air. "You're a freakin' greyhound."

It's funny, but when I turned and looked at Dan, it was as if I saw a new person. He looked like an ordinary kid who had just run the final stretch in a high school track meet and was complimenting me on my performance. It was as if it were all a game and Dan would tell me that I had run the good race, pat me on the back, and make his way home. It felt that way for a brief instant, but the feeling soon disappeared when the greasy tribe reared their ugly faces.

"You're a goner now, Davy," Bruce said, his freckles as red as his blazing crimson hair.

"Yeah, dead as a duck," Loony Tony said, practically drooling as he said it. He had a black bowl cut that was evenly parted down the middle and plastered to his skull.

Dan grabbed my neck and pulled me up. There was a small cast on his left arm, evidence of the fracture from his father. I would later wonder how Dan had managed to scale those fences with that cast on, but not at that moment. At that period of time my primary concern was whether I was going to live to see another sunset.

"When I tell you to get your ass over, you better come," Dan said, drilling his fist into my stomach. The air popped out of me like a pierced balloon, and I heaved over. "I hate it when you make me run like that." Dan slapped my face with the back of his hand, busting the dam in my nose and flooding my lips with blood. I managed to scream with what little air I had left in my lungs.

"Let's string him to a tree!" Loony said.

"Yeah, and cover him with shit," Bruce added.

"Or tar, if we can find some," Ricky said.

Dan contemplated the suggestions from his crew, devising the next step in their torture. I closed my eyes and imagined I was somewhere else—like the barbecue dinner I had smelled the afternoon before.

"Yeah, we'll look for somethin', but first he gets a wedgie," Dan said, and yanked my Hanes tighty-whities with a powerful heave. My ass and crotch burned like fire as he pulled the elastic harder, sometimes lifting me off the ground.

"Hey, stop that!" an adult voice shouted.

Standing less than twenty yards to my right was Mr. Caston, one of the residents of the neighborhood. I had only seen him a few times around the circle, mostly in his car. My mother told me he was a banker, but he looked more like a football player with his broad shoulders and bulky legs.

"Who are you?" Mr. Caston asked, closing in.

"Get out of here," Dan said, and broke away down the same path they had come. The Jerks were right behind, kicking up dust as they ran. Mr. Caston watched them take off and then walked toward me.

I undid my fly and relieved the pressure down below. The back of the underwear elastic had ripped and the cotton fabric was stretched beyond repair. I continued gasping for air.

"Are you all right?" Mr. Caston asked, still standing a good ten yards away.

"Yeah," I said, picking my mitt up off the ground. The glove, unlike my body, hadn't sustained a scratch.

"Who were those boys? Where do they live? Why were they hurting you?"

I'm not sure why I did what I did next. Perhaps it was fear of dealing with adults who just wouldn't or couldn't understand things kids went through. Perhaps it was because I was running late and missing my unwanted meeting with Mr. Phillips. Perhaps it was because I was just like Tommy and his black eye.

I just don't want any trouble, you know?

I'm not sure if there even was a correct answer, but I decided to run like the Jerks, except in the opposite direction. Mr. Caston tried to chase after me but his legs were too old for that kind of foolishness.

"Wait!" I heard him yell as I ran through the gate and down Hillwater road toward the ditch. "I want to talk to you!"

I sprinted all the way to the Vineyard, never looking back.

***

"It's about time, Davy," Jason said, firing his aspirator trigger.

"Gosh, what happened to your face?" Lucy asked.

The Gang was standing beside the scarred oak, anxiously waiting for me. They had brought their baseball gear just as I had—our parents would have grown suspicious if we had left to play ball without actually taking our equipment. Surprisingly, only Jason and Lucy had brought their bikes. I guessed Tommy, Randy, and Mikey had also thought walking was safer than riding.

"I'll tell you about it later," I said, making sure my ripped underpants were safely tucked back in. I didn't want to look like an idiot.

"Well, let's do it," Tommy said. His blond flattop looked like a fuzzy peach.

We left the two bikes beside the scarred oak and marched with our faces pointed at the cracked ground. The sky was scattered with clouds, but none of them promised rain. The clouds moved in and out of the sun's path, playing tricks on our shadows. A lonely caw sounded in the distance...perhaps the cry of the black-feathered widow still in mourning for what I had done. A short gust of wind carried the light smell of fertilizer.

I'll never forget that walk as long as I live: Mikey, casually flicking small pebbles in the dusty field, limping with his bad ankle; Randy, whistling some rock tune to himself, either Aerosmith or the Rolling Stones; Lucy with her brown ponytail sticking out of her orange cap, fidgeting with her sparkling crucifix necklace while slapping the mosquitoes off her tan shoulders; Jason, cleaning dirt out of his aspirator and blasting it to see if it was working properly; Tommy, leading the pack and strolling with an unusual calmness; and me, still feeling the pain in my nose and crotch from my scuffle with the Jerks. We were scared, but we were together. It was as if our unity made us stronger, and the problem less severe. It was a feeling that if anything happened to one, it would happen to all. I don't think I could have made that walk with just Mikey. I would have skinned out, told my mother about the baseball accident and let her take care of the rest (like she always did when I was in trouble). And I think it's fair to say that Mikey would have done the same. But Mikey and I weren't alone, and we were making that walk as a group. It was the first time we were going to face up to the consequences. It was the first time we felt like adults.

The closest I've ever come to that experience was years later, while sitting in a hospital waiting room for Susan to deliver Nick. It was a rainy August night in Los Angeles during one of the worst storms of the year and Susan was having labor complications. The doctor told me she had lost a significant amount of blood and that there was a possibility that we could lose the baby. I was a nervous wreck. I felt as if I were standing on a platform that was slowly being pulled out from under me. The one thing that kept me from slipping off and falling into the darkness was Susan's mother and father, sitting on either side of me. Their presence somehow eased my stress...lessened my burden.

"There he is," Tommy said, pointing at Mr. Phillips.

Ten yards in front of us and right beside the red-shingled house, Mr. Phillips was spray-painting a white X on the ground. A yellow plaid shirt and faded denim jeans had replaced yesterday's blue overalls, but the straw hat and thick brown boots remained on his person. Behind him, standing six feet high, lay a mound of posts and rails, a sight that both interested and frightened us.

Did he want us to build a house?

We closed in and Mr. Phillips gave us a wrinkled, sinister smile. "I'll be damned. I swore on my good mother's grave I'd never see the likes of you two hens again." He stared at Mikey and me and then looked at the others. "And not only did they come back, but they've bought their accomplices, too."

"This is everybody," I said. "Everyone that was there yesterday."

"Well, under normal cerm'stances I'd say hello and introduce myself, but this isn't supposed to be a party, is it?" We stared blankly at him, wishing he'd just get on with it. "No matter, my name is Benjamin Phillips. Mr. Blake, who are your friends?"

"This is Tommy, Lucy, Randy, and Jason," I said, running down the line. "You already know Mikey."

Mr. Phillips nodded, took off his hat and looked at the western sun. His black hair had the same disheveled, sweaty appearance. The spray paint in his hand read *Jake's Paints* in red cursive at the top.

"I suppose y'all already know about the damage you've done," Mr. Phillips said, turning back to us. "And I figured y'all know I've got some work cut out for you." We nodded. "Well, the sooner we start the better; the sun's setting." Mr. Phillips placed the can down and moved to the mound of lumber. "This here's called woodgrain. We're going use this to build a three-rail ranch fence around my property. We've got sixty-one posts and a hundred and eighty rails. Each post has to be cemented in the ground at equal lengths and each rail has to be attached at exact heights. If our measurements are off, we're gonna find ourselves up that old familiar creek without a paddle."

He looked at us and we stared at the pile. It seemed unreal...absurdly enormous.

He continued, "Now, I've got all the tools we'll need: hammers, levels, bracing sticks, measuring tapes, spools of nylon string, bags of Fastcrete, augers, clamshell diggers, and plenty of cans of Jake's famous paint. They only thing I need is a group of busy bees. That's where you Major Leaguers fit in."

We stared at the endless display of posts and rails, beginning to regret our decision to come out. The pile seemed to speak for itself, telling us it would take weeks, months, seasons to do the job.

"Y'all play baseball almost every afternoon, right?"

We nodded, despite the urge to tell him that that wasn't right...that we only played once a year and this would be the last time we would be able to make it out.

"Good, that's exactly when I'll need you," Mr. Phillips continued. "Now I know your poor parents don't know about the mess you've dug yourselves into, but I do know that you'd like to keep this our little secret. That's fine by me. What you tell your parents and how you deal with your problems is your business. But I hope you realize that there's a chance they might find out anyway. A good one, perhaps, if you're working with me every day."

He had a point. Our parents had bought the story so far, but stack up the days and one of us was bound to slip up: leave a glove at home, forget the bat in the garage, accidentally leak out info during dinner. The possibilities were endless, especially when we were talking about a project that would take as long as the one in front of us.

"How long this remains in the dark will depend on you. If your parents find out before the work is over, I'll be forced to explain myself, and that means telling them everything. The foul, the baseball, the shattered eight thousand dollar window... You hens catching me?"

We nodded.

"Yes, sir, we get you," Tommy said, affirming our position. "We'll take care of it."

Mr. Phillips grinned at Tommy's answer. He seemed content, almost delighted. "Good, we have an understanding then. Now that that's settled, let me explain the first step in our construction."

Mr. Phillips pulled a long, round cylinder from the woodpile and popped off its plastic top. Inside, he removed a rolled sheet of paper.

"Are those blue-prints?" Mikey asked, pushing his glasses to the bridge of his nose.

"Very good," Mr. Phillips said. "I take it you've seen some before."

"Only once," Mikey replied, "when my uncle Henry was building a new house. It was a big old place in Louisiana with a pool and a patio and a huge—"

Jason elbowed Mikey in the stomach and saved us from Uncle Henry's story. Mikey shot Jason a pissed glance and elbowed him back.

"Come over here," Mr. Phillips said, pointing to a flat space on the ground.

He unrolled the prints and placed a rock on each corner so that the wind wouldn't carry them off into never-never land. With a stick in one hand and his hat in the other, he pointed to the layout of the fence. It was an incredibly detailed map: his house on one end, the Vineyard on the other, and a fence in the shape of a half square in the middle. The three-railed fence hugged Mr. Phillips's house and enclosed thousands of square feet of backyard property. We were impressed at the work he had put into it.

"And this is where we'll finish up. There's sixteen feet between each post. Before we can start on cementing, we need to put X's along the strings."

We stupidly scratched our heads.

"X's?" Tommy asked.

"Yeah, y'all see those batter boards I have fixed out there?" He pointed to an area where pine boards had been hammered together in what looked like six tiny guard rails. There was one at the start and end of the imaginary fence. Four more had been built at the corners (two on each corner), and three white strings had been tied to the middle of each batter board—each string making a straight line along the yet-to-be-built fence. "We need to follow those strings every sixteen feet and mark the spot where the posts will be so we know where to dig. Otherwise, our fence will run like a crazy horse."

We still had a hard time grasping what it was he wanted us to do, and I think he read that confusion on our faces.

"You, what's your name again?" Mr. Phillips asked.

"Jason."

"Jason, go over to that box and grab me two cans of paint."

Jason made for it. Mr. Phillips removed the rocks on the blue-prints, rolled the paper up and stuck it back into its cylinder. Jason returned with the spray cans.

"Okay, over here."

We followed Mr. Phillips as he moved to the spot where we had seen him mark his first post. He removed a 100' measuring tape from his rear pants pocket and handed Tommy the tongue.

"Tommy, isn't it?"

"Yes, sir," Tommy said.

"Take this paint can and walk directly east until I holler stop."

Tommy did as he was told and stopped when Mr. Phillips gave him the call.

"That's exactly sixteen. Now spray an X on that spot. Make sure you put it on the inside of the string."

"Right here?" Tommy asked, pointing directly below him.

"You got it."

Tommy marked it and looked back for approval. Mr. Phillips nodded and glanced back at us.

"You hens understand now?"

We said that we did.

***

We worked for the next two hours, marking X's in a half square around Mr. Phillips's property. At first we were excited about the job, like we were on some secret military mission to take over an enemy fort, or to defend our base from the ruthless fascists, but by the time we were allowed to go home, after measuring and painting sixty-one spots, the boredom had hit us.

The sun, lower now, peeked over the volcano mesa to say goodnight as we staggered home. Lucy and Jason decided to walk their bikes.

"This sucks big time," Mikey said.

"You can say that again," Randy replied.

Mikey wiped his glasses and scratched his puffy cheeks. "I can't believe he wants us to build that entire fence for him. He's a loony. A friggin' nut!"

"Our baseball season is ruined, too," Tommy said, kicking a rock.

"Do you guys think we can even do this?" Lucy asked. She had removed her orange cap and had let her hair flow freely over her shoulders. The evening darkness had stolen the light from her eyes.

"Are you kidding?" I asked. "There's no way we could build a thing like that. Those blue-prints were insane. And all those posts and rails that he had stacked up? It's as tall as a mountain. As wide, too. Mikey's right. He's gone crazy."

"And how the heck are we supposed to keep this from our parents?" Jason asked sharply. "How are we gonna do this everyday? *Every afternoon?* They'll find out one day. One of us will screw up. Esto es tonto." Jason spit on the ground and stared at Mikey. "And it's all your fault, gordo."

"My fault?" Mikey replied, seeing Jason glare at him.

"Yeah, if it wasn't for your stupid foul, none of this would have happened. Maybe you ought to get your thick glasses checked."

"Screw you!" Mikey said, and pushed Jason.

"Besa mi culo, puto!" Jason replied, shoving back.

They went after each other and wrestled in a patch of dead weeds. They rolled, kicked, and cursed back and forth, forming a cloud of dust. Tommy jumped in to break it up and Lucy, Randy and I helped out.

"Knock it off, you two," Tommy said. "Quit acting like sissies."

Mikey's white khaki shorts were colored brown, along with his glasses, which were clouded with a thin, dusty layer. Jason's asthma whistled in and out of his throat.

"He started it," Mikey said.

"You started it, pendejo," Jason fired back.

"Shut up," Tommy said. "Nobody cares. Listen, it's not Mikey's fault that the ball broke that window. And it's not his fault that we have to do all this crappy work. None of us wants to do this, but it's just the way it is. No matter what we think, we're gonna have to suck it up and deal with it."

Jason inhaled from his aspirator and snuffed out the whistle. Mikey polished his lenses on his 1979 Yankee's baseball T-shirt.

"Come on, call a truce," Tommy said, standing between them like a referee in a boxing match. Mikey and Jason stared reluctantly for a few minutes and then shook hands.

"All right," Jason said.

"Yeah, yeah," Mikey said, agreeing.

"Let's move, it's getting late," Tommy said, and led the way home.

Lucy, Randy, and I, side by side, followed Tommy; Jason and Mikey brought up the rear. We trailed over the wooden ditch bridge, past Grant elementary, across Hillwater road and through the gate where I had received my unpleasant run-in with the Jerks.

I never got a chance to tell the Gang what had happened to me that afternoon. It had slipped my mind.

Chapter 12

LUCY AND THE SKY OF DIAMONDS

Our secret was safe...so far. Each afternoon, we'd change clothes, tell our parents we were going out to play—sometimes using the baseball lie, sometimes using an entirely different fabrication—and head for the Vineyard for another day's work. Progress was slow at times, almost standstill on the hard days when some of the crew was missing, like the day Lucy had a dentist appointment at the same time Randy had to visit his grandmother in Santa Fe, or the time when Tommy caught the stomach flu and spread it to us like the plague (everyone caught it except Randy, and it had held construction up for several days). But just like Tommy said, we sucked it up. After eight weeks of toil, we had dug out all sixty-one of the X's using the augers and clamshell diggers, and had planted five posts.

Installing the woodgrain posts was a meticulous, tiresome task. We first had to make sure the hole measurements were correct: the gap had to be thirty inches deep with five and a half inches to each side; if we were off by one inch, our rails would run astray like jagged teeth. We then had to put a four-inch layer of gravel in the bottom for support, place the post in, pour water in the hole, add Fastcrete, and dispense more water back on top. We had to wait thirty minutes for the Fastcrete to harden before backfilling the top with dirt. Randy, Mr. Impatient, was always trying new shortcuts to trim down the time. He once tried fanning the solution with one of Mikey's Mad magazines to see if he could make it harden quicker. It didn't.

Once the Fastcrete set, we had to check the plumb of the post to see if it needed adjustments. Like the hole measurements, there could be no mistakes in alignment. We had some hitches in this department. While working on the second post, Jason discovered that he had put the thing in diagonally. The solution, unfortunately, was too thick and hard for us to simply remove the post, so we had to dig the entire thing out of the ground to fix our problem. That mistake cost us an entire afternoon, and let me tell you, Randy had ants in his pants thinking about all the lost hours of productivity.

Daylight was another problem. Fall was in full force and the days grew shorter by the minute. In the beginning of September, we could work for a good three hours before calling it quits. By late October, we were lucky to get in two. And daylight savings, which hit this week, didn't help matters. Reality set in and we began to realize that the work was going to take a lot longer than even our longest estimate.

We were still pissed about baseball season, but our anger had diminished over time. We had come to adapt to our daily duty. It had become part of our schedule just like brushing our teeth, showering for classes, or eating our breakfast. We had penciled the fence construction into our mental planners. Time, that strange and terrifying power, had eroded our annoyance into tolerance.

School was a drag, as always, but I was doing well in my classes. For my midterm report card, I had a solid A in Mrs. Williams' Algebra class, Mr. Katts' Social Studies, and Mrs. Dawsons' English class. I had a B in PE and a B+ in Shop and Typing (I would have had an A in Typing if it wasn't for the issue I had with my eyes wandering in Lucy's direction). Coach Barr had busted out Big Red on the fourth day of class and placed it around Chris Garcia's neck. Chris wasn't overweight like Tubby, but he couldn't run worth a damn. I felt for Chris's situation the same way that every kid did: I was sorry for him, but glad that I wasn't wearing the badge of weights, sprinting around the track in front of the class like a monkey in the circus.

There are a lot of students that come out hating my guts. It happens every year, but I guess that's just tough shit.

Oh, and there was one more important thing that happened in the past two months. I was now a full-blown metal mouth. The retainer had hit the trashcan and had been replaced by a shiny new set of braces. Surprisingly, the only kids at school that made a big deal about it were pesky Timmy and Miles. Everyone else, to my relief, could care less.

***

"Davy, your friends are at the door!"

"All right, Ma," I replied.

It was Halloween night and I was ready to collect some major candy. I had my strategy planned out to the tiniest details: I would use a giant pillowcase to hold the goods, dress in the popular Indiana Jones costume to impress the neighbors—the movie was one of the biggest blockbusters of '81, a fact that was guaranteed to give me the upper hand at the door—get an early start, and hit every house at least twice if not three times. I would use my rehearsed line after ringing the bell. Screw the worn out, "Trick or Treat." I would say, "Why, your pumpkins are looking scarier than ever this year, Mrs. Yates," or "I love what you've done with the cobwebs, Mr. Sampson.

Really spooky." A bit kiss ass? Yes. A little manipulative? Definitely. But my goal was to stuff my pillowcase to the brim with sticky sweets no matter what I had to say. My mother and orthodontist had voiced their opinions on the matter, telling me to stay away from the goodies, but I didn't care. Candy apples, Sugar Daddies, Snickers Bars—let the good times roll.

"Wow, what a costume," Lucy said, staring at me. "Did you just get back from filming the movie?"

The Gang stood at my door, clothed from head to toe in different outfits. Lucy wore a white dress with a tan, sparkly pointy hat. She was either a fairy godmother or a good witch—I couldn't tell which. Mikey, of course, standing in cowboy attire for the third straight year, decided to dress up as the one and only Clint Eastwood. He looked more like a fat cattle herder than a kick-butt cowboy. Next to Mikey stood the scariest burglar I had ever seen. Tommy's outfit was simple: plain blue jeans, a white undershirt, and tennis shoes. He would have looked like a normal kid if it weren't for the freaky green ski mask over his face. It made him into an instant bank robber. Had Tommy decided to wear that mask on any other day, I would have taken him for a real criminal and called the cops. Jason had taken the half-ass route and went with a plastic Frankenstein mask that he had probably picked out of his closet from years past. Randy's costume was by far the best. He was clad in a black mask, cape, and boots. His character was unmistakable, even more popular than the great Indiana Jones. It was Darth Vader, and Randy knew exactly how to dress the part. He had a red light saber, black gloves, and a Death Star candy bag. He even had a damn voice recorder built into the mask to convert his squeaky, prepubescent voice into the dreaded Sith Lord. Consequently, I was a little upset to see him. Randy had topped me in the costume contest.

"It's not as good as Mr. Vader," I said. "Where did you get that suit from, anyway?"

"From the dark side, young Luke," a robotic Randy boomed.

"Come on!" the burglar said. "We've got to beat the rush."

I yelled goodbye to my mom and Lewis. Lewis was sitting in a chair next to the door, eating our bowl of outgoing candy. His face was smeared with chocolates.

"Save candy, Davy," Lewis said, smiling joyfully. "Me like!"

"I will, pal," I said. "Sure you don't want to join us?"

Lewis shook his head.

I smiled, understanding his fear of all the monsters he'd see, and winked at him as I closed the door.

We ran into the early night with our empty bags, dreaming of the good fortune that would surely follow. How many houses could we hit? How many treats could we collect? Would they be generous this year, or stingy like old Mrs. Helmsley, who never gave more than one Hershey's Kiss per person?

I loved that feeling, that sense that the fun had just begun. It was the same feeling I had during the summer when Tommy and I first took our pellet guns to the Vineyard field, or the time when Randy and I had set out to bicycle to Dave's Ice Cream Palace for a bubblegum snow cone. I didn't know it then, but it was an experience I would only have as a kid. That fun drained out of me as the days turned into weeks, the weeks into years. It's sad, but it happens. It's ironic that you spend your childhood wanting to be an adult, and a good part of your adulthood wanting to be a kid again.

***

"Your pumpkins are looking scarier than ever, Mrs. Patterson," I said, catching her totally off guard. It was the tenth time I had used the line, and even though the Gang had asked me to shut up just as many times, it was still working like a charm.

"Why thank you! That's Davy Blake under that hat, isn't it?" Mrs. Patterson asked, holding a bowl full of red jawbreakers. I nodded. "And that's

Tommy Smith, Jason Sanchez, Lucy Graham, Michael McNeil, and…" she giggled, "well, I'm not sure who's the man in black."

"Randy Sachs, ma'am," Darth said.

"Oh, Randy. That's quite clever of you. That's got to be one of the best costumes I've seen yet."

"Thank you, ma'am."

"Did you think of that all by yourself?"

"Yes…ma'am."

Even with the distortion of the robotic voice, we could tell that Randy was embarrassed. We chuckled at the question; it made him sound like a dummy. Mrs. Patterson gave us each a handful of jawbreakers. She had always been very liberal with the candy.

"Take care, now," Mrs. Patterson said, and waved to us as we said thanks and ran off.

"How much do you guys have?" Tommy asked, looking in his bag.

"A whole crap-load," I said, feeling the weight of mine.

"Too much," Randy said. "I can't carry it anymore."

"Me neither," Mikey added in an Eastwood impression. "I'm going to have to drop some of my load off my horse."

"Where do you plan to do that, gordo?" Jason asked. "Right here in the friggin' road?"

"No, my house," Mikey added smartly.

"I'm not going to your house for that," Jason said.

"Me neither," Randy said.

Tommy unwrapped one of the jawbreakers and popped it in his mouth. "Why don't we dump some off at the fort?" Tommy said.

We looked at each other and nodded.

"Sounds good to me," I replied.

"Yeah, and if we hurry up we might get another half bag in," Randy said. "It's only nine o'clock."

We sprinted to Tommy's cul-de-sac as a full moon illuminated our path. Along the way, flickering in the dark, we passed jack-o'-lanterns carved into vampires, Frankensteins, and werewolves. Some houses had gone all-out for the holiday—strobe lights, cobwebs, spooky soundtracks—while others hadn't done a thing. The New Mexico autumn wind was light and bitter, and it carried the hint of a fragrant aroma that was subtly pleasing, yet hard to pin its mysterious origin.

We soon reached the fort. Tommy lit an overhead gas lamp—another souvenir from Ricky Jay's dump yard—and we marked our spots. We emptied our bags carefully, making sure our candy piles didn't bleed into each other. Surprisingly, half-ass Jason seemed to have the most candy.

"How did you get more?" I asked.

"Hey, I'm a pro," Jason said, smiling from ear to ear.

"I've got the least," Mikey said, frowning at his pile.

"I reckon they got tired of Mr. Eastwood," Randy said. He had taken off his Vader mask and had perfect round beads of sweat on his brow.

"You guys wanna smoke?" Tommy asked, pulling out a tin box.

"Sure," I said, eating Mrs. Helmsley's Hershey's Kiss. One Kiss. The stingy old bag hadn't changed a bit.

"Sounds good," Randy said.

"I'll pass," Jason said.

"Me too," Mikey said.

"You guys smoke?" Lucy said, her eyes wide and terrified.

Her question took us by surprise. Lucy was a part of our group, no doubt about it, but we had forgotten that she had never spent time with us in the fort. Since Lucy lived in another neighborhood, and since it was a good ten-minute bike ride from her house to Tommy's, she had to ration her time. Sometimes, after school let out, we had invited her to the fort before going to work in the Vineyard. She always said no, and although she never said why, it was my guess that she had better things to do than sit in a smelly fort drooling over Randy's dirty collection of Peep and Lace magazines or playing poker while swapping sexist jokes. The fort was made for boys, and even though Lucy could hack it out with the best of us, and often did, she chose not to. Some activities just didn't make sense to the opposite sex.

"Yeah, every so often," I said, opening the tin can and retrieving a bubblegum cigarette.

"Gosh," Lucy said before seeing what I had in my hand. She then rolled her eyes and laughed.

"You don't have to do it," Tommy said, puffing out fake smoke. "But everyone is doing it, you know."

Lucy looked at Jason and Mikey, who were both snickering.

"My asthma kills me when I do," Jason said with a sly grin.

"And my parents would have a heart attack if they found out I'm doing this," Mikey said, reconsidering and taking one for himself.

"It's okay if you say no," Tommy said.

"Shut up and give me one of those stupid things," Lucy said, laughing. "Do you think someday they'll wonder why they made candy out of these? I mean, isn't it kinda crazy when you stop to think about it?"

"You mean first bubblegum, then six packs a week of the real stuff?" I asked.

"It could happen," Lucy answered. "Some kid somewhere who thinks they are the same and tries it."

"That's one dim dummy," Tommy replied. "He'd have a lot more problems than smoking, that's for sure."

"That sounds like Mikey," Jason added.

"Piss off," Mikey shot back.

"Hey guys, we've got to go soon," Randy said, checking his digital watch. A few insects were flittering and bouncing off the overhead gas lamp. Underneath the lamp lay a circle of six candy piles.

"We should definitely hit Mr. Sampson's house again," Jason said. "He gave the most goods."

"Yeah, and then Mrs. Patterson's place," Mikey added. "I love those jawbreakers. I only wish we could get more. Maybe she'll—"

"Shhhhhhhh!" Tommy whispered. He stared outside, one hand parting the tarp, revealing the darkness.

"What?" Mikey asked, frightened. Tommy remained silent; his face was ghostly serious. "What's going on? Is it your parents? Oh jeez, if they find out we're up here they'll—"

"Shut up!" Tommy hissed, his head still fixed outside.

We sat perfectly still and held our breath. We heard footsteps and mumbles from outside. We couldn't make out the voices, but whatever or whoever it was, it was coming closer. My heart pounded.

"Parents?" I whispered.

Tommy listened for a second and then turned to me. "No, worse. It's Dan."

There are two types of Halloween patrons: trick-or-treaters and bag snatchers. Trick-or-treaters walk door-to-door earning their candy, spending hours filling their sacks. Bag snatchers, conversely, wait until the hard work is done and then steal the bags from the trick-or-treaters. It's a dirty trick the older kids play on the younger, weaker kids. If Dan and his buddies were out on Halloween night, there was no mystery to which category they belonged.

"Get out of here," Tommy said.

"Shit, our stuff!" Randy replied.

We recklessly scooped our piles back up. Candy sprayed everywhere—the table, the ground, the chairs—and we tried to salvage as much as we could, but our hands and hearts were moving too fast. The voices and footsteps drew closer.

Mikey, with the smallest pile, was first out. Tommy followed him, and then Jason, trailing a line of chocolates and suckers behind him as he put on his Frankenstein mask—a conditioned response after doing it the entire night. Lucy was next. I left right behind her while Randy, the packrat he was, tried to rescue every piece of candy on the ground.

"Get out, Randy," I yelled in the darkness, sprinting as fast as I could.

"Hurry, they're leaving!" a voice said.

It was too dark to see where the others had gone so I made my own tracks, weaving in and out of trees and bushes. I ran with my pillowcase over my shoulder, feeling the bag bob up and down on my spine with each thump. I hit Tommy's front-yard wooden fence and frantically climbed up.

"No! Don't!" I heard someone yell. It sounded like Randy.

I jumped the fence and landed at the edge of Tommy's cul-de-sac. I raced down the open pavement, my feet echoing in the night, my bag bouncing harder. Another figure was in front of me, running full speed, silhouetted in the moonlight. A separate shape jumped out of the darkness and cut into the figure.

"Ahhhhhh!" a scream pierced the air.

It was Lucy. The shape had a hold on her bag, pulling and tugging with its long arms. Lucy held on, but she was losing the battle.

Without thinking, I ran to the fight. The figure was Bruce, smiling madly as he manhandled Lucy.

"Let go, bitch," Bruce said.

"No," Lucy replied.

With all the power in my arms, I heaved the pillowcase over my shoulder and pulled it down flat on Bruce's head. The bag hit him with a solid thud and tore in half. Bruce lost his grip, fell straight on his butt, and looked at me with terrified eyes. Candy shot everywhere. A good portion of my sweets had fallen out, but I still had enough to strike again. I did, and this time the bag came down in the middle of his face.

"Stop!" Bruce screamed out.

The bag came down again. And again. And again. I was in a trance, floating above my body, watching myself strike with ruthless abandon. My arms and legs were totally numb. The only thing I could feel was my leaking bag and Bruce's bloody face. Again. Then again. Each hit was harder than the one before. It didn't matter that the bag now only had a few candy bars inside. The force from my arms compensated for it.

"Davy!" Lucy said.

"You fucker!" I screamed.

I hit him two more times before Lucy pulled me away. Bruce was crying in a carpet of colored unopened wrappers, his face covered with blood, his hands guarding his head.

"Stop!" Bruce cried.

I stared at Bruce and watched him weep. The bully I knew had gone, and was replaced by a little sobbing kid. My bag now trailed my side, draping like a worn blankie.

"Come on, Davy," Lucy whispered in my ear.

She pulled me away as Bruce continued to cry in the darkness.

We walked under the moonlight in complete silence. A cold October breeze pushed us from behind, chilling the nape of our necks. A dog barked wildly in the distance.

We walked for another five minutes and stopped at the basketball court in the middle of the neighborhood park. Lucy and I sat on the cold pavement. She still had her sparkling hat on; I had lost the Indiana Jones hat somewhere in Tommy's yard.

"You okay?"

"Yeah," I replied, but began to cry as soon as I said it.

It came out all at once, pouring like a river.

Lucy held me in her gentle arms and whispered softly in my ear: "It's okay."

I sobbed for a good ten minutes, thinking about Dan, Tony, Bruce, and Ricky; thinking about the wedgie I had received out by the neighborhood back gate; thinking about the scrapes I had gotten after flying off my bike the day I lost my kickstand because of the Jerks; thinking about the voices I had heard while running away from the fort.

The tears finally tapered off, and I pulled away from Lucy. I felt foolish.

"I'm sorry," I said.

"Don't be," Lucy said.

"I saw him with your bag. I came to help. I guess I kinda lost it."

Lucy gave me a warm smile. "Maybe, but he deserved it all the same. He would have gotten my stuff if it weren't for you. I'm sorry about your bag, though."

"Yeah," I said, sniffling the remaining tears away. "It's okay."

"Want a lollipop?"

Lucy held up a giant swirly sucker. She really meant to give it to me, but it looked so foolishly absurd that I cracked up.

"No thanks," I laughed.

Lucy giggled with me and unwrapped the plastic off the sucker. She took a lick and handed it over.

"I can't see what kind it is," I said.

"Garlic," she replied, and we both broke up again. I took a taste and handed it back to her.

"Oh no..." I said.

"What?"

"I promised Lewis that I'd give him some of my candy."

"Your brother?" Lucy grabbed a handful of her own sweets and handed it to me.

"You don't have to," I said.

"I want to. I owe you more than that." Lucy slipped her hand in mine. Her fingers were unbelievably smooth.

"Thanks, Davy."

"Of course," I said.

She held my hand tighter and drew closer.

Suddenly, Lucy's lips met mine. They were warm and soft and magical. My body went numb again. The kiss was short, no more than five seconds, but it lasted for an eternity. Lucy pulled back and stared at me with beautiful, dark eyes.

That was the day. October 31st, 1981—Halloween night. My first kiss. It had happened in the middle of a basketball court, on cold concrete, under a diamond filled sky, beneath a bright gray moon. And it was with Lucy Graham, the same girl I couldn't say a word to at the beginning of the school year without blushing. There would be many kisses after that from other women, but none would mean quite as much as that one did. It was unexpected and innocent. From that day on, it would remind me of a time when I was young, surrounded by the truest of friends, all of us discovering life's little secrets—the beautiful and ugly.

"Come on," Lucy said, still holding my hand. "Let's head home."

Chapter 13

MR. PHILLIPS

The scarred oak had become our meeting spot each afternoon before working on the fence. We'd park our bikes at the tree, wait for everyone, and then make for the woodgrain pile. Mr. Phillips was usually outside, either working on the fence or some other project he had made for himself.

"Here she comes," Jason said.

"About time," Tommy replied, picking a sticker out of his shoelaces.

Lucy pedaled over the bridge and rolled down a bumpy hill with her hands clenched around her handlebars and her arms shooting up and down like twin jackhammers. She wore her patented yellow sneakers, blue jeans, and orange baseball cap.

"Come on, Luce." Randy waved. "We're late."

A cloud of dust covered the bike as Lucy jammed the brakes. She was exhausted.

"Sorry," Lucy said. "I had some things to do."

Tommy nodded grimly and then led the way. Randy, Jason, and Mikey trailed behind him. I gave Lucy a warm smile and waited for her to join me. She stacked her bike next to ours and grinned back.

Less than seventeen hours had passed since our magical moment, but it felt like years. Lucy and I had decided to keep it under wraps, and so far we had kept our kiss secret from the Gang as successfully as we had kept the incident of the broken window from our parents. Lucy and I had exchanged a few flirtatious glances during lunch, one of which Randy saw and dismissed with a frown, but that was the extent of our outside affection.

I hadn't heard anything about Bruce Brown and his bloody face, and I hoped I wouldn't. I doubted Bruce had told the other Jerks what had happened since he'd probably be the laughing stock of the group if he did (*Whadya say? Twelve-year-old Davy Blake did what? Kicked your fifteen-year-old ass? Ha, ha! Did you hear that, boys?*). And I didn't want to stoke the fire by spreading the story around our Gang. That tale, like the kiss, was better left untold. Anyway, I imagined Bruce probably had his own personal retaliation planned for me, something that would make my face twice as twisted as his had gotten.

Apparently, I was the only one that night who had lost candy...save the remains on the fort floor.

Tommy, Jason, and Mikey had escaped scot-free, and Randy had managed to win the tug-of-war contest with Dan Smith. Dan had caught Randy inside the fort while he was scooping the remaining lost candies in his bag. He had grabbed Randy's sack with both hands, but had been forced to release his grip when he burned his forehead on the overhead gas lamp. Randy had dashed out and disappeared into the darkness. I couldn't believe it, but right after that episode, Randy had the nerve—and the balls—to continue trick-or-treating for another half hour. It was one of the craziest stunts that anyone in our group had ever done.

"You hens ready for another day's work?" Mr. Phillips said, working on an old tractor by the woodgrain pile.

"Yes, sir," Tommy said.

Mr. Phillips grabbed his rusted toolbox and adjusted his straw hat. "Good, we've got a lot ahead of us."

We marched with Mr. Phillips to the sixth puncture. Surrounding the red-shingled house and the brown field of the Vineyard, like little rabbit burrows, were sixty-one equally spaced holes set on the inside of the white strings. The first five holes had been set with 5' ½" posts. Along the side of the remaining empty holes lay the rest of the posts for the project. We hadn't touched the mound of rails yet: it was much too early to start thinking about using them.

The work ahead still seemed intimidating and impossible. We agreed there was no way we'd be able to finish it by the close of the year. The brutal winter months wouldn't allow it.

Walking closer, we saw that Mr. Phillips had laid a bag of Fastcrete by posts six and seven. We stared at the bags, baffled.

"I bet you're wondering why I have two bags out this time," Mr. Phillips said, stopping at the sixth post, laying his toolbox on the floor. We were confused because we had only worked one post at a time up to this point. "I want Mikey, Lucy, Randy, and Jason to work on post seven, while Davy, Tommy, and I work on post six."

"You mean by ourselves?" Mikey asked nervously.

"You got it," Mr. Phillips said.

"But how are we supposed to do that?" Jason asked, his voice sounding as doubtful as Mikey's.

Mr. Phillips tipped his hat up with his forefinger, displaying sweaty clumps of hair. "You know how to do it. We've already worked on five of 'em together, so I figure you can handle your own now."

"Yeah, but what if we screw up?" Randy asked.

"It won't be the first time. Remember that diagonal post?"

Mr. Phillips looked straight at Jason. Jason blushed and looked at the dirt.

"Now, if you put your heads together, I reckon y'all do fine," Mr. Phillips continued. "Have some faith in yourself. You might be surprised what happens."

Like totally screw up, I thought. I was suddenly glad that I was working with Tommy and Mr. Phillips rather than the kiddy group. We had the pro on our team.

"Go on now," Mr. Phillips said. "You've got all the tools you need over there."

Mikey, Lucy, Randy, and Jason reluctantly walked off. I heard Jason utter a few faint curse words, and I was certain that Mr. Phillips had heard them, too.

"Let's put this puppy in, eh?" Mr. Phillips said, picking the post up. The veins in his thick hands stood out like blue roots, and his knuckles shined white. His fingernails were scratched and embedded with black dirt.

We measured the hole to make sure it was thirty inches deep, put four inches of gravel on the bottom, and poured in ten inches of water from a rusted can that Mr. Phillips had filled earlier. We then added the Fastcrete and another round of water. We rechecked the alignment of the post with our carpenter's level at the top of the beam. I had my eye on the level's horizontal oil measurement as Tommy adjusted the bottom next to the white string.

"A little to the left," I said.

"Like that?" Tommy asked, moving the post at its base.

"A little more."

"How about now?"

"More."

"Now?"

"Yeah, good, hold it there for a minute."

Tommy held it as Mr. Phillips measured the distance between the posts with his yellow measuring tape. Far above us, scratching the blue dome with a thin trail of smoke, an airplane raced west. A small humming sound faded as the plane disappeared into the afternoon horizon.

"Sixteen feet exactly," Mr. Phillips said.

Tommy released the beam and I checked the level again.

"And we're flat as a board," I said, showing Mr. Phillips the carpenter's level. Mr. Phillips smiled and looked at group two.

"How y'all doin'?"

They were squatted down beside their post. Jason was adding the Fastcrete, Randy and Lucy were holding the beam, and Mikey was supervising their work—or doing nothing at all except twiddling his chubby thumbs.

"All right, we think," Mikey said, his glasses reflecting the sun in bright flashes.

"Good," Mr. Phillips said slapping a mosquito on his arm. "Tell me when you think you've got it."

Mikey nodded and went back to staring. I sat down and Mr. Phillips squatted next to me.

"We'll wait fifteen more minutes, until it hardens, and then fill it up."

Tommy and I nodded as Mr. Phillips plucked a long strand of sweet grass and chewed on it. His baked face had deep crow's tracks around the eyes and mouth. Long horizontal canyons lined his forehead, and his black, bushy eyebrows had a hint of gray in them.

"How's school going?" Mr. Phillips asked.

School? Tommy and I thought. It was the first question Mr. Phillips had asked that didn't deal with moving posts or digging holes.

"Good," Tommy said.

"Yeah?" Mr. Phillips replied. "You two keeping good grades?"

"Yeah, pretty good," I said.

Mr. Phillips had never concerned himself about our personal lives, why was he interested now? Was he just curious, or was it something else? Maybe he wanted us to squeeze in more hours...to do more work. This last paranoid thought terrified me. If Mr. Phillips decided that the work we were doing wasn't worth eight thousand dollars, he could tack on more jobs. He could make us paint the house, weed the front garden, tend the Vineyard. He could do that and more, and we would be powerless to stop him. Once we had decided to keep the broken window a secret from our parents, we had placed our fate in his hands. We could still get out of it and spill the story to our parents, sure, but after all the work we had put in, after all the afternoons slaving away, it would be like a slap in the face. It would be all for nothing.

"I know you've heard it before, but school is one of the most important things in your life. Take it from me. It'll keep you out of work like this. Manual work I've done for more days than I can remember."

"You've done this your whole life?" Tommy asked.

The sweet grass moved from one side of his mouth to the other, as if rolling on ball bearings. "Yep, most of it at least. I was born and raised on a farm. Just like Jack Lopez."

"You knew Jack Lopez?" I asked, excited.

Mr. Phillips laughed and smiled in the afternoon sun.

"Knew him? No, I reckon nobody knew him. Kept things inside, if you catch my drift. He was a strange, wealthy man. I bought this land from him just before he passed away."

"So you talked to him?"

"Yeah...I talked to him. The last time was right after my divorce." Mr. Phillips took off his hat and looked inside it. His smile faded away. "Hard to believe how fast time passes. Seems like last week. Anyway, the old lady kicked me out of my ranch in

Taos and made me find a new roof. So, I came down here to the city slickers and that's where I saw an ad in a real estate magazine for this place. It was a little larger than I was lookin' for. Five bedrooms is a lot of space for an old cowboy with grown kids."

He watched us for a second and we nodded in agreement. Five bedrooms was certainly a mansion for one person.

"I liked the location, though, so I called the number. I was transferred around and before long I was talking to Jacky-boy himself, who invited me for a grand tour of the place."

"What was he like?"

"Jack? Well, he was short and had pitch-black hair and incredible gray eyes." Mr. Phillips laughed. "I'll never forget that about him. I had never seen a Mexican with anything but brown or green eyes before."

"Are all those stories true about him?" I asked. "How he was a potato farmer and how he drilled for oil with nothing but his shirt on his back?"

Mr. Phillips glanced at the post and checked the Fastcrete's progress. It was still a little mushy.

"I reckon they're pretty close to the truth. He was a self-made man, as far as I know. Built himself quite a business."

"Man, I bet it was cool meeting him," Tommy said.

"Yeah," I said, thinking the same.

"Cool?" Mr. Phillips frowned.

"You know, like a great experience," I explained.

"Oh...Jack? I wouldn't say that. As I said before, he was a strange camper. He always had a lot on his mind. Seemed a little disturbed. He's not the kind of man you want to invite over for chicken and biscuits."

A few months ago, the Gang and I had felt exactly the same way about crazy old Mr. Phillips. We wouldn't have stepped one foot in his house if our lives depended on it.

A mosquito buzzed on my neck and I slapped it away.

"The fella was polite, though, and did give me that grand tour." Mr. Phillips turned to the house. "I immediately fell in love with her. She had a beautiful interior that you just don't see in houses these days. Jack offered me a fair price, we shook hands, and that's how it came to be. We got the agents involved after the fact."

"Do you see your wife or kids anymore?" I asked. It was a risky question that seemed to slip out of my mouth. Mr. Phillips shot me an awkward glance, and I wished I could take it back.

"I reckon it's dry now," Mr. Phillips said and stood up. "You kids done over there?"

Randy, Lucy, and Jason still had their heads glued to the post. Mikey, the standing oddball, looked over at us.

"Almost," Mikey said. "Still waiting for it to dry."

"Once you're done, move on to post eight. We'll handle number nine." Mr. Phillips said.

We picked up the rusty water canister and our tools and made for the next hole. Another plane, this one closer, shot across the sky, trailing the same thin white tail. Two sparrows danced in its view, twisting and weaving playfully...perhaps mates in some instinctual ritual.

Mr. Phillips kept to himself the rest of the afternoon.

Chapter 14

WINTER FIRE

The weekend before Thanksgiving, Randy invited the Gang to his house for another sleepover. This time, with a little egging from me, Lucy was invited. Randy's parents agreed to it and it was up to us to convince our folks.

My mother usually didn't care if I spent the night during the weekends as long as I took care of my duties around the house. But this weekend was different. This weekend my father made an unexpected visit.

"Vrooooommmm, vrooooommmm, Dad home!" Lewis said, looking out the window.

Lewis sat at the kitchen table, clothed in a Snoopy T-shirt and brown khakis, and I was beside him, reading another one of Mikey's Mad magazines and wearing an Indy 500 T-shirt and blue jeans. We were anxiously waiting for Mom to serve up a tray of her delicious, spicy, stuffed bell peppers—one of her famous dishes that took hours to make. We could smell the peppers roasting in the oven, sizzling with juices, packed with ketchup-covered ground beef. We eagerly waited with our stomachs growling in our bellies. The peppery aroma was intoxicating.

"Don't be silly, Lewis," Mom said, slipping her oven mitts on. "Dad's not coming until next weekend, remember."

"Dad home! Dad home!" Lewis continued, shaking his head and violently banging his spoon against the table.

I looked up from the magazine and saw my father's lime green Suburban parked in the driveway. Dad was in the rear of the car, pulling his luggage from the trunk, dressed in a navy blue pilot's uniform.

"Lewis, please calm down."

"No Mom, he's right," I said, pointing out the window. "Dad's *here*."

Mom gave me a funny look, as if I had been hit too many times in the head, removed the peppers from the oven, placed them on the counter, and walked to the table.

"What in creation?" she said to herself.

She slapped the oven mitts down next to me and opened the kitchen door.

"Hey honey," my dad said, smacking her a kiss as he walked inside.

"Hey, what are you doing here? I thought you said you'd be out until next weekend?"

"I did, but there was a change of plans."

"Dad!" Lewis screamed, squirming frantically in his seat.

"Hey, sport!"

Dad rushed to Lewis and gave him a kiss on the forehead. Lewis grabbed his waist and squeezed his uniform, his arms acting as a tight belt.

"I've brought a little present for you from New York."

"Presents! Presents!" Lewis repeated gleefully.

"That's right. Hey, Davy."

"Hey, Dad," I said. I was a little taken aback, not by my dad's unexpected visit, but by the way he looked. There was something on his mind.

"I've got a present for you, too."

My mom grabbed the mitts and put them back on.

"So what were the change of plans?" my mother asked, moving back to the peppers.

"What?" my dad asked, loosening his cheap, thin tie. "Oh, I'll tell you about that later. What's for dinner?"

"Spiced peppers, but I'm not sure if there's enough. I might have to make some more."

"Spiced peppers? Mmmmm." My dad smiled at Lewis. "That sounds good, doesn't it, sport?"

"Mmmmm," Lewis repeated. "Presents! Presents!"

***

Lewis was frantically tearing through wrapping paper, licking his lips in anticipation of a grand gift. The plate of stuffed peppers was now empty and our appetites were happily satisfied. Mom had made a giant dish of apple cobbler, but she had to put it in the fridge uneaten since it was impossible for us to take a single bite without overdoing it.

"King Kong!" Lewis said, lifting up his shirt. It was a picture of the notorious giant ape scaling the Empire State Building. Kong's black nostrils were flared in a snarl and his gruesome mouth was filled with pointy white teeth.

"That's right, I picked it up just before I left," Dad said.

Lewis jumped up and stripped off his Snoopy shirt. Mom covered her mouth and chuckled at Lewis's outburst; Dad laughed with her.

"I guess it's all right to put it on here, sport," my dad joked, looking at Lewis's pasty chest. "Do you want to try yours on, Davy?"

I looked at my I ♥ NY shirt and shook my head. I liked the shirt, but I didn't care to wear it at moment.

"Fits? Fits?" Lewis asked, pointing to his shirt. The glossy King Kong shined in the kitchen lights. It was a glare that would last only through the first few washes.

"Yes, it fits, sport," Dad said.

"Davy, why don't you put yours on?" my mom asked.

"I don't want to."

"I'm sure your father spent a lot of time picking it out, please try it on."

"But Mom—"

"Don't argue with me, Davy!"

"It's okay, honey," Dad said, touching her arm. "If Davy doesn't want to, it's his choice."

My mother glared at me and then picked up her plate. *It's a bad time to ask her*, I thought. Mom would never agree to the sleepover right now, but maybe Dad would say yes. He seemed like he was in a good mood and he rarely said no. It was a Friday night, a weekend, and there weren't any rules against it.

"Hey Dad, can I stay at Randy's house tonight?"

My father polished off the last of his iced tea. "Sure, as long as your mother agrees."

My stomach tightened. It was the dreaded "as long as" proposal. I was doomed. There was no way that Mom would let me go...not now. I was beginning to regret my stance on the T-shirt issue, but it was too late to try it on now. That battle was over, and a new one had begun.

She looked at me as she flipped the sink faucet handle. Her voice was muffled, but audible. "I suppose," she said, "but first help me do the dishes and take out the trash."

I was ecstatic, even more excited than Lewis had been opening his present. I picked up the dirty plates and happily made for the sink.

"Honey, I need to talk to you," Dad said.

"What?" Mom said over the noisy water.

"I said need to talk to you," my father repeated louder, "privately."

My mother heard him the second time and wiped her hands on her butterfly-checkered apron. "Sure," she said with a baffled expression.

Private talks were never good. They were serious talks reserved for issues like the day my dad told my mother about the boat accident that had killed her sister, or the time my dad found out about the tumor in his leg—surgeons had successfully removed it, thank God. Private talks terrified me.

"Don't forget about the trash, Davy," Mom said.

I said that I wouldn't and watched her exit the room with my father. Lewis was still sitting at the table, admiring the picture of his new pet gorilla. He was supposed to help me with the dishes, but he often skipped out on the duty. Mom often let him off the hook because he was clumsy and because he had a hard time controlling his hand jitters. Lewis was a costly dishwasher: a cup or plate was destined to die in the sink basin or on the kitchen tile floor.

As I scrubbed the plates, I thought about the conversation going on in the next room. Did my dad have another tumor? Was there another accident? Another death? What if it was something I did? Maybe he had found out about the broken vase. Maybe it was Mr. Phillips's broken window!

Just thinking about what it was drove me crazy. I almost pulled a Lewis and dropped a water pitcher, but luckily I caught it before it shattered on the floor.

Right after I finished loading the dishwasher and while I was pulling out the trash liner, my mother reentered the kitchen.

"Davy, Lewis, why don't you two come in here," she said.

I dropped the trash and walked out of the room with Lewis. Lewis handed me my NY shirt and asked me to put it on. I told him later.

You boys know how much that window cost me? Eight thousand dollars.

Lewis and I entered the den and sat on a sofa opposite my mother and father. I looked at my dad to see if I could make out what he was going to tell us, but he wore the same ambiguous look he'd had at dinner.

"I don't want you boys getting upset about this, but I feel you have a right to know just like your mother." My dad stared at us for a second and rubbed his hands together. He looked to Mom and waited for an unbearable amount of time. I wanted to run out of the house and go to Randy's—play video games with the Gang, trade baseball cards, swap dirty jokes. My father cleared his throat. "I came home early because I lost my job at Skyline. The company has had some financial trouble and had to lay off a quarter of its pilots. Unfortunately, I'm one of those that got cut."

I squeezed my NY shirt and looked down at my hands. The dishwater had shriveled the tips of my fingers into raisins.

"This layoff really hit me hard. It did the same to a lot of people. I guess we should have seen it coming, but we didn't. And now we have to deal with it."

"Does this mean we are going to lose our house?" I asked.

My dad smiled. "No, no. We don't have to worry about that. I get a year's worth of severance so it will give me time to find another job. But it does mean that we're going to have to watch our spending for a while, just until things return to normal."

"How long will that take?" I asked.

"I don't know. Maybe tomorrow, maybe in a few months. The economy isn't as strong as it was a few years ago, so it might be a little harder for me, but I'll find something." My father cleared his throat again. "This really put things in perspective for me. It's strange, but it's made me confront my...other problems. It's put my addiction in the spotlight. I know I've got to stop drinking before I do something really stupid that I can't undo." He glanced at my mother and then held her hand. "I just want you boys to know we're going to work through this like a family. That things are still going to be all right. Your mother and I aren't going anywhere. Do you understand what I'm saying?"

"Yes, sir," I said.

"Lewis, how about you? You understand, too?"

Lewis was rocking back and forth, patting his Kong shirt admiringly. "Everything all right," Lewis said.

"That's right, sport, everything is going to be okay."

My mother had a tissue in her hand and was wiping the corners of her eyes. She still had her butterfly apron on. A long strand of loose hair dangled on one side of her face.

"Davy, I think it would be best for you to stay home tonight," she said.

"Awwww, Mom, come on, why?" I asked.

"Because, I just don't think it's a good time for you to sleep at Randy's."

"Honey, it's okay, let him go," Dad said. His face was tight, stern. "I don't want this to change our lives. I think it's better for him if he sees his friends." Dad stared at Mom for a second and then squeezed her hand. "Please, dear."

My mother put the tissue in her lap and furrowed her brow. “Okay, but Davy, I want you to call me as soon as you get there. It’s dark out and I don’t want you getting kidnapped or run over by a car.”

“Yes, Mom,” I replied.

“This meeting is over, then,” my father said, standing up. “Now for a family hug.”

Lewis took Dad’s left arm and I took his right. My father had long arms—that’s one thing I’ll never forget about him, odd as it is; he could hug two one-hundred-plus-pound boys and still have space to fit Mom. He held us tightly for a brief moment while my mother leaned in, dabbing her eyes. It was a bear hug, one of those that starve the air from your lungs.

He then whispered in our ears, “I love this family.”

***

I ran to Randy’s without any run-ins with the Jerks, cars, or kidnappers. Mrs. Sachs was at the door and had to wait for me to catch my breath before letting me in. Once I recovered, she led me to the den where Randy and the Gang were next to a roaring fire with Mr. Sachs, sprawled out in his La-Z-Boy—a can of Budweiser in his right hand and jar of peanuts in his lap. The entire Gang was there, including Lucy. She secretly winked at me as I joined them.

"Davy, you missed out on my stories," Mr. Sachs said, tossing a handful of nuts in his mouth. "You'll have to hear 'em some other time."

"They weren't that good," Randy said, elbowing Tommy.

Tommy, Randy, and Jason sat on the fireplace's hearthstone. Their backs faced the flames and their bare feet dangled from the shelf, just above Mikey and Lucy's heads. Mikey and Lucy lay on the floor next to a mound of sneakers. In front of the sneaker pile was a line of sleepover bags packed with a day's worth of clothes and hygiene supplies. I had brought a plastic grocery bag stuffed with a green T-shirt, a pair of blue jeans, a toothbrush, and toothpaste. I removed my Converse sneakers and tossed them in the shoe pile, lined my plastic bag up with the Gangs', and warmed my hands on the glowing embers.

"How are your folks, Davy?" Mr. Sachs asked. His blazing cheeks were a shade darker than his crimson hair.

"Good," I said. "Same as always." I thought about my unemployed dad and how I didn't want the Gang to know about it. They wouldn't say anything, but if word got out, other kids might call him a bum or a loser.

"Tell your dad we need to go out again. It's been ages since the last time."

"Yeah, sure," I said. Going out for a night of drinking was the last thing my father needed. It was another thought I kept to myself.

"Randy, throw another log on," Tommy said.

"It's too hot already," Jason replied. "I'm burnin' up."

"Then move away from the fire, dipstick," Tommy said.

Randy dropped another log on the embers and sent a storm of sparks up the chimney. Mr. Sachs stretched out his arms, squinted his eyes, and let out a cavity-displaying yawn.

"Well, I'm ready to hit the hay," Mr. Sachs said, standing up.

"Booo," Tommy said. "I thought you were going to pull an all-nighter with us."

"Yeah, right," Mr. Sachs chuckled. "At forty-seven? I'm lucky if I can make it past eight thirty."

"You've got another thirty minutes," Randy said, looking at his Han Solo watch. "It's eight on the dot."

"And that's a half an hour too long."

"Awww, come on," Tommy said.

"Maybe next time, boys. Good night, and don't stay up too late."

"Goodnight," we replied, watching Mr. Sachs mosey out of the room, one hand on the small of his back.

"What's on TV?" Mikey asked.

"Not sure," Randy said.

Randy clicked on the giant home theater TV screen. The den had a La-Z-Boy that faced the screen along with two long, fluffy couches that stood on either side of the chair. We moved to the couches and took our seats. Randy surfed for a few minutes and stopped on a lame stand-up comedy show with no-namers telling stupid jokes. They used animals, whoopee cushions, and funny-looking hats. Their props changed, but their punch-lines remained the same—flat and dull. Randy clicked the painful program off.

"That sucked," Randy said.

"Yeah, where did they get those comedians anyway?" Tommy asked.

"I think they were Roosevelt grads," Lucy said.

"Tommy, got any cards?" I asked. "I'm up for poker or blackjack."

"Na," Tommy said. "Left 'em in the fort. What about you, Randy?"

Randy shook his head. "Lost ours on a road trip in Denver. Think they fell out of our car at a rest stop."

"We could play truth or dare," Mikey said.

"I dare you to shut up," Jason said. Mikey threw a pillow at Jason's face and Jason hurled it back, knocking Mikey's glasses off.

"Hey, knock it off," Randy said. "You're going to break something."

Mikey put the pillow down and flashed Jason his middle finger.

"I know!" Lucy said, her eyes aglow. "We could make a tent in your backyard and camp out."

Simultaneously, we stared at Randy.

"I like that," I said.

"Me, too," Tommy said.

"Yeah, cool, we could even have a bonfire and roast marshmallows," Mikey said. "We'll be just like outlaws livin' in the desert."

"Tu estupido, how are we gonna have a fire?" Jason asked. "Light one in the middle of Randy's lawn?"

Mikey furrowed his brow and thought for a second. "Yeah, I guess not. But it's still a cool idea."

"Will your parents let us do it?" I asked Randy. "Camp out?"

Randy looked at us with a small smirk on his face. His expression said everything. Mr. and Mrs. Sachs' precious only child was allowed to do almost anything. Of course we could camp out...shoot, we could probably even light the bonfire, which *was* a stupid idea, but one that we could get away with if we dared it. Randy might get a slap on the hand or maybe a small scolding, but it would be nothing serious.

"Follow me," Randy said, jumping up. "We'll get the tent and the sleeping bags!"

Randy marched to the garage and we trailed happily behind him, feeling the soft carpet through our socks. One of the logs popped in the fireplace and sent a spider of sparks up the chimney.

***

It took us less than five minutes to set up the five person tent. We stabbed six ringed stakes in the lawn, ran ropes through the metal holes, and tightened the slack canvas until it ran smooth. The triangle tent door had two zipper layers—one was a screen to keep out the bugs, and the other was a part of the canvas to keep out the chilly night breezes. We unrolled our bags inside. Since the tent was meant for five grown-ups, it was the perfect size for six kids: Jason, Tommy, Lucy, and I lined ours side by side in the middle; Mikey held the rear and laid his sack perpendicular to ours; Randy ran his parallel to Mikey's and took the front, watching the door with a plastic flashlight in his hand. The inside of the tent glowed like a luminaria.

Outside, the crescent moon cast a thin layer of gray over the dying November lawn. A few crickets chirped like squeaky heartbeats and a dog barked at a passing car. Looking at the blackness through the triangle door, we felt a sense of fear and dread, as if the night had converted Randy's backyard into a deadly wilderness filled with blood-sucking creatures and fanged beasts. The tent was the only holy ground; to leave it would be to jeopardize your very life.

"Randy, where's that other flashlight?" Tommy asked.

"In my bag, hold on," Randy said. He pulled out another plastic light, this one smaller, and tossed it to Tommy. Tommy flipped the side switch and shot a white beam to the top of the tent.

"It's cold in here," Mikey said.

"That's why we have sleeping bags, pendejo," Jason replied, firing his aspirator into his metal mouth.

"Hey, Lucy, how did you convince your parents to let you sleep over tonight?" Randy asked.

"What do you mean?" Lucy asked.

Randy shifted his flashlight beam from the door to Lucy's face. Lucy and Mikey had brought pajamas in their sleepover bags, but had decided not to change into them since the temperature was near freezing outside.

"Hey, get that out of my eyes," Lucy said, guarding her face.

Randy quickly moved the beam. "Oh, sorry...I meant, didn't your parents make a big deal out of it?"

"No, why would they?" Lucy asked.

"Well, you know...you being with five guys and all," Randy said.

Lucy laughed. "Oh, yeah, well they don't know about that. I told them there'd be two other girls here."

"You lied?" I asked, surprised.

"Sure," she said, "I had to or else they wouldn't have let me come over."

"It's only a partial lie," Jason said, smiling. "You can count Mikey as a girl, too."

Everybody laughed and Mikey kicked Jason's bag. "Piss off, Jason," Mikey said.

Suddenly, a howl pierced the night and silenced us. The noise was as high as a cat's scream.

"What was that?" Mikey asked, his eyes as big as his glasses.

"Just a dog," Tommy said, pointing his flashlight out the triangle opening. Randy's light was already outside, searching for fearless creatures.

"What if it wasn't?" Mikey asked. "What if it was a coyote, or a wolf?"

"In our neighborhood?" Jason asked, looking back incredulously. "Give me a break."

"Hey, you don't know. They could wander out here. Freddy Gloski said he found a coyote at his house once, and he lives just minutes away."

"If you don't believe me, dipstick, why don't you go out and check it out?"

"Huh uh." Mikey shook his head at Jason timidly. "I'm not going out there."

"Chicken," Jason said, flapping his arms and clucking.

The howl sounded again and suddenly we all felt chicken. Freddy Gloski might have been a liar, but there was no way we'd set foot outside to check it out. Coyote or no coyote.

"Zip up the tent," Tommy said to Randy.

Randy laid his flashlight flat on his bag—with the light painfully shining in my eyes—and sealed both triangle doors. We sat in silence, our breath spilling like smoke in the cold air, and listened for another frightening cry. We listened hard but heard only the voices of busy crickets. Randy moved the light away from my face and pointed it at the ceiling.

"It's nothin'," Tommy said, laughing nervously.

"Yeah," I said, trying to find the humor but failing miserably.

"Hey, do you guys think Mr. Phillips's land is really haunted?" Randy asked. His pale, freckled face was now in the path of the light beam, making him seem like a demented ghost.

"I haven't seen anything," I said.

"Me neither," Tommy added. "Other than that piece of Indian pottery you showed us that one day."

"I asked Mr. Phillips about that Indian graveyard stuff and he said it was a bunch of myths," Randy said. "He said the land was vacant before his house was there."

"Then what about that broken pot?" Mikey asked.

Randy rubbed his nose and thought for a second in the light. I had never seen so many freckles on his face before. "I think it must have washed down the ditch or something. Maybe from up north."

"Yeah, but there's still that blood spot we found on it," Tommy said.

"That was creepy," Lucy said, shivering with goose-bumps, pulling her sleeping bag up to her shoulders.

"I think that was paint," Randy said. "It was the same color as the designs on the rest of the pottery."

"I don't know," Jason said. "That looked pretty real to me."

"Me, too," Mikey said, licking his lips. "Hey! Do you have it? We could bring it in here and try to figure it out."

"Are you kidding?" Randy asked. "I threw that crazy thing in the ditch. There's no way I was going to carry it around."

"Gosh, I wouldn't have touched it in the first place," Lucy said.

We went silent again, hearing the distant dog bark at another passing car. The mutt was relentless.

The tent had now slightly warmed up and the vapor from our breath had turned into a light mist.

"You know, it isn't so bad building that fence," Tommy said. His face was tight and serious, as if he had thought long and hard about what he had said. “It was a real drag at first, but it’s coming along.”

“Yeah, true,” Mikey said. “I mean, don’t get me wrong. I’d rather be playing baseball than putting up crappy posts, but since we have to pay for what we did...what I did, I mean...I’m glad it’s that.”

“And Mr. Phillips isn’t half as psycho as I thought he was,” I said. “I still think it’s a little odd that he works all the time, but whatever, you know.”

“What does he do when he’s inside his house?” Lucy asked.

“Paints and sculpts,” Mikey said. “Davy and I saw it the day I got my ankle wrapped.”

“Ever feel any pain in it anymore?” Randy asked.

“The ankle? Nope.” Mikey rolled up his right pant leg and pulled down his sock. The bandage was gone from his chubby leg. “Good as new.”

“Just don’t bust it again,” Jason said. “It’ll cost us another year’s worth of work.”

“How long do you guys think it will take?” Randy asked, the flashlight beam pointed right at his ghostly face.

“February,” Mikey said.

“Are you on crack?” Jason replied. “At least April.”

Tommy put his flashlight on his face like Randy. "I say the end of the school year, but it's hard to tell."

I tried to picture the completion of the fence and estimate our finishing point, but it seemed too far away. We only had half of the sixty posts up and the work wasn't getting any easier. Winter had arrived early, making the ground rock-hard. Our holes now had three months of dirt from windstorms that had to be dug out, one painful inch at a time. This slowed progress considerably. Additionally, the posts were another problem. They were as cold as ice and Mr. Phillips had to buy us three pairs of ski gloves so we could handle them. The gloves kept our hands warm, but they were thick and clumsy. Grasping the posts was a feat all in itself; our hands kept slipping and skidding. And daylight, our fickle friend, was growing dimmer by the weeks. We would soon be in December and January, where we would be lucky to get in an hour's worth of work before sunset.

My predictions were with Tommy's—late May.

"Have your parents caught on yet?" I asked, looking around the group.

"Man, mine don't have a clue," Tommy said, cupping the beam with his hands. "I could be smoking marijuana and dealing drugs for all they know."

“Same with my dad,” Jason said. “He thinks I’m having the greatest baseball season of my life.”

“Not me, I almost got caught,” Mikey said. “A few weeks ago, my mom wanted to go to one of our games.”

“Shut up!” Tommy said, staring at Mikey.

“No way. What did you tell her?” Randy asked.

“At first I didn’t know what to say. I thought about telling her we didn’t have games and that we were only practicing, but then she’d wonder why we never actually played. So I told her it would be better if she came to one of the spring games. I said that was when the playoffs took place, during warmer weather.”

“Pendejo! You said that?” Jason blasted.

“Yeah, why?”

“What are we going to do during the spring? Tell her to come to fall games? She’ll know for sure then.”

“What else was I supposed to say?”

“Great,” Randy said, “I knew this could never last. Our parents are going find out and ream us.”

“No,” Tommy said confidently, “not yet. Mikey at least bought us some time. We can figure something out in the next couple of months. Like a fake game or something.”

“Yeah,” I agreed. “We’ll pick out a day when Mr. Phillips will let us off and play baseball like nothing’s happened.”

"We can invite all our parents, too," Mikey added.

Jason took a hit of his aspirator. "No way, I'm not inviting my dad to that."

"You might have to," Tommy added quickly. "Mikey told her it was a playoff game. It'll look kind of suspicious if she's the only one that shows. Don't ya think?"

We all nodded, including Jason. I immediately wondered if I'd have to ask my mother to come. She'd see how crappy we were, dropping balls and striking out like a bunch of losers. She'd begin to question what all the practice was for, months and months of it. But on second thought, maybe not. She had never seen us play before, so she had no idea how well we played—practice or no practice. She'd smile and say, "Nice catch, Davy," or "It's okay, you'll hit the ball next time." My mother, like Tommy's parents, didn't have a clue when it came to afterschool playtime.

"Yeah, I guess we'll have to ask our folks," Randy said. "But who's gonna play us?"

"Anybody," Tommy said. "Maybe Peter and the Strikers, or Frank and the Cougars. Frankie's always beggin' for a game."

"Crap, but what if our parents start talking to them?" Mikey asked.

"What do you mean?" Lucy asked.

"Like if my mom asks Frank how often he plays with us...you know, kind of casually."

"Good point," Tommy said, "Frank would tell her that he hasn't seen us play all season."

"And we'd be toast if that happened," Randy said.

Randy reopened the tent door and pointed the flashlight out, illuminating the blackness. The bloodthirsty coyote had spared us for another day.

We remained silent, watching Randy move his beam across his yard, revealing bushes, trees, and shrubs. The vegetation took on an eerie appearance, casting long shadows into the mysterious darkness. Tommy joined him in the hunt and pointed his light on top of Randy's, doubling the beam's power.

"Well, like I said, we've got time to think about it," Tommy finally said, breaking the silence.

"Yeah, we'll come up with something," Lucy added. Lucy looked back at me and smiled. She had pulled out her hair band and had let her silky hair drape over her shoulders. She was radiant, even in the darkness. I smiled back but was a little concerned that the Gang would see me doing it.

"I'm passin' out," Jason said, fluffing his pillow.

"It's time...lights out," Tommy said, flipping his flashlight off as if he were a commanding officer ordering his unit to sleep.

Randy clicked his beam off too and the tent went black. We snuggled into our bags and listened to the chatter of the crickets. The barking dog, apparently, had called it lights out, too.

***

Thirty minutes later, I was still wide awake. I kept thinking about my dad and his job, wondering if he'd find a new one soon or if he'd end up in a welfare line getting food stamps for our family. The TV images of those long unemployment lines during the Great Depression were imprinted in my mind.

This layoff really hit me hard. It did the same to a lot of people. I guess we should have seen it coming, but we didn't. And now we have to deal with it.

My dad said we wouldn't lose the house, but I had my doubts. Anything could happen, just like the accident that had taken the life of my aunt. That came without warning, a tornado that ripped through our lives and then disappeared without a trace.

"Hey, you guys still awake?" Tommy whispered.

"Yep, I am," I said.

"Me, too," Lucy said. "Jason's passed out and so is Mikey. I can hear 'em both snoring."

"Randy's also out," I said.

Randy wasn't snoring, but I could tell he was asleep because his right hand was on top of my bag, twitching in some dream.

"You guys ever think about high school?" Tommy asked.

"Sometimes," I replied, staring at the tent ceiling. The canvas was partly transparent, and through it I could see dim spots of the brightest stars.

"Same here," Lucy added.

"Sucks we're goin' to different schools, huh?"

"Not all of us," Lucy answered. "Mikey will be with you."

"Yeah, but that won't matter. After a couple of years, we'll have new friends and won't hang around anymore."

"How do you know that?" I asked.

"It happens," Tommy said. "I mean, with Lucy at the Huckleberry Academy and you, Jason, and Randy at St. Joseph, it won't be the same."

"We'll still live next to each other, right?" I asked.

"Yeah, but that doesn't mean anything. Just look at my brother. Dan used to be good buds with Ben Klouski back in middle school. Hanging out every friggin' day like twins. But now they never see each other. They probably don't even say hi when they pass each other on the street or while gassin' up at the station. High school just changes you, that's all."

"I'll call you if you call me," I said.

"At first, Davy. But after two or three years? My house will be yesterday's news."

"It doesn't have to be that way," I said.

"No, but it just is," Tommy said. "Public school kids don't hang with the preppy kind. No offense."

"Preppy? I'm not even sure if I'm getting into the Academy. I could be with you, Tommy," Lucy said.

"Bullshit," Tommy said. "You'll get in. You're the brightest in our class."

"I've still got another semester, though. If I mess up for some reason, screw up on a final or something, I might lose my scholarship."

"That's one chance in a billion," I said. "You'll never do that. I don't know how you get that many A's, but you pull it off. Besides, even if you did blow it, the teachers like you too much. They'd give you the top grade even if you didn't earn it."

"I don't know about that," Lucy said doubtfully.

We remained quiet for a few minutes. The tent was cold again and my face felt like an ice cube. I had almost drifted to sleep when Lucy said, "Tommy, you could go to St. Joseph with Davy."

"Me?" Tommy asked with complete surprise. "Are you kidding?"

"Why not? You have the grades."

"Right, but I also have the crazy old man. I'd never get a scholarship like the one you've got and there's no way my pop would fork out for a Catholic education. Not in a million years."

"Never?" Lucy asked.

"Dead serious. One time my mother asked him if they should send Dan to St. Joseph, and you know what he said?"

"What?" I asked.

"'It's for pussies,' he said. 'Wimps and pussies.'"

"Gosh, he really said that?" Lucy asked.

"Yep, and that's what he'll say if I ask him. He went to Gregory High and as far as he's concerned, Dan and I will, too."

"It's not all that bad," I said. "It's just as good as the other schools, if you ask me."

"Yeah? Then why are you goin' to a different one, Davy?"

Tommy had me against the ropes. I desperately wanted to go to St. Joseph, and the main reason was to get out of Gregory High. Huckleberry had some fine public schools—like Huckleberry High and Westgate—but Gregory wasn't one of them. It was rated one of the most violent schools in the Southwest, and it had the second highest dropout rate in New Mexico, right behind the notorious Franklin Educational Institute. All three of Lucy's brothers had gone to Gregory and each had dropped out before senior year. Unlike Mikey's parents, who were firm believers in the public school system and determined to prove it by sending their son to Gregory, most parents in the school district resolutely shopped for substitute schools.

What I had told Tommy was, indeed, a fat lie. Gregory was nowhere near as good as the other schools.

"Well...it's college that really matters," I said, trying to worm my way out. "You'll get into a good one then at least."

"Only if I get a full ride, and I don't have the brains for that. I'm not that smart."

Tommy clicked the flashlight and covered its plastic top with his hand. The beam made his flesh glow a bright orange and outlined the bones in his fingers. Lucy and I sat up from our sleeping bags.

"There's always an athletic scholarship, baseball or football," Lucy said.

"No way," Tommy quickly replied. "I'm nowhere near the level those guys are."

"Are you kidding?" I asked. "You'll smoke the other players."

Tommy scratched his nose and shrugged his shoulders. "Maybe..." He gazed down at the flashlight and squinted at the white beam. I stared at him, wondering how in the world he couldn't realize what was very obvious to all of us. Didn't he understand that he was a phenomenal athlete? Did he forget that day he'd killed all of us on the soccer field? Couldn't he remember all the strikeouts and home runs he had had at Roosevelt and out in the Vineyard? "I'll probably be like Dan," Tommy continued. "I'll slide by with C's, stuff my diploma in my pocket and take my dad's place at the tire factory just like my old man did with my granddad. I'll be sweatin' bullets in that shitty humid factory, shooting the bull with the other drunk losers."

"That's not you," I said.

"You don't know that, Davy. It runs in the damn family. It's his dying dream to pass on that crappy job to me or Dan, and since Dan is too strung up to hold a position for more than five weeks, I'm the only one that can fill his shoes."

"It's a free country, isn't it?" Lucy asked. "You can do what you want."

Tommy gave a dry laugh and parted his glowing fingers, letting thin streams of light slice the darkness. "Not in the Smith family. Your destiny is branded on your back the day the doctor slaps you. All the pegs are lined in a pretty row and all you have to do is follow the path like a good dog."

"That's bullshit, Tommy," I said.

"Is it?" Tommy asked. "Take a good look at my dad next time and ask me that again." Tommy waited for a reply, but neither Lucy nor I wanted to give him one. We didn't want to say it, but we both knew he was right more than he was wrong. "Anyway, it's getting late," Tommy said at length. "Sun'll be up before we know it."

Tommy shut the light off and snuggled in his sleeping bag. Lucy slid back into hers and I soon followed suit.

I thought about what Tommy had told us and listened to the mesmerizing cricket chatter. After a few minutes, I drifted into a deep sleep.

***

I swore on my mother's good name that Mrs. Sachs was going to wake up before us on Saturday morning and find out about our little campout. I would've wagered twenty dollars on it. It's a good thing I didn't make that bet, because Randy had awoken first and had blown the horn for the rest of us. We had our bags rolled up and the tent stuffed back into its carrying case before sun-up—an accomplishment that surprised even Randy. By the time Mrs. Sachs shuffled into the den, wearing a blue night robe and sheep-skin slippers, we were watching the early morning cartoons: *Hall of Justice*, to be exact.

"Mornin' everyone."

"Good morning Mrs. Sachs," we replied.

"How'd you sleep?"

"Good, Mom," Randy said, giving his best freckled smile. "And you?"

"Just fine. How does pancakes and bacon sound to everyone?"

"Sounds great," Randy said, and we all eagerly agreed.

Mrs. Sachs shuffled back to the kitchen. We looked at each other and snickered like dirty thieves. Mikey put his hand over his mouth and pointed at the empty hallway where Mrs. Sachs had stood seconds before. We had successfully pulled the wool over her eyes.

***

If you don't learn from the mistakes of the past, you're destined to repeat them in the future.

The first time I heard that phrase was in my eight o'clock Social Studies class. It was on the fourth day of class and I was sitting behind Mikey, doodling on a piece of paper while Mr. Katts droned on about the War of 1812. Mr. Katts was almost as hypnotizing as Quin Tabby, the robotic Typing instructor, but unlike Tabby, Mr. Katts had the ability to make you soil your pants.

"Mr. Blake!" Mr. Katts bellowed, walking to my desk.

My head shot up in complete surprise and the class laughed at my reaction.

"Are you sleeping in my class?"

"No, sir," I replied, hiding my picture of Mr. Katts with a mustache and thick glasses.

Mr. Katts stopped beside me and tapped his foot. "Then what were you doing?"

"Nothing, sir," I replied.

"Nothing, huh?" Mr. Katts snatched my paper and inspected it. "Then what's this?"

"Oooooo, busted," the class whistled at me.

My heart dropped to the floor. He was going to give me a detention slip, or worse, send me to

Principal Pinner. I wanted to tear the paper from his hand and burn the evidence.

"A picture of me?" Mr. Katts said. "Why, Davy, I think you could have done a little better job than that."

Mr. Katts showed the class the picture and they roared with laughter.

"Are my ears really that big? What's the deal with my banana nose?"

I tried to smile, to make light of the situation, but the thought of sitting in an afternoon detention class scribbling I will not draw in class a million times kept me from doing it. Meanwhile, the class was enjoying the break from the dull lecture.

"Mr. Blake, did you hear what I just said about the battle?"

"No, sir," I admitted.

"How ironic." Mr. Katts smiled. "Can anyone enlighten Davy?"

Patty's hand fired up. She was the teacher's pet, the loud-mouth, the one with all the answers. Patty Ratty Pigtails. I couldn't stand her.

"You said that if you don't learn from the mistakes of the past, you're destined to repeat them in the future," Patty said, a prissy grin plastered on her face.

"Very good, Patty. Now Davy, do you know what that means?"

I swallowed and looked at my hands. "It means if you don't know your history, you're going to fall in the same traps as others."

"Give me an example."

I swallowed again and Patty stared at me. She was waiting for me to choke so she could rack another kiss-ass point with Mr. Katts.

"Well, like the Nazis during World War II," I said. "Hitler made the same mistake Napoleon did when he invaded Russia during the winter. The Nazi armies were crippled by the cold Russian winter and ended up losing the war."

Mr. Katts smiled. "Very good, Davy. You're a quick thinker when you're not goofing off. Do me a favor and stick to history. No offense, but you can't draw to save your life."

The class laughed at me. I blushed and closed my eyes, desperately waiting for Mr. Katts to shift the spotlight.

While the humiliation eventually passed, the history lesson stuck with me. If you don't learn from the mistakes of the past, you're destined to repeat them in the future. I understood the concept the same way I understood Mrs. Williams's algebra formulas and Mr. White's science theories. I grasped it in the abstract. I could not see a practical application for it in the day-to-day life of a kid.

I found that out the hard way that Mr. Katt's favorite adage could be easily proven. I discovered this as I was making my way home from Randy's house after our sleepover.

Had I learned a thing from my encounter with the Jerks the time I got my underwear rearranged by the neighborhood back gate, I would have pedaled my bicycle to Randy's house instead of walking the distance.

Just as I was coming around the neighborhood's park basketball courts and whistling the theme song to the show The Jeffersons, I saw Bruce Brown heading in my direction. He was moving fast, in a kind of half jog, looking straight at me. There was no doubting his intentions. He wanted retaliation for Halloween night.

I immediately darted across the basketball courts, my heart pounding. Bruce sprinted after me, his arms swinging wildly, his head forward like a raging bull. To say that he was pissed was to do him a disservice. He was furious: a devil out to kill a bratty kid.

I zipped through the grassy park, my feet slipping on the frosty, brown lawn, my breath pumping in and out in short, misty gasps. Bruce's long legs were closing the distance. He was a fast kid, probably the fastest of the Jerks, and it was only a matter of time before he caught up to me. I tried to throw him off, zigzagging between the bare willow trees, but he matched every step.

I hit Baxter road and ran directly for my house. Our subdivision was the next in line, only minutes away, but Bruce was right on my tail. I could hear his footsteps pounding on the asphalt.

I made a desperate attempt and cut into a yard full of bushy evergreens. I thought I could somehow lose him in the shrubbery; it only slowed my pace. Bruce followed me in, his stilt legs working the vegetation better than mine. Twenty feet into the yard lay a five-foot adobe wall. Beyond that wall was Mr. and Mrs. Weston's property, and I was positive that Bruce wouldn't pound on me if I were standing in the middle of their courtyard. If I could jump the barrier, I might escape the punishment.

I slammed against the wall and threw my hands over its rough, stucco top. I pulled with my arms and kicked with my legs. It was impossible to climb. The wall was too tall and I couldn't get a solid grip on it. Bruce's hand closed around my jacket collar. He yanked me down with a sharp tug.

"You little bastard!"

"Please, don't. I didn't mean to—" I begged, but Bruce's fist landed square in my gut.

"You think you could avoid me forever, ass munch?" Bruce asked. His freckles, unlike Randy's, were dark and scattered around his face like black land mines. He had a dime-sized hairy mole under his right eye. "You think you could hide?"

Bruce slapped my face and punched me in the side. The first blow had knocked the air out of me. The second felt like a thunderbolt that ripped through every nerve.

"I bet you and that little bitch had a good laugh that night," Bruce said. "Betcha even told all your freaky friends about it."

"I didn't," I said, squeezing the words out of my lungs.

"Yeah right, that's a load of shit. You sang like a canary. You bragged how you beat me up."

"I swear, Bruce, I kept it to myself. Swear."

"Yeah?" Bruce said, as if he actually believed me for a short second, creating a blissful pause in his torment. "It doesn't matter. You busted my face pretty bad that night. You see that?" Bruce pointed to his nose. It was naturally crooked; it had already received its fair share of beatings long before I touched it. Dead center was a purple bruise the shape and size of an olive.

"Your fuckin' bag did that, ass munch. You gave me a bloody one that ran for hours. Lucky for you, it didn't break."

His nose was so ugly that if I had broken it, it could only have helped. Obviously, I didn't dare proffer Bruce that opinion right there...not while he had my life in his hands.

"I don't know why you helped that brown-haired bitch."

"Stop calling her a bitch," I replied.

"Shut your trap," Bruce said and slugged me another blow. This one landed just below my ribcage.

Suddenly a miracle happened. A car rolled slowly down the circle. It was headed in our direction. We were thick in the yard, a good twenty-five feet inside, and the evergreens provided some coverage, but the driver could still see us if he happened to glance in our direction.

"Fuck!" Bruce said. "You're lucky, shit face." He pushed me into a bush and ran off.

I waited for the car to pass and then rushed off, too, thinking that if I waited in the same place, Bruce might pay me another visit.

So you want some more, do ya? Can't get enough, ass munch?

I was still out of breath and my stomach was throbbing, but considering the damage...I'd had worse. I wouldn't say I got away scot-free, because I certainly didn't, but I had gotten off easy. Bruce was a big kid, even for a fifteen-year-old, and had he decided to knock me into the stone ages, he could have done so easily. I probably weighed fifty pounds less than him and was about five inches shorter. Bruce could have squashed me like an ant.

But he didn't, and a part of me felt relieved. I had received the beating that I had been expecting since Halloween night. It had been hanging over me like a dark cloud, pregnant with water, literally waiting to rain down blows. I felt the worst was over. Sure, Bruce might decide to pound me again, after school or maybe outside my house, but at least he couldn't say that he had to get me back for the bloody nose. He had served his revenge.

When I reached our front door, I dusted off and checked my face in the side window. I didn't notice anything except a small scrape on my left cheek. It was long, but it wasn't major. That meant Mom wouldn't ask questions.

I walked inside and shut the door.

I silently promised myself I would never leave without a bike again.

Chapter 15

THE DARK HOLE

Thanksgiving came and went. We had been treated to my mother's homemade dishes for the holiday: bread stuffing, tangy cranberry sauce, sweet potatoes covered with melted marshmallows, hot rolls, and a golden baked turkey loaded with juices and intoxicating aromas. The four of us had eaten at the kitchen table, consuming as much of the food as we could handle. Lewis had loved the marshmallows the best. His face, always covered with something, had looked like a sticky snowball.

I always felt that Thanksgiving dinner was really just the appetizer for the Christmas feast. Thanksgiving was a holiday you enjoyed the day it happened, and completely forgot about the second it ended. Once the turkey was stuffed back into the fridge, where it would provide sandwiches for the next two weeks, all focus was turned to the granddaddy of months: December. If you happened to be a kid when it rolled around, whether you were Jewish or Christian, it was a month for begging for presents.

Because my dad was still unemployed, I limited my list to three items: a slingshot, a tape player, and a Wipe Out 2000 skateboard—a board I had been dying to get ever since I laid eyes on its sparkly wheels at the Kick and Run local sports store. My mother said she'd think about the skateboard and the tape player, but had reservations about the sling. It was dangerous, she told me, too risky for a boy my age. I knew it was a lot safer than my pellet gun, but I couldn't tell Mom that because she didn't know I even owned one. I had secretly purchased the ten-pump air rifle with Jason—using money I had saved from three months of lawn detail—and kept it at Randy's house in a tin storage shed in the back of his garage.

Lewis, using crayons, had made a list of his own for Santa. Lewis was still in the dark about Mr. Claus, but I had learned the truth about his existence in the third grade, when a kid named Jeffery Tatter told me about his father sneaking presents under the tree. I didn't reveal this information to Lewis since I didn't want to spoil his Christmas, and since he probably wouldn't believe me anyway. Some things were better left unsaid.

I had a hard time decoding Lewis's list for my mother—words like "chocolate" and "candy canes" were spelled "khokolate" and "kanie kans"—but after a good hour, I was able to rewrite a legible list. When my mother took us to see the jolly man in the giant red suit, Lewis was oblivious to the rewritten copy stuffed in my mom's purse.

While Lewis and I dreamed about our gifts, my father was on the phone scheduling interviews and talking to former employees at Skyline. It was strange having him around the house, yet it was nice being in his presence. He kept his promise to lay off the alcohol and helped my mom with some of those forgotten promises he'd given her while working: fixing our broken dishwasher (which had been out of order for two years), replacing the master bedroom's toilet, and repainting our tattered garage door. My mother joked that if she had the money, she'd hire him as her personal handyman. My father said he'd probably go on strike since she was a slave driver.

Dad also had a growing interest in the things I did. He had helped me with my Algebra homework and assisted me on a Shop class project—a miniature outhouse made out of wood chips, nails, and Krazy Glue. I liked the attention, but I was concerned about the secret in the Vineyard. What if Dad, like Mikey's mom, asked if he could attend one of our games? What if he wanted to see us practice, or scrimmage? He had asked me a dozen times about baseball, and I had lied each time.

How's practice with your friends going, son?

Good, Dad, I'd say. *Going just fine. Tommy hit a homer the other day. Fourth of the season, you know. He's got a great swing. He might play for high school if he gets the chance.*

I was still in the clear. Dad simply nodded at my answers and told me to keep playing, but it still made me shudder whenever he asked.

Two weeks after Thanksgiving, the day after Lewis and I talked to Saint Nick, Mikey found a little black hole in the Vineyard. He discovered it under a cloudless, brilliantly blue afternoon sky.

"Hey, guys!" Mikey yelled. "You gotta see this!"

Mikey and Randy were squatted down on their haunches, staring into a three-foot wide irrigation trench. The dirt route was one of four spillways that drained into the Vineyard from the main ditch. Tommy, Jason, and I were working on the fortieth post; Mikey and Randy were supposed to be cementing the thirty-ninth. Lucy was home, sick with the flu.

"What is it?" Tommy asked.

"Just come over," Mikey replied.

We cautiously checked for Mr. Phillips, who was busy replacing shingles on his roof, and dropped our clamshell shovels.

"Let's take a break," Tommy said, taking his winter gloves off.

Jason and I agreed and we marched over, rubbing our sore hands along the way. The gloves helped keep out the winter air, but did little to protect our hands from the wear and tear of digging into rock-hard frozen dirt.

"What's the fuss?" Tommy asked, kneeling next to Randy, trying to see what they were looking at.

"See that hole?" Mikey asked, pointing to the spot with a bony stick.

"Yeah, what about it?"

"Somethin' came out of it."

"What are you smokin', loco?" Jason asked.

"No, it's true," Randy said, his blue eyes as wide as Mikey's. "It was green and brown and slimy."

"Like a bug?" I asked.

"No, bigger," Mikey replied. "Three times that size."

Tommy grabbed Mikey's stick and moved closer to the hole. The irrigation route was usually dry during the wintertime, but last week's downfall had left it with sticky mud and scattered, shallow puddles.

"Let's see if it comes out again," Tommy said.

"I wouldn't get too close," Mikey warned. "It might bite."

"It's probably a stupid rat," Jason said.

"When's the last time you saw a brownish-green rat?" Randy asked with a raised eyebrow.

Tommy cautiously poked at the hole. The jagged stick moved in and out of the darkness.

Nothing stirred. Tommy looked back at us and licked his lips.

"Did you guys see anything?"

"Huh uh," I told him.

"What if it's a snake?" Mikey said, his eyes engulfing his face.

It was well known that Mikey was a scaredy-cat. He'd jump five feet if you tapped him on the back or brushed his hair while passing him in the hall. After years of dealing with his paranoid reflexes, we had learned to dismiss them and drown him out. If Mikey hollered, "watch out," we'd continue with our current business as if nothing had been said.

But this time Mikey's hunch had some credibility. Snakes were common in the Vineyard. Tommy had found a garter snake underneath the ditch bridge, and Mr. Phillips had found a rattler coiled inside a worn tire in his backyard. He cautioned us about venomous snakes on our third day of work, said one bite could send us to the graveyard. Since I didn't hear the ominous *chik-chik-chik* of a tail, I didn't think we were dealing with a rattlesnake, but there was a possibility it could be some other kind of poisonous creature. Maybe even a scorpion.

Tommy continued to stab at the hole, this time slower. He was hunched like a plumber. I could see every knob in his spine. He was dressed in stonewashed blue jeans, muddy sneakers, and a white undershirt. The gray sweatshirt he had worn earlier was draped over the handlebars of his bike, swaying with the breeze and waiting for its owner to return at the end of his shift.

"Come on Tommy, let's leave it alone," Jason said.

"Yeah, whatever it is, it's gone," I said, practically fainting watching Tommy risk his arm.

Tommy looked over his shoulder, "Hold on, let's see if—"

Suddenly, like an explosion, a greenish-brown phantom shot out of the hole. Instinctually, in unison, we jumped away from it. Tommy didn't see it jump out and when he felt it hit his hand, he lost his balance and slipped face first into the ditch.

"Shit, shit, shit!" Tommy said, flopping like a fish. "It's on me!"

The creature was so quick that we didn't get a good look at it. We stepped back and watched Tommy squirm. The creature was gone again.

"Where is it?" Tommy asked, doing a backwards crab crawl.

"I don't know," I said, frantically looking for it.

"Did it go back in its hole?" Jason asked.

"It's here somewhere!" Mikey yelled, looking as if he were about to have a heart attack. "I know it!"

Then, as Tommy was crawling back, the creature jumped out of a pile of leaves as unexpectedly as it had the first time. It landed in the middle of Tommy's shirt. Tommy's mouth dropped like a trapdoor.

"There!" Mikey screamed.

Like Mikey said, there it was and there it stayed. Its coffee-brown eyes staring straight at Tommy, its webbed feet marking muddy tracks on his shirt, its warty skin covered with brownish-green spots. Tommy was paralyzed with fear. He stared at it with the palest face I had ever seen.

"It's just a sapo," Jason said.

"What?" Tommy asked with a high pitched, cracking voice.

"A toad, Tommy," I said. "It's a toad."

Tommy continued to stare at the little menace as if it were going to somehow transform into a man-eating creature. Reality hit us. We roared with laughter in the dirt, rolling and kicking like mad-men, stickers and weeds pricking our skin.

"It's a friggin' toad," Randy said, holding his belly.

"That's all," I replied. I felt a cramp swell in my side, but I couldn't stop it. The image of Tommy scared witless was too much to handle.

Tommy picked the toad off of his shirt and stood up. He looked it over.

"Little bastard," Tommy said.

"Geez, Tommy, you should have seen the look on your face," Mikey said, his fleshy stomach wiggling like Jell-O. "You looked like you had seen the devil himself."

"Yeah, yeah," Tommy said, flipping us off.

We continued to twist and turn on the ground in laughter. Tommy looked at the toad again and even got a few chuckles out of it.

"You boys having fun?"

Directly above us, blocking the sun like a giant tower, stood Mr. Phillips. His straw hat was perched on his head, blacking out his face.

We immediately jumped up and dusted off. Stickers, weeds, and leaves hung on our clothes. It was impossible to remove them all, so we let a few stragglers remain.

The humor had flown out of our bodies and left us with guilt.

"We were just checking somethin' out, Mr. Phillips," Randy said, scratching his red head.

"You don't say," Mr. Phillips replied, grabbing the toad out of Tommy's hand. "And I reckon y'all have found it."

Mr. Phillips looked at the creature. The amphibian was three to four inches long. It sat patiently in Mr. Phillips's giant hand; its bubble throat expanding and retracting.

"Well, well, how did you get out here?" Mr. Phillips said.

"Is it a bullfrog?" Mikey asked.

Mr. Phillips inspected it and shook his head. "No, it's an American toad. They're common around the eastern states, but I reckon this is the first one I've seen in our neck of the woods."

"How'd it get this far?" Jason asked.

"Maybe it hitched a ride in someone's suitcase," Randy said.

"Maybe," Mr. Phillips agreed. "You boys got a name for it?"

"A name!" Mikey said, excited at the thought. "Mr. Hops."

"Mr. Hops?" Jason said. "That's the dumbest name I've ever heard."

"I found it," Mikey argued. "I'm the one that gets to name it."

"You didn't find it, Tommy's the one that fished it out," Jason replied.

"I don't want to name it," Tommy said bluntly.

"See?" Mikey sneered at Jason. "That means I get to, and I like Mr. Hops."

Just then, the toad turned in Mr. Phillips's hand and looked straight at us as if to tell us he liked the name, too.

"Mr. Hops it is," Mr. Phillips said. "You better keep an eye on him, or he'll go jumpin' into the ditch and disappear forever."

Mr. Phillips gave the toad over to Mikey, and, like magic, it hopped into Mikey's cupped hands.

"I think y'all have had a good rest break, huh?" Mr. Phillips said with a frown.

"Yes, sir," we agreed.

We ran back to our workstations and continued to dig and plant our posts in the dying afternoon sun. The wind was light and cool, and made the surrounding oak and elm trees sway their naked branches. A thin layer of snow was draped over the peaks of the Hillerman Mountains, revealing a promising ski season in the months ahead.

Every so often, I'd look across the way and catch Mikey whispering to Mr. Hops inside his flannel shirt pocket.

Mikey had found a new friend.

Chapter 16

THE SLINGSHOT

The slingshot situation was looking bleaker. Years later, I would equate my dilemma with the boy in that movie, *The Christmas Story*. I was just like Ralph, trying to convince my mother that my hunting gift wasn't as dangerous as it seemed. But that movie came out in 1983, and in 1981 the phrase, "You'll shoot your eye out, kid," hadn't made it to the big screen. That's not to say I wasn't familiar with the warning, though. In fact, my mom said the same things to me, only she'd say, "boys shouldn't use men's toys," or "you're bound to end up in a hospital."

If worse came to worst, I could always save for the sling like I saved for the air rifle, but that would mean months of lawn mowing and washing dishes—the slingshot *was* cheaper than the rifle, but it was still a good amount for a kid. I simply couldn't wait that long. Christmas was the only option, and I somehow had to persuade my mother that the present was as safe as a stuffed bunny.

Three weeks before the 25th, I came up with an idea. It was a backup plan that involved avoiding my mother altogether. I'd ask the one person that could buy it for me without getting into trouble: Dad.

I had to wait for a good day, when he was in high spirits. If I caught him in a bad mood, he would certainly say no. My father, after all, disliked weapons. Sure, he'd had his fair share of BB guns and knives when he was a kid, but he was a reformed man, a father dedicated to preserving the peace. He wanted to set a good example for me and Lewis. Nevertheless, he still had a hint of that kid inside of him, a part of his youth that wanted to break free from the walls of adulthood and shoot a tin can off a fence or stab a knife in a tree dartboard.

My chance came on December 3rd, right after school had let out. I had just come home and walked into my room, when my father ran upstairs, calling wildly for my mother.

"Nancy!" he yelled, jumping the stairs two at a time.

I dropped my backpack on the bed and walked to the hallway. My dad practically ran me over when I bumped into him outside my room.

"Davy, have you seen Mom?"

"Yeah, she's in your room with Lewis," I said.

"Thanks," he replied, and tousled my hair.

I watched as he sprinted into the master bedroom. I had never seen him move so fast before, not even during our Saturday afternoon football games in the park, where he'd sometimes take me and Lewis for a game of two-touch.

I crept to their door and eavesdropped on the conversation. It was muffled, but audible.

"I got an interview!"

"Really? With whom?"

"A small jetliner that serves the southwest. They're offering more money than Skyline. And the hours are better. I'd be home every weekend. No more three-week trips."

"That's great! When's the interview?"

"Tomorrow morning. Eight o'clock sharp."

"You better set that alarm early. The way you've been sleeping in every day, you'll probably snore right through it."

"I won't miss this. Not after waiting this long."

I heard a kiss, footsteps and some slapping on our hardwood floor. Lewis was the cause of the slapping, I presumed.

"Interbue!"

"That's right, sport. Except it's interview. Your dad's back in business."

Perfect! I thought, creeping away from the door. *This is the moment. I'll wait until he's alone and then take him by surprise. He'll say yes without even thinking about it. "A slingshot, Davy? Sure, why not, champ? Heck, I'll get one too, so we can both go out and break Coke bottles and pickle jars. It'll be a blast, just like it was when I was a boy your age. Say, let's buy them today!"*

I didn't have to worry about the afternoon Vineyard work, since Mr. Phillips had given us a three-week vacation. Playing baseball around Christmas was a little odd, he said, and we should wait until the New Year before finishing the posts. We could consider it our little present, he told us with a smile. Without hesitating, we gladly agreed and thanked him for the gift.

I opened my Algebra textbook on the kitchen table and waited for my father. But after ten painful minutes, he still hadn't come down the stairs. *What is he doing up there? Taking a nap?A shower? Crud,* I thought, *I might miss the opportunity and never get the chance again.* The slingshot dream was fading...

"Hey, Davy," my father said.

His voice took me by surprise and I jerked around. I had been so absorbed in my thoughts that I didn't hear him come down.

"Doing homework now?" he asked, grabbing a carton of orange juice from the fridge.

"Uh, yeah...got lots of work today."

"Anything I can help you with?"

"Nope, I'm okay."

Better ask him, stupid. If you don't do it now you'll be screwed forever. He'll say yes, of course he'll say yes.

"Dad?"

"Yeah, champ?"

"Do you think..." I bit my lip.

"Think what?"

I cleared my throat and swallowed. "Do you think I can get a slingshot for Christmas?"

My father laughed and took a sip of his juice. He wiped his mouth and said, "Slingshot? Well, I don't see why not, as long as you're safe."

I was so excited I almost fell out of my seat. I did it. My plan worked!

"Thanks, Dad!"

"No problem, champ." My dad grabbed his keys and made for the door. "I'm going to the store for a new tie. I've got an interview."

"I heard," I said, barely thinking about his job. My mind was in another world, filled with hunting targets. I saw myself in a movie, in the jungles of Africa, stealthily moving in and out of the palms and ferns, stalking my prey with a beautiful slingshot. The amazing Davy Blake, Jungle Warrior.

"Oh, and Davy."

"Yeah, Dad?" I said.

"Make sure it's all right with your mother. She should know, too."

He shut the door behind him and the movie went black. My heart fell to the floor. It was history repeating itself. I was doomed. A vicious tiger had killed the poor, unarmed Jungle Warrior; it had ripped him to pieces like a rag doll.

I scratched the sling off my mental list.

Chapter 17

A Gift from Lucy

The kids at school were overjoyed that it was the last day before winter break. They were energetic, talkative, and, at times, rambunctious. They dreamed about all the wonderful gifts under their trees: video games, remote-controlled cars, doll houses, footballs, new shoes... Attention spans were limited, but the teachers didn't care—it was their vacation, too. The teachers would get to spend their time reading a long-desired book, or skiing in the Rocky Mountains, or relaxing in front of the old tube near a crackling fire.

I seemed to be the only one depressed about the time off. While the other kids counted the hours until the last bell, I was busy thinking of ways to get around my slingshot dilemma. My well of ideas had run dry, though. Every road was a dead end.

"What's up, Davy?" Lucy said, catching me at the break between fourth and fifth period classes.

“Hey Lucy, nothing,” I replied. “Goin’ to shop class.”

“Is that yours?” Lucy asked, pointing at the wooden outhouse in my hand.

“Yeah,” I said, showing it to her. “My dad helped out. It took us five weeks. What do you think?”

“Looks cool.”

“I don’t know,” I said, picking at the dried Krazy Glue between the wood chips. I had seen a few other outhouses around school, like Greg Hayes’s, whose project was so picture-perfect it looked like it had been bought in a store. Greg’s dad, a Huckleberry architectural guru, had obviously done most of the work.

Lucy grabbed my hand and stopped me. We stood in the middle of the Recess Square, in front of hundreds of walking kids. It was the first time we had touched in public.

“What’s wrong?” she asked.

“It’s nothin’,” I said.

“Davy...”

“Serious,” I repeated. “It’s nothing.”

Lucy frowned and pulled on my arm.

“Come on,” she said.

“Where are we going?”

“Just follow me.”

“But we have classes, and if—”

Lucy yanked me so hard that I almost tripped over an uneven slab of concrete. She pulled me to the back of the cafeteria, which was cluttered with tumbleweeds, dead sweet-grass, and pieces of yellow newspapers. I was worried that other kids had seen us go back there, but they were so distracted—visions of sugarplums, perhaps—that they hadn't noticed.

Lucy stopped beside a large air conditioning unit and unzipped her daisy backpack.

"We're gonna be late," I said.

"Stop being such a wussy," she replied.

I nervously looked around, expecting Principal Pinner to be staring at us with detention slips in his hand. I had walked behind the cafeteria dozens of times, but it felt different that day, foreign, as if I were standing in another school. Lucy fished out a small box covered with red and green wrapping paper. A flower bow was tied on top.

"What's this?"

"What do you think it is, silly?" Lucy smiled, giving it to me.

"You didn't have to give me one."

"I know, but I wanted to."

"Thanks," I said, staring at the gift. "Sorry, but I didn't buy anything for you."

"It's okay, I didn't expect you to. So...you going to open it, or just stare like a baboon?"

I smiled, tore the paper, and opened a white box. Inside, covered in tissue paper, was a silver disk which resembled a pocket watch. It had a design of a small ship engraved on its shiny surface and silver button on its side. I pressed the button and the top flew open. Behind the shiny cover was an arrow pointing north.

"A compass!" I said, amazed at how beautiful it looked. "All right!"

"You like it?"

"Heck yeah! I've always wanted one. Where did you get it?"

"This fishing store in the heights. It was the only one they had."

"Wow!" I said, spinning around in circles, fascinated at how the needle always pointed north.

I hugged Lucy and thanked her. A crow perched on a telephone wire scolded us from above, madly cawing and squawking. It was Pinner's personal lookout for tardy students.

As the bell rang for fifth period, I kissed Lucy for the second time. It was longer this time, more sweet. Her lips were warm and soft and had the hint of strawberry ChapStick. For a short moment, I forgot about my slingshot, the Vineyard, and school. Lucy had once again taken me on a journey to her own little island, to a mysterious paradise where I never wanted to leave.

I pulled back and noticed how pretty she looked, dressed in a red turtleneck sweater, black khaki slacks, and matching red and black boots. Her silky, brown hair was draped over her shoulders, and underneath it, dangling between her small breasts, was the golden crucifix, sparkling in the cold winter sunlight.

"We're gonna get a detention slip," Lucy said.

"Stop being such a wussy," I replied.

We both laughed and ran to our classes. The crow left its wire and gave us one last raucous caw before disappearing behind a row of trees to search for more tardy students. The Recess Square was completely empty and the foreign feeling returned. Lucy blew me a goodbye kiss.

"Call me during the break," she said.

"I will," I replied, and waved back, cutting into my building.

Chapter 18

LUMINARIA BRILLIANCE

Two words described the first three weeks of winter break: cold and short. Temperature highs had dropped below freezing; snowstorms had dumped over seven inches of white powder in the Hillerman Mountains; and bitter afternoon winds, on average, had whipped up to twenty miles an hour. The deserts of New Mexico had transformed into the tundras of the arctic.

Perhaps it was the cold that made the days seem even shorter than they were. I spent most of my time indoors, helping Mom cook and clean. Lewis also helped out, but his assistance was usually counterproductive. He meant well, and my mom and I let him do his own thing as long as the damage was minimal. If we were cooking, Lewis would stir the mixing bowls, or if we were running a load of laundry, he'd fold the towels. They were simple, undemanding tasks, and Lewis enjoyed them immensely. I was amazed—and a little envious—at how content my brother could be with the littlest of things.

Mom needed me around the house since her handyman had started his new job. Dad was back on the job, although he had three weeks of unpaid hours while he trained with smaller jets than the 747s and 727s he had flown at Skyline. My mother complained about the new company's training policy and said they were taking advantage of their employees. Dad, the optimist, said that things would pick up and promised he'd be bringing home the bacon soon enough.

Because I was in the house, I didn't see much of the Gang. I had played black jack with Tommy and video games with Randy (Randy's parents had spoiled their son with an early Christmas gift—a new Atari, just like the one Mikey had), but that was the extent of my playtime. Luckily, I didn't see the Jerks, either. I still looked over my shoulder whenever taking out the trash or checking our mail. It was just habit—covering my tail whenever possible, even if I was around my own house.

The day before Christmas my mother had me unload her '78 station wagon at the front of our yard. It was packed with a ton of groceries for Christmas dinner, and it took me a good ten minutes to take it all out. Once finished, I saw a box filled with one hundred bags and candles. The bags were 6"x12" brown lunch sacks and the candles were white, 3" tall wax sticks, the same kind used in jack-o'-lanterns. I protested immediately.

"Aww, Mom, do we hav'ta?" I asked.

"Yes, we do, it's a part of the Christmas spirit," my mother replied.

"Yeah, but this many? It's double the amount we had last year."

"And it will make our house one of the prettiest in the neighborhood. Leave that box here in the driveway. We'll use the wheelbarrow to fill the bags."

I reluctantly lifted the box and dropped it where I was told. The weight of it revealed that it would take hours to set up all of the sacks.

The tradition is called the lighting of the luminarias. On Christmas Eve, people around New Mexico—and other parts of the southwest—light candles in little bags around their property in anticipation of the holiday. The bags are lined on streets, walls, and roofs. The event is a grand, glowing display that can be observed from blocks away...even miles, if we include the thousands lined all along Huckleberry's town square.

But making the luminarias was a pain. Each bag needed a candle and a heaping scoop of sand to weigh it down in case a gust of wind decided to take the bag on a journey into the night. My mother liked them on our driveway, roof, and front wall, the area where spectators would first see them if they drove down our cul-de-sac. On the face of it, the job seemed pretty easy...just a little sand and elbow grease. But when you multiplied the bags, dozens upon dozens, one begins to see the exhausting extent of the project. Making them wasn't nearly as fun as watching them.

"Hey, Lewis," I said, poking my head inside the front door. "I need some help."

Lewis jumped up immediately and ran to the door.

"Fun?" Lewis asked.

"It can be. You like to play with sand, don't you?"

Lewis nodded and clapped his hands. He followed me—and the rusty, dented wheelbarrow I was rolling—into our backyard. I stopped at a sand pile by our back fence, unloaded the lunch sacks out of the wheelbarrow, and grabbed a hand shovel.

"We need to fill each of these bags," I said.

"Each!" Lewis said, looking like the world's luckiest kid.

"That's right. Just like we did last year."

I ripped open the package of bags and gave Lewis a dozen.

"Here, unfold these like this and hand them to me."

"Yeah. I get!"

Lewis grabbed the bags and did as I said. I filled each sack with a scoop of sand and lined them on the floor. We worked for the next twenty minutes, unfolding and scooping, until my arm burned from the digging.

"Why don't you fill for a while," I said.

"I fill?" Lewis asked.

"Sure, here."

I handed him the hand shovel and took over his job. Lewis acted like he had been promoted to manager and scooped with pride. His tongue hung out the corner of his mouth and his eyes were deeply focused on the task at hand. He wore his King Kong shirt, which was already showing signs of wear with a few mustard stains on the collar and a black marker streak on the bottom.

"Davy?" my mom asked, yelling from the backyard door.

"Yeah, Ma?"

"Have you seen Lewis?"

"He's out here with me."

Lewis happily waved at my mother and she waved back. "What's he doing?"

"Just helpin' out," I replied.

My mother hated it when Lewis left the house, and I was certain she'd call him back in. Three years ago, Lewis fell out of an elm tree in our backyard and almost poked his right eye out on a protruding lawn sprinkler. He didn't break anything in the fall and he wasn't mentally scarred by it, but my mother never forgot the incident. She kept him on a tight leash after that.

"Well, okay," she said. "I'm going back to the store because I forgot the milk. I'll be back in ten minutes."

"Okay, Ma," I said, relieved she'd let him stay.

My mother left, and Lewis's shovel hit a hard spot in the sand pile, making a hollow, scraping sound. He stopped and looked at me.

"Rocks," Lewis said.

I stared at the pile and saw a concrete block protruding from its center.

"It's a cinder block," I said, trying to remove it. I squatted on the floor, wrapped my fingers around the corner of the concrete, feeling its sandpaper texture, and heaved back with all my weight. The veins in my hands shot out and the muscles in my back tightened. The block didn't budge. "You'll need to dig around it," I said, giving up on it.

Lewis did and we filled another two-dozen sacks. Right before I was about to relieve him, his shovel slipped across the concrete and cut into his palm.

"Ouweee!" Lewis screamed, grabbing his hand, watching the blood rush down his arm. He ran in circles, panicking. I looked back at the house for my mom and remembered that she had left. I grabbed him by the shoulders.

"It's okay, Lewis," I said.

"Ouweee, ouweee."

"I know, pal. Listen, sit down here, and I'll be right back."

"No leave! No leave!"

"I'm not going to leave you. I promise. Just sit down. I will be back super quick. Okay?"

Lewis looked at me doubtfully, then nodded and sat. I ran into the house, sprinted up the stairs two at a time, and made for my bathroom. I opened our medicine cabinet, grabbed a bottle of hydrogen peroxide and some Band-Aids, and dashed back down. Before I went outside, I stopped in the kitchen and tore a handful of paper towels off the holder above the sink.

When I returned, Lewis was sitting Indian-style, holding his bloody hand in fear. I sat next to him, soaked a paper towel in the peroxide, and pressed it against his wound.

"This is gonna hurt a little," I said.

I thought Lewis would scream again, but he sat passively and watched as I cleaned the cut. The scrape had looked a lot worse than it really was; the opening had already sealed itself. I pasted two Band-Aids over it and wiped off the spider web of red lines that had stained his arm.

"Davy take care of me," Lewis said.

"That's right, Pal. Just like you'd take care me, right?"

Lewis nodded and glanced at the dreaded shovel, which was sticking straight up in the sand, looking perfectly harmless.

"You dig now. Kay?"

"Okay," I chuckled. "You can have your old job back."

I wiped off the remaining stains around his wound and screwed the cap on the alcohol bottle. My mother would notice the Band-Aids, but at least it was better than before. The sight of a bloody Lewis would give her a heart attack. I'd tell her it was a simple cut...nothing big.

"Lewis, when Mom asks you what happened, just let me do the talking, okay?"

"Kay," Lewis answered.

"I'll be right back."

I quickly returned the hydrogen peroxide to the medicine cabinet and flushed the bloody towels down the toilet. I thought my mother would walk in and catch me in the act of covering up the evidence. Luckily, she never showed.

I ran back outside and started shoveling again. Lewis was up on his feet, unfolding the paper sacks and handing them to me.

We worked under a hazy sky. A few dark clouds over the western mesa promised a white Christmas. The temperature was right for it—around thirty degrees Fahrenheit—and the air was humid. I had heard the cheery songs about how wonderful it was to have snow on December 25th, but I had never experienced it. Most blizzards usually hit the Hillerman Mountains and left the Huckleberry valley unscathed. The city would get a sprinkle of snow here and there throughout the colder months, but never on the most important day in December. But I kept hoping for the storm that would dump a good foot of holiday powder over the entire valley. It was wishful thinking.

"Davy?"

"Yeah, pal."

"You's never leave, huh?"

I stopped working and stared at him. Thin traces of dried tears lined his face.

"Of course not. I'll always be here," I said.

"You's always be brother?"

"Never a sister."

"You's always give me cha-co-lots."

"If Mom's not looking."

Lewis smiled and showed me his hand. "I've got Band-Id's."

"That's right. Remember what I said about Mom. Let me do all the talking."

"Kay. I know."

As we continued to fill the bags, I thought about what Lewis had asked. I was only twelve, but I was old enough to know that someday I'd need to find my own way. After high school, I'd leave for college and live in the dorms. There was a good chance I'd end up in a new city, living a completely different life from the one I'd known for my first eighteen years. I'd come home during the summers and holidays, but then it would only be as a visitor.

I hated to admit it, but what Tommy had told Lucy and me in the tent was right. *My house will be yesterday's news*. Tommy had meant his house, but it applied to mine, too. I'd leave and Lewis would stay. That's how it was...how it was designed. Lewis wouldn't be able to understand it for the same reason he couldn't understand why I went to Roosevelt while he stayed home with my mother. He knew something was wrong, and even asked about it, but Mom told him it was because he was home schooled. It wasn't a lie for my mother. She was adamant that Lewis would live a normal, independent life someday. Unfortunately, given Lewis's progress, I had my doubts.

***

Dad came home from his training in time to help us light the luminarias. We used pocket lighters and foot-long stick matches for the job. Lewis and I had set the bags everywhere: down the length of the driveway, across the top of the front wall, and on either side of the roof. Because I had a lighter and not the long matches, I had to first take the candles out of the bags, light them, and then carefully put the candles back inside. I burned my hand half a dozen times during this process. Sometimes, if the wind picked up, the wick wouldn't catch and I'd have to light it inside the sack. One bag caught fire while I attempted this, and I had to quickly stomp it out before our entire house became a giant luminaria.

As we worked, our neighbors were out preparing theirs, too. Mrs. Gingal, the luminaria queen, lit almost twice as many as we had. Looking at all of the little flames flickering on her property, I couldn't help but think it was a fire accident waiting to happen. Mr. Franklin, the dud of our cul-de-sac, put out a whopping five bags. It was an improvement over last year, though, when his house had looked like the black hole among the other illuminated homes in our subdivision.

After an hour of jumping from bag to bag, we finally lit the last one. We gave Lewis the honor and when he was done, he clapped his hands in excitement.

"Done, done!" he said.

We moved to the edge of our cul-de-sac and took a look at our house from afar. It was so dark that the glowing bags on the wall and roof seemed to float in midair. The sacks lining our driveway looked like runway lights.

Dad hugged Mom.

"Pretty, huh dear?" Mom asked. She stood with her arms crossed and shivered from the bitter evening breezes despite her thick sheepskin jacket covering.

"Sure is," Dad replied. "Good job, boys."

"Two have gone out already," I said, looking for more incongruities in the glowing line.

My dad put his hand on my shoulder and laughed.

"You can get them when we go back."

"Looky, more!" Lewis shouted, pointing behind us.

We turned from the view of our house and stared at the festival of lights in our circle. They were everywhere, hundreds of them, outlining each property and the architecture of the houses. A car, with only its parking lights on, rolled slowly down Baxter road. It turned at our subdivision.

"Our first visitor, Dad," I said.

"Yep. I wonder what the rest of the neighborhood looks like."

I shrugged my shoulders and thought about it for a second. "Ours is the best no matter what."

My father laughed again, and said we should head in before our toes and fingers were frozen solid. We walked back as a family. Mom told us she had made a plate of tuna sandwiches inside. Lewis asked if we could have the turkey in the fridge instead. She replied that he'd have to wait until tomorrow's dinner.

I was the last one in the house and before I closed the front door, I glanced at the dark sky. Thick clouds covered the stars. My chances for a white Christmas were looking much better.

***

I woke up at exactly 5:04. I threw off the covers, jumped out of bed, and shook Lewis so hard it looked like I was trying to revive a dead man.

"Huh?" Lewis said, rubbing his eyes.

"Wake up! It's morning!"

On any other day, Lewis would have ignored me and gone back to bed. But today was different. Lewis immediately jumped out of his covers and ran out of the room without me.

"Hey, wait up," I said.

I flew down the stairs and stared at the shining tree in the corner. We could see piles of red, green, blue, and white boxes. Some were covered with huge bowties, others with strands of colored ribbon. Our stockings, hanging just above the fireplace, were bursting at the seams with various candies. Lewis went for his stocking and I made for the presents.

"Cha-co-lots!" Lewis said, emptying his candy on the coffee table.

I sorted my presents in a pile. I had only been expecting three or four, but I could see at least twice that many. I felt and shook each one. One gift was thin and heavy; another was round and light. I tried to find out if maybe, by chance, my dad had given me the one present I had been dreaming of, but it was impossible to tell. Next to the tree, with a green bow tied to it, was a Wipe Out 2000 skateboard.

"Wow!" I said, leaving my present pile.

The board was leaning vertically against the wall, its sandpaper surface glittering from the Christmas tree lights, its shiny chrome wheels reflecting the colorful array of presents on the ground. I grabbed it and spun the wheels with my fingers. They rolled effortlessly on their sleek and oiled bearings. I wanted to get on top and skate around, but remembered that I didn't know how—and learning in the house was a bad idea.

"I guess you were good boys after all," my dad said with a smile.

My father was dressed in a blue robe with black flip-flops. Mom also had on a robe, but hers was pink like her fluffy slippers. They stood at the foot of the stairs, arm in arm.

"Thanks, Dad!" I said, and held up the skateboard.

"Don't thank me, that's from old Saint Nick," he replied, winking at me.

"Oh yeah, well him, too," I said, still amazed at how cool the board looked.

Mom strolled to the kitchen while Dad plopped down on the sofa next to Lewis.

"Don't open any presents until I get my camera," my mother's fading voice said.

"It's too late dear, Lewis has already torn through them," my father replied.

"Thaf noth true," Lewis said, shoving as many candies in his mouth as he could fit.

Dad grinned at Lewis. “Hey honey, can you fix me a cup of coffee?”

“Already brewing one now, dear.”

“So, you like it?” my dad asked, pointing at the skateboard.

“It’s just the one I wanted. It’s even got the new graphite undershell.”

“Do you know how to ride it?”

“Not yet.”

“Well, you’ve got time for that, I suppose. But don’t knock your teeth out.”

I nodded. Mom returned with a camera. I put the board back against the wall and made for my presents. Mom took three pictures of Lewis and me next to the unopened gifts. She always went crazy with the camera–taking hundreds of shots on film from every angle, capturing every precious moment. More than ninety percent of those pictures would end up packed in a dusty closet or stuffed inside a clogged desk, most of them blurry or poorly exposed.

“Okay, Davy, hand out the gifts please,” she said.

“All right,” I said, licking my lips. “Here, Dad, this one’s from Uncle Greg. And this is Grandma’s, Mom.”

“Mine, mine?” Lewis asked me.

“Okay, hold your horses...here, this is from Santa.”

Lewis snatched the gift from my hands and ran for the couch. After I grabbed my gift, we ripped into the paper.

***

The paper was everywhere: on the couch, clinging to the coffee table, stuck to the pine needles in the tree. My mother had meant to put the discarded wrappings in a small trash bag, but the camera work had kept her occupied. I had opened every present save one—a small red box. The gift was from my mom and I assumed she had given me a pair of socks or underwear (toys were always listed under Santa; any present that was labeled "From Mom" meant it was boring). A small envelope was on top of the gift.

"Open the envelope first, Davy," Mom said.

"Okay," I said.

I did as I was told, thinking I was about to read another sappy love letter that was supposed to teach me about the true meaning of Christmas. Instead, I found a simple white card with neat little handwriting: Davy, please be careful. Merry X-mas. Love, Mom.

Suddenly, my eyes lit up. Did this mean what I thought it meant? No way, not from my mother...

I madly tore into the gift. I uncovered a small brown box with duct tape on top. I ripped the tape off, tossed aside the white tissue paper, and found a beautiful, red Buckshot sling inside.

"All right!"

I held the slingshot up and showed it off. It was a modern sling, much better than the ones you see on *Leave it to Beaver* or *Dennis the Menace*. Those slings were made out of wooden wishbone sticks and rubber bands. This one had a metal frame, a plastic handle, a thick elastic tube for a band, and a polished leather support hold that fit snugly around my forearm—the support hold helped distribute the tension to my arm when pulling back on the band.

I was surprised about the gift, but my dad was downright shocked. He burned his lips on his second cup of coffee.

"You bought him one?"

Mom looked at me with a cautious, tight smile. "Yeah, he really wanted it and I figured as long as he's safe, he'll stay out of trouble."

"Yes, but you said—"

"I know what I said. I guess I changed my mind."

I gripped the handle, put the support on my forearm, and gave the band a test. The elastic tube was tight and difficult to stretch, but it would loosen with enough use. I closed one eye, aimed at a target between the metal V, and released the band with a loud snap. The unnerving sound made my mother jump.

"Please, only outside, Davy."

"Yes, Mom."

"And remember what I said in the card."

"I know, Mom."

My mother sighed and my father was still looking at the present as if he couldn't believe his own eyes. Lewis was absorbed in his own world, eating more candies out of his stocking.

I ran to my mother and hugged her with all my strength.

Many Christmases later, after I had already moved out of the house, I would think about December in 1981 and wonder why my mom had given me that gift. Maybe she was just being kind and wanted to give me my dream present, or maybe she had thought that if I were safe, there wasn't any harm in it. Although these were two plausible answers, I think it was for a different reason altogether. I'm almost positive it had something to do with my father losing his job. It was only for a short time, and it didn't have a devastating monetary impact on us, but it did change the way we behaved. Before the layoff, we'd buy small luxury items without thinking twice about it. I remember one of my favorite things to do while grocery shopping was to pick out a candy bar in the checkout aisle. I was allowed one goodie with my mom—that was the rule. I'd usually get a Snickers or Three Musketeers if they were out of Hershey's bars. After my dad gave us the bad news, I stopped asking for them. It only saved us fifty cents each week, and we had enough money to make do, but I thought it could help. I suppose I was afraid that if the money well went dry and we needed an extra five dollars to pay off our monthly mortgage, my weekly fifty-cent savings might come in handy.

So did my mom buy me a slingshot just because I refrained from asking for the stupid candy bars? Yes and no. I think my mother felt bad that Lewis and I had to tighten our belts during the uncertain months when my dad was between jobs. She wanted to pay us back for it, to give Lewis and me a piece of the good life to show her appreciation for what we had done.

Of course, she had already given us that life without the gifts. As I learned later, the Hershey's bars were always on the shelves; the X-mas cards from mom were in limited supply.

***

"So how does it work?" my dad asked.

"Good, but I'm havin' trouble finding ammo," I replied.

I stood in our front yard, kicking the dirt beside our driveway. Trusty Buckshot was on my forearm, waiting for another round of target practice.

"How about this one?"

"Yeah, perfect," I said, taking the smooth black rock from my dad's large fingers.

I loaded the thin leather pouch, pulled back on the rubber tube, and aimed at a small soup can I had put up earlier. I could feel the pressure of the support band push against my arm.

"Hold it steady," my dad said. He squatted behind me, staring at the same target.

I lined the can between the metal V and closed my right eye. I released the pouch; the sling snapped and the rock fired off. A sharp crack echoed in the neighborhood as the can flipped in the air.

"I got it!"

"Sure did. Clipped the top."

I looked at my dad and he smiled back. The image of him shooting at similar targets when he was a kid reappeared. I thought he might want to give it a shot.

"Wanna try, Dad?"

My father patted me on the shoulder and laughed. "No, I'd rather keep an eye on you. Who knows what the neighbors might think if they saw me shooting at cans. They'd probably call the police."

I nodded. It *would* look pretty scary seeing a forty-year-old man marching around his property with a sling in hand. I had no doubt that Mrs. Gingal would dial the cops if she saw such craziness going on outside her kitchen window. Adults couldn't have fun the way kids did.

"Listen," my dad said, looking me square in the eyes. "Pay attention to your mother and be careful with this, it can be pretty dangerous."

"Yes, sir," I said, remembering my pellet gun at Randy's house. "I'll be safe."

"Good. I'm headed inside. Don't forget, we have to help mom prepare dinner."

"Yes, sir."

My dad left me in our driveway and walked back to the house. It was tradition in our family for all of us to pitch in for the main feast. I imagined that I'd be assigned to the cranberry sauce and vegetable platter, while Lewis would get stuck with the salad bowl. Mom and Dad handled all the cooked items.

I picked up another rock and reset my can. I glanced up to see if the dark clouds had decided to stick around, but the sky was clear blue. Those clouds had skinned out of town, taking their precious water reserves with them. Once again, the white Christmas had eluded me.

Chapter 19

BACK TO WORK

Winter break, like summer vacation, went by quickly. I spent New Year's Eve watching the ageless Dick Clark on TV, waiting for the big ball to drop in Times Square. The party in NY was lively and flamboyant, while the celebration at my house was as festive as a retirement home birthday bash. Dad was already in bed and Mom and Lewis were passed out on our den couch. I was the only one that actually witnessed '81 bleed into '82, and let me tell you, when the giant ball finally lit up, I could find little to cheer about except that I could finally go to sleep.

School started two days later. Although most kids regretted the return—with the exception of ones like Patty Ratty Pigtails, who were anxious to get back to brown-nosing— we were excited to share our Christmas stories: presents we had received, candy we had eaten, games we had played. Out of our group, Mikey and Randy had gotten the most expensive toys. Mikey received a giant Pac-Man arcade system with a mini joystick in the center, and Randy had gotten a remote-controlled car, which he claimed could do 0-40 in seven seconds. These pricey toys made the rest of us a tad jealous, but we knew we'd get to play with them soon enough, so nobody really sweated it. Jason called first dibs on the car and I claimed a spot on Mr. Pac-Man.

The holiday stories grew old after a few hours, and by lunch we began to feel the boredom of school again.

"Hey, Davy, you ready to hack it out with Mr. Phillips?" Mikey asked. He was chomping on a cheesy pizza pocket.

"Yeah, I guess so," I said, taking a sip of my soda.

We were gathered around our table: Lucy, Tommy, and Jason on one side, Mikey, Randy, and me on the other. The noon air was fresh and biting.

"What about you, Jason?" Mikey asked.

"Gee, more work after school. I'm just jumping for joy."

"It isn't all that bad," said Lucy.

"It is when you've got a new baseball bat and can't use it."

"Wow!" Mikey said, dribbling greasy tomato sauce down his chin. "You never told us you got that."

"Why would I? We're never gonna use it."

"That's not true; someday we'll play again," Tommy replied.

"Yeah? When?" Jason asked. The bill on Jason's Michigan hat was curved just above his eyes. Lunch was the only time he was allowed to wear it; Principal Pinner forbade hats in classrooms.

"We're gonna have to play in that spring playoff game Mikey told his mother about, right?"

"Crap, I forgot about that," Lucy said.

"Yeah, that's right," Jason said, frowning at Mikey. I thought for a moment he was going to tell Mikey off again in Spanish, but he held his tongue.

Tommy turned to Jason. "We'll ask Mr. Phillips if he can give us a few days to practice...you know, to get back into the groove."

"You reckon he'll let us do that?" Randy asked, a January gust passing through his blazing crimson hair.

Tommy nodded. "Sure, we've been working hard for him. It'll only be for a couple of afternoons. He'll understand. We'll ask him when the weather gets warmer. Like in March. That's when we'll put the game on."

For a minute, we sat and thought about the spring game. It was still uncertain which team we were going to play and whom we'd invite to it. It had to look like a real game or else our parents would never believe us. And what if our parents wanted to go to more games? Would we have to tell them the truth then, or keep putting on more shows like six actors? The web of lies was spinning out of control and it felt as if it would crash down on our faces at any time.

"OH, MIERDA!" Jason screamed, shooting back from the table. On top of his half-eaten pizza pocket, on the right corner of his tray, sat Mr. Hops. He had made another one of his unexpected, daredevil jumps—this time right out of Mikey's flannel shirt pocket. "Get that frog out of here!"

"He's a toad," Mikey said, cupping the amphibian gently in his hands. "He's just having fun."

"Fun? That disgusting sapo just ruined my lunch!"

"He's not disgusting. I gave him a bath in my sink this morning."

Jason's breath whistled in and out as if a bird were chirping in his throat. He retrieved his aspirator from his front pants pocket and squeezed the trigger. The bird flew off.

"Aren't you supposed to leave him around water?" Randy asked. "Won't he dry out?"

"Yeah, but I keep his skin wet all the time," Mikey said, petting his toad. Mr. Hops had a queer little smile on his brown face, like he enjoyed scaring the wits out of people. His waxy eyes were brownish-black and his webbed feet were light green. A bubble sack expanded and contracted at the base of his throat.

"He'll get taken away if you're not careful," Tommy said.

"I'll keep him hidden."

"Not if he jumps like that again," I said.

"He won't. I keep him inside my bag during class."

"I don't know why you have that pest at all," said Jason. "He belongs in the ditch."

"He likes me. Don't you, Mr. Hops?"

Amazingly, Mr. Hops croaked at Mikey as if in answer to the question. Whether or not he agreed with Mikey was another story.

"See, what did I tell you?" Mikey smiled at Jason.

Jason frowned, wiped off his pizza pocket, and continued to eat. "Stupid sapo," he mumbled.

"Huh oh," Randy said, looking behind me.

"What?" I asked.

"Here come Timmy and Miles."

I turned and saw them marching directly for our table. Timmy looked like a dwarf standing next to his ogre friend. It was almost comical how ridiculous the two of them looked together.

They stopped a few feet from our table. The white stick of another cherry sucker protruded from Timmy's lips.

"Hi-dee-ho," Timmy said with a waxed grin.

"What do you want, Timmy?" Tommy asked.

"Nothin', just coming to say hi, right Miles?"

"Yeah, comin' to say hi," Miles said stupidly.

"Why don't you take your greetings somewhere else," Tommy said. Tommy was the only one of us—or the entire school, for that matter—that wasn't afraid of Timmy's brother. It wasn't because Tommy had Dan and Dan might cover his tail if Bruce decided to pound on him. No, Tommy didn't fear Bruce because he didn't fear anybody. There's no amount of pain that Bruce or any other bully could inflict upon him that he hadn't already taken from his brother or old man. It's like the time when Miles Quincy and Sean Haggard stole our table in the cafeteria. The rest of us simply nodded our heads and accepted the fact that we'd have to eat somewhere else. It was the implied surrender, the one that said: "Sure, okay, the big guys win again. Go ahead and sit in our seats. Please let us get our stuff now." But not Tommy. Tommy was nose to nose with them, ready to break his tray over Sean's ugly face. And he would have, too, had it not been for the divine intervention of Miss Lucy. I'm certain that Tommy would have lost the fight (Sean was twice as strong and three times as mean), but that didn't matter. It was a matter of principle for Tommy.

"Hey, we're only coming to say we're glad Davy is getting married."

"What the crap are you talking about, Timmy?" Tommy asked.

"What? Don't tell me you didn't hear? Davy and Lucy are in love. They're having babies soon, you know."

A fire burned in the pit of my stomach. I looked at Lucy and she blushed. Our secret was out, but how did pesky Timmy find out?

"Get lost, Timmy," Tommy said.

For a moment I thought—and desperately hoped—that Timmy would listen to Tommy. I thought Timmy would let it rest and leave me with the burden of explaining our situation. But I knew it wouldn't happen. Timmy *never* let things go. He didn't let me be with my braces in the bus and he wouldn't dare give in now with this nugget of juicy news. The little bastard wanted to tell the world about it.

"I'm serious, we saw them kissing behind the cafeteria right before break. Huh, Miles?"

"Yup. Kiss, kiss."

The Gang was completely taken aback; they looked at Lucy and I like we were total strangers. The love bottle had been broken. There was no way to glue the pieces back together. Timmy had pounded the fragments into dust.

"Davy and Lucy, sitting in a tree," Timmy sang.

"Shut up," I said.

"K-I-S-S-I-N-G."

"I said shut up!"

"First comes love, then comes marriage, then comes the baby—"

The beady look in his eyes and the way his cherry lips resembled thick hot dogs sent me over the edge. I tackled Timmy on the pavement and strangled his neck. I thought Miles would club me in the head with one of his ogre fists, but he seemed to be as surprised by my outburst as the Gang had been about my kiss.

"I'll kill you," I said.

"Get off!" Timmy gasped.

My face swelled with blood and my heart thumped in my chest like a drum. A vein in my forehead throbbed with rage. My knees dug into the pavement rocks, but I ignored the pain. The only thing I could think about was Timmy's bright red lips singing that awful tune.

"Stop, Davy," Tommy said, pulling me away.

"You bastard!" I said.

"Get off me!" Timmy replied.

With one arm around my head and a hand on my right arm, Tommy managed to pry my grip off Timmy's neck and pull me back.

"Let me at him, Tommy!" I screamed.

"He isn't worth it, Davy," Tommy said slowly and clearly in my ear. "Pinner will suspend you."

Tommy held me in a semi-headlock while he let Timmy get up. Timmy's face was ghostly white...even his lips had paled into a light, pinkish color. Miles stood behind him, looking like an overgrown kid that was ready to cry because someone had stolen his blankie. Crowded around Tommy and me, staring in disbelief, stood the Gang.

"I'll tell my brother about this," Timmy said, wiping a small trail of blood away from his nose. "I'll tell my brother and then you'll be—"

"Get out of here before I finish where Davy left off," Tommy threatened, brandishing his fist at him.

Timmy opened his mouth again, then closed it. A small light seemed to pop on in his head. It was a dim bulb, no more than 20 or 30 watts, but it told him it would be best to leave the situation alone. Timmy wiped his nose again, slapped Miles on the arm and walked off without saying another word.

Fortunately, the other kids at school didn't notice the fight. If they had, the entire recess square would've been crammed, with all the kids eagerly placing bets on the winner as if it were Ali v. Foreman. A crowd would have drawn attention, and attention would have led to suspension.

"You all right?" Tommy asked.

"Yeah, I'm fine," I replied.

I looked at Lucy. She stared at me solemnly with her wide, green eyes, and for a moment it seemed she had forgotten about what Timmy had said. Selective amnesia, so to speak. It only lasted for a second. She dropped her gaze to the ground and I knew exactly what she was thinking.

I wanted to tell the Gang it was a lie...that Timmy had made the story up. Maybe there was a chance they would still believe me—not a very good one, but one that might be worth taking.

But the story was out, and there was no way to put the genie back in its bottle. I knew it by the look in their eyes. It was time to face reality: Lucy and I had kissed. It was the cardinal sin of middle school. Every boy knew that girls had cooties and germs, and every girl knew the same about boys. There were three levels of offenses: if you talked to a member of the opposite sex, you were made fun of; if you touched one, you were laughed at; and if you went so far as to kiss one...well, let's just say that was like sentencing yourself to life in the outcast prison without parole. Kids simply didn't do the same thing as adults. That was disgusting.

"Listen, guys, there's something you should—" I said, and before I could explain, the lunch bell sounded.

Without hesitating, we walked back to our table, gathered our half-eaten lunches and made for our next class. I wanted to talk to Lucy, to smooth things over, but she was already running to her next class, her head glued to the pavement, her hands wrapped around her daisy backpack.

I could tell she was crying.

***

That afternoon, I locked myself in my room and threw the pillow over my head. I never wanted to see the light of day again. The image of pesky Timmy ratting Lucy and I out played over and over again in my mind. Other kids would soon know the story, and before long, Lucy and I would be the laughing stock of Roosevelt. *Hey! There's the love couple! Davy, why don't you give your wife another kiss? Kissy, kissy, kissy. How was your honeymoon? Are you going to tell us when the baby comes? Kissy, kissy, kissy.*

I didn't want to go to the Vineyard, but I had to. Winter break was over, and Mr. Phillips expected us to return to our work. I tried to think of a way to get out of it: maybe tell them I was sick, or had a doctor's appointment, or had to visit my ill grandfather in Dallas. It was pointless, though. Even if I managed to escape their path today, I had to see them again tomorrow. I couldn't ignore the Gang forever.

Frustrated, I got up, changed my clothes, grabbed my baseball mitt and told my mom I'd be home before dinner.

***

When I crossed the ditch bridge on my bike, I saw the Gang already working with Mr. Phillips. Mikey, Randy, and Jason cemented the forty-fourth post, while Tommy and Mr. Phillips had the forty-fifth. Lucy was nowhere to be seen.

I parked my bike next to the others, dropped my mitt on the dirt, and headed toward Tommy. The afternoon was clear and surprisingly warm for January. The wind was calm and the air was dry. Thousands of feet above the Vineyard, lining the sky like chalk-marks on a blue blackboard, were smoke trails from jet airplanes. Some of them were puffy and jagged; others were as thin and straight as razors.

A squirrel crossed my path, stopped, and stared at me. It sat up on its back legs, its cheeks stuffed with food, and twitched its tail with curiosity. I crept toward it to see how close I could get before scaring the little guy, and only managed a few feet. It bolted off, leaping in quick, small arcs, and disappeared up a nearby elm tree.

I continued my long walk.

"Howdy, Davy."

"Hello, Mr. Phillips," I replied upon reaching him.

"How was the holiday season? You get all the toys you wanted?"

"Yes, sir. It was just fine."

Tommy and I made brief eye contact. He was busy pouring Fastcrete into a hole.

"How 'bout Lewis? Did he get what he wanted?"

"He got plenty of candy, sir. That's really all he was interested in."

Mr. Phillips laughed and rubbed his scruffy face. I wasn't surprised to see him in overalls, but I did take notice of his new brown boots.

"I'd like to meet your family some day," Mr. Phillips said. "Maybe after all this work is done. When things have calmed down."

"Maybe, sir...Did you get those for Christmas?"

"Sure did. My first boy gave me 'em. What'cha think?"

Mr. Phillips showed me his boots. They looked exactly like the old ones except for a few less scratches and nicks.

"Very nice, sir," I said.

"My boy has good taste. He gets me somethin' good every year. Here, why don't you take hold of this post and help us out."

I grabbed it and watched Tommy pour the cement. Forty-three posts were in front of me, standing toward the winter sky. They formed a large "L" which started at the edge of Mr. Phillips's house and ended about fifty yards from our oak tree. It was the first time I took notice of our work from a larger perspective. It was interesting to see something *we* had created: the first post in late September, the fifteenth in October, the thirty-fifth by mid-November. It was a physical timeline, a calendar like the rings in a tree trunk. It was odd to think of it that way, and I wondered what the fiftieth and sixtieth posts held in our future.

Once the cement hardened, Tommy and I backfilled the remaining cavity with cold dirt. Mr. Phillips handed Tommy the measuring tape tongue and walked to Mikey, Randy, and Jason. Mr. Hops sat patiently by Mikey's side, supervising their work.

"Sixteen feet?" Tommy asked.

Mr. Phillips inspected the yellow tape. "Yep, right on the mark. You can let it go."

Tommy released the tongue and it retracted with a violent zip. I had pinched my hand a hundred times doing that same trick, but Mr. Phillips somehow managed to keep his skin clear of the tape's ferocious bite.

"How you boys doing?"

"Almost done," Randy told Mr. Phillips. "Just a couple minutes and it'll be dry."

"Good," said Mr. Phillips, "maybe we can finish another one before dark. Tommy, Davy...let's get movin' on the next one."

Tommy and I dusted off, collected Mr. Phillips's toolbox and water bucket, and made for number forty-six, feeling the crunch of dead weeds and dry twigs underneath our shoes. The smell of burning wood lingered in the air. I saw smoke rising from a distant chimney in a neighborhood I'd never visited.

"There's Lucy," Tommy said, surprised.

Tommy pointed at the ditch bridge and sure enough, Lucy was pedaling down the embankment on her pink ten-speed. Her brown hair flapped out the back of her orange cap like a streaming banner.

"I didn't think she was gonna come," Tommy said.

"Me either," I added.

Lucy left her bike with ours and ran toward us. She wore a gray sweater and black khakis.

"Miss Graham! Where have you been?" Mr. Phillips asked, waving her over. "I reckoned you moved to another city during your break."

Lucy stopped in front of Mr. Phillips and put her hands on top of her cap, trying to catch her breath. "Sorry, sir...I had...some...some things at home to take care of."

"Did you have a good vacation?"

"Oh yes, sir. It was awesome."

"Awesome? That's good, isn't it?"

Lucy giggled. "Yes, sir."

Mr. Phillips smiled and scratched his five o'clock shadow, which looked closer to midnight to me.

"Well, don't you worry about bein' late. We've been making good time. The boys are actually working for a change. No more horseplay with dad-gum toads." Lucy looked at Tommy and me and giggled again. I was relieved to see her in good spirits. "I'm going to check the mail. Take my spot."

"Sure thing," Lucy replied.

Mr. Phillips walked off and Lucy squatted next to us. I wanted to say something about lunch, maybe apologize, but I didn't think it was a good time to bring it up. I didn't want to spoil her mood.

"I'll pour the cement in and you can add the water when I'm done," said Tommy. "Davy's got the post."

"Okay," Lucy said, lifting the bucket.

We worked for another half hour, watching the sun dip below the desert mesa. The horizon turned yellow, then orange, then purple. The temperature dropped a good ten notches, and my watch read 5:30.

"Time to call it quits," Mr. Phillips told us. Randy, Jason, and Mikey had already joined us at the forty-sixth post. Although the cement was still mushy, it was hard enough for us to let it dry overnight.

We stood up and stretched our aching muscles. Mikey put Mr. Hops back in his flannel home. I was amazed that the toad was still with him. I had made a dollar bet with Jason that Mikey would lose him within six weeks (Mikey was extremely clumsy, after all; he had lost his backpack a dozen times and had misplaced his glasses a dozen more). Jason had taken the high road and put his money between six and twelve weeks. So far, things weren't going in my favor. Jason gave me a cocky, confident grin with each passing day. I could see my dollar spinning in his greedy eyes.

"See you tomorrow," Tommy told Mr. Phillips.

"Until tomorrow," Mr. Phillips replied, and waved us off.

We tottered to our bikes, our feet practically dragging in the dirt. We were exhausted. We had only been on vacation for a month, but it was long enough for our bodies to forget how hard it was to hold a post for thirty straight minutes, or to lift a fifty-pound Fastcrete bag twenty times.

"Hey, guys..." Tommy said, picking his bike off the ground. We grabbed our bikes and swung our legs over the frames, making a circle of cycles. "I just wanted to say that what happened today during lunch should stay between us."

I checked to see if Lucy was looking at me. Her eyes were fixed on her handlebar rainbow streamers.

"I mean, Timmy's an annoying ass all the time anyway. So what if Davy and Lucy kissed? I don't care."

"Tommy, you don't have to say—"

"No, Davy, I do," said Tommy to me. His blond hair had grown out since the beginning of fall and it now dangled over his blue eyes. "I could care less about what happened and the rest of us feel the same. Right, guys?"

"I don't care," Mikey said.

"Me neither," Randy said.

"I do..." Jason said.

Tommy frowned at Jason.

"Gosh, just kidding, Tommy. Relax, amigo. It's no skin off my back."

Lucy looked up with a half-pleased, half-embarrassed expression on her face.

"See," Tommy said, staring at me. "We won't say a word. None of us."

"Thanks, but it doesn't matter," I said, turning my bike handle from side to side, digging my tire into the dirt. "Timmy will spill his guts anyway. I'm sure half the school knows by now."

"I don't think so," Tommy said. "Did you see him after the fight? He's not going to be bothering you anymore."

"Really?" I said, looking up, wanting to believe him.

"Huh, Mikey?" Tommy asked. "Wasn't Timmy crappin' bricks in your Algebra class?"

"Yep. Sure was. I've never seen him so afraid before."

"Me neither," Jason added. "I saw him after school. Damned loco looked like he saw the grim reaper. It was pretty friggin' hilarious, really. You guys should've seen it."

I probably would have thought the Gang was just pulling my leg had I not seen Timmy for myself on the bus ride home. He had sat in the back of the bus, something he had never done before, and I remembered him glancing at me for a brief second and then jerking his head away. He had something on his mind. Although I couldn't tell what it was, I sensed a hint of fear. He was shocked about what I had done and about the truth that Tommy didn't give two shits about Timmy's brother and wouldn't think twice about busting Timmy's jaw open if he stepped out of line again.

"Thanks," I said.

"Yeah, thanks," Lucy said. She sat on her bike seat and balanced herself with one leg on the ground.

"So, we're still buds, right?" Tommy asked, sticking his hand in the middle of our group.

"Of course," I replied, putting my right hand on top of his and keeping my left firmly on my handlebars.

"Always," Lucy added, placing her soft palm on top of mine.

Randy and Mikey agreed and joined in, too. We looked at Jason, half expecting another one of his sarcastic remarks. He might have supplied one had he not been preoccupied with his aspirator. He pulled the trigger, inhaled, and then placed his hand on top of the pile.

"Buds and locos," Jason barely managed to say.

We pedaled home under a black sky. The bitter evening wind stung our faces and numbed our fingers. The smell of burnt wood hung in the air and the image of a warm fire awaiting us at home made us pedal faster. The horizon was now a deep and dark purple. Silhouetted in the dying light, weaving in and out of the Vineyard trees, a cloud of sparrows flew in unison and moved in sudden arcs, like a school of fish avoiding an ocean predator.

Night had fallen.

Chapter 20

THE JERKS

Tommy was right: Timmy never said a word about my kiss with Lucy. I went to school each week with a queasy, uneasy feeling, waiting for the juicy story to spill. Timmy will tell. It would be a first in the history books if the king of gossip kept his mouth shut for more than five seconds. Timmy loved attention too much to let it pass. That kiss would make him the star at school; it would give him his fifteen minutes of fame as the Roosevelt reporter, so to speak.

But his lips remained sealed. That insidious fear I spoke of earlier had been implanted inside of him. I could see it when I boarded the bus in the mornings, the way he would stare blankly out the window, and while passing him in the halls between classes, when his eyes were glued to the ground or fixed on the ceiling as if hunting for cobwebs or rain stains.

Now that's not to say it totally changed the rat-faced squealer. He still sucked on his cherry Blow

Pops, goofed off in class, and bullied kids with Miles Quincy. It would take a lot more than Tommy's fist to change that part of his personality—that would entail years of shock therapy—but at least Timmy left me and Lucy alone. It was more than I could hope for.

And the same was true with his brother...at least for the last two months. I hadn't seen the Jerks since the day Bruce paid me back for Halloween. I always found it strange how they could be kicking my tail one day and then totally disappear the next. It was like they planned certain days of the month to torture us.

Okay guys, we'll give Davy a wedgie on Monday and Randy a toilet swirly on Wednesday. And remember, we've got a special treat for Mikey on the fifteenth. That's his birthday, you know. He's turnin' thirteen, so mark it on your calendars and don't forget.

Of course, all it boiled down to was being in the wrong place at the wrong time. So after two months of dodging the Jerks free and clear, it was my turn to finally slip up.

"Hello?" I said into the phone.

"Davy, it's Tommy."

"Hey, what's up?"

"You wanna shoot some cans?"

I was lying on our den couch, balancing the phone between my shoulder and ear with a long, coiled cord stretching way back to our kitchen. I was watching a lame quiz show. Lewis was taking a nap in his room and my mother was reading in the kitchen. It was a slow and boring Saturday afternoon, and I was desperate to find something to do.

"Sure. You have ammo?"

"Yep, bought some pointy pellets yesterday. Supposed to be better than the last ones. You can borrow 'em."

"Cool. I'll bring my slingshot, too."

"Okay, see ya."

"Later."

I rushed upstairs, grabbed my Buckshot sling, threw on my Cardinals baseball cap, and flew back down.

"Mom, I'm going to play with Tommy," I said.

My mother was at the kitchen table, snacking on an apple and thumbing through Ernest Hemingway's *For Whom the Bell Tolls*. She looked up from her book and stared at the slingshot in my hand.

"And you're taking that with you?"

"Yeah. I'll be careful, Mom...I promise."

I smiled the best "I'm a good boy" smile I could muster. My mother didn't smile back. A long sigh escaped her lips.

"All right. But stay away from houses, and don't kill anything with that."

"Yes, Mom."

I dashed out the front door before she could change her mind. The tension between my mother and the sling hadn't relaxed a bit. I had a constant fear she would try to trash it while I was at school—even though it had been her gift to me. She'd steal it from my room, chuck it in the garbage, and when I couldn't find it she'd simply shrug her shoulders and tell me I must have misplaced it. "You probably left it in the Vineyard," she'd say. "Oh, well. Hope it turns up." She'd smile, take a bite of her apple, and continue with her book without guilt or remorse.

I darted down my cul-de-sac, cut across Mr. and Mrs. Hampton's front yard, and hopped over Mr. Sloans's wooden fence, catching a nasty splinter on my way down.

"Crap!" I whispered to myself, stopping abruptly in my tracks.

Less than twenty yards in front of me, parked beside the neighborhood playground, was Bruce's '79 white Ford pickup. Dan and Ricky were sitting in the bed of the truck, guzzling Schlitz beer cans and smoking Reds. Bruce's butt was stuffed in a kiddy swing just beside the truck, slowly rocking back and forth on rusty chains that squealed like worn door hinges. He had a cigarette with an inch of ash dangling from his freckled lips and a tattered, dog-eared Playboy spread across his lap.

Both of the truck's cab doors were wide open, blaring the heavy guitar strings of AC/DC's *Back in Black*.

I quickly hid behind a row of hedges and watched them, my heart pounding in my throat.

"She's a fat bitch," Dan said, polishing off his can, and crumpling it between his muscular fingers. "A whore."

"What are you smokin', ass munch?" Bruce asked. "She's a lot better than Kim Kurtis."

"You can't say shit," Ricky said, taking the last hit of his cigarette and flicking the butt into the playground sand. "You never poked her."

"That's the point. I wouldn't want to."

Bruce took a swig out of his beer can and made for his front pocket. For a moment, while he tried to balance his oversized butt and remove whatever was in his pants pocket, I thought he was going to fall out of the swing. He managed to stay on somehow and retrieve a disk of chewing tobacco.

"What the shit do you know, Ricky?" Bruce mumbled, stuffing his cheek with chew. "Your balls are dry as a ten-year-old's. I *know* you haven't been with a girl."

Dan cackled at Ricky and cracked open another can.

"Screw you!" Ricky said. "I get more play than both of you."

"Yeah?" Bruce asked, his red eyebrows raised, his spotted lips greased back in a cocky grin. "Who have you laid? And don't tell me Susan Jackson, because I know that's a fuckin' lie. I asked Billy Nollan about that one. He dated her for six months and said the most he got was a titty feel. Susan's a bigger prude than Sister Alice."

Bruce's discovery must have taken Ricky by surprise, because Ricky's face was redder than a scarlet sunset. Ricky tried to pass it off and act manly by taking a chug of his beer, but he was a bad actor; he was a virgin and they knew it.

"I nailed Julie Burns last month," Ricky said, his face growing redder. "I did her at winter ball."

Bruce laughed so hard that he actually lost his balance on the swing this time and fell flat on his back. Dan was beside himself, too, and at first Ricky thought he was laughing because of Bruce's fall.

"That's another lie," Dan said. "That I know for sure. She was so sick that night her parents had to drive her home."

"I s-s-saw her old man..." Bruce said, cracking up, "pi-pi-pick her fat ass up."

"Shit, everybody saw that," Dan added. "She was practically puking on the dance floor. Nobody hooked up with her that night, not even that queer date of hers...what's his name again?"

"Ennis Capshaw," Bruce said, holding his stomach.

"Yeah, that's it. Ennis the Penis. He didn't nail her and neither did anyone else...not unless they broke into her room that night while she was blowing chunks in her bowl."

Bruce was rolling in the sand by this point, laughing so hard I thought he was going to pass out. Ricky let out a dry laugh and swallowed.

"Okay...not her, but I did screw..." Ricky said, trying to think of another girl, one that Dan and Bruce didn't know about—a mystery woman that had flown in from Alaska for a one-night stand with the old Rickster and had flown back out that very night. I could see the wheels grinding in his head. Had Ricky been a cartoon, smoke would have been pouring out of his ears. The laughter continued, and Ricky blew up.

"Fuck you, Dan!" Ricky screamed, pitching his unfinished beer at Dan's face.

The can missed Dan's nose by less than an inch and exploded on the pavement in front of the truck, spraying cheap beer in all directions.

"Whoa!" Dan said, covering his head. "Calm the shit down."

Ricky jumped off the truck and stormed off. Bruce was still roaring on the ground, wiggling like a worm.

"Come back," Dan said, chuckling as he said it. "We're screwin' with ya, dip shit."

"Yeah, w-we don't care if you d-don't get pa-pa-pussy," Bruce added over his laughter.

Ricky flipped them the bird and kept marching. He was headed in my direction. I kept low in the bushes, feeling thorns and broken twigs dig into my skin. It was bad enough that Bruce and Dan knew about Ricky's sex life (or lack of it, I should say), but if he found out that I knew, I'd be lucky to escape with my head still intact.

I held my breath as Ricky walked past me, my heart in overdrive.

"Gawd! You young punks!"

Standing about thirty yards from Dan and Bruce, clad in the same blue robe and pink, bunny-eared slippers she'd worn the day of the Jeep accident, was Mrs. Wallis. She stood at the edge of her front yard, waving her finger in disgust.

"I don't want drinkers in my park," Mrs. Wallis said. "You're nothin' but trouble."

Bruce stood up and brushed the sand off his back, no longer laughing. Dan turned to Mrs. Wallis, took a swig out of his beer, and hawked a fat loogie off the truck.

"Piss off, old bag," Dan replied.

Mrs. Wallis's face flushed Ricky-red. She was so stunned at Dan's defiance that it took her a minute to compose herself.

"I'll call the cops," she said. "Gawd, they'll lock your white fannies away and teach you a lesson. You'll see when—"

"Then call them, grandma," Dan said. "We don't give a shit."

Bruce wrinkled his lips and spit out a line of yellowish-brown saliva. Part of the line didn't quite clear his chin and Bruce wiped it off with the back of his shirtsleeve. Dan pulled out a smoke from his crumpled cigarette pack, cupped his face to light it, and exhaled a blue cloud as if he were James Dean. The sight of him smoking made Mrs. Wallis hysterical.

"You don't think I'll do it? I'll call them, don't you doubt that, young man! I'll call and—"

"Maybe you didn't hear us," Bruce said, shifting his chew from one cheek to the other. "*We don't give a shit.*"

Dan and Bruce had pushed Mrs. Wallis's last button. She marched back into her house, leaving one of her bunny slippers on the front lawn, and slammed the door. I had little doubt she would make good on her promise, and judging by the way Bruce and Dan looked, I guessed they shared the same thought.

"We better skin out," Bruce said.

"Yeah, that dumb old prune," Dan replied, taking another drag.

I looked around for an escape route. I could try to make a break behind Bruce's truck, but I'd be screwed in the open park where Dan and Bruce could clearly see me. A second option was to take the long way to Tommy's house and walk around the park. That would take a good fifteen minutes, though, and I was certain they would leave before then. I gave myself a five-minute window—if they weren't gone before then, I'd have to take the fifteen-minute scenic tour.

I sat Indian style, feeling the dampness of the ground seep into my pants, and watched as Dan finished his cigarette. I could see where Tommy got his relaxed, laid-back personality. Dan had a certain air of confidence around him, like he could predict the future and tell others what to do and when to do it. He had an overwhelming sense of assurance in the shots he called. He was fearless. It was as if he lacked the nerves and emotions that made every other human cringe in the dark and scream in the woods. The James Dean analogy is the best way to describe it. Dan was a natural leader—the unchallenged, rebellious king of the Jerks.

Tommy had inherited the same traits. You could see it in the way he pitched, so effortless and smooth, and the way he'd stood up to Timmy for me and Lucy. It wasn't that he was trying to act brave or macho, it's just that *that* was the way he was built. That air of confidence had been passed down to Tommy in some rare gene contributed by a distant Smith ancestor. And that gene *was* rare...let me tell you. I certainly didn't possess it, and kids like Mikey were light years from it. We were human. We still got goose bumps from stupid ghost tales and harmless dark closets. Sure, Tommy got scared on occasion, like the time Mr.

Hops played his little trick on him in the Vineyard, but that didn't happen often. The planets and the stars had to align perfectly for a day like that. Like Dan, Tommy just wasn't like the rest of us.

"What about Tony?" Bruce asked, finishing the last of his beer and tossing it behind the slide.

"What about him?" Dan asked.

"I told him to meet us here."

Dan took the remaining few puffs of his cigarette and flicked it over the edge of the truck bed. A light breeze ruffled his short blond hair.

"Sucks for him," Dan said. "We've got to split."

With one arm supporting himself, Dan jumped off the side of the truck and opened the passenger door. Bruce spit another yellow line of tobacco juice in the sand and made after Dan. He glanced in my direction and I immediately dropped my head to the floor.

Damn, he saw me, I thought, clenching the wet dirt in my fingers. *He must have. He'll tell Dan, they'll investigate, and then they'll lay it on me.* I waited motionless while a black spider crawled up the backside of my hand. It had long, skinny legs and a red hourglass underneath its belly. It was a black widow, the most poisonous spider in the world. I wanted to jump up and shake it off, but my muscles were frozen. My heart raced as the spider inched up my arm—from my wrist, to my forearm, to my elbow. My tongue was glued to the roof of my mouth and my toes were curled in my shoes. I stared as the eight legs edged closer to my face. I heard a car start and drive off, but I couldn't take my eyes off the creature. The black spider stopped, moved sideways, and eventually crept off my arm and disappeared into the bushes.

I jumped up and slapped at my arms and legs. The spider was obviously gone, but I could still feel it on my body: creeping up my calves, across my stomach, under my chin. It was risky blowing my cover since I hadn't actually seen Bruce's truck drive off, but I was willing to take that chance. I absolutely hated spiders, especially black widows.

It turned out Bruce did take off. The park was completely empty save an orange-breasted robin hunting for worms in the post-winter, brownish-green grass. I looked down the length of the park road to see if I could find any hint of Bruce's truck. All was clear.

I walked out of the hedges and cut across the playground, looking at the strewn cigarette butts and beer cans in the sand. The playground had a metal slide, a spinning table, a seesaw, and a three-person swing set. It was meant for kids under twelve, but older kids also came to play in the sand or take a whirl on the dizzying table. Although I rarely played there, it still made me angry seeing the garbage Dan and Bruce had left behind. It made the park look like a dump.

The police that Mrs. Wallis supposedly called never showed—at least, not while I made my way across the park. As I passed Mrs. Wallis's two-story adobe house, glancing at the lonely bunny slipper on her lawn, I considered how my walk to Tommy's house had been lined with a string of bad luck. My misfortune, however, still wasn't over, as I soon found out when I left the park and headed for Tommy's cul-de-sac. Had I not been preoccupied with the venomous spider, I probably would have paid more attention to what Bruce had told Dan before they left, for there was still one Jerk on the loose: Loony Tony Sanders.

"Awwww...crud!" I said, looking straight at Tony's cold, gray eyes.

"Hey, Davy," Tony said in a weak, creepy tone.

Like Bruce had said, Tony was on his way to the playground. I bumped into him as I turned the corner around Mr. and Mrs. Weever's redbrick backyard wall. It happened so suddenly I didn't have time to run. All I could do was stare at his pale hands and the silver switchblade he was playfully flipping in and out of the ivory handle.

"Where are you going?" Tony asked. There was something about his voice that made me shiver when he spoke...the way it sounded empty and indifferent.

"Nowhere," I said.

Tony's black hair was thick with grease and meticulously parted straight down the middle. It was so eerily perfect it was as if his head were made out of wax. His nose was small and pointy and his lips were razor thin. The thing that scared me the most about him was the sickly grin that was permanently carved on his pasty face. He was always amused.

Tony clicked his blade with an alarming snap and pointed it at my face. The sun beamed off its mirror surface and blinded me. Instinctually, I reached for the slingshot in my back pocket.

"You ain't a little Jew, are you?"

I shook my head, my eyes never leaving the blade. Tony moved closer in and I got a whiff of the burnt rubber stench on his cracked, brown leather jacket. The rancid smell brought back the image of Tony strangling the stray cat. I could see him killing the creature with the same thin grin, his fingers squeezing the feline's neck, his teeth clamped down in delight as the cat clawed at his hands in its last futile effort to save its life.

"You lying, Jew boy?"

"No," I said. My heart was pounding again and my right hand was clenched around the neck of the sling in my back pocket. Tony couldn't see the weapon, but it wouldn't do me any good if I used it against him. I didn't have ammo.

"You know what this knife can do?" Tony asked, twisting the shiny blade in his pale hands. "It can spill your guts to the floor if I cut you below the waist."

With the switchblade, Tony pointed to the area on his body to which he was referring. He made an imaginary half-circle, starting just above his right hipbone, then moving below his navel, and finishing off at the left hip. His gray eyes twinkled with delight.

"Spill your guts like spaghetti," Tony said.

His grin widened and a set of putrid yellow teeth poured from his mouth. That did it. Using my slingshot, I knocked the blade out of his hand and sent it into a nearby railroad tie. It stuck into a wooden log and oscillated like an upside down pendulum.

I darted past him and headed straight for Tommy's house. Loony Tony didn't make an effort to follow me. He simply laughed as I made tracks down the cul-de-sac.

"Like spaghetti!" I heard Loony cackle from behind.

I ran as fast as my legs could move. The slingshot pumped with my arms, its band painfully slapping the back of my wrist, and my sneakers thumped on the asphalt. I squinted my eyes closed and tried to forget about him. I couldn't, though. I kept thinking about that cat...clawing aimlessly at his hands.

***

"I don't believe it."

On our walk to the Vineyard, holding our rifles like expert marksmen, I had told Tommy about Ricky, Mrs. Wallis, and Tony. Those stories were all interesting, especially Loony's, but the one Tommy enjoyed the most was the black widow encounter.

"I swear my mother's life on it," I replied, following Tommy across the bridge. "It crawled up my arm."

Tommy snickered and shot at a nearby soup can. The pellet pierced the right corner of the can and sent it tumbling down the ditch embankment. I shot at a different aluminum target and missed by an inch.

"And you just sat there?" Tommy asked.

"Had to," I replied, adjusting the scope on my gun. "Dan and Bruce would've busted me if I moved."

Tommy laughed again and reloaded his gun. He cocked it ten times, aimed at a dirt clod about twenty yards in front of us, pulled the trigger, and sent a sharp crack across the Vineyard. The clod exploded in a cloud of dust. Tommy and I had made a promise not to shoot any birds or other animals after the day I killed the crow.

"That's awesome," Tommy said. "I bet you were crappin' big time."

"Of course. It gives me the creeps just thinking about that thing."

Tommy and I walked alongside the ditch, heading in the opposite direction of Mr. Phillips's house. The afternoon sun was on the western horizon, searing down on the open field.

"Did you catch it?" Tommy asked.

"Are you kidding?" I replied, shooting another round. "Where would I put it? In my pocket?"

Tommy laughed again and slapped his leg. He loved stories where I had to squirm to get out of my predicament.

"I would have paid anything to see your face, Davy. I bet you were as white as a ghost."

"Wouldn't you be?" I asked defensively.

Tommy didn't give an answer. Instead, he squatted down and inspected a rusty harmonica partly embedded in the ground.

"Cool, look at this," Tommy said, digging up the instrument and wiping the mouthpiece on the side of his stonewashed jeans. He played a few notes. They came out flat and distorted. There was a small crack on its orange top.

"You better take more lessons," I said.

"Maybe I can fix it," Tommy said, pocketing it.

We followed the ditch trail to the edge of the Vineyard, where the muddy water continued underneath a chain-link fence. Another irrigation route intersected the ditch at the foot of the fence, and I stopped to check my bearings with my compass.

Tommy put the butt of his rifle next to his feet and balanced its greasy barrel on his waist. "Wow, where did you get that?"

"Lucy gave it to me," I said, wondering if I should have revealed this information.

"Really? When?"

"For Christmas. It's great, huh?"

"It's killer. What does it say?"

I aligned my body to the ditch and then turned to the irrigation route. The sun glared off its surface and reflected a white ray on my T-shirt. "The big ditch is directly east, and the little one is southwest."

"What about our fence?"

I pointed it toward Mr. Phillips's house, which looked like a small toy house from where we stood, and stared at the compass.

"It's west from here."

Tommy nodded at this and spit on the ground. He picked up his gun and looked at the house through his scope. I did the same and saw our incomplete fence magnified through the lens. It was still very small, but I could make out most of our posts and the stack of covered rails.

"You think we could shoot that far?" Tommy asked.

"No way," I said. "Well, maybe...if we pointed our guns up. We wouldn't be able to find out, though."

"Yeah," Tommy said, bummed. He put his gun down, blew his long blond bangs away from his eyes and scratched his ear. Winter had stolen his tan, but he had regained some color during the first few sunny days of February. By the end of

March, Tommy's neck would look as red as Randy's hair.

"I know!" Tommy's eyes lit up. "Let's try your slingshot."

"Yeah," I said, removing it from my back pocket. "We need some rocks."

Tommy and I searched the ditch embankment for ammo. I found a couple of pebbles and a jagged piece of glass from a broken soda bottle that was small enough to fit in the sling's pouch. Tommy came up with a few rocks of his own and a cats-eye marble; he gleefully showed me the cats-eye as if he had found gold.

"You go first," Tommy said.

I loaded the leather pouch with what I thought would be the most promising rock. I aimed at our fence, pulled back on the rubber tube—feeling the tension of the support handle on my forearm—and released it with a jolting snap. The rock soared into the air and stopped well short of my target.

"Not even close," Tommy said.

"I'll try again."

I tried out the rest of the ammo. Each shot landed roughly in the same area as my first; the piece of glass turned out to be a dud and barely cleared ten feet from where we stood. I handed the sling to Tommy. Tommy's first shot flew five feet past my farthest shot; his second, third and fourth, however, weren't as spectacular.

"Try the marble," I said.

"Okay," Tommy replied, loading the cats-eye in the pouch. Tommy aimed, pulled back on the band with all the force in his lean arms, and released it with a sharp clap. The marble rocketed toward the fence, flying so high and fast that it was hard to keep an eye on it. It beat our record by a good fifty yards and landed just shy of the posts. "Man, did you see that?"

"Heck yeah!" I said. "It almost made it."

"I bet if I had another one, I could get it there."

"Maybe...see any more?"

We searched the dirt floor, hoping we'd stumble across another glass ball. Finding that first marble was pure luck, though, and we both knew it. After five minutes of kicking around the dirt, we called it quits.

"Let's move on," Tommy said.

We followed the irrigation path south. The cloudless sky spread out over our heads like a floating ocean, infinite and vast. The air was calm and dry, and the temperature was in the sixties. Spring would arrive in another month, bringing new life to the Vineyard trees and shrubs—melting the remaining snow off the Hillerman crest.

We continued to shoot at random targets, feeling the warm sun on our cheeks. There wasn't a single person or car in sight. The land, in all its glory, was ours.

***

There are certain experiences that stick with you—memories that get branded into your mind like bright flashes on the inside of your eyelids. They stay hidden in your subconscious, stealthily waiting for that ideal moment when they can jump out and slap you in the face. It might be the smell of apple cobbler that brings back the childhood image of climbing in a backyard apple tree, or maybe the pleasant hum of a car engine that summons the distant experience of water-skiing on a peaceful lake as slick as glass. It can happen at odd times. One sensory input connects with another, and then, *WHAM*, you're back at that scene again, reliving the past. Nostalgia never-never land.

Last Christmas, while I was shopping for Nick, I happened to walk by a hunting store in the mall. I stopped and stared at the fishing equipment and camping gear in the display window. There were poles for fly-fishing, waterproof tents for camping, and silver thermoses for temperature sensitive liquids. Some overpowering urge to check the place out overcame me. I wandered inside—feeling like a con trying to sneak out through the front gate of a heavily guarded prison—and I was immediately drawn to the rifles at the back of the shop. The back wall was stacked with BB guns, .22s, and double-barreled shotguns. As I glanced over the weapons, my eyes settled on a slingshot in a glass case below the guns. It was different from the red Buckshot I had owned: this one was blue and had a thinner, longer band. But...as I continued the stare at the blue Bullseye, I swear that damned thing changed colors on me. The sling transformed into a deep red, and the band contracted into the same thick rubber tube I had used in the Vineyard. It was old Buckshot, back from the past.

Did I have too many coffees that morning, or a few too many sugar-drenched doughnuts? No, not that I could recall. It was just that subconscious memory surfacing again. I've had other, not quite as vivid, experiences like that where I'm taken back to yesterday...back to the not-so-distant time when I was a kid.

Like I said...it happens at odd times.

Chapter 21

13TH BIRTHDAY

Valentine's Day was depressing. I was the only kid in all my classes that didn't receive a single card or gift. Other kids boasted about the candies they had gotten or the letters and cards they had collected, and by sixth period I was fed up with their stories. I was jealous.

But that jealousy wasn't entirely created by their happiness. I was also upset with Lucy. Ever since Timmy had opened his fat mouth, Lucy avoided me at school and in the Vineyard. Instead of sitting with me and Mikey on the bus, she'd sit in the front row by herself. In Typing, she'd stare at her computer, never taking her eyes off the screen, and while building the fence, she'd keep herself occupied with her work. Sure, she'd talk to Tommy, Jason, Randy, and Mikey, but whenever I said hello or asked her how she was doing, she'd answer me with one word. Okay. Fine. Great.

After four weeks of the silent treatment, I tried something to break the tension. I wrote her a poem. I spent several hours picking the words that would win back her heart, words that would show her how I *really* felt about our relationship. After filling my wastebasket with balls of paper, I finally settled on one I thought was worthy enough to give to her. Was it sappy? Yes. Was it gross and disgustingly pathetic—like most twelve/thirteen-year-olds would think? Possibly. But I had to try something.

Like a bee on a flower
You came to me with beauty's power
All it took was one glance
And I was in a trance
With your sparkling eyes and flowing hair
You showed me that true grace was rare
Like a little dove
You gave me love

If any kids like Timmy were to get their hands on this poem, I was certain I'd spend the rest of junior high getting ranked out behind school, wearing my underwear over my head. Writing poetry was risky. You had to be careful where and when you did it. If there's one day in the year where it is acceptable to spill your heart out on paper without casting a searing spotlight on your face, it's Valentine's Day. I probably could have come up with a better poem, but I was pressed for time. I had to get it done by February 14th.

In between first and second period, I slipped my poem inside Lucy's locker. I made sure I was alone before I did it—Valentine's Day or not, I wanted to stay clear of the horrifying spotlight. I did it quickly and skipped out of the hallway, thinking of all the wonderful things that would come from it. Maybe, while reading the romantic lines, a sudden heat-flash would consume Lucy and cause a fainting spell (with someone catching her, of course). Maybe she'd read it, grab her heart, and burst out in tears, proclaiming her love for me. Maybe she'd write a poem of her own, sealing our love forever.

But when the bell sounded the end of school, I still hadn't heard from her. It drove me nuts. Why didn't she say anything? Did she not like it? Did she not see it? What if I put it in the wrong locker?

This last thought petrified me. Putting it in the wrong locker was like committing social suicide. That kid was sure to tell their friends about the poem, and those friends would tell their friends. It would spread like wildfire, and before long the entire school would be pointing fingers and giggling hysterically.

But I double-checked her locker: number 309. There was no mistaking it—she had a red daisy sticker on the bottom of the door and a dent in the right corner. I was positive that *that* was the locker I had put it in.

So why didn't she say something?

I didn't find an answer at school or at the Vineyard. While working with Tommy and Jason on post fifty-three, I glanced over at Lucy on post fifty-two. I didn't know what I was looking for, perhaps a gentle smile like the one she had given me in the tent, or maybe a warm wink to tell me she had read my poem. I would have taken any kind of response, even if it were rejection. I got nothing. She kept her eyes focused on the post.

My mind was preoccupied with her, and quite naturally, it affected fence productivity. "Is there something wrong?" Tommy asked me when I overfilled our hole with Fastcrete. "No," I told him, trying to keep my mind on the task at hand but failing miserably. Lucy had some sort of magnetic hold over me, pulling my gaze in her direction.

I thought about asking her about the poem after our afternoon work was done, but what would I say if she said she had read it? If she had read it, she either didn't like it or didn't want to talk to me anymore. The ball had been served in her court and it was her decision to either hit it back or stuff it in her pocket and leave. I couldn't jump over the net and ask why she hadn't returned it. That was against the rules. It would result in an automatic disqualification.

There are many kids that would have said to heck with it and asked her about the poem anyway, rejection or not. I didn't have the guts to do that. I was barely able to summon the courage to write the verses in the first place...and that was like walking over hot coals for me. Actually talking to Lucy about it, face to face, was a feat beyond my ability.

A week after Valentine's Day, I still hadn't heard from her. I was angry, hurt, and confused. I had never experienced such an emotional roller coaster before. Why were adults always talking about the beauty and wonder of love when it seemed like such a dreaded nightmare? Maybe it was a lie like Santa Claus, or the Easter Bunny. It was another fairy tale devised to keep kids from misbehaving, or staying up late at night.

If you don't love your parents, young boys and girls, you'll visit the fire of eternity.

When I awoke on February 21st and looked at my reflection in my Jaws mirror—a slightly taller and bonier figure than I had seen at the beginning of the school year—I decided to block Lucy out of my mind. For today was my birthday; I was now thirteen, a teenager.

I took a shower, brushed my teeth, and put on my favorite green and red T-shirt. I walked into the kitchen with an extra spring in my step and made myself a giant glass of orange juice. The sun was out and the birds were chirping. It was a perfect day.

"Hey, champ."

"Hey, Dad," I replied.

"That's a pretty big glass of OJ, don't you think?"

"Yep."

"You leave any for me?"

My dad shook the container and poured himself a glass. I waited for him to feed me the line. He'd drink his juice, tousle my hair, and tell me happy birthday.

"Tell Mom I said bye," my dad said, putting his empty glass on the counter, glancing at his watch. "I'm gonna be late."

He did ruffle my hair, but he didn't say one word about me turning thirteen. My mother walked in shortly after he left. Lewis was behind her, playfully bouncing a rubber ball. Surely they would remember.

"Morning, Mom," I said with a big grin.

"Morning, Davy," my mother replied.

She opened the fridge and took out a half pound of bacon. She shuffled to the stove, took out a non-stick skillet, and turned the front burner on high. I moved next to her and stared as she lined the pan with thin strips, my nose practically in the skillet.

"I take it you want some bacon?" my mother asked.

"Yes, please," I said.

"Why don't you fix yourself a bowl of cereal, too."

"Yes, ma'am."

What in the world was going on? My mother had a tendency to ignore me and focus on my brother, but how could she forget my birthday? *Lewis would remember,* I thought, turning to him at the kitchen table. Lewis's mouth was sealed shut, though. He was preoccupied rolling his rubber ball from one hand to the other.

"Make Lewis a bowl while you're at it," my mother said.

"Yes, ma'am," I replied.

We ate breakfast in silence. The only topic that was discussed was the kitchen garbage. It was overflowing and needed to be taken out before I left for school. I kept expecting her to crack a smile, throw her hands over my shoulders, and wish me the best birthday a new teenager could have. It never happened. After I finished my bacon strips and slurped the last of my cereal milk, I washed the dishes and took out the trash. I couldn't believe they had forgotten.

School turned out to be the same on my birthday as it was on all the other days: slow and boring. I drifted in and out of my classes, thinking about what a crummy day it was. Nobody remembered. Desperate, I finally told the Gang at lunch.

"Davy, are you kidding us?" Jason asked.

"Nope," I replied.

"Man, happy birthday, cowboy," Mikey said.

The rest of the Gang said the same and clapped me on the back.

"Why didn't you tell us earlier, loco?" Jason asked.

I shrugged my shoulders and took a sip of my chocolate milk. "I was just waiting to see if anyone would say somethin'."

"How did you figure we'd remember when you didn't tell us in the first place?" Randy asked.

"Well...I really didn't expect you guys to know about it, but I thought my family would."

"You mean your parents forgot?" Tommy asked.

"Yep, didn't say a word this morning, and they didn't make any plans in the days before, either."

The Gang was shocked. Our lunch trays were filled with fish sticks, shoestring French fries, and sliced peaches. Tommy was the only one that had brought his lunch—a ham sandwich, a pickle, and an apple—and he was also the only one drinking a soda.

Lactose intolerance is a bitch.

"Wait a minute," Randy said, "I know how this works."

"Huh?" I asked.

"This is the perfect setup for a surprise party. They don't make plans for you before it happens and they don't say anything the day it comes. They're gonna surprise you."

"You think?" I asked.

"Did they tell you to come straight home after school?"

I sipped my chocolate milk again and thought for a second. "No, but yesterday my mom did say she needed me to go grocery shopping with her this afternoon."

"That's it," Randy said, slapping his hands together. "While you're at the store with your mom, your dad will fix the house up. They'll keep you busy so you'll have no idea."

"Yeah?"

"Sure, what do you guys think?" Randy asked, looking around the table. Mikey, Lucy, and Tommy nodded. Jason shook his head.

"I don't know," Jason said.

"What?" Randy asked.

"If that were true, why didn't they invite us to the party? Doesn't it make sense to invite his friends, too? I mean, I didn't get an invitation."

"Me neither," Mikey said.

"I never saw one," Tommy said.

"Neither did I," Lucy added.

"Maybe it's just a family thing today, and the big bash is later on," Randy said. "That happened to my dad once a couple years ago."

"Maybe," I said, picking at my fish sticks. I wanted to believe Randy, but I just couldn't see my parents going through all that hassle on my birthday.

"Don't worry, Davy," Tommy said. "If they forget to give you a party, we'll throw you one. Right, guys?"

"Right," the Gang said in unison.

"Thanks," I said, feeling like the biggest loser at school. I regretted bringing the subject up.

"It'll be a country hoedown, partner," Mikey said in another Eastwood impression.

"Shut up, Mikey," Jason said.

"No, you shut up," Mikey replied.

"I told you first, gordo."

"I told you second, and two is bigger than one."

"Both of you shut up," Tommy said.

Mikey stuck his tongue out at Jason and Jason returned the gesture. Lucy looked at them and laughed. Seeing Lucy break up made me giggle, too. It felt good letting go. I didn't want to worry about whether or not my parents had planned a party for me; I just wanted to enjoy my day.

But after lunch, my mind returned to my parents. Were they planning to surprise me as Randy had suggested? Would I come home from the grocery store to see a kitchen full of balloons and streamers and presents, or would I come home to a dark and barren house? The curiosity was gnawing at my brain.

***

While at the grocery store, I studied my mother's face to see if I could find a trace of a preplanned party. If she were hiding something, she was a damned good actor because she had the same determined look she always had while shopping for bargains. My mother was an avid coupon user, a fanatic by most standards, who loved to save her pennies whenever she could manage it. She'd hunt through magazines, newspapers, and junk-mail solicitations to find the lowest discounts. According to her, name brands were slick marketing scams designed to up the ante on common products and fatten the pocketbooks of big corporations. If I wanted Kellogg's Frosted Flakes, and if she had a coupon for Deds' Frosted Puffs, it wasn't tough to guess which cereal would end up in our cart. The fact that Deds' Frosted Puffs tasted like dirt didn't matter either. My mother only savored the sweet taste of savings.

So I followed Mom and Lewis up and down the aisles, keeping my eyes and ears open for any hints of a surprise celebration. I questioned every food item my mother picked off the shelves. *Coke? Chips? Ice Cream? What's she buying these things for? It must be my party: she knows how much I love soda and how I die for chocolate chip ice cream.* Of course, the fact that my mother bought these items all the time never entered my head. I was too caught up in my own little world, one with thirteen blazing candles flickering atop a white frosted cake, with friends crowded around me, singing merrily at the top of their lungs, and presents piled high on the kitchen table.

"Davy!"

"Huh?" I said, staring blankly at my mother in confusion.

"What's wrong with you? I said hand me that milk carton."

I grabbed the half-gallon carton my mother pointed at and continued to follow her down the next aisle. Randy was right...they wouldn't forget. How could they? They were my parents.

***

I walked inside our dark kitchen—carrying two paper sacks of groceries—and waited for the lights to click on and everybody to jump out from behind the furniture. They'd shout and I'd look surprised to see them.

Happy birthday, Davy, old buddy old pal. You didn't think we'd forget the day you turned thirteen, did you? I bet we fooled you, huh?

But the kitchen remained dark...

Maybe they were waiting for me to flip on the lights. I put the groceries down, pressed the wall switch and lit the room. Still nothing. Maybe they're in a different room. I ran to the den, to the living room, to my bedroom upstairs, clicking on all the lights. Nothing. Every room was empty save for the furniture.

"Davy, what are you doing?" my mother screamed from downstairs.

"Nothing, Mom," I said, looking behind my bed.

"You're not finished yet. Help Lewis carry these bags in."

"Yes, Mom," I replied, shutting off my light.

Dad came home from work just in time for dinner. Mom served us tacos with spicy ground beef and refried beans. I ate in silence. My mother and father talked about work, the neighborhood, and the news. "Can't believe that kid got shot today," my dad said, pouring himself a glass of water. "He was just eight years old."

"It's a cryin' shame, isn't it," my mother responded. "Makes me worry about Davy when he's out with his friends. Just shows how dangerous the streets are these days."

After dinner, I washed the dishes, wiped the kitchen counters off, and helped Mom sweep the floor. I went to my room after my chores were finished and locked the door. I collapsed on the bed and buried my face in my pillow. I wanted to fall asleep, to wake the next morning without the awful memory of today. Birthdays were stupid. I never wanted to have one again, and if any kids at school dared to gloat in front of me about theirs, about how many toys and games they had received, about how many friends had shown up at their grand fiesta, I'd punch them in the face. Why should they be happy?

I counted sheep; I said the alphabet backwards; I practiced multiplying prime numbers. Nothing worked. My eyes were wide open. I eventually came to the conclusion that if there was one thing that could make me tired, it was homework, so I unzipped my backpack and did Monday's assignments on Friday night. It must have been the first time in history I had attempted such a feat. I was a huge procrastinator, sometimes putting off my math problems and English readings until ten minutes before class. I had completed over three dozen assignments on the bus ride to school, and dozens more during lunch with the Gang. Homework was a bore, and it was just the thing I needed in a crisis like this.

I finished Mrs. Dawsons' English assignment within a half hour. English always came naturally to me. Unlike most kids in class, I didn't mind grammar questions and essay summaries, and I even enjoyed the in-class short story readings—which were usually about murder or mayhem. They were stories my mother would promptly slap out of my hands if she caught me reading them. Math, however, was a different story. It took me forever to work through Mrs. Williams' Algebra problems. Some of the formulas had so many X's and Y's and Z's I couldn't keep them all straight in my head. Luckily, I had a good grade in the class so far, but that was one grade I had honestly *earned.* On the good days, one assignment usually took me an hour to slug through; on the bad days, I could be at my desk for a three-hour stretch. It was painful. We could find the odd numbered answers in the back of the textbook—simple solutions with no tips from the author on how he solved the problem—but Mrs. Williams wanted to see the work. She was so picky that if you messed up on just one part of the formula, she would mark the entire question wrong. She was meticulous, and that meant we had to be as well.

So I opened the textbook and started the math assignment. The Indiana Jones clock on my wall read 9:30. By the time the clock struck ten, I was fast asleep.

***

"You gonna shoot it?" Tommy asked.

"Huh?" I asked.

"The crow, you dummy, you gonna kill it or not?"

I stood next to the scarred oak in the Vineyard, staring at Tommy and the black, greasy gun he was holding. It wasn't a pellet gun, but rather a .22 rifle with a giant scope perched on its top. I was armed with a slingshot, a yellow cats-eye marble sitting in the sling's leather pouch. The marble felt slick and fleshy, like a real eye.

"I dunno," I said, looking up the oak. The crow swayed gently on a bony twig, the wind ruffling its glossy, ebony feathers.

"Don't be a wuss," Tommy said. "If you don't get it, I will."

I aimed the slingshot at the bird and pulled back on the rubber tube. The bird stared back at me with familiar, oily eyes. They looked hollow and dead. It screamed a raucous caw and flapped its wings.

"Looks angry, doesn't it?" Tommy laughed.

"Yeah," I replied, trying to muster a laugh, too, but my throat was dry and sticky. I lowered my slingshot. "I don't think I can shoot it, Tommy."

"No?" Tommy asked. "Okay."

Tommy pointed his rifle at the crow, curled his finger around the trigger, and pulled back. The gun exploded next to my head—ringing in my eardrum—and the crow screamed out in pain. The bullet pierced its chest and blood poured from the hole like a fountain. It stayed on the twig, though, staring back at us with glowing red eyes and a pointy beak as sharp as a surgeon's knife. If it was angry before, it was pissed as hell now.

"Tommy, let's split," I said.

"No way, I'm droppin' that sucker."

Tommy loaded another brass bullet in his gun and got off another shot. The second hit struck the bird's head, knocking out its right eye. This time the bird dropped...but not straight down as we had expected. It was diving at *us*.

"Crap! Get down!" Tommy screamed, dropping to the ground.

I hit the dirt and covered my head. The crow landed on me and tore at the back of my neck with its scaly claws. Its beak pecked at my skull like a woodpecker.

"Get it off! Get it off!" I begged, blindly throwing my marble behind me.

Tommy tried to hit the bird with the butt of his gun, but it took off before he could strike it. Blood trickled down my neck and back. I stared at the crow circling in the cloudy sky, still feeling its beak digging into me. The bird dove again, still targeting me, and landed on my chest. It was no longer a seven-inch crow. It was now a three-foot feathered beast with a worm twitching in the socket of the eye Tommy had shot out. Its other socket held my cat's-eye marble, glaring at me in deadly lust.

I grabbed the bird's glossy neck as it tried to hammer my face. Blood spilled from its beak as it cried its revenge.

CAW! CAW!

"Help! Tommy!"

"I'm trying," Tommy replied, pulling on one of its giant claws.

The beast pecked my chin, cheeks, and lips. It continued to hammer relentlessly... with a beak that had transformed into Loony's switchblade.

"Get it off!"

The worm dropped out of its socket and burrowed into my right eye, wiggling and squirming its way into my iris.

CAW!

"Get it off!"

"Davy?"

CAW! CAW!

"Tommy!"

"Davy!"

I jumped up from my desk. My mother stood beside me, looking concerned. Lewis and my father were behind her, dressed in their pajamas.

"Where is it?" I asked.

"What?"

"The crow, where is it?"

"It was just a nightmare, champ," my father said moving to me and putting a hand on my shoulder.

On top of my desk was a blueberry muffin with a candle stuck in its center. The clock on the wall said 11:55 P.M.

"What are you all doing here?" I asked.

"We're so sorry, Davy," my mother said, hugging me. "It completely skipped our minds."

"Yeah, I don't know how we forgot," my father added.

It took me a moment to figure out that I had fallen asleep on my desk. I was only asleep for two and a half hours, but it felt like days.

"Bedtime now?" a sleepy Lewis asked. He was in his PJs, and I could tell he'd been woken up for this.

"Not just yet, Lewis," my mom replied. "We've got to light the candle. Davy, we don't have a cake for you right now, but we'll buy one first thing tomorrow. The biggest one we can find. And you'll have presents, too."

I stared at the blueberry muffin. It was almost comical seeing it on top of my desk, its crooked candle sticking out at an awkward angle.

"It's okay, it's over anyway," I said.

"Well, technically, you've still got five more minutes," my dad said, pointing at the clock, winking at me.

Mom took out a box of matches, removed one, and struck it on the box's sandpaper side. She lit the candle and shook out the flame.

"You ready?" my mom asked.

"Yep," my dad replied. "One...two...three."

As the clock changed to 11:56, my family sang happy birthday. Lewis, as always, was off-key, but it was beautiful nonetheless. They sang as I stared at the flickering flame, trying to summon up the best wish I could think of. The song ended, I blew out the lonely candle, and they hugged me.

"Happy thirteenth, Davy," my mother said. "Sorry it turned out this way."

"Thanks, Mom," I said, staring at the thin trail of smoke petering out of the wick. "It's okay."

My dad threw his arm around my neck and gave me a light noogie. "Oh-oh...you're a teenager now. Soon you'll be driving a car, taking chicks on dates, and drinking beer."

"I don't think so," I said, chuckling.

"No? That's what I did back in my days. It was a blast."

"Honey!" my mother said, furrowing her brow. "We don't need to motivate our son to drink."

"Oh, Davy's a good kid," my dad said, defending himself. "He knows better. Listen, champ, I've got a special treat for you tomorrow."

"Really?" I asked.

"How would you like to go flying with me?"

My eyes lit up. "Would I!"

Mom looked at Dad with surprise. It was obviously something they hadn't discussed together. "Are you sure Davy can go with you?"

"I'm still a pilot, right? I hope there's nothing you know that I don't."

My mom took the skirt off the muffin and handed me a large piece. Lewis licked his lips and held out his hand for some. "You know what I mean," said my mother.

"It's fine," Dad replied, sitting on my bed. I had never seen him sit on it before; the single size bunk looked so tiny and frail under his bulky frame. "Davy's old enough now. It's the little ones you have to worry about."

My mother sighed, handed Lewis a quarter of the muffin and gave me the remaining part. "Just make sure you strap him in, okay?"

"But how is he supposed to do handstands on the wing?" my dad asked, smiling at me.

"Honey..."

"I know, I know, we'll be careful. Right, champ?"

I nodded eagerly, my lips stained with blueberries.

"Before you two leave, I want us to have a birthday lunch. I'll pick up a cake at the store."

"Cake!" said Lewis.

"Not right now, hon," Mom said. "That's tomorrow."

Both of my parents were in matching blue robes and sheepskin slippers. Lewis's PJs had patterns of Curious George from his ankles to his shoulders. Mom stretched her arms, yawned, and glanced at her watch.

"We better get back to bed."

"Yep, we've got a big day ahead of us," my dad agreed.

My mother kissed my forehead and shuffled out of the room with Lewis. Dad got off the bed, the mattress springs exhaling in relief, and nudged my shoulder.

"You want the lights off, champ?"

"Yes, please."

I got in bed as he flipped the switch and grabbed the doorknob. Before he shut the door, he glanced back at me, a small ray of light seeping into my room.

"And Davy..."

"Yeah, Dad?"

"Love you."

"Love you too, Dad," I said.

He closed the door and sealed my room in darkness. I stared at my ceiling and thought about flying ten thousand feet in the sky. Within minutes I was asleep again, this time dreaming of better things than one-eyed killer crows.

Chapter 22

SOARING ABOVE

The next day I dug into a supreme pizza for lunch, which included all of my favorite toppings: onions, mushrooms, bell peppers, tomatoes, sausages, and pepperonis. A giant chocolate cake followed—thirteen candles spelling out my age—along with three presents. My mother bought me a deck of Bicycle playing cards and new sneakers; Lewis gave me a Knight Rider toy car, which I'm sure he had picked out with my mother that morning while shopping at the mall.

"You ready for my gift?" my father asked.

"Heck yeah!" I said, practically choking on the cake in my mouth.

My father grabbed his car keys, gave me my jacket, and kissed my mother good-bye.

"Please be careful up there," Mom said.

"Why is it you're so concerned about my safety when Davy tags along, but you could give two bits when I'm up there by myself?"

"I just want to make sure he doesn't get hurt."

My father rubbed my head and smiled. "Are you gonna jump out of the plane or something?"

"No, sir," I said, shaking my head.

"Well there you have it," my dad said to my mother and walked out.

I hugged Mom and followed Dad to the car. Lewis was already tearing into the Knight Rider package, eagerly waiting to race Kit across the kitchen table.

"Be careful," my mother said, waving from the door.

***

Jumbo jets thundered over our Suburban as we pulled into the airport parking lot. The planes zoomed on and off the runway, the noise rattling our car as if it were a tin can. My dad turned into a back lot, an area specifically reserved for pilots and airport employees, and pulled the car into a numbered slot.

"Wow, you get your own space, Dad?"

"Neat, isn't it?"

We walked inside and my dad introduced me to a few people. Each person shook my hand and told me how much I looked like my father. We eventually ended up on the tarmac where my dad showed me to our plane.

"That's a Piper Cherokee."

"Awesome," I said. It was tiny compared to the 747s I had flown in when taking trips with my family; those jets were superbly massive—flying buildings with wheels, wings, and engines. This plane had one propeller engine, four seats, and three tires that were no bigger than the wheels on our Suburban. I could see why they named it Piper. You could fit five of them inside one of the jumbo jets.

"Sorry, no trespassers allowed."

I turned and saw a man in engineer boots, black slacks, and a greasy blue shirt. His hair was slicked back in a tight ponytail, with hints of gray peeking out at the roots. Pacific Air was written in cursive on his breast pocket.

"Hey, Cliff, I didn't know you were workin' today," my dad said, shaking Cliff's soot-caked hand.

Cliff's hand engulfed my father's. My dad was no small man, six-foot one and weighing over two hundred pounds, but he looked like a kid next to Cliff, who I guessed was probably around six-six or six-seven, and three hundred plus pounds. Cliff's mouth was as big as my face and his giant ivory teeth were blinding white dominos.

"Yep, they're workin' me to the bone."

Cliff looked at me and frowned. Had my father not been with me, I would have made tracks back inside the building, my tail hiding firmly between my legs.

"Your son, I assume," Cliff said.

"That's right," my father replied, patting me on the back. "I'm taking him up today."

"You have clearance?"

"Yeah, it's all taken care of. Have you checked her out yet?"

Cliff coughed and spit on the tarmac. "She's set and ready. Gave her gas this morning."

My father made a lap around the Piper, doing his own inspection. I stood next to Cliff, feeling like a midget in a circus freak show. My father returned after a few minutes, satisfied.

"You ready?"

I nodded anxiously.

While the plane thumped down the cracks in the runway, my father pointed at cockpit instrument panels. I was strapped in the passenger seat next to him, my legs dangling above the floor. Both of us wore headsets with small microphones under our chins.

"That's the clock, this is the air-speed indicator, the horizon indicator, and that last one is the altimeter. Do you know what an altimeter does?"

I shook my head.

"It measures the plane's altitude. Without it, I'd have no way of knowing how high up we were over the sea or ground. We might smash into a mountain if I had to fly in foggy weather."

I nodded again, praying that we wouldn't find ourselves in that situation. It was a clear day, thank God.

"And down here we have a turn and bank gauge, a gyrosyn compass, and a rate-of-climb dial." My dad paused for a second and stared at me. "You getting all this?"

I shook my head.

"You better, because I'm gonna have you land the plane."

I nervously stared at the controls. It was nothing like our Suburban, which had three simple gauges: gas, speed, and oil. Any dummy—especially a thirteen-year-old dummy—could figure out what they were for; when the needle said E, it was time to gas up; when the little oil lamp was full, our gears were getting lubed. That knowledge didn't require a driver's license. The plane's gadgets, however, reminded me of the Star Trek episodes where Scotty was busy punching hundreds of red and blue flashing buttons, trying to boost the Enterprise's power so Captain Kirk could warp away from the warmongering Klingons. The controls all looked the same. They weren't as bad as the gauges in a jumbo jet, which would probably even give a pro like Scotty a heart attack, but they were intimidating nonetheless. And the most frightening instrument was the control wheel on my side of the cockpit. It was exactly like the one in front of my father. I stared at it, wondering if that was what I'd have to use to land the plane.

My dad eventually winked at me. "Don't worry, champ, this ride's on me."

He pulled the Piper behind two planes that were not much larger than ours. I checked to see if any 747s were preparing for takeoff. All of them were parked at their gates, loading and unloading luggage, surrounded by crewmembers that were doing checkups underneath the wings and engines.

The first plane in our line turned onto the runway and took off. Minutes later, the second plane sped away and lifted into the blue sky. When it was finally our turn, I was beginning to regret my decision to come along. What if something happened? What if we ran out of gas? What if that allmeter, or atmeter, or whatever in the world it was called failed and we ran into foggy weather? My mother would read about us in the paper, perhaps in a small column at the bottom of the front page, next to a picture of a demolished plane in the Hillerman Mountains.

Two males died yesterday in a plane crash, likely due to foggy weather. Sources said one of the victims was a small boy that couldn't help his father land the aircraft. Witnesses claimed the plane was flying too close to the ground.

"You all strapped in?" my dad asked.

I nodded my head frantically, staring at the line of concrete in front of us which stretched into a small point. Was it long enough?

"Flight 303, you're clear to go."

"Roger," my father replied.

The propeller spun faster, seeming to rotate one direction and then changing to the other. I gripped my seatbelt and felt the pressure against my back. Even with the headset on, the ear-deafening buzz of the plane drowned out all other sounds. The aircraft accelerated down the runway, thumping over the concrete cracks, and as we moved faster, the thumps grew closer together. Before long the bumps were impossible to count. I could see the end of the runway closing in. We weren't going to make it. We needed more space.

I closed my eyes and bit my lip.

Then I felt the plane lift. The thumping disappeared and the buzzing noise tapered to a low hum. I reopened my eyes and saw us rising over the brownish-green Huckleberry landscape.

My dad smiled at me. "You okay over there?"

"Yeah," I said, looking at the buildings and cars beneath us. They looked like props in a toy train set.

"Pretty neat, huh?"

"Yeah," I said.

I felt more secure in the air. We had narrowly escaped disaster, and the papers wouldn't be writing about our ill-fated takeoff. Whether or not we would encounter bad weather or land safely was another question. We were up, and that's all that mattered at the moment.

"See the Rio Grande?" my dad asked, turning the plane.

"Is that it?" I asked, pointing.

"Yep, that's the one."

"It's so small from up here."

The river split the city in half, with houses lined on both the east and west sides of the embankments. There were only two bridges that crossed the Rio Grande—the northern four-lane Kyser overpass, and the southern two-lane Santa Fe viaduct, which also extended over a good part of the valley. The viaduct was a historic bridge that was built in 1924, during the years of Calvin Coolidge's presidency; the Kyser bridge, however, was only a few years old.

"Can you see our house?" my father asked.

"Huh uh, where is it?"

My father turned the wheel and pitched the plane. The sudden drop made my stomach curl, summoning the pizza and cake to the top of my throat. I swallowed the food down, and my dad leveled off. He pointed to the valley below. "Right there."

I followed his finger to the Vineyard. We were too high up to make out the fence, but Mr. Phillips's red-shingled house was recognizable. The ditch, running from east to west, was just north of his property, starting behind a cluster of bushy trees and emptying into the Rio Grande several hundred yards downstream. Several smaller waterways and irrigation routes crisscrossed throughout the Vineyard, looking like snakes in a brown field. On the other side of the ditch lay Grant elementary, and next to that was our circular neighborhood. The houses looked unreal, almost comical in their size.

"Is that it?" I asked, pointing.

"Yep, that's it. Looks different up here, huh?"

"Sure does," I said, wondering what my mother and Lewis were doing at that very moment. Maybe watching TV in the den, or napping upstairs. It was surreal to think that they had no idea we were flying above the house right now, just a few thousand feet up.

"Wanna go over the mountains?"

"Sure," I replied.

My dad turned the plane again, aiming the nose of the craft directly at the Hillerman Mountains. The propeller buzzed along. Occasionally, the aircraft would shake from a bubble of turbulence and the control wheel would rattle in my dad's hands. The disturbances were short-lived, although they were long enough to remind me that the only thing separating us from the hard ground below was a thin layer of plastic, wood, and metal. Our lives were at the mercy of a single gas engine.

The plane climbed as my dad pulled the wheel down, and soon we were zooming over Hillerman Mountains. Thin traces of winter snow were still visible on the peak. Jagged rocks and cliffs protruded from the mountain and reached out toward the sky. I caught sight of a gray goat ascending the back of a large boulder.

We flew over the crest and made a U-turn. Then, slowly, Huckleberry unfolded before our eyes as we flew back over the peak. We could see everything—the valley, the river, the downtown buildings, the western desert volcanoes.

I looked at my father and smiled. He smiled back without saying a word. It was a view he had seen before, perhaps hundreds of times. It was a sight that never grew old. It was his world up here, his sanctuary.

We flew back toward the city, watching the land move beneath us. The propeller hummed and the sun winked off the plane's wings. My hands were clenched tightly around my seatbelt strap and my eyes absorbed the beauty below.

We were soaring.

Soaring far, far above.

Chapter 23

The Final Post

It comes in like a lion and goes out like a lamb. My grandfather used this common idiom to describe the month of March, but I'm positive that, during his lifetime, he hadn't seen the kind of unusual weather we were currently experiencing. The beginning of March did not start out stormy and gray, but warm and calm. The girls at school brought out their spring flower dresses and white sneakers, and the boys wore shorts with T-shirts. The sun's welcomed return made us antsy in class, and there wasn't a kid around who would rather stay inside instead of play games in the sunshine in the spectacular weather—well...except for Patty Pigtails.

The days had grown longer and the Vineyard work had become easier. We could now stay out until six thirty before heading in. The once-frozen ground was now soft again, which made the re-digging a cinch.

By March 5th, we were on our last three posts.

"What the heck is that?" Jason asked.

"It's a house," Mikey replied.

"What for?"

"For Mr. Hops. He needs a place to stay."

We were gathered around the scarred oak, next to our parked bikes, getting ready for another afternoon's work. The sky was clear and the wind was moderately breezy. Birds, squirrels, and other small creatures were taking advantage of the mild weather, collecting nuts, seeds, and insects.

Mikey had taken a small wooden box out of his backpack. It was made out of particleboard pieces, with glue and nails sticking out at odd angles. A small hole was carved in its front—Mr. Hops's door, I presumed—and it had a pretend chimney on its top.

"Tu eres un tonto—frogs don't have houses," Jason replied.

"How cute!" Lucy said, kneeling next to Mikey.

The Gang crowded closer to Mikey to get a better look. The box was a slipshod job. Had Mikey built it for Shop class, he would have gotten a fat F on the project. Cute was not the word I would have used to describe it.

"Great, huh?" Mikey asked, adjusting his thick glasses. "Watch! Mr. Hops loves it."

We watched under a warm sun as Mikey laid the box on the ground and retrieved the toad from his pack. He placed him near the box's hole and waited patiently for him to jump in. Mr. Hops, however, had other things on his mind. He sat perfectly still, exhaling and inhaling his bubble throat.

"Come on...you can do it," Mikey said, tapping Mr. Hops's rear.

"Forget it," Jason said. "He's not gonna get in that stupid thing."

"He's done it before," Mikey said, licking his lips. His plump cheeks were rosy-red, and his trunk-like neck was already slightly sunburned. "Come on, big guy."

Finally, after what seemed to be an eternity, Mr. Hops leaped in the hole. He cleared it in perfect form—a feat that would make any animal trainer proud. Mikey gave us the fattest grin I had ever seen, and stuck his tongue out at Jason.

"Hah! I told you," Mikey said.

"Wow, looky there," Randy said.

"Yeah, yeah," Jason replied, walking away. "I don't know why you keep that stupid sapo."

Lucy picked up the particleboard box to get a better look at Mr. Hops's new home, while Tommy, Randy, and I followed Jason into the Vineyard. Mr. Phillips was already working on the fifty-eighth post, wearing his trademark straw hat, engineer boots, and blue overalls. He didn't see us walk up until we were a few feet away.

"Howdy," Mr. Phillips said, removing the hat, wiping beads of sweat off his forehead. "Beautiful day, isn't it?"

"Sure is," Tommy replied. "Great day for a baseball game."

"Yeah, I suppose it is. I bet all those other kids are havin' fun."

"I bet," Tommy said, smiling at Mr. Phillips. Tommy was now always kidding him about other things we could be doing rather than working in the Vineyard. In turn, Mr. Phillips would remind him how much he had loved his stained-glass window, how it was the most precious thing he had owned. It was a game they loved to play with each other.

"You hens ready to finish the posts?" Mr. Phillips asked.

"Think we'll do it today?" Randy asked.

"Sure, if we hurry up. This one's finished, so we only have three more. I reckon we can get in the last one before sundown."

Mikey and Lucy ran up behind us. Mikey had left Mr. Hops and his home back by the oak.

"Randy, Tommy, and Mikey—you guys get this next post. Jason, Davy, and Lucy, you can take number sixty."

"You gonna help us?" Lucy asked.

Mr. Phillips put his straw hat back on and scratched his leather face. "Na, I'm afraid I can't today. I've got some things around the house that need tending to. But give me a holler 'fore you do the last one. I wanna be there for it."

Mr. Phillips tipped his hat at us and walked off. Randy, Tommy, and Mikey made for their post, and we went for ours. I was a bit angry that I had been assigned to Lucy's group. Since we still weren't talking, it was awkward working with her. She'd either completely ignore me and focus solely on the job, or she would talk to the other person in the group and make like I wasn't there. Mr. Phillips tried to rotate the groups as often as he could so we could all work together, but he sometimes got confused as to which one we were in the day before. For the past three days, I had worked with Randy and Tommy, and that was fine by me. At least *they* could talk to me about school, sports, or good movies they had seen at the dollar theater. Working with Lucy was like washing dishes with my mother—all work and no play.

"Jason, you hold the post in place; Lucy, you pour the water," I said. "I'll take the cement bag."

"Okay," said Lucy.

"Lo tengo," Jason added.

I ripped open the bag and got right to the job. *Two can play at this game,* I thought. *If Lucy wants to ignore me, then I'll do the same to her. All work and no play, yes sir.* I poured the cement as Lucy added the water.

"I heard Pinner suspended Frank Gleeson and Joey Wilson this morning," Jason said, hovering above our heads with the post clamped between his hands. His shadow was over my face.

"That's what I heard, too," Lucy said, crouching next to me, the sun reflecting off her bucket of water, the golden crucifix kissing her neck. "Some say they tried to call in sick to school."

Jason laughed, revealing his silver grin. His Michigan hat was turned backwards. "Yeah, Mikey told me they tried to act like their parents when they made the call. Heard they were at Frank's house when they did it."

"Lucy, keep pouring," I said, irate that she was ignoring my silence.

Lucy adjusted her bucket. "How did they get caught?"

"Mikey told me Frank made the first call. He impersonated his mom's voice and said that her son was very sick."

Lucy cackled and spilt all over the edges of the hole.

"Lucy, the water," I said again, growing angrier.

"Okay, okay," Lucy replied, straightening out. "So wait...what did Joey do?"

"Get this," Jason said, barely able to control himself. "Joey called in minutes later, and acted like his mother. He said the same friggin' thing Frank said." Both Lucy and Jason were roaring. The post was swaying and the water was spilling again.

"Guys," I said.

"The school was suspicious, so they called Frank's house minutes later," Jason continued, laughing. "They asked for an emergency number and Frank gave 'em Joey's home number."

"No," Lucy said, astonished.

"That's what I heard," Jason laughed. "Then they called Frank and Joey's dads at work. They were so busted."

"Oh my gosh!"

"Guys," I repeated louder.

"Frank's dad left work, went home, and stormed into the house. He caught both of 'em red-handed in Frank's room, playin' Monopoly. He dragged 'em back to school and that's when Pinner slapped them with three weeks' worth of detention slips."

"What dummies," said Lucy.

"Pendejos of the year," Jason said. Jason and Lucy looked at each other and cracked up again.

I couldn't take it any longer. "Do the damn thing yourself!" I said. I ran off, furious with rage.

"Where you going?" Jason asked.

"Davy, come back," Lucy replied. "We're sorry."

Sorry or not, I didn't care. I was tired of dealing with it. I'd rather stay home and watch TV or listen to the radio. Never mind if I *had* to be in the Vineyard, I just wanted to get away from everyone, to hide in a hole.

Lucy ran up and caught me.

"Davy, come on," Lucy said, grabbing my elbow.

I twisted my arm loose and grabbed my bike off the oak, almost smashing poor Mr. Hops's house with my rear tire.

"I'm going home," I said.

"What? Why? Why are you so upset?"

I glared at her. Her long brown hair was caressing her soft cheeks and her bright green eyes looked at me in confusion. Staring at her pretty face almost made me forget why I was even mad in the first place.

"Because of you," I said.

"Because of me?"

I thought about riding off, but I couldn't now. I had opened the door and I'd only be satisfied if I let it all out.

"Yeah Lucy, the way you ignore me!" I said, my face red, my lips white and pressed together.

"Ignore you? What about me? Ever since Timmy, you've avoided me like the plague. I don't sit next to you on the bus because you treat me like I'm some jerk."

"That's a lie."

"Yeah? Then why don't you talk to me in the halls anymore? And what about lunch? You're more than willing to talk to the others. Telling stories and carrying on like you do. But never once do you say something in my direction. Heck, you won't even sit next to me at the table."

"I don't because you don't want me to."

Lucy frowned. The Gang was staring at us, spectators in our little feud. "What gave you that impression?"

I gripped my handlebars and thought about riding off again. Why was she playing me like an idiot? She knew damned well how I felt. I didn't want to bring it up, but I didn't have a choice.

"Why didn't you say something about my poem?"

Lucy's thin eyebrows shot up in shock. Her mouth dropped open as if someone had told her she'd won a million dollars.

"Poem?"

I felt like the biggest fool in Huckleberry. She was going to make me crawl through the mud, make me repeat the embarrassing lines. It was rejection all over again. I was glad the Gang was too far away to hear us. At least that would salvage whatever dignity I had left.

"You know what I'm talking about," I said. "The one I wrote for you on Valentine's Day. 'Like a bee on a flower, you came to me with beauty's power.' That one."

"You wrote a poem for me?"

Suddenly, I realized she wasn't pretending. "Yeah, I slipped it in your locker. You mean you didn't get it?"

"No! I never saw one."

"Come on, don't give me that."

"I'm serious, Davy! I swear my life on it. I haven't seen anything but my books."

My stomach dropped to the floor. The image of me putting it in the wrong locker returned. Someone else had read my poem and had passed it on to their friends. They had known about it for weeks now, and it was probably tacked up on some bulletin board—everybody laughing at Davy the love sap...spilling his guts out.

"But it's 309, right?" I asked, begging her to say yes.

"Yeah, of course. That's mine all right, but I never saw it."

I stared blankly at the ground, pondering the whereabouts of the Valentine gift.

"Then what happened to it?" I asked softly.

"Maybe it's inside one of my books."

"Maybe...but you would have seen it by now."

Lucy scratched her light brown neck, leaving thin, white tracks on her skin. "Perhaps it fell out while I was opening it. I might have missed it if I was putting my backpack inside."

I pictured the scenario: the poem falling out by her feet; students inadvertently stepping on it, kicking it around; the white paper turning brown with footprints; ending up in a pile with a stack of paper trash at the end of the day; a night janitor noticing it while sweeping; picking it up; reading the lines to himself; pocketing it; later reciting the poem to his wife, perhaps claiming it as his own.

That was the best scenario I could think of. The others were too upsetting to ponder.

"I can't believe you wrote me a poem," Lucy said, smiling with her smooth lips.

"Yeah, well, it was a dumb idea."

"That's the sweetest thing."

Lucy threw her arms around me. It caught me off guard and I almost tripped over my bike. Her hair smelled like shampoo; her arms were warm from the afternoon sun. It was great to touch her again, to feel her embrace. I was mildly aware that the Gang was still staring at us, probably wondering if we were going to make out in front of them.

Euuuueeeeee! There they go again! I see tongue. You guys see it? Hey, you two! Get a room.

Lucy withdrew from me. "I'm sorry I didn't get to read it. I'll check around, though, maybe it will turn up."

"Yeah," I said. It was wishful thinking, but it was all I had. "It wasn't very good anyway."

"I doubt that," Lucy said, smiling at me. "I hope I find it... Sorry about the way I acted, too."

"Yeah, same here," I said. There was a long silence and we both didn't know what to say next.

"So, you gonna get on that bike, or come back?"

I had forgotten it was in my hands. I looked at it blankly. "Oh, yeah," I said.

I parked it next to the tree, this time paying special attention to Mr. Hops's domicile, and walked back with Lucy. My steps were light, and the sun felt good against my T-shirt. Mikey, Tommy, and Randy were back at work. Jason was still staring in our direction, anxiously waiting for us to return before Mr. Phillips noticed our departure.

It was time to finish the three last posts.

***

We sweated in the afternoon sun. For the last four months our perspiration glands had been on break, but now, with the temperatures creeping up into the high eighties, and with the wind as still as a frightened mouse, our skin was shouting for relief. The heat drove the birds and squirrels to their shaded homes, and the insects took refuge in the cool earth. Mr. Phillips was working in his garden, pulling weeds and checking his crops. I glanced at him from time to time, envying the straw hat perched on his head. Jason was the only one smart enough to bring a baseball cap.

I wiped my forehead with my T-shirt and wiggled the post. The cement solution had hardened.

"I think it's ready," I said, looking up at Jason.

The tape measure was in Jason's hand. Lucy stood at Tommy's post, holding the tongue of the long yellow tape.

"Sixteen feet?" Lucy asked.

Jason double-checked the tape and glanced over.

"Looks like it to me," Jason replied.

Tommy, Mikey, and Randy were done with their post, taking a break on a small patch of spring grass.

"You guys done yet?" Tommy asked, a long strand of grass poking out of his mouth.

"Yeah, yeah," Jason said. "We would have been done sooner if it wasn't for Davy's friggin' temper tantrum."

Jason walked the measure to Lucy and I followed him. New life was sprouting around us: dandelions, weeds, and grass.

"What are you doin' sitting on the job?" I asked Tommy.

"Waitin' for your slow butt," Tommy replied. "If you were this slow every day, we'd be working out here until retirement."

"You guys wanna get Mr. Phillips now?" Lucy asked.

"We better hurry up," Mikey said, glancing at his watch. His thick neck was now as red as a Huckleberry sunset. I could feel the sunburn just looking at him.

Tommy put two fingers between his lips and let out a deafening whistle. Mr. Phillips waved at us from his garden, threw a handful of weeds aside, and made his way over.

"I sure am thirsty," Randy said.

"Me, too," Jason replied.

"You guys want me to grab the bottles?" Mikey asked.

We winced at Mikey's suggestion. Each afternoon, six small water bottles were left for us in a cardboard box by the first post. We used them constantly, but the cool water Mr. Phillips filled them with at the beginning of the afternoon was usually lukewarm by the time we needed them. We drank them hesitantly, forcing the heated liquid down our throats.

"Man, what I wouldn't pay for a cold Coke right now," Jason said.

"I'd take a lemonade," Tommy said. "A tall, icy glass of it."

"Yeah, a lemonade..." Lucy said, her eyes wide.

I wasn't thirsty before, but now that the Gang mentioned it, I was suddenly licking my lips, dreaming of my own frosty glass.

"Y'all done?" Mr. Phillips asked, tipping up his hat. His white undershirt was drenched with sweat, sticking to his skin and overalls.

"Just one more to go," Tommy said.

Mr. Phillips smiled and nodded. "Well, let's do it then."

He started walking over and when he noticed we weren't following he looked back in confusion.

"Well? Come on. Don't tell me you're quittin' on the last one."

"We're kinda thirsty, Mr. Phillips," Tommy said.

"Y'all know where your drinks are at."

We looked back at the cardboard box as if we hadn't seen it before. We could see the sun bearing down on the bottles, heating them to a near boil.

"Do you have any cold drinks, sir?" Tommy asked.

Mr. Phillips put his hands on his hips and looked at his house. An orange-breasted robin landed next to his feet. It was a brave bird, standing no less than ten inches away from his engineer boots. If Mr. Phillips were to take a step in the wrong direction, the robin would see the business end of his shoe.

"Not sure...I could use a cold drink myself," Mr. Phillips admitted. "But I don't have anything in my fridge."

We lowered our heads in defeat. The ice-cold drinks vaporized. We could manage the heated bottles again...shoot, we had put up with them this long, what's one more day?

"But I could make us a pitcher of juice."

Our hearts lifted.

"You have any lemonade mix?" Mikey asked, sounding a bit rude. Jason elbowed him in the ribs.

"Think I do," Mr. Phillips answered. "Is that what you guys want?"

We nodded our heads eagerly. The robin pecked at the soil until it finally snatched up a pink earthworm. It took off with its prey dangling in its beak.

"Come on, follow me."

***

We wiped our feet on the welcome mat. Mr. Phillips didn't ask us to, but we felt it was the appropriate thing to do before entering. It was, after all, the first time the Gang had all set foot inside his house (Mikey and I, of course, had entered the day we had broken the window). I saw Mr. Phillips's paintings and sculptures for the second time. There was a picture of a cowboy lassoing cattle on one wall, riding under a desert storm, his horse kicking up a cloud of dust. On the opposite wall, set in an alcove, stood a clay sculpture of a hand holding a ball. We passed a dozen more art pieces—all initialed by BJP.

Mr. Phillips led us to the kitchen where he asked us to sit at a table while he prepared the lemonade.

"Wow, did you do all this?" Lucy asked, looking at the paintings.

"Not all of it," Mr. Phillips replied, emptying ice cubes into a giant glass pitcher. "A few of 'em are from my ex-wife. She let me keep them after our separation."

"That's nice of her," Randy said.

"Yeah...I suppose after taking my house and furniture, she felt obliged to give me something."

We sat and watched as Mr. Phillips opened a canister of lemonade mix and poured five heaping spoonfuls into the pitcher. We could taste its tangy flavor on the tips of our tongues. One pitcher didn't seem like enough...we would down it in seconds.

"That's weird. Why do you do it?" Mikey asked.

We frowned at Mikey for asking the rude question.

"You mean make art?"

"It's okay, you can just ignore Mikey, Mr. Phillips," Tommy explained. "He gets a little carried away sometimes."

Mr. Phillips laughed and placed the pitcher under his sink faucet. "Heck, I don't mind the question. I'm not sure why I do it, to tell ya the truth. It's my form of entertainment, I guess. I've been doin' it for so long it's almost habit now."

"Habit?" Mikey asked.

"Yeah. Instead of watching TV or movies, I do this. I suppose a kid your age thinks that's pretty strange."

"Oh no, sir," Mikey said, smiling. "I mean, when I said it was weird, I meant it in a good way. It's kinda cool, actually. It's not sissy or anything."

Tommy kicked Mikey's shin underneath the table and Mikey jumped.

"Sissy?"

"Yeah, you know...you do stuff about cowboys, ranchers, and gunslingers," Mikey continued, rubbing his leg. "That's cool."

Mr. Phillips took the pitcher out of the sink, stirred it and grinned at Mikey. "I guess it is, huh?"

We licked our lips at the beautiful lemonade swirling inside the glass. In another minute we were going to rush him and snatch the drink away like savages. Mr. Phillips grabbed a handful of red Dixie cups from inside a cabinet and made for our table.

"That looks good," Jason said, mesmerized.

"Sure does," Randy added, a bead of sweat rolling down his freckled neck.

Mr. Phillips poured each of us a glass and handed them around the table. We drank quickly, feeling the cool liquid slide down our throats. Our Adam's apples bounced up and down like rubber balls. I finished mine in a matter of seconds and handed my cup to Mr. Phillips before he finished pouring himself a glass.

"Calm down, son," Mr. Phillips told me. "You're gonna choke on your tongue."

I tried to give him a smile, but was too busy catching my breath. After he topped off his cup, he refilled mine. I quickly gulped the first half down and let out a satisfied sigh. Even though it wasn't freshly squeezed, it was the best lemonade I had ever tasted. The rest of the Gang downed their glasses, too, and asked for seconds. Mikey was the last to finish his cup, and by the time Mr. Phillips filled it back up, the pitcher was empty.

"Y'all are as thirsty as stranded sailors," Mr. Phillips said. "It's a good thing your parents weren't here to see it. They'd think I was tryin' to kill ya."

Mr. Phillips walked back to the sink and flipped on the faucet. We smacked our lips at the table and wiped our mouths with the back of our hands. Savages, stranded sailors, rude kids—whatever one wanted to call us, we fit the profile.

"Speaking of your parents, how's it goin' with them anyway?"

"Our parents?" Tommy asked, taking another sip out of his cup.

"Yeah, is everything going all right with them?"

Tommy looked at us and we shrugged our shoulders. "Sure, everything's fine."

Mr. Phillips rejoined us at the table. He sat down in an empty seat next to Mikey and Lucy and gulped a quarter of his juice down. "It's still a secret with them, right?"

Mikey nodded. "Yep, they don't know a thing about it."

"Really?" Mr. Phillips asked, furrowing his brow, obviously a bit suspicious of Mikey's answer.

"Yes," said Tommy. "We've had a few snags here and there, but we've done a good job hiding it from them."

Jason poured himself a third cup. I thought about pouring myself another glass, but I felt I'd float out of Mr. Phillips's house if I did.

"To tell the truth, I never thought y'all would get away with it," Mr. Phillips said, taking off his straw hat and scratching his head. "I swore it would last a few weeks at most before they'd find out. I would have wagered my house if someone were to bet me you'd make it this far."

"You didn't think we'd do it?" Tommy asked.

Mr. Phillips swallowed down another gulp. "Six kiddos trying to keep one secret? No way. Not a chance on God's green earth."

He laughed at us and we stared at him, shocked.

"So you never expected us to build it?" I asked.

"Hate to admit it, but yep...that's about on the money. I thought either they'd find out or you'd fade off one by one, and I'd be stuck building it by myself."

"You mean you wouldn't have called our parents if we walked away?" Mikey asked, his green eyes bigger than his glasses.

"I'm not sayin' that," Mr. Phillips replied. "I would have called them had that happened. You *did* do quite a bit of damage, after all. All I'm sayin' is that I just didn't think you'd get the chance to pay it off yourselves. There were too many cards stacked against you." He took another sip out of his cup and stared at us. "How did ya do it, anyway? Keep it from your parents, that is."

"A lot of lyin'," Tommy said.

"Yep, lots of it," Lucy added.

The rest of us nodded and played with our cups. The half-melted ice cubes bobbed up and down in the pitcher like little buoys.

Mr. Phillips nodded. "I thought so. I feel bad about that—really bad. I figured you'd told your share of fibs to your folks before all of this had ever started. Last thing I wanted was to add to it. Secrets can be nasty."

"It's not that bad," Mikey said. "I make up stuff with my parents all the time."

"You do?"

"Yeah, just last week I told my dad I was going to—"

Another foot struck Mikey's shin again, and his mouth slammed shut.

"What Mikey means is that it's not as bad as it seems," Tommy explained. "We've done it for so long now, it's sorta like a game to us."

"A game, huh?"

"Yeah, it's not like we're doing something wrong out here. We're helping you out, and I don't think our parents would throw a fit about that. If we were smokin' and drinkin', that would be a different story. But we're just building a fence, you know. We're only playing a little game of 'Don't Tell' so that we can finish what we started."

Mr. Phillips polished off his cup and looked at Tommy with a skeptical eye. Tommy was stretching the truth quite a bit, and we all knew it. Whether we were building a fence, a garage, or a house, our parents would still kill us just the same. A lie was a lie, and no bit of rationalizing would change that.

"Maybe so," Mr. Phillips said, putting his hat back on and glancing out his kitchen window. "It'll be dark soon. We better finish that post while we still have time."

"Can we take our cups with us?" Mikey asked.

"Sure. I don't see why not."

We refilled our drinks and walked out to the sixty-first post. The sun was on the edge of the horizon, telling us that we had less than an hour to finish in daylight. We worked as a team, taking turns pouring and holding. While we cemented, we talked to Mr. Phillips about school and baseball. Even though it was only the beginning of the season, Mikey, as usual, thought the Yankees were going to win the World Series. Randy was pulling for the Braves, and Tommy and I took the Dodgers. Lucy and Jason didn't have an opinion about it, and just listened to us argue about which team had the best outfielders and pitchers. Occasionally, we'd take sips from our Dixie cups, which were scattered on the floor around us, and relished the cool breezes that would sometimes blow by. Since the sun was no longer scorching our heads, an unbearable afternoon had transformed into a pleasant, early evening.

When the cement hardened, we checked the alignment. It was imperfect—a little less than sixteen feet from the next post, and an eighth of an inch from the string—but not enough to throw our rails off. Mikey, using a carpenter's level, verified that the top of the post was even with the ground.

"Then that's it," Mr. Phillips said, smiling at us.

We smiled back, and took a long look at the work we had completed. Sixty-one posts. Sixty-one light-brown poles standing straight up toward the sky. It was living proof of six months of sweat and toil. It was hard to believe that we had done the work ourselves. The posts made a perfect half-square, following the line of string Mr. Phillips had put out the first day we had started. It was laid out exactly as the blue-prints had specified. How could it be the work of a bunch of thirteen-year-olds? Certainly an expert had helped us out.

But it was *only* us.

We had completed the first half of the fence under the guidance of Mr. Phillips. What had once seemed to be a stupid, impossible, time wasting project, was now an interesting challenge. If we made it this far, couldn't we make it the rest of the way?

Mr. Phillips retraced the fence backwards, counting the posts as he went, and we followed behind him. We formed a long line: Jason in the front, tapping the posts with the Michigan hat in his hand; Tommy next in line, strolling as if taking an early morning walk in a park; Lucy trailing behind, her hair blowing in the wind, her soft fingers brushing against the woodgrain posts; Randy behind her, counting to himself as he walked; me following Randy, striking each one with the palm of my hand; and Mikey bringing up the rear, skipping along happily, whistling some unknown tune.

Fifty percent was finished. The other half was just around the corner.

Chapter 24

It Hits the Fan

Trouble was bound to hit the Vineyard. We could all feel it, like a dark thundercloud forming over our heads, waiting to strike at a moment's notice. Six months was a long time to keep a secret and something was bound to give. We didn't know how, where, or when, but we knew it would happen. Sooner or later.

The first problem came a week after we had completed the posts. It happened on a hot Thursday afternoon. New Mexico was going through a dry spell, one that had already lasted over two months. It was abnormal weather even for Huckleberry, which usually averaged around twenty inches of rainfall annually. Temperatures rose to record highs and the air was uncomfortably dry. Neighbors set their lawn sprinklers to water twice a day—sometimes thrice, depending on how brown their grass looked. The heat shriveled spring flowers and killed off the early fruit tree blooms. The mayor issued a code green state of emergency—there were three stages: green, yellow, and red, red being the worst—calling for all Huckleberry residents to ration their water. Because the city was essentially an oasis in the middle of a desert, water had to be used sparingly. The warnings rarely worked, though, and they usually had the opposite effect on motivations. Nervous residents would soak their gardens or crops, sure that the water would soon run dry: it was *the better get it now before it runs out* kind of attitude.

On that blistering Thursday, we were nailing the rails on the fence. There were three rails for every two posts, and special divots were at each end where a four-inch nail would eventually attach the rail to the post. Hammering rails was easier than cementing posts, but it was still hard work that required a person at each end. Tommy worked with Jason, Mikey with Randy, and I was with Lucy. We attacked the fence, drinking more water than the mayor would approve of, and sweated like dirty pigs. When the heat got too much for us, we'd take a break under the scarred oak's shade.

At the end of the day, I happened to glance over my shoulder while waiting for Lucy to hammer in her side of the rail. At first, I couldn't believe what I saw. I was sitting on my haunches, and about seventy yards to my right, propped up on the ditch embankment, was a figure of a man. The heat waves rising from the ground made the figure unreal, like a mirage playing tricks on my eyes. The person walked across the ditch bridge and moved closer to us. I stood up to get a better look. My heart raced, for no one had ever seen us working in the Vineyard before, at least no one I could recall. I squinted my eyes and my jaw dropped to the floor.

"Oh, crap!"

"What?" Lucy asked, her eyes still on the rail.

The person stopped in his tracks. He was far enough away to keep a safe distance from us, but close enough to reveal his identity.

"What's goin' on, Davy?" Lucy asked, this time staring at me.

"See that guy?"

I pointed to the figure. The rest of the Gang crowded around me, obviously as curious as I was.

"Damn, is that who I think it is?" Tommy said over my shoulder.

"Sure looks like it," I replied.

It was Loony Tony Sanders. I would recognize his greasy hair, scarecrow frame, and pasty skin anywhere in Huckleberry. I couldn't make out what he was doing, but it was clear that he was staring at us–probably with the same freaky grin I had seen on him a hundred times before.

"What does he want?" Lucy asked.

"Nothin'," Tommy replied. "He's just snoopin'."

After a few minutes, Tony crossed the bridge again and disappeared over the embankment.

"Crud, we're screwed now," Jason said, angrily kicking a dirt clod.

"He'll tell for sure," Mikey said, shaking his head. "He'll sing to Dan, Bruce, and Ricky, and before long, everyone in the neighborhood will know."

"Including our parents," Randy added glumly.

We stared at the floor. Tommy opened his mouth in an effort to console us, but closed it dejectedly without uttering a sound. There was nothing preventing Tony from telling the others. Had it been another kid from the neighborhood or from school, we might have stood a chance of chasing him down and stopping the damage before it was too late—catch the brat by the collar and threaten that if he didn't keep his lips zipped, he'd suffer the consequences. But not Loony. Loony would whip us if we tried that. The fact that it was six against one didn't matter either: he was psycho, and we all knew he wouldn't think twice about jabbing that ivory switchblade deep into our stomachs.

Spill your guts like spaghetti.

"Come on," Tommy finally said, "let's get back to work."

***

For the next two weeks we waited for things to hit the fan. It would come in the form a phone call, probably from Tommy, telling us that Dan had told his mom and dad what he'd heard from Tony. The phone soon became our worst enemy. We would jump at every ring, thinking it was the inevitable call that would ruin our plans. I couldn't count the number of times I wanted to rip the menacing device out of the wall.

The call never came, though. After two weeks, Loony, for some reason, had kept what he had witnessed to himself. We frequently talked about it while working in the Vineyard. Mikey guessed that Tony just didn't know what we were doing out here and therefore thought nothing of it. Jason thought that the person we had seen maybe wasn't Tony after all, but just a passer-by, taking a casual stroll along the ditch. I was certain the person we had seen was Tony, and so was the rest of the Gang. As I said before, you can't mistake a creepy figure like that. You can almost *feel* his dark presence.

Randy came up with the best theory. He thought that Tony had probably figured out why we were out here and had decided to use the information against us at the perfect moment, when we were almost done with the fence. "Why rat on us now when he could wait until we were on the last dozen rails?" Randy asked us. He could screw us right before finishing the project. Randy's guess was a stretch, but it fit Tony's personality perfectly. The plan was evil and calculated. Tony, unlike Bruce and Ricky, was a thinking cat. I had heard a rumor that Loony had taken an IQ test and had scored close to one hundred sixty. I wasn't sure whether that information had any truth to it, but it was certainly believable. You could see it in his cold eyes. I'd seen it the day Tony showed me how to kill a man by cutting his stomach open. Only Loony would know something like that. If Ricky and Bruce were to get in a fight, they'd simply stab the sucker—three or four quick jabs to the chest. Tony worked on an entirely different level, one that made him the scariest kid on the block. If given the choice between Dan and Tony, I'd take Dan any old day of the week. No doubt about it.

Whether or not Tony would eventually tell on us was out of our control. We couldn't do anything to stop it, and worrying about it was pointless. All we could do was build our fence. Progress moved along smoothly. We had put up forty-five out of one hundred and eighty rails and it looked like we would be finished with the project before the end of the school year. Mr. Phillips occasionally complimented our work. "She's takin' form," he'd say, and "It's one amazing beauty." He tried to help out when he got the chance, but the jobs in the garden and around his house kept him away most of the time.

Just when things were returning to normal after Tony's visit, we got more bad news. It came at the end of March, and it didn't come from Dan, Bruce, Ricky, or even Tony. It was Mikey. His mother wanted to see us play baseball.

"She's gettin' antsy, guys. We better put this game on soon," Mikey said.

We were sitting beside the scarred oak, taking one of our afternoon breaks. Mr. Hops was in the middle of our semi-circle, bathing in a small Tupperware dish filled with water—a luxury Mikey had given him to fight off the dry sweltering heat. His coffee-brown eyes stared at us with curiosity, and his bubble throat moved in and out in rhythmic motions. Every afternoon after work, Mikey placed Mr. Hops inside his toad house and left him by the scarred oak, and the following day, to our surprise, we'd find him in the same spot. Mr. Hops was a very unusual amphibian.

"Yeah, I guess he's right," Tommy said, chewing on a grass strand. "It's 'bout time."

"Are we gonna play Frankie's team?" Jason asked, inhaling from his aspirator.

"Nuh uh, Frankie sprained his wrist last Wednesday," Tommy replied. "Looks like they won't be playing for three, maybe four weeks. I was thinkin' the Strikers."

"Adam's team?" Randy asked. "But they're awesome."

"Yeah, they've only lost two games this year," I said. "They'll absolutely kill us."

Tommy chewed the grass and thought about it for a second. If we were going to make it a legitimate game, one with all of our parents standing on the sidelines, we had to look like real players. Our dilemma was simple. We hadn't practiced since September, and if we played against Adam's team, they would make us look like idiots. My mother didn't know two bits about baseball, but if we were matched up against the Strikers, it wouldn't take a genius to figure out which side spent their afternoons in a grassy ball field and which spent theirs in a field filled with weeds and posts. And if my dad showed up, you could forget about it. We might as well tell them about our Vineyard secret.

"What about Billy's team?" I asked.

"Not enough players," Tommy replied. "We're gonna need at least three extra men on our team if we play, and they barely have nine."

"I heard Kevin's got his own team this year," Mikey said.

"I heard that, too," Randy said. "We should ask him."

Tommy nodded at the suggestion and spit on the ground. Forming teams at Roosevelt was an art. Kids came and went like flies. Teams were always splitting up and changing sides. One week it would be Gregory and the Lightning Rods, the next it would be Luke and the Slammers. Loyalty was a rare commodity. Kids always wanted to play for the winning team, and consequently most teams barely made it past one season. The only exception was Adam and the Strikers, which had been going strong for the past three years.

"Then Kevin it is," Tommy said with authority. "I'll talk to him on Monday. We'll set up the game for next week or something."

"Should we tell our parents about it?" Mikey asked.

"No, not yet. Wait until I clear it with Kevin first. That way we know it's for sure."

We agreed with the plan and made our way back to the fence. Our five-minute break had become a fifteen-minute chat period. Mikey left Mr. Hops in his hot tub; the little guy was happily bathing in paradise.

***

Tommy never got a chance to talk to Kevin. He wasn't given an opportunity because Randy dropped a bomb on us on Sunday morning that changed everything.

My doorbell rang at exactly ten o'clock. I heard it while eating a ham omelet brunch with my family at the kitchen table. Lewis clapped with delight.

"Someone here! I get, I get!"

"No, stay here, honey," my mother replied, wiping her hands on her butterfly-checkered apron and shuffling toward the door. "I've got it."

My father's eyes never left the sports section of the Sunday paper, and I continued to eat and read Mikey's newest edition of Mad magazine. I had to pay Mikey twenty-five cents for the rights to read it before Jason and Tommy; Mikey, of course, always charged more for first dibs on his subscription. I was absorbed in a juicy article about a woman who had given birth to five werewolves. Quality reading.

Traditionally, our Sunday brunch was followed by a trip to the Huckleberry Catholic Church, where we'd sit for an hour as Father Stevens warned about the sins of premarital sex, drug abuse, and compulsive gambling. That was our usual schedule, but because Uncle Larry's flight from Houston was due in at eleven-thirty, we were going to miss out on Father Stevens' lecture. Uncle Larry, an unmarried electrical engineer, was my father's younger brother. He frequently flew to New Mexico to ski the mountain slopes of Hillerman, Santa Fe, or Taos. Hillerman's snow was melted and so was Santa Fe's, but Taos still had another three feet at its base. It wasn't good skiing—unless you liked slush during the mornings and ice during the afternoons—but it suited Larry just fine. As long as he got his annual ski trip in, Larry remained in good spirits.

"Davy!"

"Yeah, Ma?" I asked, looking up from the magazine.

"It's for you."

My dad looked at me and I shrugged my shoulders. I wasn't expecting any visitors. "Okay, Ma," I replied.

Randy stood at our front door, wearing his Sunday best: tan khaki slacks, a white polo shirt, and brown loafers. Mikey and Tommy were beside him, clad in regular T-shirts and blue jeans.

"What's goin' on?" I asked.

"We need to talk," Randy told me, looking frightened.

"About what?"

Randy shuffled his feet and glanced at my mother standing behind me. Tommy had the same terrified expression as Randy, and Mikey looked like he had suffered a stroke.

"I can't say here, can you come to the park with us?"

"Well, I'm eating right now and my uncle is—"

"It's really important, Davy," Tommy said.

I glanced at Mikey's pale complexion again, nodded, and asked my mother. She told me it was okay as long I came back in time to join her in picking up my uncle. I rushed upstairs, slapped on my sneakers, and flew back down.

"I'll be back soon," I told my mom, shutting the door.

We walked to the edge of my driveway in silence, where it seemed like a safe distance to talk. I couldn't hold out until the park.

"What's goin' on?" I asked.

"We're screwed," Mikey said.

"What do you mean?"

Randy stared at Mikey and Mikey glanced at Tommy.

"Come on, guys," I said. "Spit it out."

"My mom knows," Randy finally said.

Suddenly, my knees buckled and I stopped cold in my tracks. A lump the size of a bowling ball was caught in my throat. "What do you mean?"

"She knows about the Vineyard work."

"What! How? Was it Tony?"

"No, he wasn't the reason," Randy said. "It was my fault, but I didn't mean it to happen. I swear, Davy."

"What happened?"

Randy swallowed and scratched his crimson head. "My mom and I stopped by the grocery store after church. We do it every Sunday and I hate goin', but she always brings me with her. Anyway, while we were in the bakery aisle, we saw Mrs. Jackson—you know, Glenn's mom. Mrs. Jackson and my mom started talked about this and that, and before long they were discussing our baseball games. My mom told Mrs. Jackson about our game with Glenn's team last Wednesday. It was a lie, of course, but I'd completely forgotten I'd even told her about it. Mrs. Jackson frowns at my mom, real confused, you know, and tells her she thought Glenn went to band practice that day."

"Oh no," I replied. "What did you tell her?"

"I had to make somethin' up fast, so I told her that Glenn left the game early. It was a stupid thing to say and I wish I could take it back, but I couldn't think of anything better. They were breathing down my neck. So then my mom says I told her that Glenn hit two homers that day. I was caught in my own lie, Davy. I friggin' pinned myself. Mrs. Jackson became dead serious and asked me to tell the truth. 'Did Glenn skip out on band practice that day?' she asks. What was I gonna tell her? I couldn't say we just made the whole game up...then my mom would wonder why I lied to *her*. So I said yes, that Glenn skipped out."

"Crap," I said, squeezing my hands into two hard fists.

"After we got home from the grocery store, Glenn calls. He wants to know why I lied like that, and is beggin' for me to bail him out. His mom is pissed as heck at him. Gonna whip him, he says, if he doesn't start telling the truth."

"So you talked to her?"

"I had to, Davy. I couldn't let Glenn sink like that."

"Damn!" I said.

"Friggin' incredible, ain't it?" Tommy asked, pounding his fist in his hand.

"Mrs. Jackson then talks to my mom," Randy continued, "and my mom asks why I made it up."

"You told her everything?" I asked, screaming it. "Everything about the Vineyard?"

"Sorry, Davy. I tried to get out of it. I swear! I cross my heart and hope to die. I really, really tried. But I just couldn't lie to her face like that. Not my mother."

As much as I wanted to knock Randy's teeth out, I couldn't blame him. The Boy Scout king couldn't lie worth anything. Honesty was a part of his sacred oath. The fact that we had made it this far without getting caught was nothing short of a miracle.

"Man, what do we do now?" I asked.

"First we gotta tell Jason about it, too," Tommy replied.

"What about Lucy?"

"She's out of town," Mikey said, squinting his nose underneath his glasses. "Visiting family in Roswell."

I stared at the ground and watched a lone black ant crawl up my shoe. My size eight sneaker looked like a mountain compared to the tiny insect.

"We're really screwed this time, Davy," Tommy said.

I looked up and saw Tommy's frightened blue eyes. Seeing that lost look in his eyes and hearing his drab, hopeless voice made my blood freeze.

Tommy was our steady rock, and if *he* said we were out of luck, we had to brace for the mess that would follow. "What if we don't tell our parents?" I asked, trying to find an out. "What if Randy just tells his mom that we told them?"

Randy shook his head. "She'd find out anyway. She'll ask your dad, or Mikey's mother, or maybe Jason's old man. They'll find out whether or not we tell them."

"Yeah, and it's a lot better if they get the news from us," Mikey said.

Randy nodded and Tommy agreed. I tried to see it from their perspective, but I simply didn't agree that things would go easier if my parents heard the lie from me or from Mrs. Sachs. My folks were going to ream me one way or the other, and as far as I was concerned, the longer it took for them to find out, the better. "I can't believe you told her about it!" I said, turning my anger to Randy again.

"I didn't have a choice," Randy said. "I didn't think that—"

"We had a pact, remember? The secret would stay between us."

"I know, Davy, I remember. But you had to be in my shoes."

"Try being in my shoes when my dad brands my ass red," Tommy said.

"Mine, too," Mikey added.

Randy's pale blue eyes moved from me, to Mikey, to Tommy, and eventually settled on his fumbling hands. He had blown it, and we couldn't help but feel sorry for him.

"I'm sorry, guys," Randy said.

We remained silent while a cool breeze blew past us. Clouds were rolling in from the west, and the morning sun would be covered by early afternoon. A humming-bird zoomed in front of us, its wings flapping a hundred beats per second, and took off as quickly as it had appeared. The smell of freshly cut grass hung in the air.

"We'll deal with it," Tommy said, patting Randy on the back. "We better get Jason now."

Randy tried to smile at Tommy but his quivering lips wouldn't let him. "Okay," Randy replied.

We made our way to Jason's house, picturing every possible punishment that lay ahead. Whippings. Groundings. Scoldings. Imagining what would happen was worse than actually going through it.

***

Jason took the news better than we thought he would. Had his aspirator not been stuffed in his mouth, he might have screamed Randy's head off. He triggered a record seven hits after hearing Randy's story. He was gasping so hard that at one point we thought we might have to call an ambulance to take him downtown; he eventually regained his breath and color, and told us it was just a bad attack. He *did* share a few four-letter words with Randy, but he was more concerned about how he would break the news to his dad.

I stayed with the Gang as long as I could. Going with my parents to pick up Uncle Larry was the last thing I wanted to do at that moment. I needed more time to think about what I would tell my parents. If I could somehow downplay the Vineyard work, making it a small project, I could maybe get off with just a scolding.

We just got in a little trouble, Mom. Mikey only broke a window, that's all. We're only payin' off a small debt. We'll be done soon.

It was wishful thinking. The fact that the window had cost Mr. Phillips eight thousand dollars would not be taken lightly. There was no way to successfully broach the subject without my folks flipping out.

After spending a good thirty minutes in Jason's backyard, pondering my fate with my friends, I decided to head home. Randy, Tommy, and Jason split up, too. Home was the last place Mikey wanted to go. He talked of such foolishness as running away, or living in Mr. Phillips's house. "He won't mind," Mikey told us. "He's got plenty of empty rooms in there." Mikey was in panic mode, and any thought that entered Mikey's thick skull, no matter how illogical or unsound, gushed out of his sweating lips in a chaotic downpour. You could see the terror in his magnified eyes, moving side to side, searching for an answer.

Once we broke up, I checked my watch and sprinted home. I was running five minutes late.

***

"Hurry up, Davy," my mother yelled, standing beside our green Suburban in the driveway. "You'll keep Uncle Larry waiting."

I jumped into the back seat and strapped myself in next to Lewis. My father shot me an irritated glance in the rearview mirror and sped off in a cloud of dust.

"You know how we hate to be late to the airport," my mother said.

"I know, Ma, I'm sorry," I replied, barely hearing what she had said. Lewis was playfully running a toy car along the edges of his window. He was dressed in a tight red-and-white striped shirt and green khakis.

I told my parents right away. It was akin to the old Band-Aid method—one quick rip and it would be all over with. Procrastination was usually my favorite route, but I couldn't take that road this time—the weeds of deceit were growing out of control, coiling their nasty, fingering roots around my neck, literally choking the truth out of me. It wasn't the best time to break the news to my parents since they were already upset, but I couldn't wait any longer. Not anymore. Not after seven months of suppressing the secret.

"Mom, Dad, I have something to tell you," I said, swallowing as I said it. The words escaped my mouth, and there was a part of me that wanted to grab them and put them back where all the dirty lies were kept—deep inside.

"Can't it wait?" my mother asked, thumbing through a bed catalog. She had talked my father into buying a new mattress because their old one hurt her back.

"I wish it could," I said. My father glared at me in the rearview mirror and my mother turned around. I had second thoughts about telling them as soon as I saw my mother's impatient face. *It's too late to back out now,* I thought.

"What is it?" my mother asked.

I swallowed and wiped my sweaty hands on my legs. "Well, I guess I should start at the beginning," I said.

And so I told them. I spared no details: how Mikey's foul ball had broken Mr. Phillips's window; how we had tried to get away but had been caught when Mikey sprained his ankle; how Mr. Phillips had told us about the damage we had caused; how I had been working with Jason, Randy, Tommy, Lucy, and Mikey on a three-rail ranch fence for the past seven months to pay Mr. Phillips back for the money that we had cost him.

My father asked me to repeat this last bit of information.

"How much?" he asked, his voice a little faint.

"Eight thousand, sir," I told him. I was glad that I could only see part of my father's face in the mirror. If he was gnashing his teeth or wincing in pain, it was unknown to me. My mother's reaction, on the other hand, was perfectly visible. She was completely appalled.

"Why did you lie to us?!" my mother blasted at me. "Why didn't you tell us from the start?"

"I would have, Mom, but I was scared," I said. "I was gonna tell, but it was a secret between all of us."

"You're in big trouble, Davy Blake!"

"But Mom, it wasn't all my fau—"

"Shush! I don't want another word out of you until we get home. We're going to have a serious talk about this, young man. Oh boy!"

My mother turned her back to me and threw her catalog to the floor. My father was gripping the steering wheel so tightly that his knuckles were bone white. I stared out the window and secretly cursed at myself for telling them. I wondered if Tommy and Jason and Mikey had told their parents yet. Randy was already out of luck since his mother would certainly tell his father. Lucy, however, had it easy—she still had another day before finding out that disaster had struck, and another day seemed like an eternity at that moment.

Uncle Larry was at the curb with his luggage. We could tell that he had been waiting for some time, which obviously didn't help matters for me. We loaded his luggage, exchanged our hellos, and jumped back into the car. The ride home was filled with conversation about work, family, and old friends. I politely answered my uncle's questions about school and sports, but that was the extent of my input. My mother's frequent glares made it clear that I was to keep my mouth zipped until she could let me have it at home.

When we arrived at the house, I rushed upstairs and shut my door. I buried my head under the sheets, closed my eyes and tried to think of better things. Every thought, though, funneled into what my punishment would be. Unfortunately, Mom and Dad were busy talking with Uncle Larry downstairs. It made the wait unbearable; if they were going to whip or yell, I wanted them to do it right away. But it wasn't going to work that way. It was their turn to wait it out. I had put off telling them for seven months, and now I was getting a taste of my own medicine. They wanted me to squirm, to suffer. I was at their mercy, and it was their plan to show none.

I felt every painful minute tick slowly by.

Chapter 25

THE MEETING

Pat'O pulled the bus beside me, swung the door open, and greeted me with a warm, Irish smile.

"Top of the mornin', Davy," Pat'O said, his red afro swaying like an autumn hedge on a windy day.

"Morning," I said.

I waved, boarded the bus, and made my way to the back. Mikey was hunkered in a window seat in the second to the last row. I sat next to him and stuffed my green backpack underneath the chair in front. Mikey took off his glasses and stared at me with beady little eyes.

"You tell 'em?" Mikey asked.

"Yep, you?"

"Yeah, they're grounding me until May."

"Really? You got it easy. I'll be lucky if I can play again before school's out. My parents screamed at me for almost two hours last night. I've never seen them so worked up before."

"Did they hit you?"

"Na, yours?"

"Nope. I thought they would give a spanking or something, but I guess I'm too old for that now."

I nodded. My father had only whipped me two times. The first happened when I was very young, and it was for something minor yet potentially deadly: crossing the street without permission. The second thrashing occurred when I was nine years old. I was tinkering around with my dad's tools in the garage and accidentally stumbled upon his gas-powered chainsaw, a twenty-five-inch tree cutter. The teeth of the saw were sparkly and sharp, and it had a red plastic handle with a black trigger. Green streaks lined the stainless steel cutting blade from top to bottom—evidence of the blood from tree limbs and shrubs that had crossed its ferocious path. I thought it would be neat if I gave the cord a good yank to see what would happen. I'm not sure if I actually thought it would start. It looked much too deadly and dangerous to be activated simply by pulling on a string. I held the handle with my left hand and pulled with my right. It fired up on the first try. The saw vibrated to life with a riveting sound that made me fall backward. I watched the beast shake on the ground as smoke poured out of its exhaust vent—the chain wasn't spinning, thank goodness, for I had to pull the trigger for that. I desperately wanted to shut it off, but I was too afraid to touch it in fear that it would take off my hand. I stared hopelessly for what seemed to be hours before my father shot through the door and snuffed the machine out with a flip of a switch. Smoke had filled the garage and I was coughing and choking. My dad opened the garage door, dragged me outside, and laid it on me in our front yard. He stripped off my pants, took off his belt, and stung my cheeks in broad daylight. He whipped me seven times. That's a number I'll never forget as long as I live. Each slash was worse than the one before it. I cried and bawled and begged for mercy as my father scolded me. When he was done he ordered me to my room, and told me to stay in there until dinnertime. I obediently complied.

But that was four years ago. Mikey had a point. We *were* too old for that now. There comes a time when parents can't teach you that way anymore. You grow a little too tall and get a little too heavy, and before long, there's a fear that you might strike back.

But some parents never lose that intimidation factor. Tommy's dad, for example, would sooner die than let his kids have the best of him. Mr. Smith was the head bull and if Dan and Tommy so much as thought about hitting him back, he'd come back with a shotgun and show them what it was really about. It went back to that chain of command thing, with the leader calling the shots.

"They're having a meeting," Mikey said, polishing his glasses and fixing them back on his face.

"What do you mean?" I asked.

"Jason's dad called my parents last night. He wants the parents to meet with Mr. Phillips."

"You sure? We didn't get a call about it last night."

"Yeah? Well, you probably will today. They're gonna round up everybody. Talk about what's been goin' on for the last seven months."

The thought of all the parents getting together with Mr. Phillips made me shudder. Our situation kept getting worse. "Oh no, this really sucks," I said, staring at the passing scenery.

"I wish we would have told them from the beginning."

Pat'O slowed the bus to an ear-numbing, screeching stop, cranked the door open, and waved at Lucy.

"Top of the mornin', Lucy."

"Hey, Pat'O, how's it going?" Lucy asked, climbing inside.

"Not too bad. How 'bout ye self?"

"Okay for a Monday, I guess."

Lucy made her way back, wearing pink shorts, a white collared shirt, and white sneakers. Her golden crucifix lay hidden under her silky brown hair.

Mikey spotted her. “Oh no, I forgot about Lucy.”

“Yeah, me too,” I said, staring at her walk toward us. It had completely skipped my mind that Lucy was still in the dark. She was going to get the information for the first time from me and Mikey, and we hadn’t bothered to think about how we were going to break it to her.

“Hey guys,” Lucy said, sitting next to me.

“Hey, Lucy,” I replied.

I looked at Mikey and Mikey stared at his chubby hands. Mikey would never tell. Not in a million years. His lips would remain cemented just like the time Mr. Phillips had caught us trying to escape. He was more than comfortable shooting his mouth off when talking about food or stupid jokes, but when it came to saying the important things, things that took courage to say, he suddenly lost his voice.

“Lucy, there’s somethin’ we need to tell you,” I said.

Lucy flashed her brilliant green eyes at me. Her skin looked incredibly smooth. “Yeah?”

I looked at Lucy and thought about Randy’s guilty face when he broke the news. I pictured Jason’s shocked expression when we retold the story to him. I tried to imagine the way Lucy would respond after I told her. I took a deep breath. “I don’t know where to start or how to say it.” I looked at Mikey for support, but found none.

Mikey's tail couldn't be tucked any further between his legs. "Our parents know about the fence."

"I know," Lucy said.

I looked back at her in surprise. "You know? How?"

"Jason's dad called. It was about an hour after we got home last night from our trip. I answered and when he asked to speak with my dad, I knew it wasn't good."

"What did he say?" Mikey asked. The weight on his tongue had mysteriously been lifted.

"Not sure exactly," Lucy said. "I think he basically told my dad what you guys already know. That we had been lying to them for the past seven months. That we had broken an expensive window. That he wanted the parents to meet with Mr. Phillips tonight."

"Tonight!" I said. "He said that?"

"Yep, at seven o'clock."

"Oh no," Mikey said. "Crud, Davy, we're gonna get it now. Oh man. Oh geez. We're never gonna see sunlight again. They'll lock us away and throw away the key. They'll—"

"Shut up, Mikey," I said. "Are you sure it's tonight?"

"Positive," Lucy said. "My dad told me right before he sent me to my room. I think they want us there, too."

I stared blankly at the daisies stitched on Lucy's backpack. I wasn't sure if having us there would help matters or make things worse. On one hand, nothing was more nerve-racking than our parents meeting with Mr. Phillips while we waited impatiently at home for the jury to return the verdict. On the other hand, it could be worse if we were stuck in the boxing ring with them. Our very presence might stoke the fire.

"I wonder if Jason's dad has called my parents yet?" I asked.

Lucy shrugged her shoulders and scratched her chin. "Not sure. Probably so. He's callin' everybody."

The bus turned into Roosevelt's parking lot and pulled to another screeching halt. Pat'O ordered us out and we unloaded single file. I followed Lucy off, and Mikey trailed behind me. My watch read 8:15, but it felt closer to noon with the spring sun bearing down on us from the eastern horizon. It was going to be a hot day, and possibly a hotter night.

***

The rumors were confirmed during lunch. Jason's dad had called our parents and had arranged a meeting at Mr. Phillips's house at seven o'clock. Jason, confirming Lucy's words, said we were to join our parents. It was going to be a giant slugfest, with the kids and Mr. Phillips in one corner and the angry parents in the other. Unfortunately, referees wouldn't be there to stop the fight when things got out of hand...when it got too bloody. It would go a full twelve rounds until there was a winner. No holds barred.

"What do you think's going to happen?" Mikey asked.

We were seated at our regular table, chomping on greasy grilled cheese sandwiches and shoestring French fries. Tommy had to pass on the dairy special and settle for last week's meatloaf, which looked about as appetizing as Jason's worn and sweaty Michigan hat.

"Who knows?" Tommy replied. "Whatever it is, it can't be good."

"You can say that again," Jason said.

I took a sip of my soda and stared at Randy, who was still feeling bad about what had happened.

"Maybe they'll just talk about it," Lucy said, brushing her hair away from her face. "You know, chat about what's been going on."

"Chat?" Tommy asked. "Yeah, we wish. They'll be doin' a lot more than that. I'll be lucky if my old man doesn't knock someone's nose in."

"Me, too," Jason added. "I've never seen my dad so pissed before. He's grounded me for the rest of the school year. He even ripped my phone cord out last night. He said he never wants me callin' you guys again. I know what we did was wrong, but man...he's gone friggin' loco."

We glanced at Jason. We all had it pretty bad, but Jason arguably had it the worst. If his dad had gone out of his way to call our folks up, it was a pretty safe bet that Jason's house had been the center of the storm last night. Jason wasn't physically beaten (none of us were, not even Tommy), but the verbal abuse was probably severe enough to give a priest a heart attack. Jason's dad was more than pissed; he was crazy, or loco, as Jason had said.

"I wonder what Mr. Phillips is going to tell them?" Lucy asked.

"Same here," Tommy said. "I wonder if he's going to show them the pieces of that broken window."

"Pieces? Do you think he kept them?" Jason asked.

"Maybe," Tommy replied. "You know, in case he had to use them as evidence against us."

"What do you mean?" I asked. "Why would he do that? We're on friendlier terms now than we were before all of this happened."

"Don't count on it, Davy. I mean, just think about it for a second. All of our parents are going to show up and talk to this strange man that they've never met before. None of them know what we've been doin' with him all this time. To them, he looks like some sicko that's been using us as child labor. Sure, we've gotten to know him better, but that doesn't mean jack shit when it comes to our parents. You remember when he fixed Mikey's ankle and dropped you guys off? Well, he basically lied to your parents that day. He told them you guys were late because Mikey had a bike accident. *That was true*, but he didn't say a thing about the window. Whether or not you call that a lie is one thing, but you can't say that's going to look good tonight. It's cover-your-ass time, and Mr. Phillips has to deliver his best case against us...about why he withheld that information."

Despite what Tommy thought about himself, he was a bright kid—a lot brighter than most people gave him credit for. What he said at the lunch table blew us away.

"Damn, you're right!" I said. "Crap, Tommy. My mother's gonna kill him for that."

"Oh crud, I didn't think about that," Mikey said, the wheels in his head now in overdrive. "He straight out told my ma a friggin' lie. And she'll remember that, too! She never forgets. She's remembered a hundred things my dad's done wrong. Like things that happened ten, fifteen years ago... Oh no. Oh geez!"

Tommy stared at the table and made rings on the warped wood with his Coke can. It was the last day of March, but it felt more like June. Huckleberry's drought still hadn't lifted; the mayor had upgraded the water emergency from code green to yellow. Three heat records had been broken so far and more were expected. Local chili farmers prayed for relief for their thirsty crops, and nervous residents filled churches and synagogues to say their own personal prayers. Scientists and meteorologists attempted to explain the unusual weather, some pointing at rare seasonal anomalies, others at the abnormal atmospheric pressure conditions.

We continued to eat our lunch while pondering the meeting. Our efforts to guess the outcome were about as good as the efforts to predict the weather. Outside forces controlled our fate.

***

I almost went crazy waiting for the clock to reach seven. My mind kept returning to what Tommy had said, and I kept wondering whether my mother would remember her brief encounter with Mr. Phillips. Like Mikey's mother, she was unlikely to forget something like that, but there was always a chance—a very slim one, perhaps—that it might slip her mind.

Jason's dad did get around to calling my parents. I figured that he must have called during the morning, right after I left for school. My mother agreed to the meeting and right after she got off the phone, I guessed, she must have called my father. It probably took less than five minutes to set the stage for tonight.

Eventually, after hours of painful waiting, my parents opened my door; I was grounded and couldn't leave my room.

"Come on, we're leaving," my dad said.

"Okay," I replied, immediately jumping off my bed.

"If you're asked to talk, you better tell the entire truth," my mother said sharply from behind my father. "Understand, young man?"

"Yes, ma'am."

I followed my parents down the stairs and into the garage. Lewis was taking a nap in his room. Uncle Larry hadn't left for his ski trip yet, and he agreed to stay at home until we returned. I desperately wished I could do the same.

***

Driving to Mr. Phillips's house took longer than biking there. Since the car couldn't take the same shortcut over the rickety ditch bridge, the only access to the house was through a long dirt road on the west side. It felt strange traveling down the dusty street, a path I had only seen a glimpse of while working on the fence. Maybe it was the night and the blackness that surrounded our car, or maybe it was the way our headlights illuminated the barren road; whatever it was, it seemed like we were a thousand miles away from our house, in the middle of nowhere.

Four cars were already lined in Mr. Phillips's driveway. It was too dark to make out the first three, but the fourth was unmistakable. It was Blue Streak, Mr. McNeil's shiny BMW. It was at the front of the line, which meant that the McNeils had been the first to arrive.

I trailed behind my parents to Mr. Phillips's front door, walking reluctantly on legs that felt like lead. A sudden instinct to run entered my brain. I could sprint away, shoot straight through the Vineyard, dash over the ditch bridge, and find another home. For a brief instant, Mikey's plan to run away and live life on our own didn't seem all that unreasonable.

"You must be Mr. and Mrs. Blake, I reckon," Mr. Phillips said, opening the door.

"That's correct," my father said, and shook Mr. Phillips' hand.

A handshake, I thought. *At least it's not starting out badly.*

"Yes, well, we've been waiting to meet with you," my mother said, frowning. "It seems we have a lot to discuss."

"You couldn't be more correct, Mrs. Blake. Please, come in."

We entered Mr. Phillips's house and were led to the back. While my parents absorbed the plethora of art pieces decorating the ceiling, floor, and walls, I scoped out the area, looking for the

Gang. I didn't see anyone, although I could hear voices coming from Mr. Phillips's den.

"This is absolutely beautiful," my mother said, her mood slightly brightening.

"You are too kind," Mr. Phillips replied. "I hope it's not hard on the eyes."

"Are you kidding? You could sell this stuff for a fortune. Is it all yours?"

"Yes. At least, most of it. Some of it's my ex-wife's. That part of it is a long story."

My mother stopped and stared at a sculpture of a cowboy lassoing a bull. She ran her fingers over the clay figure, feeling its texture, its delicate, crafted frame. She had forgotten the reason why we were here.

"Honey, just look at this," my mother said, nudging my father.

"I see it," my father replied.

"It must have taken hours to do this."

"Weeks, actually, Mrs. Blake," Mr. Phillips said with a smile. "I had trouble with the bull's head. See this area here?" Mr. Phillips pointed to a section of the sculpture where the clay looked slightly incongruent with the body. "Little bugger broke off six times. I almost called it quits, but I finally got it on the seventh try."

My mother touched the very spot Mr. Phillips pointed to and nodded in appreciation. She then straightened herself and pressed her lips together.

"Yes, well, that's very nice. Where is this meeting, now?"

"Oh, right this way."

Mr. Phillips took us to his den. It was the largest room in the house, with circular walls and four gray couches set in a semi-circle around a cherry wood handcrafted coffee table—another art piece designed by none other than the man who enjoyed wearing straw hats. Mikey sat between his parents on one couch on the right side of the room and Randy was with his folks on a sofa next to them. Jason was on the same couch as the Sachses, with his hands in his lap and his father standing beside him. Mr. Sanchez was clad in a black suit, a gray tie, and a wrinkled face that looked about as angry as a person could look without blowing a few gears upstairs. Lucy was on the third couch with her mother and father on either side of her. Tommy was plopped on the forth sofa, alone.

"I reckon you know the McNeils, the Sachses, the Sanchezes, the Grahams, and Tommy Smith," Mr. Phillips said, introducing everybody. My parents nodded that they had met before, and Mr. Phillips pointed to Tommy's couch. "Please, have a seat."

We took our place, and I exchanged a brief glance with Tommy. *Where were Mr. and Mrs. Smith?*

"Now that the Blakes are here, I think we should get started," Mr. Phillips said. He wore a white dress shirt, bright blue jeans, and brown loafers. His thick hair was parted to one side and his face was perfectly shaven. I had never seen him look so sharp. “But first, Tommy? Are you sure your parents aren’t going to make it?”

Tommy looked up and shook his head. “They’re busy tonight,” Tommy said, swallowing. “They’ve asked me to come so I can report what happens tonight.”

Mr. Phillips rubbed his hands together and looked at his watch. “Fair enough. I should begin so I don’t keep everyone past bedtime.”

He paced around for a minute and then stopped and raised his gaze. “The whole mess began at the end of last summer. I was in my kitchen skimming through a catalog I had picked up for the purpose of buying more material for a ranch fence I wanted to build around my property. Your children were playing ball in a field not far from my house. I knew it because could hear their distant hollers and laughter...a sound I had heard many times over the course of several years. Anyway, I was there reading, not thinking much of their playtime activity, and the next thing I knew I heard this terrible crash from my second floor. It sounded like someone breaking into my house. I suppose I would have thought the same had it not been for the glass fragments I saw come raining down on my roses in my backyard garden. They were pieces of an expensive stained-glass window I had purchased from a famous artist in Santa Fe. A powerful hunch hit me at that moment. I knew running up the stairs was the wrong decision. My gut told me I had to dash outside to seek answers for what had happened. Sure enough, my gut proved right. I saw your kids in a wild panic, fleeing the field as fast as their skinny legs would take them. I took off after them. Now, I'm the first to admit this was a dumb decision on my part. My joints have seen more replacements than the limbs on the bionic man. The fragments in my rosebushes could have easily complemented the plastic fragments of my knees and shoulders as I attempted such a foolish feat at my age. I'm long past my prime football years, let me tell you. But run I did, and God's good grace carried me all the way to where your kids were playing ball without falling on my face. The culprits were on their bikes at this point, making dust. Watching them, I knew I didn't stand a chance on foot, and I was positive all I was going to do was shake my fist and yell in vain as they got away. Only it didn't turn out that way. One boy came crashing down his bike. Another stopped to help him. Divine intervention struck yet again. Those two boys were Mikey and Davy."

Mr. Phillips paused his story and looked at both me and Mikey. He shook his head and exhaled a soft laugh. "Davy had the fear of death in his eyes when he saw I had caught them. It was a sight to see, I tell you... Now, a few of you folks here already know that Mikey had injured his ankle and that I had helped patch him up in my house. What you don't know is that I ordered all of the kids back to my property so they could own up for what they did and right the wrong they had caused. To be honest, at the time I really didn't know what I was going to have them do. Simply having them sweep my house, do my dishes, or perform some other trivial task didn't make sense at all. That window cost me eight thousand dollars, you see. I needed a larger project. It had to be something that really fit the damage they had caused. So that night, after I had dropped off Mikey and Davy, it came to me while I was in my kitchen as I picked up the catalog I had dropped on the floor in fright when the incident happened. *The ranch fence*. It was perfect. The project was large, fairly easy to understand, and it would completely make up for the debt they owed. I explained all of this to the kids at our next meeting. They agreed with the plan, and that basically takes us to where we are today. I want all the parents here to know that I do feel terrible about the lying that resulted because of it. I should have worked this arrangement out with the parents, too, and I take full responsibility for any pain I might have caused as a result of my decisions. I ask for your forgiveness in that regard."

Mr. Phillips stopped his story and glanced around at the group. It was now the parents' turn to fire back, and Jason's dad wanted the first strike.

"Like hell do you have my forgiveness," Mr. Sanchez thundered. "I feel no sympathy for what you have done! It's one thing for our kids to lie about this, but for an adult to help instigate it? It's ridiculous! You've had our kids slaving away in your backyard for well over half a year. And for what? A stupid damned window?"

"Mr. Sanchez, please understand...it was more than just a window, it was—"

"I heard what you said and I know the stupid price tag. Frankly, I could care less. I'm sure it was a *grand* piece of art."

There was a hint of sarcasm behind Mr. Sanchez's voice as he put emphasis on the word "grand." I could see where Jason had inherited his wiseass mouth.

Mr. Phillips opened his arms in a peaceful gesture. "I think if you saw it from my perspective, you'd have a better appreciation of the situation. I think that you'd—"

"Don't you dare tell me I would do the same thing! You and I are nothing alike. I've been taken advantage of hundreds of times in my life, working for meager pay-checks and taking crap from bosses who were as dumb as stones. I've worked my tail off to get where I'm at, and it will be a cold day in the pit of Hades before I let my son go through the same thing. Consider yourself fortunate if I don't press charges. Vamonos, Jason!"

Mr. Sanchez grabbed Jason by the arm and Jason tried to shake off his grip.

"But Dad, I don't want to—"

"Cállate. I said come on, boy!"

Jason reluctantly followed his father, and shortly after they left the room, we heard the front door slam. Mr. Phillips furrowed his brow and the parents stared at each other in shock. I thought it rather ironic that the man who had called the meeting had been the first to walk out on it.

"I handled that well," Mr. Phillips said, forcing a smile. Lucy's mom smiled back at him. It was a warm smile from a stunningly beautiful woman. I saw where Lucy had gotten her looks and grace.

"Mr. Phillips, my wife and I didn't come here today to threaten you," my dad said. "I think like most of us here, we want to reach a reasonable solution." My father looked at the other parents and they nodded with him. "In fact, I spent some time talking to my wife about all of this before coming out here, and we don't entirely disagree with what you did. They *did* break your property, and whether or not it's worth all the time building this fence is really none of our business. It was a part of your house and they destroyed it. Now, as you mentioned, I can't say we agree with the lies that have been told in the process, or the way the work has progressed secretly, but I can say that you've given our kids a valuable lesson. A better one, I'm sure, than simply grounding them as we would have done."

"I agree with Mr. Blake," Mr. Sachs said. "I'm actually glad you made these kids work for you. I think it teaches integrity. Heck, Randy talked to us for three hours last night about some of the things you've taught him. Said he learned a lot about cementing posts."

Randy blushed and picked aimlessly at his blue T-shirt. His face was one shade lighter than his hair.

"Yes, we are in the same boat," Mrs. McNeil said. Both Mr. and Mrs. McNeil were short and round and looked like larger versions of Mikey. "And our son just feels awful about hitting that ball. He sometimes thinks this entire thing is his fault." Mikey glared at his mother, obviously angry she had told the group this fact.

"We're all at fault," Tommy said bravely for the Gang. "Not just Mikey alone."

Mr. Phillips scratched the stubble on his chin. "Tommy's right. All the kids were out playing baseball that day. Mikey shouldn't feel bad about it. I'm even a part of this now. And I agree with Mr. Blake. I think the best thing for us to do is find a reasonable solution to this mess."

"Do you have any suggestions?" Mrs. Graham asked.

We stared at Mr. Phillips as he paced for a minute, lost in thought. He finally stopped and rubbed his calloused hands together. "I've had some time to think after I got off the phone with Mr. Sanchez last night. I must be honest with everyone here and say that when the fence project started, I never thought it would go the distance the way it has. I assumed the parents would find out in a matter of days and that that would be the end of it. But for some strange reason, it didn't happen that way. These kiddos managed to secretly build a mighty fine fence over many months, and they've helped me out in more ways than I can say. They've done a job worthy of any award at school, if there was one for buildin' fences." Mr. Phillips started pacing again. I quickly glanced at Tommy, remembering his parents were at home. Busy. "I think they've more than learned their lesson. They've paid their debt and it's fair to say their job is completed."

"You mean you don't need them around at all?" my father asked.

"Yes, Mr. Blake, that's what I'm getting at. I can handle things on my own now. It'll take a bit, but I can complete the rest by myself. I'm very appreciative of their service, and, regarding tonight, your understanding and forgiveness for my own faults."

I couldn't believe what I was hearing. Quit? Now? We couldn't do that. Not after all the work we had put in.

"And you'd completely strike the large debt they owe you?" my father asked.

"Yes, sir," Mr. Phillips replied. "Consider every cent paid and then some."

My father smiled and looked at the other parents. "Well, that sounds like a reasonable deal."

"Yes, it sounds like a great solution to me," Mr. Sachs added.

"We like it," Mr. Graham said, glancing at his wife.

Mrs. McNeil nodded. "Us, too."

I don't, I thought. *That sucks.* I waited for Tommy to say something for us again, to tell them what was so obvious to me. I waited but didn't hear a peep out of him. Randy, Mikey, and Lucy were silent, too.

"Well, I guess that's it, then," Mr. Phillips said. "Is there anything anyone wants to add that hasn't already been said? I've got thick skin, please vent if you need to." There was no reply. I once again waited in vain for the Gang to pipe up. "Well, I guess we're done here."

And with that, the parents stood up. Soon, everyone in the room was standing except me.

"I'm glad we had this meeting," my father said, shaking Mr. Phillips' hand.

"Me, too. I just wish it could have been under better conditions."

Suddenly, I leapt to my feet. "Wait!" I blurted out. Everyone turned around, and my mother glared at me with fierce eyes. I felt like the entire world was watching me.

"Yes, Davy?" Mr. Phillips asked.

"This is no good at all," I said. "We've come all this way, and I want to finish the job! There's nothing wrong with us bein' out there. I don't see why we can't continue."

Mr. Phillips walked over. He was a giant compared to me—roughly the same size and height as my father. He put a hand on my shoulder. "Davy, you don't have to work anymore. I know you're only saying this because you feel guilty."

"I'm not. I swear." I stared at the Gang. "I mean, I don't know about the rest of us, but I wanna do this. It's shitty to quit now."

"Davy!" my mother said. "Watch your mouth!"

"Sorry, Ma, but it's true. Huh, Tommy?"

I desperately hoped that Tommy felt the same way, and was relieved when he nodded. "Yeah, I was kinda lookin' forward to seeing this thing through. I sort of don't want to stop, either."

"Me, too," Randy agreed. "It seems like a waste of time if we did."

"Yeah," Lucy said, looking at her mother. "It's funny, but I don't mind going to Mr. Phillips's house after school. I've gotten used to it."

"That's how I am," Mikey said, adjusting his glasses.

The parents were speechless. A thin grin formed across Mr. Phillips's mouth.

"Y'all aren't pullin' my leg, right?" Mr. Phillips asked, and we shook our heads. "Well, I don't have a problem with it, but it depends on what your parents think."

There was some mumbling in the room.

"It's okay with us," Mikey's mother said. "But Mikey can only return after his grounding is up."

"I don't mind. Do you, dear?" Mr. Sachs asked his wife.

"Well..." Mrs. Sachs wavered, then shrugged. "I suppose there's no harm in it. If the kids want to do it, why not let them?"

Mr. Graham looked at his wife. "We're proud of Lucy. She can continue. Of course, we'll still have to punish her for lying, though."

I stared at my mother, who was still angry at my outburst. My father lightly placed his hand on her arm.

"What do you think, honey?" my father asked.

"I don't know," my mother answered. "I still don't like it."

"Yes dear, but Randy does have a point. It does seem like a waste if they couldn't get the chance to at least finish it. It's a big deal to the kids."

My mother glared at me. She then sighed and rolled her eyes at my father before facing me again. "You are still in deep water, young man. You know that, right?"

"Yes, ma'am," I said, elated she was okay with us continuing.

Mr. Phillips winked at me and cleared his throat. "Wow... Okay... Well, your children can come over whenever they want. If they want to work on weekends rather than weekdays, it's fine as long as they get permission. If you feel more comfortable supervising their work, you can come over, too."

Whatever tension had existed in the room at the beginning of the meeting had flown out the door with Jason and his father. Our parents were beginning to see the side of Mr. Phillips we had grown to know since the start of our school year.

"It's late, we better get going now," my mother said, nudging my father.

Mr. Phillips checked his watch. "Yes, of course. I've kept y'all much too long. Please, follow me."

And that was the surprising end of it. Mr. Phillips showed us to the door, said his goodbyes to the parents, and restated his apology. We had made it through the dreaded meeting without pandemonium. Sure, there was the incident with Jason's father, and we were *still* going to be disciplined at home, but at least we could return to the Vineyard. And returning to the Vineyard, as surreal as it might seem, made us the happiest kids in Huckleberry.

***

JOURNAL DATE: 8/30/01

It's been almost five hours since Nick and I checked out of that shady motel room in Needles. The manager with the crooked teeth bid us farewell at the front desk. "Es got everything you's need? Es nice, no?" I said it was everything I was looking for, which wasn't a complete lie since I wasn't expecting much from a place with a green neon sign that read Nice'n Comfy Inn.

Nick and I then headed west on I-40, passing Topock, Kingman, Seligman, and the small town of Williams. We hit Flagstaff at one o'clock, with full bladders and empty stomachs. Nick said he was craving Taco Bell, so I took the first exit off the freeway and searched for the fast-food restaurant. I easily found one.

It's now one thirty. After consuming three burritos and two tacos, I'm beginning to think I might need to take another trip to the boy's room. Note to self: never eat a flour tortilla stuffed with beans and cheese during a road trip. Our restaurant table, which is roughly the same size as the kiddy desks that litter Nick's fourth-grade classroom, is filled with wrappers, empty hot sauce packets, and used napkins. Nick is drawing and coloring in a sketchbook, and I'm trying to color in the next Chapter in my story—a pink scar has replaced the bandage around the top of my injured thumb.

I'm officially on vacation and I should feel relaxed, but Susan's absence makes me nervous. It's only the second trip I've taken alone with Nick, and our last retreat together was cut short. Two years ago Nick and I took a three-day hiking vacation at Mammoth Mountain. It was Labor Day weekend—a beautiful, sunny September holiday weekend—and since Susan was visiting her mother in Oregon, I figured Nick and I could spend some time with each other while camping in the woods. Unfortunately, Nick took a nasty fall on a steep hill and broke his leg.

Even though that incident happened two years ago, the memory of Nick's fall is as vivid and real now as it was on that Labor Day weekend. I break out in cold sweats whenever he strays more than five feet from me. "It was just an accident," Susan often tells me. "There was nothing you could do about it." *Maybe so,* I'd think, *but nothing like that has ever happened on her watch.* The most Nick has ever sustained under Susan's supervision was an inch-long cut on his chin from falling off the monkey bars, a cut which didn't even need stitches.

Even now, while Nick is coloring a page in his sketchbook, I can think of a hundred things that could go wrong. *What if he falls out of that chair and breaks his nose? What if the straw he's chewing on somehow ends up lodged in his throat? What if he gets food poising from that bean burrito he just ate?* I think it's the same heightened paranoia my mother had with Lewis. Everything is a lurking danger: sharp knives waiting to cut, light sockets eager to shock, plastic bags ready to suffocate.

But it's pointless to think about those dangers. I've got to let it go like Susan said and ignore my fears and phobias. I can tell I've made some progress already on this trip doing just that. I let Nick play with my Swiss Army knife in the car, and while gassing up in Needles, I allowed him to pump the gas, something I would have never done in San Diego. Maybe this trip is not only about helping me remember my youth, but also about helping me forget about being an adult. Maybe it can show me how to have fun again—to let Nick do the things kids do without worrying about all the consequences.

To let him play like I once did with my friends.

Chapter 26

Jason and Mr. Hops

The next day at school, while eating a homemade peanut butter and jelly sandwich at our regular table, Jason told us his father would not permit him to work on the fence anymore. "He's beyond pissed," Jason explained. "He'll never let me come out again." We tried to cheer him up and said his dad would soon see things differently, but Jason had his doubts. He said he had never seen his dad so upset before, not even when his older brother had stolen the family car to go joy-riding with his friends.

Jason wouldn't be the only one missing from the Vineyard. Mr. and Mrs. Graham grounded Lucy for the next three weeks, and Mikey's parents, as Mikey had already told me on the bus, wouldn't allow their son to work until May. For the first three weeks of April, it would be me, Tommy, and Randy working with Mr. Phillips. My mom only let me return on the condition that I understood that a simple grounding wasn't good enough—she had other forms of punishment on her mind.

"Can you take care of Mr. Hops?" Mikey asked me.

"Only if you pay me fifty bucks," I said.

Mikey's magnified eyes stared at me for a second, pondering whether he could afford such a high fee, and then he realized I was ribbing him.

"Just messin'," I laughed. "Of course I'll take care of him, dipstick." I thought about the silly bet Jason and I had made on Mr. Hops. We had both lost. More than four months had passed and Mikey still had the brown toad.

"Remember that he likes flies and crickets. And don't forget to refill his bath once a week. He dries easily."

"Yeah, yeah, I know. I've seen you feed him before."

"Hey, Tommy, did you tell your parents what happened last night?" Randy asked.

Tommy's face tightened. "Yeah, I told them. Why? You don't think I did?"

"No, just wondering, that's all."

Tommy frowned. "Why'd you ask, then? Because I *did* tell them, you know. I told them just like you guys did."

"Relax, Tommy, I believe you," Randy said. "You wouldn't make that up."

Tommy regained his composure and took another gulp of his soda. The thought that Tommy had not told his parents had crossed my mind more than once. When Jason's dad called the Smiths, he only got an answering machine—something Jason had told me between classes. Tommy could have erased that message and kept it a secret. He had all the motive in the world, since telling his old man was like a death sentence.

But Randy was the only one that questioned him about it. I'm certain if it had been another member of the Gang in Tommy's place, more eyebrows would have been raised. Had it been someone like Mikey, he would have been drilled like a suspect in an interrogation room. But not Tommy. It was different with him. Perhaps it was because we trusted him, or perhaps it was because of his cool and collected nature. It was blind faith, I suppose. I didn't find out the details of what had really happened at Tommy's house until weeks later, when he and I went shooting in the Vineyard.

"I'm kinda glad it's in the open now," I said, glancing around the table, feeling my braces with my tongue. I still hadn't gotten used to them in my mouth.

"Same here," Lucy said. A light breeze pushed her hair up behind her neck like a brown parachute. "It feels like a weight has been lifted. I've had trouble sleeping for the last two weeks, but after the meeting, I slept like a baby."

"I've had nightmares," Mikey added. "One's where I wake up sweatin' like a pig."

"That's 'cause you *are* a cerdo," Jason replied.

"Screw you," Mikey replied, throwing a balled up napkin at Jason's sarcastic grin.

"I feel the same as Lucy," Randy said, slapping a fly away from his freckled cheek. "I'm glad I don't have to hide this stuff anymore."

"You can thank Mrs. Jackson for that," I said, "next time you're at the grocery store."

Randy shook his head profusely. "Are you kidding? I'm never goin' again. My Mom can do her own shopping."

"Man, you're one terrible liar," Jason said to Randy.

"You can say that again," Tommy replied, snickering. "Out of all the ways it could have happened, it was at the friggin' grocery store."

"In the bakery aisle," Randy repeated, shaking his head again.

We burst out laughing, picturing Randy at the supermarket, staring dumbly at the loaves of bread while trying to weasel his way out of his own lie.

***

During the next two weeks, Mr. Phillips, Tommy, Randy and I slaved away to keep the fence work going. It was impossible to keep the pace we had started with since our labor force had been stripped in half, but we puttered along, slowly but surely.

We managed to nail thirty rails in ten days, bringing our total to seventy-five. We could have nailed forty to forty-five had we not had problems with the last rails we hammered in. Mr. Phillips had a row of five-foot cypress trees next to our rail pile. The drought that had hit Huckleberry was also taking its toll on these evergreens, and Mr. Phillips was forced to run the hose over them at least once a week. To protect the pile from the water, and small creatures that like to chew on boards, Mr. Phillips covered it with a blue tarp. He had bought the tarp at a flea market for five dollars. The seller had assured Mr. Phillips it was the best money could buy. Perhaps a more accurate statement was that it was the best five dollars could buy. After weeks of watering his cypress trees, with the water innocently splashing against his tarp, Mr. Phillips discovered a little hole no more than an inch wide. He pulled up the cover and revealed layers of warped rails underneath. Some of them were so crooked they looked like props for lightning bolts right out of a grammar school play. The ones that weren't visibly damaged had to be tested to see if they could be salvaged. We spent a good portion of our time aligning the rails to the posts and guessing whether we could save them.

Aside from the slower pace and loss of hands, something else was missing, too. It wasn't the same without Jason's sarcasm, Mikey's slipshod

Clint Eastwood impressions, or Lucy's humor and graceful smiles. I couldn't help but glance at the ditch bridge from time to time, expecting them to ride up on their bikes, the dust kicking up from their rear tires, the wind tossing up their hair as they pedaled down the ditch hill. But they never came.

That's not to say they weren't interested. Lunch hour was news time, and Tommy, Randy, and I would update them on the recent developments: the progress; the stories Mr. Phillips had told; the newest adventures of Mr. Hops and his grand toad house; and the weather in the Vineyard, which was always hot and dry. Our stories captivated everyone, especially Jason. He'd hang on our every word, listening with his metal mouth agape and his brown eyes as wide as pool balls. Once we'd finish he'd trigger a shot of his aspirator and ask more questions, then probe for more information. We tried to answer all that we could. We felt sorry for his situation. We were all equally at fault for what had happened, but he was being punished the hardest for it. It didn't seem fair that he should have to sit at home while we worked. I guess Jason felt the same way. It was a punishment the wiseass wouldn't tolerate.

On the third week, while hammering a rail with Randy and Tommy, Jason yelled at us from behind.

"Hey guys!"

We jumped at the sound of his voice, and the rail we were holding went crashing into the dirt. Jason laughed at our surprise in his usual Ernie chuckle: Hee-hee-hee.

"What are you doing here?" Tommy asked, looking as if he had seen a ghost.

"I've come to say hello. Whatcha think? I've come to kick your culo, Tommy?"

"You're not supposed to be here," Randy said. "What about your dad?"

"Yeah, well, he's at his job right now, and what he doesn't know can't hurt him."

"Man, you have some balls bein' here, Jason," I said.

"Bigger cojones than yours, my friend...bigger cojones than yours," Jason told me with a cocky, silver grin.

Jason squatted down and grabbed Randy's hammer. He then picked up one side of our rail and leveled it to Tommy's post.

"You guys gonna help me or not?" Jason asked, his Michigan hat sitting backwards on his head.

"I don't think this is a good idea," Randy replied. "I mean, if you get caught with us, we could be in some serious—"

"Who's gonna tell?" Jason asked sharply.

Randy looked to Tommy and Tommy stared at me. We shrugged our shoulders. Whether or not Jason was supposed to be out here or not was no concern of ours—that was Mr. Sanchez's problem. We wouldn't say a word.

"What about Mr. Phillips?" I asked.

Jason dropped the board, fished for his aspirator, slapped it against his palm, and took a hit. He inhaled and exhaled and replaced the device in the seat of his pants.

"I'll just hide when he comes," Jason said. "I can see that sombrero de paja comin' from a mile away. He won't know a thing."

We nodded. Yes, it was no concern of ours. Tommy joined Jason at his side of the rail, and Randy and I made for our side.

"Hey! What am I supposed to hammer with?" Randy asked.

Tommy and Jason snickered, elbowing each other. "You'll just have to hold the rail, then," Jason said, giving Randy the same cocky grin he had given me. Randy frowned, and I got a few chuckles at his expense. We aligned the rail and fixed it to the posts.

***

Things went on like that for the next few days. Jason would make an unexpected appearance, join us at the posts, and dash off when Mr. Phillips reared his face. Jason would hide out behind the scarred oak, beside Mr. Hops's house, and wait until the coast was clear. Sometimes it would only be a false alarm—Mr. Phillips moving from one side of his house to the other, watering his garden or trimming his bushes—and Jason would return within minutes; other times Mr. Phillips would join us at the fence, and Jason would be stuck chatting with Mr. Hops for a long spell.

I think it was during these chats that Jason found a new appreciation for the classy amphibian. One day, on a sweltering Huckleberry afternoon that rose into the triple digits, Tommy, Randy, and I took a break from the heat. Mr. Phillips was the one that actually made the suggestion. He had been working with us for over an hour and told us that we should take fifteen while he checked his mail. We gladly agreed. Our shirts were soaked with sweat that felt as warm as engine oil and our sopping hair was pasted against our skulls. We collected our water bottles and made for the oak's shade.

"I don't believe it," I said, pointing.

"Crap me a house," Tommy said, staring in the same direction.

There in front of us, lying flat on his belly like a fish, was Jason, nose to nose with Mr. Hops's water dish. He was refilling the Tupperware tub with a silver canteen of water. Mr. Hops was sitting beside his wooden house, patiently staring at his pool with warm, brown eyes.

Jason quickly scrambled to his feet as soon as he heard our voices.

"Oh, hey guys," Jason said, dusting his legs. "I wasn't expecting you."

"You don't say," Tommy replied, plucking the canteen from his hands. Tommy tipped the silver canister and poured a puddle of liquid in his palm. "Is this water I see?"

"Yeah," Jason admitted, fidgeting with his backward hat.

"Now why would you be pouring water in Mr. Hops's dish? Isn't that Davy's job?"

Randy put his hand on my shoulder and pointed at the floor. "Maybe he slipped on that dirt clod there and it accidentally fell in," Randy cackled. "Surely he didn't do it on purpose."

"Maybe," I agreed, joining in. "Or maybe he's just drinkin' out of the dish himself. You know, see what's it's like to live the fancy life of a toad."

We stared at Jason's flustered face and cracked up. Jason's lips were pressed so tightly against his braces that we could see the outlines of the brackets and wires against his skin.

"All right," Jason said. "Vete al carajo. The slimy freak's bath needed water and I put some in. He looked hot and I felt sorry for him."

"Felt sorry?" Tommy asked, probing further. "How could Senor Jason Sanchez feel sorry for a sapo?"

We chuckled for almost five minutes as Jason cursed us in Spanish. We repeatedly tried to stop, but the image of Jason on his belly kept fueling our laughter. Mr. Hops had made a new, unlikely friend, and we wished on our mother's good names that Mikey could have been there to see it.

And so the responsibility of taking care of Mr. Hops quickly passed to Jason. He brought the little guy his flies and crickets, and when needed, he'd refill his bath with a fresh pool of water. Mikey couldn't have done a better job himself. An American toad never had it so good living in the high desert. By some odd twist of fate, and by some unknown path, Mr. Hops had traveled hundreds of miles to the foreign climate of Huckleberry, and had managed to find a house, a spacious backyard and a pool thrice the size of his body. He was perhaps the luckiest of all toads.

Unfortunately, as saying goes, all good things come to an end. Mr. Hops's fortune was destined to change.

Chapter 27

Two Phone Calls

Jason might have been able to skip out on his punishment, but there was little I could do to escape the wrath of my mother. There was a cost for letting me work in the Vineyard. She made me sweep and scrub the kitchen floor, polish the toilet bowl, remove the green mildew stains off the shower tile walls, and repaint the discolored garage door. She tacked on a hundred other tasks to my list of chores as well—jobs such as dusting the den bookcase, pruning the backyard trees and shrubs, and removing the ashes from the living room fireplace. My mother's mind held a plethora of tiresome, tedious jobs, and she wasn't hesitant about assigning them to me.

She worked me ruthlessly: in the mornings, in the afternoons after the fence work, and on the weekends. I took shelter wherever I could find it. Sometimes my dad would bail me out and take me to get a chocolate ice cream cone or a forty-ounce soda at the nearest 7-11. Sometimes it was Lewis that came to my rescue, asking for help tying his shoes or putting together a puzzle. I graciously accepted the breaks since my mother wasn't half as generous as Mr. Phillips in giving them. I had lied, and that was a cardinal sin to her. Begging for mercy was useless; punishment was the only entrée she cared to serve—at least until she felt I'd learned my lesson.

I also wasn't allowed to visit my friends outside of the Vineyard or have sleepovers. Phone calls, incoming and outgoing, were strictly forbidden. One exception was a call from Lucy on a Saturday afternoon. I had spent six hours doing odd duties around the house with my mother—mopping, sweeping, scrubbing—and was currently digging up weeds in the backyard. The call came at about a quarter till three.

"Davy, it's for you," my mother said.

"Who is it?" I asked, my knees black with soil, my hands throbbing from the stickers of the uprooted plants.

"It's Lucy, I think," my mother said. "She sounds upset."

I stood back up, my knees cracking like two dead branches, and shuffled inside with one hand against the small of my back as if I were three decades older. "Hello?"

"Davy? It's Lucy."

There was a tension in her voice. It was slight, but audible.

"Hey, what's up?"

"Can you meet me at the ditch bridge?"

"Why? What's it about?"

"I don't want to talk about it over the phone. I just need someone to talk to right now."

I picked at the scabs around my hands. One stubborn weed had left a nasty slash on my right hand between my forefinger and thumb. It was on the webbed area of the skin, and every time I opened my hand, it would reopen the wound with a sickening tear that I could feel in every nerve of my body.

"I'll have to ask my mom."

"Okay. Give me a call if you can't make it. If you don't call, I'll meet you there in fifteen minutes."

"All right," I replied, and hung up.

I strolled back outside and asked my mother. I was certain she'd say no.

"She wouldn't have called if it wasn't serious. You better go see her, Davy. Don't spend too long, though. You've got more weeds to work on."

"Yes, ma'am," I replied, staring at the dreaded plants in my mother's garden. The weeds had literally grown out of control.

I made for the garage, grabbed my ten-speed, and pedaled to the ditch. I bit my lip as my sore legs and hands protested against the cycling.

***

Lucy beat me there. She was sitting in the middle of the wooden ditch bridge, wearing a black dress and matching black sandals, tossing yellow dandelions into the trickling water below. She had almost a dozen golden flowers in her lap, and they seemed so bright sitting against the black background that they almost glowed like miniature suns.

"Hey, Lucy," I said, laying my bike on the floor next to her pink ten-speed.

"Hey," Lucy said, looking at me with a warm, yet gloomy smile.

I sat next to her, feeling the heat of the bridge seep through my shorts, and stared at the water. It wasn't muddy like it usually was when I passed over it on my way to the Vineyard. It was clear—so clear I could see smooth, colored pebbles and sparkly sand on its rippled floor. Lucy tossed a dandelion in the slow current and we watched it bob and dip down the stream.

"Thanks for coming," Lucy said with eyes fixed on the floating flower.

"Anything to get away from my mother," I replied. I found a small twig next to me and snapped it.

"She's workin' ya hard, huh?"

"Yep, all day long. Just look at my hands."

I showed her the scars, feeling a little proud in doing so. She touched them delicately in a way only a girl could.

"That's pretty bad. I'm glad my parents haven't gone that far yet."

I nodded, withdrew my hands and tucked them in my lap.

"Why are you dressed like that?" I asked.

Lucy flashed her green eyes at me. I remembered the vivid image of her on the bus the first day of school—pacing down the aisle like a model. "I was at my granddaddy's funeral today. He passed away a few days ago. Kidney failure, they said. It happened very suddenly." She took her eyes off me and turned back to the stream.

"I'm sorry. Was it the same one you stayed with last summer?"

"Yes. Hard to believe, huh? I was with him less than a year ago..."

"I'm sorry," I repeated, not knowing what else to say.

We sat in silence for a moment, watching the stream. "I really loved him, Davy. He's the only person I've known that has died. He wanted to be buried in Huckleberry. My mother says he's in a better place now. Somewhere where he isn't old anymore. Somewhere peaceful."

Lucy dropped another golden flower into the stream. A light breeze pushed it to the side of the embankment, where it bounced off mossy twigs and long, drooping grass strands.

"Do you believe in that?" Lucy asked.

"What?"

"Heaven. Do you think it's real?"

I looked at my hands again. I went to church with my parents every Sunday, and there was always talk of angels and demons and the afterlife. If you did wrong in this world, they told me, you went to a place of eternal fire. If you had faith and behaved, you joined God in his limitless kingdom.

"Yeah. I think so. I mean, it seems odd if this is all random, you know?"

"My mom says heaven is a place that has streets of gold and a wall of jasper. She says that when you pass away, you'll stand before gates of pearl so high they are like sky-scraping towers. It's then, she said, when you enter this kingdom, that you'll see your loved ones who have chosen the same path. Your family."

Lucy tossed a flower in. For a moment, while sitting on that bridge, I could almost see those golden streets—sparkling and twisting beyond the eye's reach. I could almost see that wall of jasper and those beautiful towers of pearl. It was a pleasant, almost intimidating thought that took me away from the crappy ditch bridge I was on and left me in a land of paradise, where no one gets old.

A distant train blew its horn and brought me back to Huckleberry.

"I wrote something for you," Lucy said, taking a folded piece of paper from under her leg. "I hope you like it. I spent some time writing it out. It's probably the best poem I've ever written. That's probably not saying much, but hey, I had to give it a shot since you did. Right?"

I took the white folded paper from her and stared at it blankly.

"Thanks."

I started to open it and Lucy stopped me with her soft hands.

"No. Not now. Read it when you get home...please."

"Okay," I replied, folding the paper two more times and carefully placing it in my front pocket.

Lucy continued to add the sun-like flowers to the stream and I continued to watch. The water's rippled reflection danced on our bare legs, and the sun poured on our heads from an untainted blue sky. Sometimes Lucy would comment on her grandfather, sometimes she'd talk about school or the Vineyard, sometimes she'd say nothing at all and playfully kick her legs over the passing water. I lent her the best ear I could.

Sometimes you just need a shoulder to lean on.

***

A week after Lucy phoned me, I received another call. This one was from Tommy and he wanted to know if I could go shooting in the Vineyard. Sure, I told him, I could go. I had put in enough overtime at the house to satisfy my mother for the next few days— clearing the weeds in the garden, pruning the cherry and apple trees in our front yard, mopping the floors squeaky clean. My punishment wasn't over, my mother warned me, but I could start seeing my friends again.

I met Tommy just outside of Randy's house. I had cautiously grabbed my pellet gun in the Sachs's storage area behind their garage; it was hidden behind a stack of old encyclopedias—an area where Randy kept a pile of his forbidden Peep and Lace magazines.

Tommy had a fresh purple bruise over his left eye and a split lip.

"Whoa, what happened?" I asked.

"I'll tell you later," Tommy replied, walking past me, his eyes fixed on the floor.

I followed him out of our neighborhood, past Grant elementary school, and over the ditch bridge. We shot at random targets along the way— tin cans, broken jars, and bottle caps—and remained silent.

Huckleberry's drought was worsening. Not a drop of water had fallen in the past three months. The mayor was one step away from issuing a code red emergency. Dark clouds, heavy with rain, floated teasingly over the city, waiting to drop their baggage on other areas where water was already abundant. Daily highs were between one hundred and one hundred and ten degrees. Humidity was nonexistent, and any plants that weren't artificially watered stood a good chance of dying under the ruthless sun.

Tommy and I walked to a shaded spot in the Vineyard, not far from where we'd found the cats-eye marble, and staked out a seat on two dead branches. Three elm trees shielded us from the sun.

"Need ammo?" Tommy asked me, twisting open a new disk of pellets.

"Na, still got half of mine left," I answered, checking my disk.

We loaded our guns and hunted for targets. Tommy found an abandoned blue sneaker caked with mud and placed it on a rotted log in front of us. We took turns shooting at it, betting quarters on each shot. I hit it four times, Tommy six.

"That's fifty cents, buddy," Tommy said.

"Wanna go again?"

"Sure, but let's try somethin' different."

We searched the dirt. After spending a few minutes looking around, I came up with a Coke bottle.

"Look what I have," I said, holding it up.

"Cool, put it up. We'll use this can next."

I replaced the sneaker, and sat back on my branch. Tommy cocked his gun, took aim and fired.

"Dang," Tommy said, loading another pellet.

"I get next shot," I said.

I held the greasy rifle to my face, aligned the bottle in the crosshairs of my scope, and pulled the trigger. The bottle shattered with a quick pop that sounded like a ladyfinger firecracker.

"Bastard," Tommy said, grinning.

"I'm only down a quarter now. Put the can up."

Tommy agreed and replaced the broken bottle with a half-crushed red soda can. He then took his seat and reloaded his gun.

"I told my parents, you know," Tommy said.

"Huh?"

"About the Vineyard. I know you guys don't believe me, but I told my parents just like you guys did."

"I believe you, Tommy. You don't think I do?"

Tommy shrugged and spit on the ground. His split lower lip was twice the size of his upper one. "You wanna know what my dad did when I told him?"

I gripped my gun tightly and stared at him. "What?"

"Nothin'," Tommy said. "He grunted, mumbled about me bein' a loser, and did nothin'."

It was Tommy's turn to take a shot, but I could tell he wasn't going to take it. I shot for him.

"I hate him, Davy. Isn't that messed up? I fuckin' hate my own father."

I laid my rifle in my lap and hit the safety button. "That's not true. You don't mean that."

"I do, man. I hate him worse than my brother. At least it's normal for your brother to lay it out on you. You want to know how my face got like this? My dad ran out of beer, that's how. I was watching TV in the garage and he walked in and socked me straight out. Two hits. He showed me two empty cans and blamed it on me. Said he knows I've been drinking them. The screwed part about it is I know he knows it wasn't me. I saw it in his face, man. He know it was Dan. All the way. But Dan wasn't around, so he needed someone to lay out."

I stared intently at the scope on my gun and pretended to fix it. I was at a loss for words.

"He doesn't give a shit about what I do. Not in the Vineyard, not at school, not anywhere. He cares more about that wrecked Jeep than he does about me. He despises me, Davy."

At that moment, Tommy cried in front of me for the first time. He wept silently, holding much of his anger inside. He held his gut with clenched fists and rocked on his branch. After a moment, he swallowed and stared at me, tears still fresh on his cheeks.

"If I ever have kids, I'll never hit them. Not once. I swear my damn life on it."

"Of course," I said. "You're not like that."

"Sometimes I am, though, Davy. Sometimes I'm worse." Suddenly, Tommy grabbed his gun and fired at the can. He hit the target dead on, and it exploded off the log. A group of sparrows shot out of one of the elms and flew off. "I'll kill him one of these days if he keeps pushing me. I swear I'll do it."

"Come on, Tommy, you're acting crazy. Don't say—"

"It's the truth, man. I'm not sure I can take it next time. I'm tired of hiding. I'll do him good. It'll be quick. A stab or a shot. He'll finally get what's been coming to him. I'll do it, and that will be the end of his bullcrap."

The scariest part about sitting with Tommy that day wasn't hearing those words. It was seeing the look in his glazed eyes. It was a look that said Mr. Smith could die a thousand deaths and Tommy still wouldn't be satisfied. He'd keep coming back to haunt Tommy's dreams. Mr. Smith was a permanent part of Tommy's life; there was no killing his memory. Not with a stab. Not with a shot.

I had known Tommy for almost seven years, but he seemed like a complete stranger that day. He had *changed.* I began to believe, as Tommy had suggested, that Mr. Smith had finally shoved his son over the edge. Tommy made threats against his brother all the time, but never once did he say he was going to kill him. When Dan bullied Tommy, Tommy's brand of retaliation was to make promises to spray paint Dan's hair in his sleep, or shave off his eyebrows, or punch him between the legs where it hurts boys the most. Tommy used these threats as a defense to guard against further bullying. But a premeditated plot to kill his father was an entirely different story. Worst of all, I had a deadly intuition that Tommy might actually follow through with it if pushed.

"Come on, let's find another target," Tommy said, jumping up.

"All right," I agreed, searching with him.

Chapter 28

FACE-OFF

April flew by, and by the beginning of May, Lucy and Mikey had rejoined our group. We were fifty-two rails from completion. The fence was taking form and we could finally visualize, without looking at the blue-prints, what it would look like once we finished. There was a good chance that we could complete it by the end of May, too, since school let out on the 21st. That meant we had three more weeks of working afternoon shifts, and then ten days of working full day shifts.

We desperately needed a change of pace. The afternoons had become almost unbearable. The Vineyard, which had frost on the ground only months ago, was now a blazing oven. Our breaks under the scarred oak's shade became more frequent, and we doubled our water intake. Mr. Phillips had to refill our bottles at least twice a day. The water was still piss warm and nasty, but, as they say, beggars can't be choosers. We gulped the bottles down and drenched our faces. There were times I wished we were building a pool rather than a fence.

Mr. Phillips tried to ease the strain of the work and heat when he could. One afternoon he brought us a cooler of icy sodas and juices. We dug into the refreshing chest like wild beasts and drank most of the drinks within minutes. Randy consumed the most—almost three sodas in ten minutes. On another afternoon, when the temperature was a record one hundred and eleven degrees, Mr. Phillips unscrewed his front yard hose sprinkler—one of those rotating blades that oscillate on lawns—and set it up in the Vineyard. His backyard hose wasn't long enough to reach our work area, so he put it by the covered rails, making sure it was far enough away to prevent further warping. Needless to say, we weren't very productive that day. We spent most of our time goofing off under the fountain, playing games like slip and slide and dodge the waterfall.

Aside from the heat relief, Mr. Phillips had given us another gift. It was a small AM/FM radio. We placed it between the posts we were working on, and an orange, seventy-foot extension cord provided power from inside Mr. Phillips's house. It was tuned to 104.3, The Beat. While we were squatted on our haunches hammering our rails, we jammed to Bruce Springsteen's *Hungry Heart*, and Rick Springfield's *Jessie's Girl*. Other hits included *Eye of the Tiger* by Survivor, *Comfortably Numb* by Pink Floyd, and the Gang's favorite, *Heroes* by none other than the legend himself, David Bowie. We rocked to the music and sang the lyrics that we knew. Mikey was by far the loudest, and our ears hurt more from his off-key voice than our constant hammering.

Jason, taking a note from rebellious David Bowie, continued to defy his father. He worked with us every afternoon. Mr. Phillips caught him doing it a week ago. None of us saw him coming. We were busy fixing the rails to the posts and humming to the radio, when suddenly the shadow of a straw hat loomed over our faces. Jason was busted. Mr. Phillips was concerned that he was with us, but not upset. Jason begged him not to tell his father. Mr. Phillips said he wouldn't, and to our surprise, added that he could continue to work. "I don't know you're here," Mr. Phillips warned Jason, "got me?" Jason said he understood and eagerly stated that he'd take full responsibility if his father ever found out about it.

Other than Jason's covert appearances, all of our secrets were out in the open, and it felt great. I think Lucy put it best. It *did* feel like a weight had been lifted. I had gotten dizzy keeping my stories straight—whether I was playing baseball, football, or videogames. We were now honest workers. I actually looked forward to working in the Vineyard after school, and I think we all did. Just as we stated during the meeting, we wanted to see the fence built...in its entirety.

And then, just as we were beginning to enjoy the work, we were paid an unexpected visit. It wasn't from Jason or our parents. It was the Jerks.

The fence construction was definitely out in the open, and it was only a matter of time before one of the Jerks figured it out and spread the word to the other numbskulls. It might have been Loony that sang. He was, after all, the first to know about the fence, and maybe he couldn't hold it in anymore. Or it might have been Dan, getting the word directly or indirectly from his parents. It's equally possible it that could have been Bruce or Ricky. None of us were sure who it was or how it happened, but we were certain that the '79 white Ford pickup parked no farther than ten feet from the ditch bridge spelled trouble.

BLAM!

"What the heck was that?" Tommy turned quickly. Tommy, Jason, and I were nailing the rails on one side, and Lucy, Mikey, and Randy were working on the other. Mr. Phillips had left for the afternoon to run an errand in downtown Huckleberry.

"It came from over there, I think," I said.

"It sounded like a gunshot," Mikey yelled over.

"That wasn't a gun," Jason replied. "I know what a gun sounds like, and that—"

BLAM!

The second explosion was louder than the first, making our eardrums ring and the ground shake. Standing on the top of Bruce's truck, like four stupid oafs, stood Dan, Bruce, Ricky, and Loony. A Molotov cocktail was in Dan's right hand; in his left was a green cigarette lighter. Between our group and the Jerks was a square patch of fire burning in the field. Smoke swirled in the air.

"What the piss are they doing?" Jason asked.

"What does it look like?" Tommy answered, tossing his end of the rail into the dirt. "Being buttheads, is what."

Without hesitating, Tommy marched toward the ditch bridge. Unlike him, we had more important things on our mind, like keeping our noses straight and our teeth intact.

"Well?" Tommy asked, looking back at us. "You guys gonna come or not?"

"I'm not sure if we should do that," I said. "They've got weapons."

Tommy lifted the hammer in his hand. "So do we. They can't fight all of us with these. We outnumber them. Come on."

Tommy made his way over and we stared at each other. We couldn't bear to watch Tommy go by himself—that would make it four against one. They'd slaughter him. Of course, if we joined in we'd likely get slaughtered, too, but at least then we wouldn't have our consciences to deal with.

"Crap," I said, grabbing my hammer, heading in the same direction.

"Double crap," Jason added, trailing after me.

Lucy and Randy joined us. Mikey, the old yellow tail, remained at his post.

"Wait!" Mikey said. "I dunno about this, guys!"

"Come on, Mikey," Jason said.

Mikey waited as long as he could, and then hesitantly picked up his hammer. "Aw crud, I can't believe I'm doin' this. This is a bad, bad idea! Aw man..."

As we made our way over, Dan lit another cocktail and launched it at us. We watched the bottle fly toward us in slow motion. We could see the flammable liquid splashing inside the glass. We could hear the deadly flap of the lit handkerchief stuffed in the neck of the bottle, sounding like a blowtorch turned on high.

BLAM!

A huge fireball exploded not ten feet in front of us, roughly in the same spot as the first two bombs. We shielded our eyes from the brilliant brightness and protected our faces from the searing heat, a heat five times stronger than the sun that was roasting Huckleberry.

"Holy cow!" Tommy said, rubbing his eyes.

"I can't see," said Randy.

Over the crackle of burning weeds and sticks, sounding as terrifying as the fireball we had just witnessed, came the cackles of Dan and Bruce.

"Did you see their stupid faces?" Dan hollered, slapping Bruce's shoulder. Dan was clad in a white A-top, tan shorts, and muddy sneakers.

"I think they squirted in their drawers," Bruce replied, spitting a stringy line of yellowish-brown chew juice over the side of the truck. Bruce wore an Indy 500 T-shirt that read *Peelin' Rubber*. "Those ass munches. They squirted so bad it ran down their legs, I bet."

Ricky and Loony were also laughing, though not quite as loudly as their two accomplices.

"That was great," Loony said, his hair greased in the same plastic part.

"Yeah, Dan, that was really something," Ricky said.

"Wasn't it?" Dan asked, looking at his three accomplices for confirmation that he had almost barbecued six bratty kids. "Too bad I have only three left, huh?"

"Yeah," Bruce answered, spitting his chew juice again. "Should have made some more at the house."

"Hey, buttheads!" Tommy yelled, raising his hammer. "What's the deal?"

The first two firebombs burned an isolated square of dead foliage. *Thank God for that,* I thought. Even with the drought, the fires would soon die out. Had Dan thrown the firebombs closer to our fence, where there was more fuel to burn, Mr. Phillips's property would have lit up faster than a puddle of gasoline.

"We'd thought we'd pay you guys a visit," Dan replied. "To see your retarded fence."

"The only one retarded here is you, Dan," Randy replied.

"Good comeback, pecker face," Bruce said. He pointed at Randy and nudged Dan. "Hey, Dan, you think his crotch is as red as his head?"

Dan slapped his A-top and snorted. "Yup, it's a fire crotch. Ten bucks says I could stick this bottle down there and light it up."

The Jerks hollered at Randy. Tommy walked around the fire patch and approached the bridge.

"Get out of here," Tommy demanded. "You've done your damage, now get lost. Mr. Phillips is coming back soon and when he sees that fire you started, he'll call the cops."

Dan laid the flammable cocktail in the bed of the truck next to two other bottles, and jumped off. The Jerks followed him and made their way toward the bridge. We were one step behind Tommy.

"Shut your crybaby mouth, Tommy-boy, before I come over there and rub your ugly face in the dirt."

Tommy stopped at the foot of the bridge and his brother halted at the other end. Tommy picked up a rock the size of his fist.

"You cross this bridge and I'll put this between your eyes," Tommy said sharply.

Dan licked his lips and glanced at his buddies. "You try that and I'll make you wish you were never born." A thin smile creased Dan's face.

I looked at Jason and then at Randy. I could tell by their pale faces and wide eyes that they were as scared as I was. My heart was beating so fast and high in my throat that I felt I could stick my hand in my mouth and touch it. Lucy looked the same, and Mikey was one step away from passing out. We could hear the low crackle of the fire behind us.

Dan took a step on the wooden bridge and Tommy raised the rock in his hand. "Don't do it."

Dan's smile widened. "You wouldn't do it. You're too big of a puss, little Tommy-boy. You *know* I would kill you at home."

"Maybe, but not out here you won't. Not with this in my hand."

Tommy's face was completely serious, and there was a flicker in Dan's eyes that said he understood that seriousness. But it *was* a faceoff, and Dan was the last person who would walk off without a scuffle. He took another step and Tommy hurled the rock. It was a pitcher's throw, fast and deadly, and it would have hit Dan's nose had he not twisted aside. The rock grazed Ricky's lumpy head instead.

Dan's smile vanished. "Son of a bitch. You almost hit me with that, you prick."

"That bastard!" Ricky shouted, rubbing his ear. "He nicked my head. You see that, Dan?"

Tommy grabbed another rock, this one smaller and more manageable. "I won't miss on purpose again," Tommy replied.

Ricky glanced back at the truck and I was frightened that he might try to grab one of the bottles. They could end the standoff right here and now. One cocktail explosion and you could say goodbye to Tommy and the rest of us. My gut told me that *that* was too crazy even for the Jerks to try, but my mind told me they had already crossed that line by creating the bombs in the first place. Who in the world made Molotov cocktails for kicks?

Dan paused for a moment, staring his brother down, and took another step. Tommy made good on his promise and pitched the rock. It was as sweet as one of his fastballs. It struck Dan in the center of his forehead with a solid thud. The sound was sickening, like the noise a baseball makes when hitting a concrete wall at full speed, and when I saw Dan plunge straight into the ditch, I was certain he was dead.

"Oh shit!" Bruce said, looking into the water.

"Damn!" Jason added, staring in the same direction.

We gathered around the bridge, the Gang on one end, the Jerks on the other, and waited for Dan to surface. The seconds passed like hours. We stared at the current, which was no longer as clear as it had been on the day I had met Lucy, but was as muddy as the Mississippi draining into the Gulf of Mexico. We waited for a hand to surface, a leg, a shoe. Nothing. Everyone was stunned except for Loony, who was staring with that greased, freaky grin, probably hoping that Dan would spend the rest of his days sleeping with the fishes.

"Tommy!" I screamed. "Get him!"

Tommy was one step ahead of me and was about ready to dive in when Dan's head finally exploded out of the water. He gasped for air and grabbed a nearby tree branch to stop himself from drifting.

"Dan, jeez, you okay?" Bruce asked. The nasty chew inside his mouth was gone. He had swallowed it whole.

Dan mumbled something and put his hand over the gash in his forehead. Blood streamed down in two thin lines that emptied into his eye sockets.

"Get me out," Dan barked.

Ricky clumsily stumbled over and threw his arm down. "Grab my hand," Ricky said.

Dan seized it blindly and hoisted himself out, almost pulling Ricky into the drink with him. Once on dry land, Dan checked the blood on his forehead and glared at Tommy with eyes that burned like fire.

"Oh, you're gonna pay for that, dickhead," Dan said, his A-top matted against his chest, his shorts dripping on the dirt.

Tommy picked up another rock, roughly the same size as the last one. Dan, for the first time in his life, had a flash of intelligence. Tommy had won this battle. It was best to back off.

"Wait until we get home, prick. Your ass is mine then. Just you wait."

Dan made his way back to the pickup, wobbling as he went. The Jerks followed. We watched as they loaded into their truck, Bruce and Dan in the cab, Ricky and Loony in the bed, and peeled out in a cloud of dust. We continued to stare until the truck disappeared around the bend.

"I can't believe you did that," I said, looking at Tommy.

"Damn, Tommy, did you see how hard you hit him?" Jason asked. "Pow! Right in the friggin' noggin."

"Wham!" Mikey added, slapping his fist in his hand. "I thought you killed him."

"I thought I did, too," Tommy added with a hollow look in his eyes.

"Are you okay?" I asked. "You still look shaken."

Tommy didn't give an answer. The hammer in his left hand slipped out and fell to the ground, the claw end sticking in. He made his path back to the fence. Randy retrieved the hammer and chased after him. Jason and Mikey trailed behind Randy, reenacting the fight and Dan's near death. Lucy and I brought up the rear, occasionally looking over our shoulders to see if the Jerks had decided to come back. We never saw them.

We grabbed our water bottles and emptied them over the scorched square. The fire had already burned itself out, but, as Randy warned us, hot coals could be worse fire hazards than open flames. Better safe than sorry.

Once we made sure the charcoaled square was completely drenched, we returned to work. The Gang continued to chatter about the face-off, each person adding their own twist to the story. Mikey claimed the rock Tommy had thrown was the size of a bowling ball. Jason swore that Tommy had cracked Dan's skull. The story would mutate and eventually scatter throughout school the next day, no two tales alike.

Everyone was talking about it except for Tommy. He sat silently and hammered his nails. He didn't utter a sound for the rest of the afternoon.

Chapter 29

The King Roller

Dan paid Tommy back. It was expected and unavoidable. Tommy never told us what Dan did, but we figured it must have been serious. He was absent from school for two days and he didn't work in the Vineyard for an entire week. Strangely, his face wasn't marked and his arms weren't bruised. It was as if nothing had happened to him at all. That wasn't the case, though. We were positive about that. Dan had used Tommy as a punching bag, and if we couldn't *see* the evidence, it was covered underneath his shirt or shorts: maybe a row of Charley-horses on both thighs, or a line of scrapes and scratches down his back.

Tommy had creative ways of hiding his wounds, especially from the teachers. He had used his mother's powder and concealer to hide the black eye and split lip his father had given him. He layered the stuff on, spreading it as thickly as he could. Up close you could always tell it was makeup because it looked strange—like he was a kid preparing for a lead part in the school play. But from far away, you couldn't tell the difference. As a result, Tommy never sat at the front of the classroom and he avoided one-on-one teacher interactions at all costs. As far as the school faculty was concerned, Tommy was just another kid finishing his last year at Roosevelt. They were either oblivious to Tommy's troubles at home, or dismissed what they saw in person as common injuries. Kids, after all, broke arms and scraped knees all the time. A simple split lip or dislocated shoulder didn't mean that there was child abuse. How could it? It was impossible to find *that* out without probing further, and in the days when America was becoming increasingly sue-crazy—taking teachers to court for simply looking at their students the wrong way—probing further was the last thing educators wanted to add to their list of duties. It was best to mind your own business.

We never asked Tommy about what Dan did to him. Quite frankly, we had other things on our mind while working in the Vineyard, such as keeping our eyes and ears open for the Jerks. Occasionally we'd hear or see something strange and halt our hammering to check it out. Mikey was usually the first to issue the warning. "You guys hear that? It came from over there...by the ditch bridge. It sounded like a truck!" Mikey's trucks were typically passing planes flying close to the ground, or nearby Amtraks rumbling down Huckleberry's rails. Mikey was as jumpy as a grasshopper, and his paranoia got so bad that we learned to tune him out like background music.

One of those warnings came while I was hammering with Mikey on rail number one hundred and eighteen. Randy and Tommy were tackling the middle rail, and Lucy and Jason had the bottom. Mr. Phillips was out running another errand. Mikey stood up and looked around with frightened, magnified eyes.

"I heard something!" Mikey said. No response. "Did you guys hear that?"

"Shut up, scardie, and get back to work," Jason replied.

"Na, I'm serious this time. I heard something."

"Yeah sure, just like yesterday when you heard an explosion at Mr. Phillips's house, right?" Tommy asked.

Mikey furrowed his brow and stared at Mr. Phillips's driveway. He looked like a deer sniffing the air for danger. A rather portly deer, that is.

"There! I heard it again!" Mikey urged.

"Cut the crap, Mikey," I said, hammering away. "Pick up your friggin' end of the rail. I can't work with it down like that."

Mikey retrieved the board and aligned it to its proper position. My four-inch nail was bent and I had to use my hammer's claw to straighten it out. After spending some time jimmying the nail, I got it back into a workable position. Before I could take a whack at it, though, Mikey dropped his end again and sent the entire rail crashing to the ground. My nail spit out like a dart.

"Mikey, look what you did!" I said, pissed.

"There! I see it!" Mikey yelled, pointing at Mr. Phillips's driveway.

I had no choice but to look where Mikey was pointing. *He's going to be wrong again,* I thought, *and I'm going to strangle him when it turns out to be his stupid imagination.* I stood up and stared at the driveway, which was barely visible from where we were working, more than a hundred yards away.

"See, dipstick, nothing there," I said. "Just like yesterday and the day before that. Now pick up your side and—"

But at that moment I *did* see something. It was bigger than a truck, and it was kicking up a dust storm from its rear. It moved slowly, bouncing and dipping down the long, bumpy driveway.

"Crud, guys, he's right," I said. "Something's comin' our way."

The Gang shot up. My warnings had more weight than Mikey's. The vehicle rolled closer, and soon we could see its shiny chrome bumper, its oily wheels, its tall antenna sticking up like a tower, and its creamy, tan paint job. It was an RV.

We ran toward it, taking our hammers for safety. We didn't think it was the Jerks, but since we weren't absolutely positive, we didn't want to take any chances.

As we approached the driveway, we saw Mr. Phillips sitting in a brown leather chair, his straw hat perched on his head. He let out two booming honks and waved out the window. He parked it at the front of the driveway, and we stopped next to it, flabbergasted.

"Awesome!" Jason said.

"That's tops!" Randy added.

"Y'all like it?" Mr. Phillips said, sticking his head out of the window like a dog.

"Are you kidding?" Tommy asked, running his finger over its tan hood. "This is incredible. Did you buy it?"

"Yep, this baby's mine now. I've been checking her out for the past few weeks."

"So this is the errand you've been working on," Jason said, retrieving his aspirator. The run over had taken its toll on his lungs.

"Wanted to surprise you fellas. She's used, but you can't tell. I got her at a great price. Come around the side and I'll show you what she's got."

Mr. Phillips opened a wooden paneled door, revealing three metal steps. We climbed in, Randy first and Mikey in the back, and our hearts raced at all the goodies before our eyes.

"She's got a microwave, a gas oven, a TV, a radio, a refrigerator, three beds, and a bathroom with a toilet and a small shower," Mr. Phillips said, pointing out the accessories.

"Can we touch it?" Randy asked.

Mr. Phillips let out a hearty laugh. "Sure. What do you think this is? A museum?"

We raced around, opening doors and cabinets.

"Look, you can stick Cokes 'n stuff in here," Randy said, sticking his head inside the fridge.

"And this kitchen bench converts into a bed, too," said Jason, lifting the padding.

We felt like pioneers discovering uncharted territory. The feeling was similar to opening a Swiss Army knife—each new part served a different purpose. The cabinets above the kitchen sink held the dishes; the drawers in the rear of the RV, next to the bathroom, contained the linens. We had seen RVs on the road before, but we had never been inside one. It was amazing, a mobile house that allowed you to travel across the country, state to state, over a thousand miles without having to check into a motel.

"Can we sit in the driver's seat?" Randy asked.

Mr. Phillips took off his hat and wiped a line of sweat from his brow. The crow's-feet around his eyes looked like deep canyons. "Sure, but you can't pull forward until the state of New Mexico changes its driving age to thirteen."

Randy raced to the front. We followed him, pushing and shoving to get in line.

"I got second dibs!" Jason yelled.

"I call third," I said.

"I'm after Davy," said Lucy.

Tommy and Mikey took their respective places. We waited anxiously for a chance to sit in the royal seat. It was an intoxicating feeling. The steering wheel was made out of the same brown leather as the chair, and it had the words *King Roller* written in silver cursive in the middle. A pine tree air freshener dangled from the rearview mirror, and the sun shone off the slick, black dashboard. As soon as Jason got out, I hopped in. I gripped the wheel, feeling the warmth of the fresh leather between my fingers, and checked the round gauges: the odometer read 29,458; the gas was three-quarters full; and the speedometer said zero, but I imagined it cruising at sixty-five, with the window rolled down, the radio cranking out one of Springsteen's hits, the road stretched out like a never-ending gray carpet. The driver's seat somehow transformed me into a king on the throne of the mighty King Roller.

"Come on, Davy, get your butt out already," Lucy complained. "It's my turn."

"Okay, okay," I said, stealing one last royal moment. I sadly relinquished my power.

"Pretty neat, huh?" Mr. Phillips asked with a wink of the eye.

"Sure is, we should camp in it sometime," I replied.

"Yeah!" Randy said, his eyes aglow. "That's tops! We can do it when school lets out. We've only got two weeks left. After that, we can work all day, camp out, and finish the fence. I'll even bring the tent from my house."

"And we'll eat hotdogs and hamburgers," I replied. "Make it like a barbecue. That is, if it's okay with you, Mr. Phillips."

"Sure, it's fine. But you'll have to ask your parents. I don't want to create more trouble by going around 'em again."

"Of course," Randy said. "We'll ask them tonight. They're done grounding us. Right, guys?"

"I've finished my punishment," I said.

"Me, too," Lucy said.

"I can do it," Tommy replied.

"Same here," Mikey added.

Jason adjusted his Michigan hat, his somber face pointed down. "I don't think my dad will agree to it. Shoot, I'm not even supposed to be here right now. There's no way he'll let me spend the night."

Mr. Phillips nodded. "You're probably right. Judging from the way he blew out of my house that night, I don't think he'd let you get my mail, let alone sleep in my RV. I'd make a call for you if I thought it would do any good, but I don't think it will mean diddlysquat. Your pa's pretty much made up his mind."

Jason agreed. We could hear the distant chirping of a robin just outside the camper. I tried to think of something to tell Jason, but came up empty.

"Maybe you can sneak over," Tommy said.

Jason glanced at Tommy. "Yeah, maybe. We'll see."

Mr. Phillips took the RV keys out of his denim overalls and broke the silence that had followed Jason's reply.

"Do y'all wanna take a ride?"

Our eyes lit up.

"Now? Really!" Randy said, licking his lips.

"Sure. It'll give you a break from that damned sun. It feels so hot these days that I'm afraid my fence will spontaneously combust."

Mr. Phillips dropped into the leather chair, strapped himself in, and fired up the engine with a loud cough. We took our seats around the van, Randy claiming shotgun. The RV lurched forward and made a wide U-turn across a barren opening in Mr. Phillips's front yard. The King Roller straightened out and bumped down the long, dusty driveway, the dishes clanging against the cabinets, the white window curtains swaying back and forth. We stopped at a paved street, carefully looked both ways, and slowly headed north.

There's the road, I thought, *stretched out like a never-ending gray carpet.*

Chapter 30

THE LAST TWO WEEKS

Junior high was coming to an end. We only had two weeks left, ten actual school days, and then we were freshmen in high school. Technically, of course, we wouldn't really be freshmen until the fall, but we didn't see it that way. High school started when the bell sounded our last day at Roosevelt. We could see the next four years on the horizon: driving to movies, late-night dating, championship football games, prom, homecoming, new teachers, and a new principal. We would no longer fear Principal Pinner and his shiny bald head. *Strict Discipline Makes An A Student*—not anymore, Mr. Pinner. He and his motto could kiss us where the sun doesn't shine. We were free as birds when that glorious bell rang.

But that final bell seemed years away. Classes dragged on, and the teachers could care less that summer was just around the corner. They had courses to teach, and some of them were running behind. That only meant more homework to cram in, like the five Chapters we had to cover in Mrs. Williams' Algebra class, and the six Chapters in Mr. Katts' Social Studies. In addition to the stress of extra homework, we had final exams, too. They were worth a quarter of our semester grade. The thought of bombing a test sent shivers down our spines and gave us nightmares at night, those dreams where you end up missing all of your exams and flunking every course.

My tests were scheduled during the last three days of school. I had finals in English, Algebra, and Social Studies. Because PE, Typing, and Shop didn't have exams, I spent my time preparing for the other classes. I thought I had seen the worst of Coach Barr and the notorious Big Red. I was wrong.

The night before my Algebra exam, I stayed up past midnight working out problems and reviewing twelve Chapters. I got less than four hours of sleep, and when I awoke at seven in the morning, I felt like someone had beaten me with a sack of potatoes. I hastily threw on a pair of jeans and a wrinkled T-shirt, skipped my morning shower, wolfed down half a blueberry muffin, and caught the bus as it was pulling away from the curb. By the time I got to school, my eyelids felt twice their weight. I wanted to stay in the back of the bus, lie down, and take the exam in my sleep.

I dozed in and out of Social Studies, hearing the annoying voice of Patty Ratty Pigtails in my hazy head, gleefully spitting out answers. Mikey tried his best to keep me awake, tossing paper wads in my face, but it was impossible. Mr. Katts eventually caught me and threatened an afternoon detention. I told him it wouldn't happen again and when it did, he promptly gave me a pink slip.

While the pink slip was bad, it was nothing compared to Big Red. Our daily routine in PE was to run five laps around the track, do fifty sit-ups, twenty-five push-ups, and finish it off with ten chin-ups. I never made it past the laps.

It started during my second lap around the track. The running had chased off my sleepiness, but as soon as that problem disappeared a new one hit me like a train. It felt like someone twisting a dagger in my side. I had cramps like I had never had them before.

"Davy! You betta move your butt!" Coach Barr bellowed from across the track.

I limped a few feet and stopped in the middle of the running lanes, doubled over. "I can't, Coach," I said, grabbing my side. "I'm hurtin'."

Barr marched over while the class lapped me. I looked at Barr, hoping, in spite of all I had seen and known about the military man, for some shred of sympathy. Instead, I saw the unmerciful abyss of his black sockets and the twitching beetle-like irises. Big Red was slung over his lean shoulders, the ruby-red weights kissing his whistle.

"Don't give me that garbage. You kick those feet up now."

I tried to obey, but my feet felt like they were in cement shoes. The pain in my side intensified. It must have been the blueberry muffin. I should have had more for breakfast.

"I can't, I need to sit down."

"If you sit your skinny butt on my track, I plant my foot in your mouth. I'll give you five seconds to get a move on. One, two, three."

"But Coach—"

"Four, Five."

I remained doubled over, massaging the cramps as best I could, trying to feed the starved muscles oxygen. Barr removed Big Red from around his neck and dropped it on mine. It felt as if I had loaded every book in my backpack, including the six-inch roach-killer Algebra text, and stuck the straps around my neck.

"Coach, I swear. I've got cramps in my—"

"Son, I don't give one turd about what you have. I've seen a man crawl for miles with one of his legs shot off. I've seen a blind man run into a field filled with mines. Don't give me this shit. I'm adding five more laps to your four. If you don't get going now, you're going to spend the rest of the day out here. Got me?"

I got him. Arguing with Barr was akin to persuading Principal Pinner to close school early. It was pointless. I had little doubt that Barr had witnessed such ghastly war scenes (how else could he have ended up the way he was?), and if I thought my cramps were on the same pain level as a soldier's in battle, I had a serious lesson to learn. I would either suck it up or land in Pinner's office with two pink slips in one hand and a bag of ice for my aching neck in the other. I chose the former.

I bit my lip and hobbled around the track. The pain was fierce, but I soon found there was a threshold, a point where it couldn't get any worse. Big Red beat on my chest, cracking against my ribs, telling me to quit, to give it up. I didn't. It took me most of the class, but I finished those nine laps. I finished with the intense heat of the Huckleberry sun baking my brains, the weight of the rope tearing into my neck, and the cramps clawing into my side. I finished and gave Big Red back to Barr.

"It's done," I told Barr, exhausted.

"Good, I sent everyone into the locker room. Go get changed."

I did as I was told. I spent the rest of that period not really thinking or saying much about what had happened. It wasn't until later in the day, during the middle of my Algebra exam, that I returned to it.

I was racing through the problems, feeling the confidence only a person who has spent hours preparing for the material can feel. I was going to ace the exam; I could feel it. The answers just seemed to come to me, one after the other. And then, for some reason I can't properly explain, I looked up from my paper and glanced around the room. The class was madly scribbling away, their noses glued to their desks. It was strange seeing them like that, like I was witnessing some sort of sacred ritual in a foreign country. I guess I was lucky Mrs. Williams didn't catch me looking up, for she could have torn my up exam and branded me a cheater. Fortunately, she was too busy grading our homework—a pencil tucked behind her right ear—marking X's and checks with a red marker on the papers. In that brief moment, I thought about Coach Barr and Big Red. I saw myself getting cramps. I saw Barr throwing those weights around my head and ordering me to move it. I saw myself finishing those laps in that miserable heat.

And then I thought about something else, something Barr had told us at the beginning of the year. *Most of you will never want to see my face again after you go. There are a lot of students that come out hating my guts. It happens every year...*

A thin smile creased my face.

Not me, Coach. Not this kid.

***

It took forever, but the last day of school finally arrived. We had completed our texts and taken our exams. I felt as good about the finals in Social Studies and English as I did about Algebra.

Much like the day before winter break, the school was filled with eager students waiting to bust out of their classes like corks in champagne bottles. The teachers were now just as ready to get out, and most of them gave us the day off—like Mr. Katts, who let us watch the movie, *Jaws*, and Mrs. Dawson, who allowed us to talk the entire period "as long as we kept our voices down." By lunchtime, our heads were nearly splitting with excitement.

"Two more hours!" Randy said gleefully.

"Heck yeah!" Jason replied. "Two more hours and we never have to see this joint again."

We were seated at the lunch table: Tommy, Jason, and Lucy on one bench; me, Randy, and Mikey on the other.

"Two hours," I said, chomping on a slice of pepperoni pizza. The cafeteria had made pizza, chocolate chip cookies, and strawberry ice cream. It was their best way of wishing us the best. Had they served meatloaf or fish sticks, it would have meant goodbye and good riddance.

"Why don't they just let us out now?" Mikey asked. I saw the reflection of the blue sky on his glasses. "It's not like we're gonna do work today."

"Don't be so sure. Quin Tabby had other thoughts," I said.

"Man, Davy, that was awful, wasn't it?" Lucy agreed.

Amazingly, Lucy and I were forced to work in Typing, the easiest class we had had all year. Quin Tabby, with his robot voice, read three pages from a phone book. He made the class type every name and number. It was a torture I wouldn't wish on my worst enemy. My fingers were so numb by the end of the period that they felt like chopsticks.

"We can't get out early because of Pinner," Tommy said. "He won't let us off easy like the other schools."

"I'm glad I'll never have to hear his name again," Jason said, adjusting his hat.

"You can say that again," Lucy added. "I wonder what our high school principals are going to be like."

We silently stared at each other. It hit us at that moment. This *was* our last day together at Roosevelt. Lucy would go to Huckleberry Academy (she'd passed the entrance exams with flying colors), I would head to St. Joseph with Jason and Randy, and Tommy and Mikey would pack up for Gregory High. I would no longer see Mikey or Lucy on the morning bus, or pass Tommy's friendly face in the halls. The Gang as I knew it, as we knew it, wouldn't be the same. It didn't feel like it was ending, but it was. It had to.

"There'll never be another Pinner," Tommy said with a slight grin.

"You can bet on that," I added, looking around the table, a cool breeze brushing my black hair.

"You guys gonna miss this place?" Mikey asked.

"Not a chance in the world," Jason said, letting out an earth-shaking belch. "I'm never lookin' back at this basurero."

Randy nodded. The sun made his blue eyes pale and transformed the freckles on his face into darker, browner spots. "Me neither. I've had *waaay* too many detentions. If I had to stay here another year, I'd go nuts."

"I'll miss it," Tommy said bluntly. "Not today, maybe not tomorrow, but someday. It's kinda cool having you guys around. I'm worried I'll have to hang with blockheads like Timmy and Miles next year." Tommy took a sip out of his Coke and made his patented condensation rings on the warped wood.

"If you hang with them, you don't know us," Randy joked.

"Screw you, Randy," Tommy said, snickering. "You know what I mean."

"At least you guys will know someone," Lucy said. "I'm goin' to a new school by myself. I'll be the freak on campus."

"Not unless you change your looks," Tommy replied. "You'll make friends with all the guys on campus. You'll have more boyfriends than you'll know what to do with. No offense, Davy."

“Piss off,” I told Tommy, and the Gang laughed at me, including Lucy. I threw a bottle cap at Tommy’s face, and he dodged it with a smirk.

“Missed me,” Tommy said.

“I won’t next time,” I replied, smiling back.

The sun beat down on our necks. Huckleberry’s drought had entered the highest state of emergency, code red. The mayor had issued it a week ago, along with the restrictions on water consumption: lawns could not be watered for longer than one hour, car washes were strictly forbidden, sidewalk pressure hoses were not allowed in residential zones, and toilets and showers were to be used in “a reasonable manner.” Violators would be fined five hundred dollars for the first offense, and two thousand for the second. The mayor meant business, and if any residents took the phrase “a reasonable manner” too loosely, he was determined to give them a good slap in the face that would make them think twice the next time they went crazy with the water.

The local Channel 4 meteorologist predicted a strong storm coming from the west by late afternoon. So far, the possibility of rain seemed about as real as the movie where Godzilla fights the Giant Praying Mantis. There wasn’t a cloud in the sky.

“Is everybody gonna make it tonight?” Tommy asked.

"For the campout?" Randy asked. "Yup, I'll be there. I've got our tent, too."

"My parents said it was okay," I said.

"So did mine," Lucy said. "It took me awhile, but I convinced them."

"What 'bout yours, Mikey?" Tommy asked.

"Yeah," Mikey replied. "Mr. Phillips has to call them once I get there, but they're down with it."

"Jason?"

Jason shook his head. "Nope. My dad said no flat-out. He was even pissed I asked him at all. There's no way he's lettin' me out there."

We stared at our food trays. We were thirty rails from finishing our fence. Our plan was to camp out in the Vineyard for two nights inside Mr. Phillips's RV and Randy's tent. That would allow us to work all day tomorrow and the next—if we needed another day, that is. It was a perfect plan, but we still had to solve the issue with Jason's dad.

"You can still sneak out with us tomorrow," Tommy told Jason.

"Yeah, I guess," Jason replied, picking at his braces with a toothpick. "Maybe I'll try it tonight, too."

"You think you can pull it off?" I asked. "Won't he catch you?"

Jason squinted his eyes at me. "Maybe not, if I do it quietly. Pero mierda, my dad would *kill* me if he found out. If he saw me sneakin' off like that."

The bell rang and sounded our last lunch. We returned the cafeteria trays and headed for our classes. In less than two hours we would be out for the summer. And in less than two days we would be done in the Vineyard

At least, that's what we thought.

Chapter 31

By the Fire

Riiiiiinnnngggggg!

The long-awaited sound echoed down the halls and through the classrooms. Kids shot out of their classrooms in a frenzy, running around like wild rabbits. I was no exception. I practically knocked a sixth grader on his face while running to my locker—he caught his balance on a nearby handrail, gave me the finger, and told me to piss on an electric wire. I cleared my locker out with one giant swoop of my hand, throwing my books and a year's worth of paper, gum wrappers, and other garbage into my backpack. I then darted out the door and ran to the bus, glancing at the Roosevelt Middle School sign for the last time.

The remaining part of that afternoon was spent packing for the two-day Vineyard campout. Mr. Phillips told us to meet him at seven o'clock, just after sundown. "I don't want you working right after your last day of school," he had told us. "Since y'all are going to work a full shift, it would be better if you saved your strength for the next day."

I emptied the contents of my backpack on my bed and restocked it with shorts, socks, tighty-whities, and a Cardinals baseball cap. I then went into the bathroom and stuffed a toothbrush and toothpaste inside. Before I sprinted down the stairs, I snatched a deck of Bicycle playing cards from my dresser—the same cards my mother had given to me on my birthday—my baseball glove, and a dozen licorice sticks.

"Packed already?" my mother asked. "You've still got three hours, I thought?"

"Yeah, well, I wanted to get an early start," I said, clicking the TV on.

My mother was sitting on the den couch with Lewis, trimming his fingernails. Lewis hated having his nails cut, and my mother was the only person that could do the job without sending him screaming out the front door. My father had once tried the duty and ended up with a bloody nose.

"Did you enjoy your last day?" my mother asked.

"Yes, it was okay," I replied, flipping through the channels.

Lewis fearfully squeezed his eyes shut as she clipped his right thumb. There were three quick snaps and Lewis reopened them, relieved that the remaining part of his finger had been spared.

"You're gonna have a lot more time on your hands...now that school's finally out." This time, it was my eyes that were closed. I knew where she was heading. It was that dead-end road where all mothers like to take their children. "You can help me out more. I sure need an extra hand around the house."

"Aww, Ma," I complained, "do I have to do that stuff this summer?"

"Yes, until you're old enough to get a job. I think you owe it to me after what you pulled this year."

Great. It was just as I thought. She was going to use the Vineyard lie against me until the day I died. My mother knew how to stack the deck in her favor. Like Mikey's mother, she had a long and vivid memory: promises that had been broken, lies that had been told, mistakes that had been made. She'd use any one of those against me to get her way. *Remember that promise you made to me about washing the car? I sure hope that's not some lie. You remember the last time you made that mistake?* She was a master at it, and because she was my mother, there was no arguing with her.

"Yes, ma'am," I said, stopping the TV on Scooby Doo, one of my favorite cartoons.

It's funny how time passes when you're watching TV. It seems to slip away through some large crevice that opens once the tube is clicked on. The three hours I spent watching cartoons blew past me, and it was time to head out. I clicked the tube off, grabbed my bag, kissed my mother and brother goodbye, and went out the garage door. I hopped on my ten-speed and pedaled off into the early evening light, thinking about the roaring fire we would create for the campout.

***

As I rolled over the ditch bridge, I could see the flicker of a fire next to Mr. Phillips's RV. The van was parked beside his red-shingled house, roughly fifteen feet away. The Gang was already there, and when I rode up to the campsite, I saw Tommy, Randy, and Lucy unfolding the Sachs's tent. Mikey was forming hamburger patties with Mr. Phillips, part of the dinner barbecue feast. Jason wasn't around.

"Hey, Davy," Tommy said, the fire dancing in his eyes. "About dang time."

"I'm only ten minutes late," I said, glancing at my watch and parking my ten-speed next to the row of bikes.

"Give us a hand with this," Randy said. "Grab that end."

I took a corner of the tent's canvas and helped stretch it out. Less than a foot behind Randy, reflecting the day's last light, were six ringed metal stakes.

"Stab one in each corner, and in the middle of both sides," Randy said in his authoritative Boy

Scout *I'm the King of the outdoors* voice. He tossed us each a stake.

"Whoa!" Lucy said, jumping back from the spike. "Careful where you throw that thing. You almost took my foot off."

"Don't be such a girl," Randy said, snickering at Lucy. Luckily for Randy, Lucy snickered back.

"Hey! You guys want hot dogs, too?" Mikey asked.

"If we have some," Tommy replied.

"Mr. Phillips bought a pack of twenty. I think he also has sausages. Right?"

"I've got six of 'em," Mr. Phillips replied, tossing three patties on the metal rack above the fire. The blazing sun had retired for the day and so had his straw hat, which now sat on a small hook on the outside of King Roller's wooden paneled door.

I wasn't hungry when I left the house, but now that I smelled the intoxicating aroma of the burgers and heard the juices sizzling over the flames, I felt as if I could eat a cow. My stomach growled and rumbled, and my tongue and lips were wet with saliva. I felt like a mangy mutt foaming at the chops.

"Make sure you guys put 'em in deep," Randy said, stabbing his stake into the ground.

"We've done this before, remember?" Tommy replied.

Randy, Tommy, and I secured our sides of the tent. Lucy was having trouble with hers. “Crap, I’ve got a hard spot,” Lucy said. She was wearing a black tank top and white shorts. I could see the outline of her tricep muscles as she put all her weight on top of the stake. Her face twisted in pain and her bent knees hopped up and down. She took a break and winced at her red hands.

“Hold on, I’ll be right back,” Randy said, running off.

Randy returned seconds later with one of our work hammers. He pounded Lucy’s stake into the dirt. Each hit let out a sharp crack that echoed around the dark Vineyard. It spooked a flock of sparrows off a distant cottonwood tree.

“There,” Randy said, “now use this on the middle two.”

Lucy took the hammer and did as she was told. We then ran the ropes through the canvas, the ringed stakes, and erected the tent. We pulled until the tent took its form and secured the ropes with a double knot. Randy unzipped the two triangle doors.

“There it is,” Randy said proudly, looking at his Han Solo digital watch. “A little over four minutes.”

Because of Lucy’s mishap, it wasn’t a record breaker, but it wasn’t bad by Randy’s standards.

“You guys ready for the burgers?” Mr. Phillips asked.

We nodded eagerly and darted for the cooked patties. Mr. Phillips had stacked the burgers on a small table along with condiments: ketchup, mustard, onions, relish, tomatoes, lettuce, mayonnaise (for those strange characters like Mikey who love to layer that stuff on), and pickles. Mr. Phillips also put out a giant bag of barbecue chips and a dozen chilled sodas.

Our outdoor feast was now ready.

***

We had stuffed ourselves like pigs, clearing out ten hamburgers, fifteen hot dogs, and the entire bag of potato chips. I had eaten my share of the lot, two burgers and a hot dog, and was now paying the price. I felt like I would burst if I attempted to force down another chip or take another gulp of my soda.

We were gathered around the fire, watching the flames dance in the cool night air, listening to the pops and hisses of the burning logs and the distant, calming buzzing of cicada. The afternoon heat had passed and the desert temperature had dropped thirty degrees. Lucy, Randy, and I were sitting in lawn chairs; Tommy was squatted on his backpack; Mikey was sitting on the dirt with Mr. Hops, who was happily sleeping in his toad house; and Mr. Phillips was perched on a log he had found next to his RV. A pile of sleeping bags was stacked between Lucy and Randy, bags that Mr. Phillips had brought from inside his home. We sat and stared at the mesmerizing flames. The fire felt good on our cheeks.

"This is the way to start our summer," Tommy said, chewing on a twig.

"Yeah..." Randy said, his hands behind his freckled head. "This is tops."

"I bet this is the way Clint Eastwood did it," Mikey said. "Out in the open. Nothin' but the fire and his six-shooters. I bet it was just like this."

"Clint Eastwood probably never slept in the desert," Tommy said, moving the twig across his mouth. "He's not a real cowboy. He's an actor, remember?"

"That doesn't mean he hasn't done it," Mikey fired back. "He's been out in the desert before. I guarantee it. You can tell he's a real hard-ass."

"You like western movies, eh?" Mr. Phillips asked Mikey.

"Yup. Seen all the classics. *Shane, Butch Cassidy and the Sundance Kid, Hang 'Em High,* all the Roy Rogers and John Wayne flicks."

"It's pathetic," Tommy said.

Mr. Phillips laughed, rolled up the pants on his right leg, and scratched a mosquito bite. We saw a long scar down his calf.

"Holy cow, what happened to your leg?" Mikey asked, pointing.

Mr. Phillips studied it as if he hadn't seen the scar a thousand times before. He ran his index finger over it.

"This? It's a rattlesnake bite."

"Cool!" Randy jumped in. "Was it out here?"

Mr. Phillips shook his head. It was strange seeing him without his hat. "No. This happened back in Roswell, when I was only a kid. Probably pretty close to your age now."

"Was it in the desert?" Tommy asked.

"Huh uh, it was at my father's ranch."

"Tell us about it," Randy asked.

"I don't think you hens want to hear it."

"Please," we begged in unison.

Mr. Phillips sighed. "I was helping my pop fork hay for the horses. We did it every Monday, you see, right before sunrise. My father had a strict schedule for all the days of the week and he tried his best to stick to it. That day was different, though. The work around the ranch kept him occupied. Chasing stray cattle, watering crops...and such. It was late afternoon by the time we got around to the forkin'. The sun was coming down and the horses were gettin' edgy. I thought he'd put it off until the next morning, but my father was a stubborn man. Like I said, he had his schedule. The forkin' had to be on Monday. That was his rule. So we were out in the afternoon, you see, feeding the horses out of the back of my pop's pickup. He drove while I forked. We hit a bad bump in the road and got a flat. My pop stopped the truck and got out cursing, claiming that the good Lord was punishing us for not going to church the previous Sunday."

"Flat tires suck," Mikey said. "We had one last week. It took my dad over an hour to change it." Mikey licked his lips and laughed. "Man, you should have seen the look on his face. He was so—"

"Shut up, Mikey," Lucy said. "Nobody cares about your story."

"Oh, yeah," Mikey replied, pushing his glasses back up to the bridge of his nose. "Sorry, Mr. Phillips."

Mr. Phillips nodded and took a drink out of a soda can. "So we had a flat and I helped him unscrew the hubcap. My father always worked with gloves on, but he had to take them off to get a grip on the bolts to get them unscrewed. A gust of wind hit us at that time and one of the gloves tumbled off. He told me to get it. Next thing I know, I'm searching for that glove in this pile of rocks and I hear this rattle." We stared at Mr. Phillips, our eyes glued to his face. The fire popped and sent a streak of sparks into the air. *He was my age at the time,* I thought. *That scar happened when he was thirteen.* I pictured myself searching for that same glove, hearing that same *ch-ch-ch*. "I knew about snakes and I had heard about rattlers. One of them had killed a kid at my school a few years before I arrived. I had heard about them, but I had never *seen* one before, you know? So I didn't think much of it when I heard the sound. I thought it was a bug or maybe a small squirrel. I was wrong. I stuck my foot in the wrong spot and that damned thing fired out of its hiding place and struck my leg." We grimaced at the thought, holding our calves as if we had been bitten. "That son of a gun hurt. Man, did it ever. It sunk its teeth so deep I swear I could feel its fangs brush against my bone. I screamed and my father immediately came to me, picking me up while avoiding getting bit himself. Luckily, he had fixed the tire in time and was able to drive me downtown to the Roswell General Hospital. By the time we arrived, I was running a high fever and was feeling faint. My leg had swollen to three times its size, and there was so much pressure on my arteries that my foot wasn't getting blood. The doctors had to cut my calf to drain the fluid." Mr. Phillips pointed to the jagged scar. "And that's where this mark came from."

"What about the venom?" Mikey asked.

"The doctors gave me antivenom. I got lucky with that. Several hours later, they stitched up my leg and sent me packing." Mr. Phillips laughed and rubbed his belly. "All that trouble for a simple glove."

We sat motionless, the constant chatter of the crickets filling our ears. Tommy threw his twig on the fire, and we watched it turn from brown, to bright red, to gray. The greasy smell of cooked hamburgers and hot dogs lingered over our campsite.

"That's tops," Randy said.

"Yeah, what a cool story," Mikey said. "Did you go back to find that snake?"

Tommy furrowed his brow at Mikey. "Why would he do something stupid like that?"

"I don't know. Maybe have it as a trophy. You know, kill it and hang it in his room for everyone to see."

Mr. Phillips laughed. "No. I never saw that thing again, and that's fine by me." He got up and checked his watch. "Uh oh, we better hit the hay. We've got a long day ahead of us. Where are you kids sleepin'?"

"Lucy and I called dibs on the trailer," Tommy said. "Mikey, Davy, and Randy are in the tent."

"Very well," Mr. Phillips replied. "I'll let you kids alone. I'm headed in for my soft bed. I'm afraid my back isn't as young as it was in the days when I got this scar."

"Isn't it better to sleep on a hard bed if you have a bad back?" Tommy asked.

"Yeah, that's what they say. I've never agreed with it, though. I tried it once and sleep never came. Tossin' and turnin' all darn night."

Mr. Phillips gathered the condiments, which were still sitting on the small table with an empty bag of barbecue chips, and put the containers inside his RV fridge. We helped him clean up, and told him goodnight.

"Be ready at six o'clock," Mr. Phillips said.

We nodded. "Sure thing," Tommy said, waving at him as he left.

Soon after Mr. Phillips retired, Tommy and Lucy made their beds inside the van and Mikey, Randy, and I unrolled our sleeping bags in the tent. Mikey wanted to throw another log on the fire, but everyone agreed it was best to let it die out. We didn't want a stray spark flying into a bush while we were sleeping, especially in the middle of a bad drought. After a few lame ghost stories and a dozen dirty jokes, we called it quits for the night. I thought about Jason as I drifted to sleep.

He never showed.

***

"Rise and shine, fellas!" I heard a voice bellow outside our tent.

It took me awhile to figure out where I was and what I was doing sleeping in a sack. Through the triangle zipper door, I saw Mr. Phillips standing in the dawn's coal gray light. The crickets were gone and the fire was a heap of smoldering ashes. I sat up and rubbed my eyes. Mikey turned in his bag, mumbled something inaudible, and threw his pillow over his head. Randy was already dressed and ready for the day's work—Mr. Boy Scout at his annoying best.

After spending fifteen minutes waking Mikey—slapping his round face until it was bright red—and eating a cereal and banana breakfast inside of the RV, we headed for the remaining unfinished rails. Mr. Phillips had work to do around his house and said he'd join us in the afternoon. The sun was now peaking over the Hillerman Mountains, casting golden rays over the desert mesa like long fingers. The Vineyard robins and sparrows were actively chirping and hunting for an early meal.

"I'll work with Davy," Tommy said. "You guys take the other end of the rail."

Lucy, Mikey, and Randy nodded. Mr. Hops was patiently balanced on Mikey's shoulder, and a sudden vibrating croak escaped from his bubble throat. He seemed to agree with the arrangement, too.

For the next six hours, we hammered under the rising sun. Yesterday's stormy forecast, like most of Huckleberry's forecasts, never materialized. Channel 4's meteorologist claimed that a cold front from up north had delayed the rainy weather and that the storm was actually due in the early evening. I had my doubts yet again. The blue dome over Huckleberry was unscathed, and there wasn't a hint of rain on the horizon.

The heat started to take its toll by noon. It beamed down on our knobby spines like the burning ray from a magnifying glass. Our necks were red and our mouths felt as if they had been stuffed with cotton.

"I gotta take a break," I said, rubbing my throbbing forehead. On top of the heat, the hammering had given me a dull headache.

"Yeah, same here," Tommy replied, dropping his hammer.

Mikey, Lucy, and Randy gladly agreed. We collected our water bottles and took a break under the scarred oak's shade. We drenched our heads and soaked our shirts. Mikey shared his bottle, giving Mr. Hops a bath of his own, pouring the water over his coffee-brown eyes. A rare and welcomed breeze swept by and chilled our skin.

"Hey, is that Jason?" Randy asked, looking at the ditch bridge.

Tommy took a mouthful out of his bottle and nodded. "Yeah, that's him. Man, look at him go."

I had never seen a person ride a bike as quickly as Jason was at that very moment. Had he been in the Tour de France, and kept that pace, he would have won by a landslide. He was standing on his pedals, firing his legs like pistons, using all the weight in his one hundred and twenty pound frame to accelerate. I was amazed the wind didn't steal the Michigan cap off his head. As he rode closer, we could see he had been in a scuffle. He had scrapes on his chin and elbows, and his right ear was caked with blood.

Jason slammed on his brakes and filled the air with dust.

“Man, what happened to you?” Tommy asked.

Jason’s lungs wheezed and whistled. He opened his silver mouth and blasted four shots of his aspirator. The strange noises in his lungs tapered off.

“The Jerks,” Jason said, looking back at the bridge. “The Jerks...”

And that was all he needed to say. We took cover behind the oak and Tommy rushed off to get his backpack. Tommy didn’t say what it was he had hidden in there, but I was hoping it was dynamite or grenades. It was a ridiculous wish, but it didn’t seem that absurd at that moment, especially with the Jerks looming beyond the edge of the ditch embankment.

“Where’d they get you?” I asked.

Jason took another blast and stuffed the breathing apparatus in the seat of his shorts. “By the neighborhood gate. They were in Bruce’s truck, drinking beer and doing shots of whiskey. I thought I could skin by without ‘em noticing, but Bruce caught me. He broke into a sprint. Man, he’s a quick runner. That bastard knocked me off my bike and tossed me on the pavement. The next thing I knew all the Jerks were on top of me, kicking and callin’ me concha. I don’t know how I escaped. I was friggin’ lucky. A car came by and they had to lay off. I got back on my bike and booked it. Damn, you should have seen Dan. He was friggin' loaded. He wanted to kill me."

Tommy returned with his pack. He unzipped it, tossed aside yesterday's clothes, and took out a seven-inch gutting knife. He unfolded the blade from its black plastic handle. Our faces reflected off its deadly, mirror surface. Its razor-sharp edge shone in our eyes. It looked far deadlier than dynamite or grenades.

"I brought this," Tommy said with a tight face, "just in case..."

"Holy smokes, Tommy, that thing's huge," Randy said, staring at it fearfully.

"I stole it from the old man. I thought they might come back. Did they follow you?"

Jason shook his head. "I dunno. I know they were on my tail for a bit, but I didn't look back." Tommy nodded and took a look at the ditch bridge. All was clear, so far. "They were drunk, guys," Jason continued. "Real friggin' borracho. Dan was nuts and so was Loony. Loony tried to get me with that switchblade. Callin' me a puto and a dirty Mexican Jew. Shit, I'm not even Jewish."

Tommy wiped the blade with his A-top. A patch of light spilled through the oak's thick shade and made Tommy's blond hair golden. "That doesn't matter," Tommy replied. "They're just lookin' for an excuse. When Dan beat me up for knockin' him in the water, he told me you guys were next. And it isn't only my brother. Bruce,

Ricky, Loony—they're all on the war-path. They want to get us back for that day at the ditch."

"Bastards," Jason said, pounding his fist in his hand.

"Can't they leave us alone?" Mikey asked, his magnified eyes filled with fear. "Haven't they done enough already?"

A dry laugh escaped from Tommy's mouth. "After what I did? Are you kidding? It was over for us when I hit Dan with that rock. Yeah, they left after I hit him, but I *knew* they would come back. They wouldn't just leave and call it quits. No way. They wanna see us at the bottom of that ditch like Dan. Except there's one difference..." Tommy paused and stared at us with dark eyes that made me shudder. "They never wanna see us come back up."

Tommy twisted the knife in his hand. We watched it and felt its cold metal sharpness. We sensed its lethal presence.

"Let's tell Mr. Phillips," Lucy said. "He'll protect us. He has a shotgun! I know, I've seen it inside his house. If they try to get us, he'll shoot 'em."

Tommy shook his head. "Can't do that. You see, he might guard us today, but what about tomorrow? Is he gonna follow us around the neighborhood wherever we walk or play? Be our personal bodyguard? How is he going watch after all of us?"

Our gaze dropped. Tommy had a point. Telling Mr. Phillips would do us more harm than good. It would be impossible to guard six kids around the clock.

"And this is our problem, not his," Jason added, looking up. "We've gotta stick together and watch our backs."

Tommy spit and nodded. He picked up a rock, a stone almost the same size as the one he'd hammered Dan with. "That's right. We'll keep watch together. If they come here, we'll give it to them." Tommy slammed the stone against the oak with a solid thud. The sickening sound gave me goose-bumps.

"Give it to them," Jason repeated, picking up another stone.

We gathered our ammo around the tree and kept a careful eye on the ditch bridge. There were birds and small scurrying lizards looking for shelter from the blazing sun, but no Jerks. We waited thirty minutes until Mr. Phillips called us in for lunch. We left our rocks behind us and retreated to the RV.

The temperature continued to rise.

***

My watch read 4:45. *It's late afternoon,* I thought. By early evening we would be finished. We were only fifteen rails away. The thought made all of us ecstatic, but the heat was truly unbearable.

Mr. Phillips walked over from his house. “Fifteen more, eh?” Mr. Phillips asked, counting the lumber pile. A broken sewage pipe under his front lawn had prevented him from joining us after lunch as he had planned.

“That’s it,” Tommy said proudly.

“Fifteen more,” Mikey repeated.

We paused from hammering, our foreheads covered with sweat, the backs of our T-shirts completely soaked. Randy was the only one that had stripped off his shirt, and judging from the scarlet color of his back—a burning red as deep as merlot wine—Mikey, Jason, Tommy and I were glad we didn’t have it quite as bad. Randy was going to experience some serious pain tonight.

“Y’all need a break?” Mr. Phillips asked.

“Heck yeah,” Mikey blurted out. “We’re roasting like ducks out here. Over-cooked ones, too. It’s waaay worse than it was this morning.”

“You can say that again,” Jason said, licking his dry lips. “Can we play under the hose again?”

“Got a better idea,” Mr. Phillips said. “How ‘bout we get some ice cream?”

We jumped up at the suggestion. Mikey was so excited that he almost lost his glasses.

“That’s tops!” Randy said.

“Oh boy!” Mikey added. “Can we get a Giant Frosty Bubble at Dave’s Ice Cream Palace?”

“Sure,” Mr. Phillips answered. “Whatever you guys want. It’s on me. We’ll take the RV.”

We sprinted to the van, leaving Mr. Phillips and our hammers in the dust. We could already taste the ice cream on our lips, and feel the ice shavings numbing our tongues and freezing our throats. We shouted our orders to each other: Tommy and Jason went in with Mikey on the Giant Frosty Bubble, Lucy wanted a strawberry snow cone, Randy craved either three scoops of vanilla or chocolate chip, and I had my eyes set on a large cup of rocky road.

We loaded inside the sweltering RV, which felt like a sauna set on the highest setting, and Mr. Phillips fired the engine with a turn of the key. The van roared to life. He shifted gears and plowed his path down the bumpy driveway, the oversized vehicle tottering as it rolled.

At first, I didn't believe my eyes. I thought I was imagining it the same way I had imagined my rocky road ice cream melting in my mouth. But I took a second look and realized what I was seeing was real. On the edge of the western desert mesa, billowing like a line of black sheets, was a thunderstorm. It was miles away from the Vineyard, but I could see jagged streaks of lightning bolts finger down from the ominous clouds, striking with brutal violence.

Huckleberry's drought was finally coming to an end.

***

Dave's Giant Frosty Bubble was a work of art. The recipe was simple: ice shavings, a brown sugar cone, and artificial flavors. The ice shavings were rolled into a softball-sized bubble, the bubble was stuffed on top of the brown sugar cone, and both the cone and the shavings were layered with a rainbow of flavors—cherry, orange, grape, lemon, lime, and peach. The result was a chaotic, sticky mess that left your hands and lips with purplish-black bruises. But the taste...well, the taste was high heaven. Each section of the bubble had a different flavor, and biting into it was like biting into the fruit itself. It was artificial flavoring, but the fruits tasted as if they had been freshly plucked from a tree branch or vine. It was the best dessert in Huckleberry.

"Whatcha want, honey?"

A teenage girl behind the register glared at Tommy with impatient disdain. She was chomping on an unusually large wad of bubble gum, and the pin on her blue and red uniform read Sally. *Service With A Smile* was written in cursive on her blue hat. We were at the front of a very long line, and it was my guess that Sally didn't give two bits if Tommy and the rest of the line walked out the front door and dropped dead on the street.

"Ummm, I'm going to have a Frosty Bubble and so are two of my friends," Tommy said, pointing at Jason and Mikey, "and we also want two strawberry snow cones and a large cup of rocky road ice cream."

"Don't forget the three scoops of chocolate chip," Randy said, elbowing Tommy.

"Oh, yeah, and that, too."

Sally mechanically punched the order in the register and read the orders with a deafening high-pitched shriek. Three employees scurried around the freezers, ice cream buckets, and blenders to make the desserts.

"That's ten fifty, sweetheart," Sally said, blowing a bubble.

"Let me get that," Mr. Phillips said, handing Sally a ten and a five.

Sally snatched up the money, punched the amount in the register, and dropped the change in Mr. Phillips' hand. She then shoved over the desserts, almost spilling two of the Frosty Bubbles on the ground.

"Next!" Sally blurted out, giving her version of *Service With A Smile*.

We sat in two large booths—Tommy, Randy, and Mikey in one; me, Mr. Phillips, Lucy, and Jason in the other—and ate our desserts. The ice cream froze our tongues and rolled down our throats. We didn't say much except "ahhhh" and "ummmm" at the booth. It was paradise, but it wasn't entirely pleasurable. Brain freezes were common. I got one so bad it felt as if my head was being tightened in a vise.

"I have to say," Mr. Phillips said while eating the last of his strawberry snow cone, "this was the best dessert I've ever had."

"Same here," Lucy agreed, finishing her strawberry cone.

"You should have tried the Frosty Bubble," Mikey said with purplish-black lips.

"And look like that?" Mr. Phillips asked. "I reckon I'll pass."

Tommy and Jason had the same mess on their face and hands, and they snickered with Mikey. Lucy pointed at me and giggled.

"You've got chocolate everywhere," Lucy said.

I laughed at myself, knowing I too was a mess.

"And, Ra-Ra-Randy..." Jason said, holding his bouncing stomach. "I wonder if he got any in hi-hi-his mo-mo-mouth."

Mr. Phillips' jaw dropped open like a trap door and a booming laugh escaped his throat. The lines around his eyes and forehead deepened. His face flushed rosy red.

"Y'all are a damned sight to see," Mr. Phillips hollered. "I wish I had a camera."

We continued to laugh and it got so loud at one point that bubblegum-chewing Sally glared at us with fiery eyes that could melt all the ice cream in the store.

"You hens better clean up 'fore you get in my van," Mr. Phillips said. "I don't want my seats looking like that."

We nodded and made for the restrooms, still snickering as we went. We quickly cleaned up as best we could, gathered a handful of napkins for the road, and followed Mr. Phillips to the RV. We could still see thin traces of the desserts outlined around our lips.

"I guess this is finally it," Mr. Phillips said, starting the van and revving the engine. "Fifteen more and that's all folks, as Bugs Bunny would say."

"You think we can get it in before nightfall?" Mikey asked. "It's getting pretty dark. And look at those clouds."

Mr. Phillips shifted his dash gear to D and glanced at the horizon.

"Looks like a nasty storm, doesn't it? It's rolling in fast. Figure it will be here in the next few hours. 'Bout time we got some rain. Y'all are going to have to hurry it up if you want to complete it today."

The thought of nailing the last rail excited us, but the dark clouds held our attention. The storm was closing in. Bright lightning bolts flashed around the outskirts of Huckleberry and left blue marks on the inside of our eyelids. The booming vibration of thunder accompanied the flashes and warned of the danger ahead. The clouds moved with an eerie slowness that unnerved us.

Chapter 32

THE STORM

"Hijo de puta!" Jason shouted, sitting shotgun in the RV.

Jason cursed loud enough for all of us to hear him, including Mr. Phillips. Under normal circumstances, Mr. Phillips might have told him to watch his mouth or asked for an apology, even if the foul language was in Spanish.

"Damned assholes!" Mr. Phillips added.

It was the first time we had heard Mr. Phillips swear, and when the words hit our ears, Tommy, Lucy, Mikey, Randy, and I darted to the front of the RV.

"Oh no," Lucy said, covering her mouth.

"Bastards!" Tommy shouted, looking through the windshield at the same spot.

Mr. Phillips parked the RV no less than twenty yards from the destruction. Two of our posts had been ripped from the ground and ten of our rails were in pieces. Four of those rails had been snapped in half and one was standing vertically in the ground, looking like an upside down L swaying in the wind.

We flew out of the van, smelling the rain in the air, and ran to the damage. Bits and pieces of woodgrain were everywhere. Tommy picked up a severed end to a rail. Randy rolled over one of the uprooted posts. Jason held a spray can that had been used to deface a post. Lucy pointed to the remains of the AM/FM radio, which had been smashed into countless pieces (the orange extension cord—looking like a dead snake in the dirt about ten feet away—had been rudely yanked out).

"Dan," Tommy said, pounding his fists against his thighs.

"And the rest of them," I replied, looking at a hammer where the claw had been planted on top of one of the rails.

"They left us a message, too," Jason said, pointing at the defaced post.

Tommy, Mr. Phillips, and I circled around Jason. Using a pencil, they had drawn a fat smiley face on top of the post, and underneath it was a note: "WE JUST MISSED YOU GUYS. WE HELPED OUT WITH THE FENCE." Underneath the message was a red spray-painted swastika.

"Who do you think drew that?" Tommy asked.

"Who else?" Jason replied, running his finger over the paint. "The lunatic who hates Jews, that's who."

"Are these the same boys that burned the square in the field?" Mr. Phillips asked, pointing to the area where the Molotov cocktails had exploded.

"Yes, sir, the same ones," I said.

Lucy and Randy walked to the defaced post, bringing more pieces of shattered rails with them. Suddenly, Mikey screamed from the oak tree. He was howling at the top of his lungs, but the wind was so strong that his voice barely carried the distance between us. He was on his knees, his face in his hands.

We rushed to him as our hearts pounded in our throats. I had the sudden fear that the Jerks might still be in the Vineyard, perhaps waiting to ambush us. I thought about Tommy's knife. I couldn't remember what Tommy had done with it. Did he put it back in the pack, or did he have it on him?

"They killed him, guys," Mikey said, weeping madly. "Those rotten bastards."

Mr. Hops's house was in front of Mikey's knees...at least, what was left of it. The top of the roof had been kicked in and the front wall was completely missing. Fragments of particleboard littered the ground like chips on a sawmill floor, and the luxurious Tupperware pool was smashed in a half-dozen pieces. Mr. Hops was nowhere to be seen.

"They took him and killed him," Mikey repeated.

"Maybe not," I said, kneeling next to the destroyed house. "Maybe they let him go."

Mikey didn't believe me, and to tell the truth, I didn't believe myself. If they had taken Mr. Hops, he was as good as dead. They'd either run over him using Bruce's truck, or had used him as target practice with one of Ricky's shotguns. I hated to think it, but there was a ninety-nine percent chance that Mr. Hops was no longer with us, and a part of me was glad they had spared us the ghastly sight of seeing the poor toad dead.

Lightning ripped the sky and the rain poured down. Drops pounded on the dry soil. The wind howled through the Vineyard, and the scarred oak creaked under the intense gusts, sounding as if it might crack in two like one of our destroyed rails. Thunder boomed and shook the drought out of Huckleberry.

"We've got to get out of this," Mr. Phillips yelled, the rain rolling off of his straw hat like miniature waterfalls.

We nodded and he led us back to the RV, with Mikey sadly bringing up the rear. The field was already muddy and the ditch was filling at an alarming rate that suggested the possibility of a flood. A flood, no doubt, would spell disaster for our fence. If the water rose above the ditch embankment, the Vineyard would fill up and wash away the last eight months of our work. The remaining rails and posts that hadn't been destroyed by the Jerks would end up floating to the lowest point in the field, drifting with the current like logs in a river. Worst of all, if such a disaster happened, the damage to Mr. Phillips's house would be considerable—ruining his property inside and out.

We sought shelter in the RV. We sat in silence and listened to the drumming of the rain on top of the van's roof.

***

The rain was relentless. Three hours after it had started, it was still pouring with brutal force. We said little in the RV during that time. Our thoughts were on the fence and our parents. We had little doubt that our parents were worried sick, but we also knew that there was no way to reach them without a phone or other means of communication. Driving was out of the question since there was a good possibility that the roads were flooded. We were completely isolated. Our campsite was only minutes away from our neighborhood, but in this fierce weather, it might as well have been miles.

"Once this storm lets up, I'm calling the police," Mr. Phillips said. He was sitting sideways in the driver's seat, looking back at us with grim eyes. We had piled in the RV's kitchen: Tommy, Randy, and Lucy sitting on a bench; me, Jason, and Mikey hunkered Indian style on the floor. A naked fifty-watt bulb between the kitchen and the bathroom supplied the only light in the vehicle.

"I guess that's best," Tommy replied, running his hand through his damp hair. It had dried some since we had first gotten in, but it still looked brown instead of blond.

"We'll settle here for the night. It'll be tight, but we'll manage. I'm going outside to get your sleeping bags. They're still in the tents, right?"

Randy nodded. "Yeah, I packed them inside."

"Good. It'll make it easier for me."

"Wouldn't it be safer if we made a run for your house?" I asked. "I mean with that ditch and all, we could get flooded out here."

Mr. Phillips calmly shook his head. "We're fine in here. It's going to have to rain like this for a long time for that ditch to give way. And I mean a really long time. We will be safe by staying put."

We glanced at each other, not entirely convinced by his claim, but we silenced our reservations. Mr. Phillips turned the handle and a gust of wind ripped the door open like it was a piece of cardboard, tossing it violently from side to side. Before he closed it, a burst of lightning lit up the cloudy sky.

"I should have brought Mr. Hops with me," Mikey said solemnly. "I could have saved him."

"Don't say that," Jason replied, patting Mikey on the back. "How the heck were you to know? You're not psychic."

"That's right, Mikey," Lucy said. "It was the Jerks that did it, not you."

"You think they were all in on it?" I asked.

Tommy spun a penny on the kitchen table and waited until it slowed and settled at a corner next to Lucy, Lincoln's head up. "Yeah, they must have been. Dan and Loony couldn't have done all that themselves. No way. They had to have had help from Bruce and Ricky. I bet they did it as soon as we left to get ice cream."

"You mean they were waiting for us to leave?" Lucy asked. "Spying on us all that time after they attacked Jason?"

Tommy spun the penny again. "Yeah, I think so. Ripping out one of those posts takes time. A friggin' long time. You guys ever tried budging one of those things? They're heavy as shit, especially with that cement. I bet it took 'em fifteen to twenty minutes to get those two posts out. At least that long."

Mr. Phillips reentered the RV and tossed in three sleeping bags.

"The wind's too strong for me to take down that tent," Mr. Phillips said, closing the door behind him. His overalls were drenched and his thick black hair was dripping on the van's carpet.

"It's a strong tent," Randy said. "At least, that's what the salesman said when my parents bought it."

Mr. Phillips wiped his face with a paper towel. “I hope so, that wind’s blowing something terrible. It’s one rager out there. It seems like all the other storms that missed us have been rolled into one giant storm. I’ve never seen lightning like that before.”

“Think it will keep up all night?” Jason asked.

Mr. Phillips tore another paper towel from above the kitchen sink. He dried his head as best as he could and shrugged his shoulders. “Hard to tell. Sure hope not. Are you guys hungry?”

We shook our heads. Our appetites had disappeared the moment we had seen the broken rails.

“Me neither,” Mr. Phillips said. “Well, it’s late anyway. Perhaps it’s best if we just went to bed. I’m afraid you have no choice but to stay with us, Jason.”

I had forgotten about Jason’s dad. It was almost nine-thirty and Jason’s father was surely home from work by now. This was bad on two levels. Not only would he notice that Jason was missing, he wouldn’t know *why* he was missing. If Mr. Phillips wanted to talk to the police, it was in his best interest to do it tonight. Tomorrow morning, the cops would be working on a missing person case.

“Yes, seems so, sir,” Jason answered.

Mr. Phillips sighed, obviously thinking about Mr. Sanchez. He made his way to the back of the RV and opened a cabinet full of blankets.

"Everyone already has sleeping bags, but you can use these if you need them. I've got extra pillows in the same cabinet."

Mr. Phillips took one blanket and handed Jason the rest. Mr. Phillips then headed to his bed in the driver's seat. He then reclined his chair and covered his face with his hat.

We followed suit, unrolling our bags and fluffing our pillows. Jason and Randy set up the kitchen table bed, transforming the two benches into one mattress. Lucy made camp in the back with Tommy, and I took the kitchen floor with Mikey.

A moth bumped and flittered against our lonely fifty-watt bulb. Tommy eventually shut the light off with a flick of a switch, leaving the moth and us in the dark. The rain continued to drum on the King Roller as thunder hammered Huckleberry.

***

The sky was filled with crows. There were hundreds of them, perhaps thousands, flapping their glossy wings and flying in a massive black circle. They flew counterclockwise, issuing their shrieking caws down upon a giant scarred oak standing in the middle.

"Come on, Davy," Tommy yelled back, sprinting toward the tree with a pellet gun in both hands.

"Wait," I replied, following his lead.

We ran across a muddy field. Our shoes splashed in the muck, layering our shorts and bare legs with black sludge. As we reached the eye of the feathered hurricane, the caws grew stronger and the birds flew faster. The force of their circular flight created a twister around the scarred oak, placing the tree inside the hurricane's eye. The funnel looked like an upside down cone: the top was fat and filled with garbage (leaves, soda cans, pieces of newspaper, and plastic baggies) and the bottom was as skinny as a needle. The thin end of the tornado spun violently, moving from side to side, stripping branches and bark from the oak.

Tommy stopped at the tree and pumped his gun.

"Get 'em, Davy! Get 'em 'fore they come down."

I stared at Tommy, feeling the slick grease of my rifle in my hand. The air was thick and moist and carried the putrid smell of decaying trash. I tried holding my breath to guard against the stench, but my lungs continued to take air.

CAW! CAW!

The cries shot down and pierced our ears. I glanced at the swarming birds, which were now circling at a dizzying speed. They were closing in on us, shrinking the center of the tornado. A cloud of fiery red eyes beamed at us. *There's hate behind those eyes,* I thought, fearfully pumping my gun, a hate so fierce I could feel it in the pit of my stomach.

CAW! CAW!

"Hurry, Davy! Get 'em 'fore they come down."

Tommy pointed his rifle at the sky and shot at the storm of eyes. One bird dropped out of the black mass, and a dozen more swooped down at us. I threw my arms over my face and felt the sharp pain of beaks puncturing my skin. Feathers slapped against my cheeks and claws tore at my hair. I slapped and kicked until the crows finally withdrew.

"Now, Davy!"

Tommy took another shot and dropped another feathered beast. This time two dozen dropped from the circle. They attacked again. Their beaks felt like little knives stabbing me in a hundred spots. Their claws ripped into my skin with vicious force. Blood trickled down my arms and legs, and my tongue felt a beak embedded in my right cheek. Just when I thought they would kill me, they withdrew.

"Don't shoot them, Tommy!" I screamed. "Don't shoot or they'll come again."

Tommy ignored my plea and continued to reload and cock his gun. His eyes were wildly searching the black sky, thirsting for more blood.

"Get 'em 'fore they come down," Tommy repeated, gnashing his teeth.

Irrationally, I aimed my scope at the feathered cloud and fired. Another bird dropped. Then, like a swarm of giant bees, the entire cluster swooped down. Glowing red eyes ripped past me and an ocean of beaks and claws tore at my skin. I blindly reloaded my gun and fired.

"Get 'em!"

CAW!

I fired again. And again. And again. The birds slammed into me with a riveting force that almost forced me backward to the muddy ground. I could hear familiar voices around my body, whispering among the swarm of crows. Again, I fired. And again.

Then, suddenly, the black cloud rose from the ground and disappeared in the vortex. The sky became blue and clear, and the sun shone on my blood-soaked shirt, which was riddled with holes.

"They're gone, Tommy," I said. "They left us."

Tommy didn't reply. I turned and found him on the ground. But it wasn't Tommy anymore. It was *Jason*. He had a deep hole in the middle of his chest.

"Jason!" I cried, dropping my gun.

I sprinted to where he lay. The mud was now gone, and the ground was scorched and dry. The only dampness around Jason's body came from the blood spilling from the hole in his shirt. I knelt down beside him and put my hand under his head. His brown eyes stared blankly at me, his mouth agape.

"Amigo, you shot me," Jason said in a whistling asthma voice.

His hands closed around the center of my shirt and pulled me closer. His grip was so tight I could see the veins pulsing in his hands like throbbing blue wires. I stared at his ghastly white face as he drifted away. The strength in his hands faded and his eyes rolled white. He was dead.

"Davy?"

"Jason!" I shouted, opening my eyes.

"Shhh!" Randy whispered. "You'll wake Mr. Phillips."

"It was only a dream, loco," Jason said, squatting next to Randy.

"What?" I replied in confusion, sitting up.

My eyes darted around the RV, half-frightened that a crow would shoot out from the darkness and dive-bomb me. I didn't see any, and Jason was still alive, sitting with the Gang in the kitchen.

"What's going on? What time is it?" I asked, feeling my chest. The holes were gone. So was the rain outside, I noticed.

"It's midnight," Tommy replied.

"What are you guys doing up?"

Tommy looked at the others and pursed his lips together. "We're gonna get the Jerks back."

"What? Now?" I asked, suddenly wide awake.

"Yep, tonight," Jason said, staring at me. "It's friggin' payback time."

"Why didn't you wake me?"

"Sorry, we would have, but we weren't sure before," Tommy said.

"Those bastards are going to pay," Mikey said, fidgeting with his glasses. I had never seen Mikey as serious as he was at that moment. "We've got to do it for Mr. Hops and the fence."

Jason nodded. "And all the other crap we've been puttin' up with."

"What about Mr. Phillips?" I asked. "And the storm?"

"He's completely passed out in the driver's seat," Tommy replied, thumbing at Mr. Phillips, who was snoring under his hat. "If we do it quickly and quietly, he'll never know we were gone. The worst of the storm is over. The roads should be clear enough to walk by now."

"What about the police?"

Jason let out a dry laugh. "Are you kidding? There's no point waiting until tomorrow for them."

"Why not?" I asked.

The snoring abruptly ceased. Our hearts stopped and we stared at Mr. Phillips. He rolled from one side of the seat to the other, coughed, and resumed sleeping. We let out a sigh of relief.

"Because, Davy, what do you think they're gonna do?" Tommy whispered. "Book 'em and toss 'em in the slammer? They broke a fence that was built by a bunch of stupid kids, and killed a worthless toad. What kind of crime is that? And even if cops were to do something, they probably couldn't pin it on the Jerks if they tried. What evidence do they have?"

"They might find something," I said. "A fingerprint or shoeprint."

"Davy, it's not like someone was murdered or something," Randy replied. "We'll be lucky if they even come out and file a report. They don't have time for things like this."

Tommy nodded. "That's right. Either we get the Jerks or they get away with it again like they always do. And they'll never stop if we don't hit 'em back. They'll keep on doin' this shit for as long as it pleases them."

It became obvious to me that the Gang had been up for quite a while. It's possible that they never went to sleep, and spent the last two hours discussing it while I was battling it out with the crows.

"What are we gonna do?" I asked.

As swiftly as a cat, Tommy removed the gutting knife from his pocket. He unfolded the deadly blade and showed it to me with the same wild eyes I had seen in my dream.

"I'll explain outside. Come on, let's get out of here."

***

The rain *was* gone, but the lightning wasn't. A brilliant display of pyrotechnics illuminated Huckleberry's sky: bolts of jagged lightning stabbing in chaotic flashes, some bolts joining with others; pockets of clouds igniting like a light behind a gray curtain; sporadic bursts of arching bolts shooting from one end of the sky to the other, never touching down. It was as mysterious as it was frightening.

We snuck out of the RV, one person at a time—Tommy leading. Jason was behind Tommy, Lucy followed Jason, and Randy and I were next. Mikey was the last one out of the van, and he shut the door with a loud clap that we swore had awoken Mr. Phillips.

"Estúpido," Jason whispered.

"Sorry," Mikey said, putting his fist in his mouth.

Tommy quietly crept to the front of the RV and peeked through the windshield. He made a circle with his index finger and his thumb and led us through the Vineyard.

It was muddy. "The dang ground is drenched," I whispered to myself, wondering if my dream was really a dream at all. Yes, the crows were gone, but the sky was still black and the air was still thick and moist. *Was it a bad omen?* I shrugged off the superstitious thought and kept my eyes on the group.

Tommy stopped at the defaced post and picked up a loose spray can that had been used to paint the smiley face and swastika. He held it up as a bolt of lightning flashed behind him. Tommy looked like Moses, holding up a spray can instead of a stone tablet of the Ten Commandments.

"We'll give 'em a taste of their own medicine," Tommy said, pressing the red spray button. Its blast sounded similar to the discharge of Jason's aspirator.

"How do you know where to find them?" I asked.

Tommy stuffed the can in his shorts and tapped his watch. "It's game night. Dan and the group always play poker Saturday night. All of 'em are at my house."

"And so is Bruce's truck, right Tommy?" Jason asked, the lightning reflecting off his silver mouth.

"Yep, it's there. It always is."

And so the plan came to me. A spray paint can. A knife. Four Jerks bottled up inside one house. One fine white pickup truck. Giving them a taste of their own medicine was right. We'd get them right under their noses the same way they had gotten us. Inside Tommy's house, the Jerks would have no clue what damage was being done on the other side of the wall.

"I'm having second thoughts about this, guys," Mikey said, looking back at the RV, which looked about a million miles away from where we were standing. "What if Mr. Phillips wakes up?"

"Stop bein' scared," Jason said. "Tommy checked on him. He's knocked out cold."

Tommy nodded and led the way. "Right. Come on. To the ditch."

We made our path in the muck, the lightning flashing overhead like a strobe light. We crossed the ditch bridge, hearing the wooden boards creak under our weight, and looked down at the unusually high current rushing below. We then passed Grant Elementary and its empty playground, which looked haunted with its swings eerily swaying in the stormy, chilly wind and its seesaw rising and falling with no riders in its seats. We heard the rusty hinges on the back gate squeal as we entered our neighborhood. We stealthily cut through the residential circle, dodging two cars on the circular road and one loose dog in the park. Fifteen minutes after we had left the RV, we arrived at Tommy's cul-de-sac.

"There it is," Tommy whispered, pointing ahead of us.

"I see it," Mikey said, shouting it a little too loudly.

Bruce's truck was in the front of the Smith's gravel driveway, with the bed facing us. Streaks of lightning shone off its rear chrome bumper.

"Be careful and follow my every move," Tommy said, moving slower.

We edged closer to the house, creeping single file. The house was dark except for two windows: the kitchen and the back bathroom. Tommy bent down and moved cat-like across his front lawn, toward the kitchen window. We matched his steps, trying our best to stay as low as he was. Tommy stopped at the window, looked back at us to make sure we had made it safely, and peered inside.

"Wha-what ya-ya-you see, Tommy?" Mikey asked, shivering with fear.

"Shhh," Tommy whispered. "Dan and Loony. Sitting at the table."

"What 'bout the other two?" Randy asked, cupping his mouth with his hand.

Tommy shrugged his shoulders. "Not here. Maybe smokin' some pot in the back. They light up together all the time. Listen, you guys stay here. I'm gonna search around the house for 'em."

We nodded and Tommy crept out of sight. We took turns at the window, and just like Tommy had said, they were playing poker, drinking beers, and smoking cigarettes. Dan had a half-burned Red dangling from his lips and Loony had a 40oz bottle of Joe's malt liquor, the same shitty beer they had been drinking earlier.

Tommy returned minutes later, exhausted. We were scared that someone had seen him.

"Well?" I asked.

"Don't know," Tommy said. "Didn't see them in the house. I looked through every window. They must be in the garage."

"Should we wait?" Jason asked, holding up the can of spray paint that Tommy had given to him on the walk over.

"Huh uh, the quicker we do this, the better."

We crept back to the truck. Tommy took out the gutting knife and unfolded its shiny seven-inch blade. My heart raced and a vein in the middle of my forehead throbbed. I watched with the Gang as Tommy jabbed the knife inside the truck's left front tire. We winced as air hissed out of the rubber like air from a pressure hose. *SSSSSSSSS*

"Oh shit," Mikey said, shaking his head frantically. "Shit, shit, shit."

"Man, Tommy," I said, not believing my eyes. "They're gonna be pissed."

"Look, it's open, too," Randy said opening the driver's door.

Tommy withdrew the knife and stared at us with a disturbing determination in his eyes. "Come on! Let's fuckin' do this!"

Suddenly, we turned into a vandalizing mob. Jason spray-painted the eggshell hood bright red, and Lucy and I helped smear the paint over the pickup's front and rear chrome bumpers. Randy removed a Swiss Army knife from his pocket, a gift he had received in Boy Scouts during his first year, and stabbed the blade in the truck's leather seats. He put one hand on the fuzz-covered steering wheel and one foot on the edge of the truck's brake, and then yanked at the knife with all the weight in his skinny one hundred and twenty pound frame. The leather made a sickening ripping sound that made me quiver, like the noise a pillow cover makes when torn in half. Mikey opened the passenger door and layered the inside of the pickup with a heaping mass of nasty mud. It smelled so vile that one whiff almost forced my lunch out the wrong tube. Then, right after Tommy destroyed the truck's right tires, two white beams turned into the cul-de-sac.

"Car!" Jason yelled, making tracks.

"Damn," I replied, running the same path.

Mikey followed me, while Randy, Tommy, and Lucy darted in the opposite direction. I dove into a row of hedges, cutting my cheek and almost taking out my right eye. The vegetation obscured my vision, but I could still see headlights pull into the gravel driveway and shut off. I heard a car door slam and the sound of crunching over the gravel. Another door, presumably the front one to the house, slammed soon after, and the noises disappeared. I waited a good five minutes, holding my breath, before deciding they hadn't seen us. The danger had passed.

"Jason?" I whispered. "You around? Randy? Mikey?"

"Yeah?"

"Mikey? That you?"

I crawled out of the bushes and felt the gash in my right cheek. It was deep, painful and bleeding badly.

"Where are the others?" Mikey asked, wiping his glasses on his shirt.

I looked around, but saw only darkness. "Don't know, come on."

I didn't feel safe returning to the truck just yet, so I led Mikey to the western side of the Smith house. Bushes covered the entire side except at the far end, where a window lit up and shone on a patch of grass.

"Isn't that Tommy's room?" Mikey asked.

"I think so. I wonder who's in there?"

We kept our backs to the bushes and slowly crept sideways to the window. We then peeked inside and saw the shock of our lives.

"Holy shit!" I said.

"Oh geez!" Mikey added.

I had seen a thousand things that day I couldn't believe—portions of our fence smashed into oblivion, rain falling on Huckleberry, Randy (Mr. Straight Arrow himself) vandalizing Bruce's truck—but what I saw in Tommy's room knocked the wind out of me. Bruce was standing beside Tommy's bed with his pants off and his boxers around his ankles. And there was Ricky, kneeling on the floor, jerking Bruce off with a funny little grin on his face.

"Oh crap, Davy—" Mikey said, covering his mouth.

"Shit," I repeated, staring with eyes as wide as saucers.

And then something hit me at that moment, something Bruce had told Ricky the day I had run into them at the park: *I* know *you haven't been with a girl.*

I suddenly realized why Ricky had stormed off that day. It wasn't because he hadn't slept with a woman, which was most likely true, too. That wasn't it at all. It was because he was gay, and Bruce knew it. That's what was really going on. A dozen questions popped in my head. Was Bruce gay or bisexual? Was Dan completely in the dark about Ricky and Bruce? What about Loony? Was he in on their secret, too? Was he also gay? I was terrified looking through that window, more afraid than I had ever been at any other time I bumped into the Jerks. But I couldn't move, either. I was frozen...petrified with fear. My legs felt like wooden stilts, cemented to the ground like our posts in the Vineyard.

"Man, there you guys are," Jason said, stepping out of the bushes, into the path of the window.

"Jason!" I shouted, but it was too late. Bruce and Ricky had seen him. Their jaws dropped to the floor and Bruce immediately went for his boxers. Jason looked behind him and saw what it was that he shouldn't have seen.

"Mierda!" Jason said.

Ricky plowed toward us with a look of death on his face. I grabbed Jason's collar and yanked him away just before Ricky threw open the window and swiped at Jason like a tiger clawing its prey.

"You're fuckin' dead, punk!" Ricky bellowed.

"Get outta here!" I cried, running.

My knees hit my chest and my arms pumped like pistons. I passed Mikey, cornered the house, and ran by Tommy, Randy, and Lucy, who were standing by the pickup, blankly staring. As soon as they saw me in full stride, they hit the panic button. No questions asked. Our feet crunched down the gravel driveway and clapped down the paved subdivision. I heard a door slam open and a voice, probably Dan's, scream from behind.

"There, I see 'em!"

We split up at the end of the cul-de-sac. Lucy ran my direction, toward the park, and Tommy took a detour through Mr. Ridley's grassy backyard. I didn't see Jason, Randy, or Mikey, but from the sound of their footsteps, I was positive they weren't far behind.

Lucy kept up with my pace as I bolted across the park, running no more than three feet to my right. Lightning flashed overhead and the booming vibration of thunder shook my body. The rain started to fall again, first a drizzle, then a downpour. The drops were fat and bitterly cold. My lungs ached for air, but I couldn't stop, not in the rain, not with the Jerks ready to tear my head off. I glanced behind to see how many were following us, and saw two figures. The closest looked like Randy, about twenty feet back, running like a loose scarecrow. The farthest was a blinking silhouette, appearing only when the lightning flashed. It was too slow to be Dan or Bruce.

A shrieking scream pierced the darkness.

"Th-through here," I gasped, slapping Lucy's arm, and pointing at a shortcut.

Lucy nodded and followed. We shot past elms, oaks, and cottonwoods. We sliced through rose bushes, evergreens, and hedges, collecting more than our fair share of scrapes and thorns.

Lighting struck. Thunder clapped. Rain poured. I blindly searched out my path, cutting and weaving, fearing that a hand would soon close around my neck and stop the race. I hit the muddy, barren clearing leading to the back gate, the same area where the Jerks had given me the monster wedgie, and sprinted with every last ounce of strength in my legs. *They're going to catch me again,* I thought. Mr. Caston, the broad shouldered banker, wouldn't be there to stop it this time. They'd finish the job where they had left off, wrapping the stretched underwear elastic around my throat, choking the last breath out of my lungs. Game over.

But I made it. I ran through the gate like a marathon runner hitting the yellow tape at the finish line. I collapsed a few feet from the chain-link fence door and gasped for air. The rain pelted my soaked body and the fierce wind slapped my face. The pyrotechnics continued overhead, flashing and booming.

"Lucy?" I yelled, clenching the mud underneath my chest. "Lucy?"

There was no response. I called again, and then again. I waited for what seemed like an eternity, feeling foolish in the darkness. I didn't see Lucy or anyone else. It was as if I had sprinted by myself. But she *was* behind me. They *were* behind me. Weren't they? I couldn't remember where I had last seen Lucy or the others...where I had lost them. Maybe they had found another route to the Vineyard. Maybe they had already beaten me to the RV. That couldn't be, though. I had taken the shortest path possible. Tommy's detour would have taken him to the far east side of the circle, and it was impossible to cut in front of me from that route unless he was on a bike, and even then, it would be difficult.

One thing was for sure: I couldn't wait for them where I was. By no means was I out of harm's way. Just because I was on the other side of the gate didn't mean that the Jerks would melt into puddles of toxic waste if they crossed the neighborhood threshold. They could still make lethal use of my Hanes elastic.

I called Lucy one last time and then made my way back to the RV. Shivering and probably one degree away from hypothermia, I walked past the deserted elementary school, marched over the ditch bridge, and sloshed through the muddy Vineyard. I reached the King Roller and checked around. No one.

The rain grew stronger and I took cover in Randy's tent, which had held up surprisingly well during the storm. Randy's carryover backpack was still inside. I unzipped it, tossed aside a T-shirt and a pair of shorts and socks, and grabbed a flashlight. I had expected to find the light in there since Randy always brought one when he camped out, but what I hadn't expected was a beach towel.

I flipped the light on, dried myself off and waited for the others, listening to the pitter-patter of rain on the canvas above my head.

Where were they?

***

Lucy was the first to arrive. I saw her limping across the Vineyard and I first mistook her for Randy because of her skinny legs and pulled-back hair.

"Who is that?" I asked, peering into the dark with the dim beam of my flashlight. The rain was still steady, although not as strong as it had been earlier.

"Cold..." Lucy said, ducking inside the tent, shivering.

Relieved it was her, I removed the towel from my legs and handed it to Lucy. "Here, this'll make you feel better." Lucy dried herself. She tried to smile, but it came out as more of a twisted grin. "What happened to you?" I asked. "I thought you were right behind me."

"I was, but I hit my leg on a tree stump by Mr. Caston's house. I smashed it real bad. Hurts like crazy."

She showed me her wound and I nodded. It was purple and swollen. "Did you see the others?"

"I saw Mikey when I made it to the gate. Someone was still chasing him. Maybe Loony. I wanted to make sure he was all right, but I was afraid they might catch me, too. What are we gonna do if the Jerks come here, Davy?"

I flashed the light outside the triangle canvas door and watched the darkness. A paralyzing fear enveloped me. Someone was out there. I could feel them. They were watching us inside the tent, waiting for the perfect time to get us. "I don't know. I think we should run to the RV. At least Mr. Phillips is there."

Lucy tossed the towel back to me. The shivers had left her, and terror took its place. “We shouldn’t have done this. I knew it was a bad idea and I should have said somethin’. The Jerks are furious now.”

I nodded solemnly. Lightning flashed, and another figure appeared, silhouetted like a walking zombie. My heart thundered inside my chest. The figure swayed in the mud, stumbled, and got back up. Fearing the worst, I clicked the light off and held my breath. Lucy did the same, clenching my arm tightly.

“Who is it?” Lucy whispered.

“Dunno. Might be one of them. Stay low.”

We crouched and stared at the frightening figure. It staggered clumsily, and slowly made its path toward the RV. My heart raced faster.

“Tommy? Davy?” it whispered.

“Mikey?” I called out, clicking the flashlight back on. “Mikey, is that you?”

“Yeah, where are you guys?”

“Over here. In the tent.”

Mikey jogged over, falling face-first two more times in the mud, and then collapsed inside the triangle door.

“I’m so-so fri-friggin’ tired,” Mikey wheezed. “I’ve na-never run that ma-much in my life.”

We let Mikey dry off and catch his breath before firing questions at him.

"Did you see Tommy, Jason, or Randy?" Lucy asked. "What about the Jerks?"

"They caught him, guys."

"Caught who?" I asked. "Tommy?"

"Nu uh. Jason. I think it was Bruce that nabbed him. It happened in the park. My glasses were fogged and it was rainin' pretty hard, but I'm bettin' it was Bruce. He was big and fast as hell."

"Are you sure it was Jason?"

"It was dark and all, but yup...pretty sure. You guys hear that scream?" Lucy and I nodded, we had heard it in the park. "That was him. I heard him callin' for help. I wanted to do something but friggin' Ricky was right on my tail, too. He followed me the entire way here. I'm lucky I escaped. He's as fast as the others, if you ask me."

"Did he follow you to the Vineyard?" I asked, seeing my spotted reflection in his glasses.

Mikey bit a sticker out of his palm and thought for a second. "No. I lost him by the gate."

"You still better keep an eye out there," Lucy told me, glancing at the flashlight.

I nodded and pointed the beam back out, pondering the situation. Jason was in serious trouble. If Bruce had caught him as Mikey had suggested, he wouldn't hesitate to wrap his fingers around Jason's neck and squeeze the life out of him. Jason was the first face, maybe the only face, that Bruce and Ricky had seen through that window. They knew he *knew*, and that above all things put Jason in the greatest danger.

"Turn that light out!" a voice screamed from outside.

A figure jumped through the tent door and knocked the light out of my hands. I immediately threw my arms around the intruder and placed him in a headlock. The figure kicked and squirmed, with one foot painfully landing in my crotch, but I kept my hold.

"Davy! Stop! It's me...."

"What?" I asked, not hearing his words.

"Raaandy," he gasped.

I released my grip. "Randy? Man. I thought you were Ricky. Why did ya have to—"

"Shhhh! Quiet! He still might be out there. Turn that light off."

Lucy grabbed the flashlight and fumbled with its switch. Its beam shot around the tent like a scared bird trying to find its way out of a cage. She finally clicked it off. We watched the darkness for any signs of motion. Lightning flashed in three quick bursts. The relentless drumming of the rain continued to beat on our canvas shelter.

"I think he's gone," Randy whispered.

"Who?" I replied. "Ricky?"

"No. Bruce."

A brilliant bolt split the sky and lit Randy's freckled face. His right eye was black. "Bruce?" I asked. "How could he be out here? Mikey said he caught Jason."

"They might have trapped Jason, but it wasn't Bruce that did it. I know because Bruce chased me through Mr. Ridley's backyard. He was screaming and cursing and callin' me a dead punk. He was a mad-man, you know? I ran as fast as I could, but he kept gaining. I hid behind some bushes in the Silvers's front yard and prayed he'd run by. I waited five minutes and thought the coast was clear. It wasn't. He caught me again and chased me all the way out here. He would have had me had he not hit his head on a tree branch. I hit mine on the same branch. Not quite as hard as he did, but still hard enough to make it hurt like crazy. Man, you guys. I've never seen him so pissed before."

"Wait, was it you who screamed?" I asked.

Randy touched his bruised eye. "No. I thought that was you?"

I shook my head. I was more confused than ever. If Bruce hadn't caught Jason, then who did? Did the scream come from Tommy, instead? What if it wasn't one of the Jerks? I suddenly remembered the car that had pulled into Tommy's driveway. I was certain that *that* was Mr. Smith coming home from the bars, and if my hunch was right, it was equally possible that he might have seen the damage done to Bruce's truck, gone inside to see what the hell was going on, and then heard the commotion in Tommy's room as Ricky screamed at Jason through the window. Had that happened, Mr. Smith might have sprinted out the door with the Jerks. Then another question entered my mind. Goose bumps the size of dimes covered my body.

"Crap, you guys!" I said, my eyes darting around at their dark faces. "What if Mr. Phillips isn't asleep?"

"Didn't you check on him before coming in here?" Randy asked.

"No. I just assumed he was sleeping. I never thought about doing it."

"Wait, you think he's waiting up for us in there?" Mikey asked.

"Don't you see," Lucy said, looking at Mikey, her mind one step ahead of his, "If he woke up and found us missing, he wouldn't just sit around. He'd have no idea that we snuck out. For all he knew, the kids that did this to our fence might have done something to us."

"All of us?" Mikey asked. "Inside the RV? He wouldn't think that."

"Not in the van, dummy," I said. "Outside. If someone came back, and we found out about it, we might have gone outside to check it out. Investigate it without him."

"Shoot," Randy whispered, "and if he thought we were in trouble, he might call our parents. Or worse, the police. Man, Davy, you think he did that?"

"I don't think he called the cops, but I'm not sure about our parents," I said, standing up. "Only one way to find out, I guess."

"Wait, where are you going?" Mikey asked, grabbing my leg.

"Where do you think? To check the RV. I'll be right back."

"Be careful, Davy," Lucy said. Her brown hair was still half-wet and uncombed, but looked surprisingly pretty in the dim light. Her lips were soft and her eyes were warm. I nodded at her and made my way to the King Roller.

The pyrotechnic show continued, though the thunder had died to a low rumble. Bolts stabbed and forked around Huckleberry and the Hillerman Mountains. The rain had slowed to a sprinkle. I glumly stared at the broken segments of our fence, vaguely wondering if we'd ever finish it.

I then gazed at the empty field between the fence and the ditch bridge. A surreal terror rippled down my spine as I watched the hauntingly vacant space flash from black to white with each lightning blast. I felt as if something would pop up with each brilliant stroke of light. Something out there. Something closing in on me.

I suppressed the thought and made my way to the RV. A new fear seized me: Tommy's knife. Tommy still had the weapon. He probably had it clenched in his hands, waiting for the perfect opportunity to use the good end of it on one of the

Jerks. And what if he ran into his dad instead? Mr. Smith would stare at Tommy with the same brutal eyes he had used on a hundred other occasions before beating the crap out of his son, and gently persuade Tommy to lay the knife on the floor. *Come on boy, you don't want to get hurt, do you? Just put it down and come home. We'll talk it all out. Father and son. What do you say?*

But Tommy wouldn't do it. He'd get a good grip on that black plastic handle, charge at his father, and stop the abuse.

I'm tired of hiding. I'll do him good. It'll be quick. A stab or a shot. He'll finally get what's been coming to him. I'll do it and that will be the end of his bullcrap.

That thought was worse than the fear of the unknown in the flashing field. And if that wasn't enough to think about, there was the situation with Jason and his father. Was Mr. Sanchez searching the neighborhood, too? Would he do something drastic if he caught his son? I didn't think Jason's father was crazy enough to hurt Jason, but then again, I had seen stranger things all night.

I crept up to the front of the RV, craned my neck, and peered through the passenger window. The glass was too foggy to see past the passenger seat. I crouched back down, snuck to the other side of the vehicle, and placed my hands flat against the King Roller's cold, wet frame. I slowly straightened myself, inch by inch, and brought my eyes level with the driver's side window. Like the other side, the glass was fogged and spotted with rain. It was too dark to make anything out and I wasn't tall enough to see the driver's seat, so I searched around my feet for a stepping-stone. I found a piece of jagged concrete and placed it at the foot of the door. The rock teetered under my weight, and I slowly balanced myself into a good viewing position. I peeked through the dark glass. I had a horrible fear that something would shoot out at me from behind the window, a monster of some sort, with teeth as long and sharp as steak knives.

No monsters, though. Just Mr. Phillips, sound asleep.

"Thank God," I whispered to myself.

Then, unexpectedly, a cold hand fell on my shoulder. I slipped off the rock and fell backwards in the mud. My blood went as cold as the hand that touched me. I squirmed in the muck, losing my balance on the slippery floor. I eventually scrambled to my feet and was about to run toward the tent and scream as loud as my lungs could muster, when another hand grabbed my collar.

"Davy, don't freak. It's me..."

I stared at him in the blinking light.

"Tommy?" I gasped. "Damn...you scared the crap out me. Where were you?"

"Shhh." Tommy motioned with a finger to his lips. "You'll wake him. He's still out, right?" I nodded. "Good. Is everybody in the tent?" I nodded again. "Come on then, I'll tell you about it in there."

I walked with Tommy back to our hideout. Randy yelled, "Who goes there," as we approached, as if he could actually do something to stop us if we were one of the Jerks.

Tommy replied, "Your mother," and stepped through the door. We gave Tommy our towel, which was as wet as a dog after already drying four bodies off. Tommy told us his story: that Dan had chased him across the circle, and he had gotten away from him by hiding out for ten minutes; that he had heard the scream, too; that he had seen someone catch Jason; that he didn't see anyone follow him into the Vineyard; and that he had no idea if the Jerks were still after us.

"Maybe we should go after him," Randy said.

"Not now," I replied. "We don't know if they've called it quits yet. They could be waiting for us to leave.

"Davy's right," Tommy said. "We've got to wait it out longer. See what happens. He might show. Heck, look how long it took me. Hey Randy, keep that flashlight pointed outside, okay? We've got to give Jason some light so he knows where we are at."

"What if the others see it?" Mikey asked.

Tommy took out the knife, unfolded the blade, and pointed it at Mikey as if he were going to use it on him. "Then they'll get this."

Tommy carefully placed the knife in his lap and threw the towel over his head. Randy aimed the beam of light outside and searched the area like a prison tower sentry shining his spotlight for potential escapees. The rain fluctuated from drizzle, to downpour, to drizzle again, and the wind adjusted with the changes—sometimes blowing so hard we felt our tent might take flight, sometimes slowing to a cool summer breeze as gentle as a whisper.

We sat without saying a word and waited for Jason.

***

Jason stumbled inside our tent roughly thirty minutes after Tommy had arrived. He was bitterly cold and exhausted. His skin felt like ice and his lungs wheezed in and out with a gruesome rattle that made our own lungs cringe. Since he was too weak to get the aspirator himself, Lucy helped remove it from his back pocket and triggered three blasts in his mouth. Tommy warmed him with the towel and Randy gave him a fresh shirt from the backpack. We huddled in a circle. The flashlight was in the middle and its beam shot toward the top of the tent. After ten minutes of pampering, Jason came back to life and spilt his portion of the story.

He had gotten away, but it hadn't been easy. Jason had sprinted down the cul-de-sac and had taken the same detour that Tommy had chosen.

Before Dan was on Tommy's tail, he had wrestled with Jason in Mr. Ridley's front yard. Jason had absorbed his share of shots in the stomach and chest, but eventually came out on top with one solid slug between Dan's legs. He then escaped from Dan only to be pursued by Tommy's dad.

"Shut the hell up!" Tommy said. "My father was out there?"

"Swear my life on it," Jason answered. "He was drunk as piss and cursing like a street bum. I was more afraid of him than Dan. He was friggin' mad, Tommy. Plain loco. Boy, was he! I screamed when I saw him."

"So that was you," I said. "We thought someone had caught you in the park."

Jason shook his head. "Huh uh. I was never near the park. Once I got away from Dan, I took cover in Mr. Ridley's bushes. Dan saw his old man coming, too, and took off down Tommy's path. I guess that's when he ran into you, Tommy... Anyway, I hid while Mr. Smith walked right by me, reeking of booze. I waited in those bushes forever, probably over a half hour. I know now that I waited too long, because by the time I blew my cover, the Jerks were walking home. They saw me come out."

"All of them?" Mikey asked.

"All four of the ugly bastards. I ran for my life, jumping fences, climbing walls, diving through bushes. Shit, if they caught me, I wouldn't be here talkin' to you guys right now."

"Friggin' right," Randy said. "How did you get away?"

"Tommy's dad, that's how. While I was sprinting toward the back gate with the Jerks friggin' on my tail, I ran into Mr. Smith again. I could do two things. It was either run at Mr. Smith or take the beatings from the Jerks. I ran. Holy cow, Tommy, I barely blew by your old man. I was so close that he actually reached out and touched me."

"And what about the Jerks?" Lucy asked.

"Dan wasn't taking any chances with Mr. Smith, and neither were the others. They called it off."

"You're a lucky bastard," Mikey said, letting out a dry laugh.

"Sí," Jason replied. A thin silver grin stretched across his face.

"We're all lucky," Tommy added. "The part I still can't believe is Ricky and Bruce goin' at it."

"I swear my life on that part, huh Davy?" Jason asked.

I nodded. "He's telling the truth, Tommy. Mikey and I saw it, too. I sure wish I hadn't. It's burned in my head now."

"Man...you guys know what would happen if that story leaked out at Gregory High?" Jason asked.

"We'd end up at the bottom of that ditch, that's what," Tommy answered. "We've already paid them back for the fence. What we did to the truck was enough. We don't need to go blabbin' to people about Bruce and Ricky. It's none of our business what they do together. We're gonna keep that part of the story to ourselves."

Mikey leaned forward. "But Tommy, do you know what—"

"I mean it, Mikey," Tommy said sternly. "We gave them their due. We are square now. That shit stays with us."

We stared at Tommy and nodded doubtfully.

"Everyone promise..." Tommy said, sticking his hand over the flashlight beam in the middle of our circle. "And I mean everyone."

"I promise," I said, throwing my hand in.

"Bueno, promesa," Jason said.

"Scout's honor," Randy added, putting his freckled hand on top of Jason's.

"Got my word," said Lucy.

Mikey reluctantly looked at the pile of hands and eventually caved in. "Yeah, yeah, I promise...I still think we should rat those bastards out, though."

We sat with our hands in the center for that brief moment of time—the lightning flashing outside, the light drafts brushing against our tent like a cool sea breeze stroking a sail. We would eventually call it a night, sneak back inside the

RV—where we would find Mr. Phillips still safely asleep—and roll up in our sleeping bags and blankets. We would close our eyes in the darkness and drift off into our own world of dreams and fantasies. But before we fell asleep, before we returned to the van, we were hand in hand. Friends forever.

Chapter 33

STOLEN INNOCENCE

An explosion ripped through the back window and sprayed liquid flames inside the RV. The smell of gasoline and smoke quickly filled the vehicle. I shot up from my sleeping bag, rubbed my disoriented eyes, and stared at the dancing flames in the back of the van. Horrifying, piercing screams cried in all directions. Mikey grabbed my arm and yelled something at me. Jason was rolling on the floor, consumed by an asthma fit. Randy was standing behind me, blankly staring at the destruction, frozen as stiff as a block of ice. I squeezed my eyes shut, but the smoke stung them so badly it felt as if my eyelids were on fire. I heard the side door smash open.

"Help, please!" a voice cried from the back.

"Get out!" another voice bellowed.

I collapsed on the floor next to Jason. My oxygen-starved lungs burned more than my eyes. The fire in the back spread quickly, and the fierce heat of it singed my leg hairs and melted my right

T-shirt sleeve to my arm. I painfully reopened my eyes, absorbing more smoke, and caught sight of the wicked inferno: curtains were ablaze, dripping fire on the burning, black carpet; the burning bathroom door was ajar and swaying jarringly from side to side like a loose porch screen door on a windy summer afternoon; the ceiling was layered with soot; the air was filled with billowing clouds of black smoke; and the back of the RV, the center of the firestorm, was a blinding, bright hellhole with flames flickering in chaotic flashes.

"Help! I'm burning!"

A hand grabbed me by the back of my shirt and yanked me through the RV's side door. Tears streamed out of my burning eyes and my lungs begged for oxygen. I staggered to my feet, dry-heaved three times, and spit out the soot that had filled my mouth. A steady rain beat on top of me, and I welcomed the cool drops on my burning skin.

"Davy, you okay?" Mikey screamed in my ear.

I felt like I was going to pass out, but I nodded anyway. I glanced up with watery eyes and saw the bonfire spitting out of the RV. The back of the vehicle had completely caved in, and flames and sparks spewed out of the opening like fireworks in a tin can. Fire danced in the windows and smoke seeped through the cracks in the King Roller's frame. Mikey and Randy stood next to me, their faces painted black. I saw Mr. Phillips bravely dart back into the burning structure and return minutes later with Jason cradled in his arms. Jason wheezed and moaned and cried for his aspirator. Mr. Phillips laid him at our feet and turned back to the fire. He dove back into the smoky door, never hesitating for a single second over the fact that his own life was in danger by doing so.

"Tommy and Lucy!" Randy cried, grabbing my shirt. "Davy...Tommy and Lucy!"

I stared at Randy's frightened blue eyes. There was a terror behind them that sent it all home for me. Tommy and Lucy had slept in the back. That's where the explosion happened, where I had seen and felt the brightest flames. There's no way they could survive that kind of heat.

"They're okay!" I screamed, trying to hide the doubt in my voice but failing miserably.

A violent explosion shot from inside the van and blew out the remaining windows. Smoke poured from the new openings. The fire crackled, hissed, and sent sparks into the air like strings of light. The heat was intense even from our distance; I couldn't begin to imagine what it was like inside the vehicle.

"They're dead!" Mikey screamed. "Oh man, guys! They're dead. They're—"

"Shut up, Mikey!" I screamed. "No, they're not! Mr. Phillips will bring 'em both. He'll get them."

Tommy and Lucy, I repeated to myself. *Tommy and Lucy. Tommy and Lucy.*

The fired burned and more time passed. I couldn't stand to watch the van burn. "Come on! We've gotta help them!" I took a step toward the RV and felt the searing heat smack my face like a red-hot frying pan.

"It's too hot, Davy!" Randy said, pulling me back. "We can't do anything!"

My mind swirled. There's got to be something. I can't just watch them die. Not like this. I considered approaching from a different angle when suddenly Mr. Phillips burst out of the black door. He was coughing wildly and his face was a mixture of red and black. Tommy was limp in his arms, dangling like a puppet. Mr. Phillips staggered to where we were watching and collapsed.

"You have to go back in, Mr. Phillips!" I cried, pulling on his shirt. "Lucy's still in there. You have to go!"

Mr. Phillips stared back at the fire and shook his head in resignation. "I can't, Davy."

"No you have to!" I cried, tears streaming down my face. "She's in there, damnit! She's still in there!"

"The fire's too strong now," Mr. Phillips said, coughing as he said it. "I barely made it out with Tommy."

Another explosion ripped through the RV and spit a hand of angry flames at us. We retreated from the heat, stepping back ten more feet. The rain offered some relief, but the wind countered it and stoked the fire.

Water, I thought. *More water.* I searched frantically at my feet, realizing the rain was all I was going to get. The hose in Mr. Phillips's garden was too far to reach our campsite, and filling buckets would take too long.

It finally dawned that we were going to watch the RV burn. All of it.

"Lucy!" I cried, running toward the fire and getting stopped again. "Lucy! Luuuuuuucy!"

I fell to my knees in the slick mud. I gazed at the flames that would haunt my dreams for years to follow. I watched with absolute powerlessness as Lucy burned.

Chapter 34

By the Ocean

The fire department arrived fifteen minutes after Mr. Phillips pulled Tommy from the RV. It took them an hour to contain the flames. The nearest hydrant was over one hundred yards away, in the playground at Grant Elementary, and a large amount of time had been spent just attaching the hose.

In the end, all that remained of the King Roller was the metal frame at the bottom and the front quarter of the vehicle from the driver's seat on. The walls and the ceiling had caved in and had burned into a smoldering pile of ash, save the remnants of a half-dozen metal panels. The wheels had melted into a thick puddle of black tar, and the furniture had gone up in a cloud of smoke. Strangely, the only thing in the back of the RV that survived was the fifteen-inch black-and-white TV, which was sitting where the bathroom once stood, its screen coated in a thin layer of soot.

Huckleberry's thunderstorm had blown east. By early dawn, about the same time the police arrived, the only clouds lingering in the sky were over the Hillerman Mountains. The violent winds that had fueled the fire had died to a serene whisper, and the black night had transformed into a light gray morning. The air was thick and sticky, as was the mud at our feet.

I barely noticed any of these climate changes. The same was true regarding the events that followed the fire. It felt like I was in some sort of nightmare, floating above my body, and I'd soon awaken to find that everything was all right and that Lucy was alive. But I wasn't asleep. Not this time. Lucy was as dead as the ash that held her remains.

The police encircled the campsite with yellow caution tape and compiled their report. I sat with the Gang on a wool blanket provided by the Fire Department and watched as the lead investigator, a tall and heavily built man named Lucas Robbins, scanned the area. A much shorter and thinner man followed Lucas's steps, snapping pictures as he stomped through the mud—the crime scene photographer.

We sat mutely and stared as they examined the scene. I did everything in my power not to think about Lucy. The horrific images of what had happened to her were too much for me to handle. I felt I would shatter into pieces if I accepted the reality of it. Instead, I kept my focus on the one thing that steered my mind in a different direction: how the fire had started. Were all the Jerks involved in it? Was it Dan's idea, or had one of the others suggested the evil plan? I played through many different scenarios, and each seemed as plausible as the next. What could bring about such brutal and cold retaliation? Was it all for a stupid truck? And if they had wanted to strike at us that night, why didn't they do it right away, while they were chasing us?

Then, like a punch to the face, the answer hit me. I came up with the plan that stood out above the rest, the one that seemed to fit the puzzle perfectly. It involved only Bruce and Ricky and the deadly Molotov cocktail that had exploded inside the RV.

Bruce and Ricky had been shocked to their core when they saw Jason standing outside their window. Someone had caught them in their sexual act, and it was their primary goal to catch that someone before his tongue had a chance to flap in the wind. They had flown out of that window like bats out of hell, sprinting through Tommy's front yard and down his cul-de-sac. There was a good chance—a great chance, possibly—that neither Bruce nor Ricky had noticed the damage to the pickup. They were focused on the pursuit, and they probably had passed right by it without ever wondering why we were at Tommy's house in the first place. Had they stopped to ponder the question, they would have easily realized we were paying them back for the damage done to our fence. Had they done that, they might have had a look around to see exactly what we had done. But they weren't concerned about that. Not at that moment. Both Bruce and Ricky were chasing me, Jason, Mikey, and Randy for an entirely different reason, and after an exhausting half-hour pursuit where they came up empty-handed, they had called it quits and headed home.

It was then that they had probably run into Dan. I wasn't sure whether or not Dan had noticed the damage to the pickup, but I was almost positive that if he had known, he hadn't told Bruce or Ricky about it. I knew because of what Jason had told us in the tent. He said he bumped into the three of them as they were walking home. Jason said they were walking, not running. Had Dan told Bruce about the damage, Bruce's natural reaction would have been to sprint back to where his truck was parked. Wouldn't anyone do the same if someone told them their car had been vandalized? It could be argued that they were too tired to run since they had already raced around the neighborhood chasing Tommy and Mikey, but that argument didn't hold up when you consider their second wind once they saw Jason come out of the bushes. They had enough energy to run after him. Why wouldn't they have run to Tommy's house?

I was certain that it was after they chased Jason that they found out about the truck's damage. They must have seen it as they entered the Smith's driveway, after calling off the pursuit. That sight of the vandalized truck would've been a double blow to Ricky and especially Bruce. Not only had we caught Bruce with his pants around his ankles and Ricky with his hand on Bruce, but we had also destroyed Bruce's truck in the process: spray painting the hood, layering the cab with putrid mud, and stabbing three of its tires. It was like throwing kerosene on the fire. Ricky would have freaked and Bruce would have gone nuts. Dan and Tony would have been surprised, too, but they might have been expecting to see something like that. Dan and Tony, after all, were probably thinking a lot clearer than Bruce and Ricky. It was my guess that Dan and Tony had called it quits for the night and had decided to crash, while Bruce and Ricky were determined to get us back. Maybe Bruce was examining his destroyed pickup and happened to glance at the three Molotov cocktails in the bed, three gleaming bottles just begging to be used. Maybe the idea hit Bruce at that moment, and he told Ricky about it. They might have then made their fateful walk with one or two of the homemade bombs splashing in their deadly bottles, and a book of matches in the seat of their pants.

It was the best explanation I could fathom. There were a few holes in it, but I couldn't think of a better one. It wasn't until a week later that I got the entire story, and I was wrong on one crucial fact.

"Your folks are on their way," Mr. Phillips told us. His face was still black with soot and his voice was deep and sorrowful and unfamiliar.

"What about Lucy's parents?" Tommy asked.

Mr. Phillips glanced back at the RV. Smoke continued to seep through the ash. "The police are making a trip over to tell them in person, and I'm going with them when they do."

We sat and stared at the remains of the King Roller. "What can we do?" Tommy asked.

"Nothing. The detective is going to ask you boys some questions. Make sure you tell him what you can. Understand?"

"Yes, sir," we replied in unison.

Mr. Phillips turned and shuffled off. It hurt to the pit of my stomach seeing him walk away like that. He looked old and defeated. *The fire was our damn fault,* I silently told myself. If we hadn't snuck out, none of this would have happened. The RV would still be in one piece and so would Lucy. Because of our foolishness, our dumb fucking pride, he had been forced to risk his life just to save ours. At that moment, it didn't feel like our lives were even worth saving. It seemed like it would have been better had we all perished in those flames—everyone except for Lucy.

The detective came and asked all the questions the law would allow him without having our parents present. "They're only inquisitive questions," he told us, "nothing designed to elicit an incriminating response."

We told him everything about the last twenty-four hours. Detective Robbins furrowed his bushy eyebrows and jotted down the facts in a yellow, college-ruled notepad. He asked us the full names of the other kids and we freely told him: Dan Smith, Anthony Sanders, Bruce Brown, and Ricky Adams. We even told him about what we had seen in Tommy's room. Our group promise to keep it a secret seemed ridiculous in light of the current situation.

Our parents arrived shortly after our statements. They parked their cars in Mr. Phillips's driveway, some cars skidding to muddy stops, and sprinted toward the yellow tape. Jason's father was the first to pull in, and one of the officers had to hold him back as he stormed toward Mr. Phillips. His sleeves were rolled up and his face looked like it was ready to explode. He was more than ready to rearrange Mr. Phillips's face. It wasn't until Detective Robbins told him that Mr. Phillips had saved his son's life that Mr. Sanchez regained his composure.

"Is that true?" Jason's father asked Jason.

"Yes, sir," Jason said, his eyes aimed at the floor.

"According to the boys, he rushed inside a blazing inferno to pull him out," Detective Robbins said, pointing at the remains. "Judging from the looks of what's left, it must have been one hot mother in there. Never seen anything quite like it before in all my years. It's because of this man that your son is here with you now."

The color returned to Mr. Sanchez's face, although it was still a shade of red, this time from embarrassment. Mr. Sanchez made a rare apology, then asked if he could take his son home. The detective asked a few follow-up questions, and then Jason's dad angrily left the scene, pulling Jason by the arm.

I then saw my parents jogging over with Mikey's folks. My heart dropped and a lump the size of a bowling ball formed at the top of my throat. Mikey embraced Mr. and Mrs. McNeil with tears flowing down his cheeks. I tried my best to keep myself from crying, but couldn't hold out when I felt my parents wrap their arms around me. I couldn't bottle it up anymore.

***

Lucy's funeral was held on a cloudy Wednesday afternoon. The storm was a smaller version of the one that had ended Huckleberry's drought, and the weatherman predicted that it would head out by tomorrow morning. The air was dry and cool. The wind drifted with delicate ease and carried the sweet scent of rain.

Lucy was buried in a small, grassy graveyard less than ten miles north of our neighborhood, the same cemetery her granddaddy had been buried in less than three months ago. There were flowers surrounding her casket: radiant white orchids, beautiful yellow chrysanthemums as bright as the morning sun, fresh red and blue roses with deep green leaves, lilies, and a rainbow of daisies. We were all there at the service, dressed in black suits and matching black ties, our hair perfectly parted. Our parents were with us, as well as Mr. Phillips. Mr. Graham was standing stoically with Lucy's three older brothers, the boys standing tall and looking like a line of sharp troops. Mrs. Graham was bawling in a wooden chair next to the gaping hole in the ground. Little Heather—Lucy's three-year-old, brown-eyed, curly blonde sister—was busy hunting for dandelions on the grassy floor. She had snatched five of the yellow suns in her small hand, and had tucked two more in a tiny front pocket inside her black dress. Looking at her brought back the image of Lucy sitting on the ditch bridge, casually tossing flowers in the clear, serene stream.

Standing in that peaceful graveyard felt absurdly unreal. The wind that whispered in my ear seemed like the breath of someone trying to wake me up, and the priest's eulogy was an inaudible mumble. My tongue was numb. My eyes stared at the wooden coffin, waiting for someone to open it up and show me that it was empty. *It's a joke, Davy. That's all. No harm done, we're just pullin' your leg. See, there's Lucy, standing behind you. Man, we had you fooled, huh?* I looked behind me. There was nothing but scattered graves.

"Davy?" my mother said softly, lightly touching my shoulder.

"Huh?" I looked up, dazed.

"It's your time to read."

I stared blankly at her.

"Can you still do it?"

I nodded instinctively. I looked back at the casket and was suddenly relieved that it was closed—as if, for some reason, it would be otherwise, forcing me to look at her burned remains.

I walked to where the priest was standing and took the Bible, the page mark on *Matthew 19:14.* The wind picked up and a faint caw sounded in the distance.

A crow, I thought. *That was a crow.*

***

More rain visited Huckleberry that day. I watched it fall from inside my room. With my window raised and my arms outstretched, I felt the soft water sprinkle over my dry skin. I was still clad in my white dress shirt, black slacks, and slick black loafers. One drop landed flat on a freckle, magnifying it to twice its size while another landed at the crook of my elbow, inches away from where I had rolled up my sleeve. They dotted my arm, and were cold and clear. The storm carried no lightning or thunder this time. The pyrotechnic circus had packed up and left town for another show, perhaps in some small town in Texas or Louisiana.

"How you doin', champ?"

The voice caught me by surprise and I jerked away from the window.

"Hi, Dad," I replied.

He walked into my room and sat at the edge of my bed. The mattress springs once again wheezed and protested under his bulky weight.

"Raining a lot these days, eh champ?"

I glanced back out the window and then stared at the spots on my arms. "Yes, sir."

"It's good. This city needs it. Never seen it so dry before."

I heard my mother talking to Lewis downstairs. She was patiently reading him a kid's book about a boy that travels to the nine planets of our solar system. He read with her, and although he couldn't sound out some of the words, he did a fair job keeping up.

"Do you feel like talking about it?"

A gust of wind found its way through my window and pushed my half-drawn plastic shades out. The shades swung back and slapped against the glass. I shook my head.

"You sure?"

"Yes, Dad."

My father stared at me for a moment and then looked back at the open door, as if to confirm that it was still there.

"It's a terrible, awful thing, Davy. What happened to Lucy. I really don't know what to say because I've never been in your position before. Not with something like this. But I want you to know it wasn't your fault. You know that, right?"

"Yes, sir."

"People do that, you see. They start thinking that they are responsible for these kinds of evil acts. But they're only beating themselves up, Davy. I don't want you to ever think that. She didn't die because of what you kids did that night. The sin of her murder is on someone else's hands."

"Yes, sir."

My dad looked at me again, opened his mouth and then closed it. He gave me a forced smile, patted me on my leg, and got up.

"Maybe you should take a walk around the neighborhood. You've been cooped up ever since this happened. I think it would be good if you got out."

"Maybe, Dad," I said, staring out the window.

He left me alone. I sat for another ten minutes in silence and watched the rain grow stronger outside.

Then suddenly, I couldn't stand to be in my room anymore. I felt confined, imprisoned, and I darted for my door and shot down the stairs. My mother looked up from Lewis's book, staring at me with terrified eyes.

"Davy?"

I hit the kitchen door and threw it open. It slammed against the back wall with a vibrating crack that echoed through the house. Mom sprinted after me.

"Where are you going?"

The rain stung my cheeks as I ran down our driveway. The wind whipped past me and I heard my mother yelling from behind. She jogged a few steps and stopped when my father called after her.

"Let him go, dear," my father said. "Just let him..." and his words trailed off as I bolted down the subdivision. My knees hit my chest and my fingers dug into my palms, forming impenetrable fists. I squeezed my eyes closed and listened to the clap of my black loafers striking the pavement. I ran to the only sanctuary I had left.

***

The rain was pouring by the time I reached the Vineyard. It came down in dime-sized drops that splashed in puddles like pebbles thrown into a pond. I fired across the ditch bridge, cut left, and ran in the opposite direction of Mr. Phillips's house. The mud was slimy and slick. My right loafer caught the edge of a concrete block and it sent me flying face-first into a pile of soaked leaves. I skinned my forearm and punctured my left palm on the broken end of a dead branch. I ignored the pain. I got back up and dashed for the shaded area where Tommy and I had sat and shot at targets only weeks before.

The wind pushed against my face and forced my hair to stand on end. A gray mouse, no longer than five inches from head to tail, scurried across my path and dove down the ditch embankment. The mud exploded under my feet. My drenched, muddy dress shirt stuck to my skin, and the black slacks covering my legs were heavy with dampness.

I came to the shaded refuge and collapsed on the same branch I had sat on beside Tommy. It might have been the mud, or maybe the way the clouds strangely blocked out the afternoon light, but the place seemed different...transformed. It was as if I were in a different spot altogether, in another field. *But it has changed*, I thought. *Hasn't it?* It would never be quite the same. Not how I once knew it. Not how any of us knew it.

I tried to picture Lucy in the heaven she had painted for me. I tried to see those golden streets and that beautiful pearl gate. But all I could see at that moment were flames dancing like wild demons, spitting sparks and burning debris. I could only visualize billowing clouds of smoke, clouds so black and thick it hurt my lungs just to think of them. Instead of that heavenly paradise, I only saw evil—vicious and crude and pointless. Never again would I get to see the way the sun shined off her brown, silky hair, or the way her golden crucifix necklace winked in the afternoon light. Never again would I feel her warm, soft lips or her smooth, delicate hands.

I removed a white sheet of paper from my back pocket, the same sheet Lucy had given me on the ditch bridge. The paper was a tad wet and its corners were dog-eared, but the words remained untouched. I unfolded the sheet and reread the poem. The lines didn't hit me in my room after the funeral. I had re-read the verses on my bed with emotional indifference, the shock of the funeral still weighing on me. But now, while sitting on a jagged tree branch with a throbbing pain in my left palm, the words hit me. It finally broke the dam. Salty tears streamed down my face. Lucy *was* alive again. She was *here*. It was her voice, forever locked on the page.

Take my hand and show me where the red daisies give new life
Where the scent of rebirth is still fresh in the air
Take my hand and lead me to the wondrous white expanse of the desert

Where the sand stretches beyond the limits of our eyes and where the stars shine brightly
Take my hand and show me the path to the blue ocean
Where there are no borders and no divisions
Take my hand, Davy

The wind howled and the rain poured. About a hundred yards to the west, the yellow caution tape around the RV could be seen. The broken fence was there, too, as well as the scarred oak where Mikey had found the remains of Mr. Hops's house. It was all still in the Vineyard. And so was I, crying with my face in my hands.

Chapter 35

JUSTICE

The investigation was at a standstill. All leads had turned into dead ends. Bruce Brown, their lead suspect because of the Molotov cocktails in the bed of his truck, adamantly denied involvement in the murder and had a solid alibi to back up his claim. It was a receipt. Since driving on three flat tires was not only dangerous but plain stupid, he'd called for a cab at Tommy's house. The wrinkled cab fare receipt read 1:36. That was the time he arrived at his house, and according to the statements given by Bruce's mother and father, that was where he had spent the rest of the night.

Ricky had spent the night in Tommy's room (this time with his pants on, I'm sure). Dan declared that Ricky had never left the room and Ricky stated the same about Dan. Since there wasn't evidence to the contrary, the police were left empty-handed. They were in the same boat with Tony and Mr. Smith. Both of them denied knowing anything about the incident and both claimed to have gone to bed before two in the morning. Detective Robbins had drilled Mr. Smith for a good six hours in a room the size of a jail cell, asking what a drunken adult had been doing wandering around the neighborhood with a bunch of kids. The answer was simple, Mr. Smith had told him, suppressing his notorious temper. He thought his house had been broken into and was only chasing after what he thought were the burglars. The fact that nothing was missing from his house didn't matter. Unlike Dan and the others—it turned out I was right about them not finding out about the vandalized pickup until later on—Mr. Smith had seen the damage to Bruce's truck and had reason to believe that something had been done to his house.

The case seemed hopeless. There were no fingerprints on the broken Molotov cocktail bottle, no prints around the RV, and no useable shoeprints in the mud that hadn't been washed away in the heavy rain. Six days after the murder, they were beginning to think the case would remain unsolved. The local media, which had been following the investigation closely, dubbed the murderer "Midnight Madman." The reality that the murder actually happened at four thirty in the morning was of no concern to the reporters. Midnight Madman made for better headlines than Four Thirty Joe. So Midnight Madman was still at large, and the situation seemed grim for Detective Robbins.

But the next day, four days after Lucy's funeral, the police got a huge break. One of the officers, a young man named Justin, was scanning the area, searching for more shoeprints, and accidentally stumbled across a shiny object embedded in the mud about twenty yards beyond the yellow police tape. At first, Justin thought it was a quarter. He bent over, dug it up, and then realized what he had on his hands was worth a lot more than twenty-five cents. He had found an ivory switchblade.

It didn't take long to find out to whom the weapon belonged. They then went to the owner's house, rang the doorbell, and showed him the evidence they had uncovered in the Vineyard. "I was wondering where that went," Tony told the police, a queer grin on his face.

"Strange coincidence, huh?" they replied. The weapon wasn't enough to convict him, and it wasn't even enough to make an arrest. All they had was an unlawful possession of a switchblade, a petty misdemeanor in New Mexico, but what they didn't have Tony provided himself. For reasons only God really knows, Loony spilled his evil secret. He might have been excited about what he had done. Perhaps he was even proud, and had wanted to share his glorious achievement with the world. Perhaps he thought he'd get caught eventually anyway and decided to end the game on his own terms. Or maybe it was his conscience that got to him—although I really doubted that one; in all the years I had known Tony, never once did he strike me as a man who spent his time worrying about what's morally right or wrong. Whatever the reason, Tony fessed up. He told them how he had taken the bottle from Bruce's truck when Bruce had left in the taxicab. He explained to Detective Robbins how he had made his walk to the Vineyard, cradling the lethal cocktail in his arms. He confessed how he had waited three hours by the ditch bridge, watching the RV in the fierce thunderstorm, with the rain pounding his head and the wind blasting his face. He admitted to deliberately lighting the Molotov and tossing inside the RV's back window. He told the police all of this with that same crazy smile, and when he was finished, they arrested him, read him his Miranda rights, and tossed him in the back of their squad car.

I heard the news on Channel 4's ten o'clock broadcast that same Sunday, and got the complete details over the next few weeks. Had I read the signs better, I would have realized it couldn't have been Ricky or Bruce, as I initially suspected. It went back to what was said before: Tony worked on an entirely different level than the other Jerks. You could see it behind that creepy smile and behind those lifeless, gray eyes. He was cold, calculating, and twisted.

The part of the story that really chilled my blood was that Tony waited for three hours before making his move on the RV. *Three hours.* That's one hundred and eighty minutes that he waited in that awful storm as the rain pelted his skin and the lightning lit up his pale face. He sat patiently like a phantom in the field, an apparition, contemplating the best way to carry out his sinister plan and deliver his sadistic message inside that bottle. While sitting in the field, he could have replayed the image of our pain and screams a thousand times before he actually carried it out. And then, an even scarier thought than that, after he delivered his liquid message, he might have watched as we burned inside that flaming trap, picturing us clawing at the door like the cat that had clawed at his hands.

Spill your guts like spaghetti.

So it was Anthony Sanders. Midnight Madman. Loony. It was him and him alone. He had meant to kill us all in that RV, and if he had the power, I absolutely believe he would have done so. But he only managed to get one, and now the District Attorney wanted to try sixteen-year-old Sanders as an adult for first-degree, premeditated murder. If convicted, something that looked highly likely given Tony's confession, Tony could face life imprisonment or even the death penalty, which was allowed in the State of New Mexico if the conditions met certain aggravating circumstances. Given the choice, I wasn't sure which one I wanted him to get. A horrible part of me wanted him to die the way Lucy had. I guess it goes back to that eye-for-an-eye business. He had taken a life, and as a result, had forfeited his. But there was another part of me that wanted to see him rot in prison. Capital punishment seemed like a quick escape, an easy ride out. Why should Tony get the benefit of avoiding a life behind bars when there were thousands of other prisoners that were slaving their time away, serving their sentence while sleeping on rock-hard bunks and eating miserable food. No, to me it seemed like a life sentence was much worse.

Whatever the verdict, there was a terrible reality to face. Lucy's smile was still gone. Her sharp green eyes, her soft, gentle voice, her silky brown hair—it was all a memory now. Whether or not Tony was in prison or executed would never change that fact. Lucy Graham, the Roosevelt graduate that had aced all of her classes, the student that was listed for fall enrollment at the Huckleberry Academy, the only Graham that had a solid shot at going to college and possibly further, was dead. Lucy had been stolen from us. And there was nothing that I nor anyone else could do to change it.

Chapter 36

A VISIT FROM TOMMY

The hours bled into days, and the days into weeks. More thunderstorms passed over Huckleberry, making up for all the days they had spent sightseeing in other cities. I spent most of my time locked inside my room. My concerned mother assigned me odd chores around the house in an effort to get me out: washing dishes, dusting for cobwebs in the attic, mopping and waxing floors. I obediently did my duties and when I was finished, I'd shuffle back upstairs and lock my door again. After four weeks, my mother was beginning to think there was something seriously wrong with me. "You need to get out get some sun, dear," my mother told me. "Why don't you call up your friends? I'm sure they'd like to play. Maybe you could go to the park." I told her I'd think about it. It wasn't a lie. I stared at the phone and seriously thought about dialing Tommy or Randy. But I could only manage to pick up the receiver and put it back in its cradle. I couldn't play with the Gang. It didn't feel right doing that without Lucy. Truth was, after her death nothing felt right anymore—the thought of playing poker in our fort, tossing a football in the park, or listening to Jason's dirty jokes. It all seemed pointless now.

Two days after my mother had tried to get me out, Tommy paid me a visit. I was in my room, reading a lame science fiction book about a Russian cosmonaut who falls in love with an alien on Mars. It was stupidly titled *The Space Bachelor* and why I was reading it was a question even Patty Ratty Pigtails couldn't answer.

"Davy?" my mother called from downstairs.

"Yeah, Ma?" I replied, looking up from the book.

"You've got a visitor."

"Okay, Ma."

I tossed the book on my bed and went downstairs. Tommy stood at the front door, clad in blue shorts, a red-and-green striped T-shirt and white Nike tennis shoes that looked like they had seen their share of miles.

"Hey, Davy."

"What's up, Tommy?"

"Man, we were bettin' you moved out of town. We've been calling you for weeks."

"Yeah? Well, I've been busy around the house."

"I thought you were dead or somethin'."

An awkward silence stood between us. Tommy swallowed in embarrassment. "Wow, I can't believe I just said that. Sorry, Davy, you know what I—"

"I know. It's okay."

I walked out the front door and sauntered with Tommy down our driveway. Scattered clouds passed over the sun like puffy cars on a sky highway, darkening and brightening our shadows.

"How you doin'?"

"Good," I said, feeling the warmth of our paved driveway seep into my soles.

"Did you hear what Randy got for his birthday?"

"Huh uh, what?"

"A friggin' new pinball table."

I stopped walking.

"Shut up."

"Swear my life on it. I saw it myself last week. It's awesome, Davy. I played it for hours." Tommy scratched his head, and a dry laugh escaped his throat. "Even got the high score."

"That's not hard," I snickered. "Randy sucks at pinball. Even Mikey could beat him."

We walked again and eventually came to a railroad tie at the end of our driveway. We took a seat and stared at a line of red ants crawling on the floor. Some had pieces of leaves clenched between their giant pinchers; some were carrying grains of sparkly sand. Tommy took a metal disk out of his pocket.

"They found this in the ashes."

He handed it to me and I stared at it as if he had given me a golden nugget. "I forgot I had brought it there."

"Mr. Phillips gave it to me when I went back see how was doing after that...that night."

I pressed the disk's brass button, which still had a layer of soot on it, and saw the needle inside, always pointing north.

"Thanks," I said, pocketing the compass.

"Mr. Phillips is working on the fence again. He's bought new rails and posts to replace the broken ones." I nodded at Tommy and looked at the ants again. It amazed me how many there were. I saw hundreds of them, each one working toward the collective goal of the hill, to nourish the queen. Each one knew their purpose in life, their path. Beautiful, clear instinct. "We're gonna help him, Davy," Tommy said at length, staring at me with dark, blue eyes. "Me, Mikey, Randy, and Jason. We want you with us."

I tossed a rock down our driveway and watched it skip over the pavement. "No thanks," I replied. "You guys can finish it yourselves."

"What the heck are you going to do?"

"Other things."

"What other things? Don't tell me you're busy around your house, because that's a sack of shit. I know it."

"I just don't want to go, okay?" I said, skipping another rock and standing up.

I started to walk away and Tommy grabbed my arm. I fought off his grip. He caught me again, and then we started wrestling. We fell to the floor and rolled like two logs on the warm pavement, grazing our knees and nicking our elbows. I had his arm pinned around his back and his neck locked between my forearm and bicep. Tommy squirmed out of the headlock and gave me one in return. His arm tightened under my chin and forced a crack that rippled down my spine to my tailbone. I kicked at his shins.

"Get off!" I screamed.

"Not until you stop kicking."

I kept at his shins until his grip became so tight that I could hardly breathe.

"All right, all right!" I shouted in anger.

Tommy kept his hold for a couple seconds longer, to make sure I *had* given up, and then released me. I grabbed my chafed neck and gasped for air.

"I'm sorry, but don't pull this on me, Davy." His forehead was wrinkled and his lips were white and thin and pursed together. "You can do it to your parents, but not me. I know what you're thinking. Don't you think we thought the same thing? You're asking 'Why does the fence matter?', right? Well it fuckin' matters, Davy. Not because we had to do it at one point, or because we wanted to do it. But because we *need* to. We gotta go back there to show them they can't beat us that way. We gotta show them we'll never be defeated like that. We never quit, Davy. That's not *our* way."

I stared at Tommy's penetrating gaze, then found myself bawling again. I felt foolish doing it in front of him, but I couldn't help myself. The dam I thought I had repaired had somehow sprung a leak.

"I miss her, Tommy," I cried. "I really, really miss her."

Tommy put his arm around me and lent me his shoulder. The clouds rolled overhead, and the summer breezes brushed against our cheeks. As the day inched forward, our shadows changed back and forth from black to light gray.

It was my turn to lean on someone else.

Chapter 37

MEN

I worked my way through the thick fog, following the raucous call of the black bird. Marble headstones brushed my feet as I drifted closer to the beckoning sound. Lightning forked overhead, webbing the night sky with brilliant, twisted bolts.

CAW!

"Lucy?" I called, searching the flashing darkness.

A hundred feathered wings beat around me, flying behind the misty blanket. I plowed my way forward with my arms outstretched and my face pointed toward the grassy ground. I had the terrifying fear a pale hand would shoot out of the green carpet and wrap its bony fingers around my ankle, a hand with splinters embedded in its fingernails after clawing through its wooden prison. Distraught, I yelled for Lucy again. A girlish laughter answered my cry.

CAW!

I followed the laughter and the bird's shrill voice, stumbling over the scattered headstones. My fingers searched the foggy air and eventually fell upon a solid box. The mist cleared and revealed the casket of Lucy Graham. The laughter returned—reverberating from inside the wooden coffin. It was deeper this time, more distant, as if echoing inside a sarcophagus. My heart thundered and my tongue curled in my mouth, much like a dog's tail curls between its legs when it's frightened. I heard another cry from inside. Not laughter, but a voice...a girl's voice. It was light, but audible.

"Davy? Is that you?"

Lightning lit up the sky and revealed a brass handle at the front of the casket. I felt my hand close around it. It was painfully cold, as if it were made of ice. I desperately wanted to release my grip, but a petrifying curiosity held me to the flashing tomb.

"Let me out, Davy. Please."

I slowly opened the front of the casket, inch by inch. I expected something to jump out at any moment. Something not quite like Lucy anymore. Something horrible. But when the lightning finally flashed again and exposed the inside, I only saw a black crow. It was standing at the bottom of the empty coffin, staring directly at me with dark, sticky eyes. I could read its thoughts. The score was now even between us.

CAW!

I awoke inside a dark and empty room. My alarm clock read 2:37 am. The wind howled outside my window, and a tall elm in our backyard cast a terrifying shadow of a bony hand on my wall. It swayed with the wind and looked like the hand of some giant witch waiting to lock me in her death grip and steal me away in the night. I hid underneath my covers. I soon realized, after slipping back asleep, that the crow nightmares were over. I would never dream of those feathered creatures again.

***

I met the Gang at the scarred oak early the next morning. The sky was still filled with scattered clouds, but the puddles on the pavement had evaporated and the mud in the Vineyard had hardened. I was the last to arrive at the tree. Tommy, Jason, Randy, and Mikey were beside the oak, breaking twigs and flicking small stones. I rode over the ditch bridge, feeling the boards creak under my heavy tires, rolled down the bumpy hill, and came to a slow stop in front of the others. They stood up and looked at me as if they hadn't seen me in years.

"Hey, Davy," Randy said, stuffing his hands in the seat of his short pockets. Everyone was clad in shorts, T-shirts, and sneakers.

"Hey, guys," I said, laying my bike next to theirs.

"I knew you'd show!" Mikey smiled. "Jason didn't believe me, but I knew it."

"I was just kiddin' ya, loco," Jason said, elbowing Mikey. "Of course he'd show."

Tommy smiled, threw his arm around my head and gave me a noogie. "Davy wouldn't skin out like that. Not if he knew what was good for him. We're buds, remember?"

I fought out of Tommy's grip and smiled back. "Yeah, well...are we going to work now or just pick our noses?"

All of us snickered at the thought. It was good to see the Gang again.

"Come on guys, we gotta get Mr. Phillips," Tommy said seriously, picking up a white box next to his bike.

"What's inside that?" I asked.

"You'll see," Jason replied. "It's a little present we picked up yesterday for Mr. Phillips. Mikey bought it for us."

"Mikey?" I asked, shocked.

Mikey shrugged his shoulders. "I had to buy it for him when I saw it. I think Clint Eastwood would have liked it."

"What is it?"

The Gang showed me and I smiled. We then made our way toward the fence. Our cheerful mood changed as we saw the remains of the broken rails and posts. The destruction was just as we had left it almost a month before: two uprooted posts; a broken radio smashed into a thousand plastic pieces; an unplugged, lonely orange extension cord looking for its lost friend; and a vertical, L-shaped rail. We walked to the center of the devastation. The remains of the King Roller had been towed away and the yellow caution tape had been removed, but we could still see the ash and feel the flames of that terrible night. We slowly stepped past the scene with heavy hearts and weak eyes. Mr. Phillips had tried to return the field to its normal condition, removing the RV and the burnt furniture, but our memory remained fresh. We would always return to that fiery van, with sparks spitting from its roof and thick smoke seeping from its windows.

Seconds later, we rang the front door-bell.

"Think he's up yet?" Mikey asked.

Tommy nodded. "He should be. He's always up at the break of dawn."

We patiently waited as Mr. Phillips shuffled to the door. He was awake, but was still dressed in white long johns and sandals.

"Well...hello," Mr. Phillips said, a bit shocked. "I wasn't expecting to see y'all."

"We should have called," Tommy said. "But we thought it might be better if we saw you in person." Mr. Phillips furrowed his brow. He scratched his head, which was covered with tangled black hair.

"In person for what?"

Tommy glanced at us. He didn't look like he wanted to be the one to talk about it, but none of us were brave enough to volunteer for the job. "You saved our lives, sir. And you tried what you could for..." Tommy checked himself. "We owe you everything for that. And we owe you our deepest apology for causing what happened. Had we stayed put, Tony might not have started that fire. And maybe—"

"That's bull. You're no more responsible than I am."

This time it was Tommy that was surprised. "How could *you* be responsible?"

"Because I could have stopped you kids from going. I knew about you hens sneaking out."

"You knew?" Mikey asked, his magnified eyes looking like melons.

"Sure. I heard you leaving the camper. Y'all were pretty noisy, I might add. You could have woken a man in a coma. I thought about stopping you, but I got to thinking about when I was your age. I know you've been dealing with those older boys all school year. I've seen ya show up with bruises and scrapes and cuts, and I know it wasn't from fallin' off your bike or tumbling from a tree house. Those older boys have been picking on you for a very long time. And there comes a time when you get fed up with the bullshit. I had an older brother, and he was pretty mean to me. Hittin' and callin' me names. He wasn't as bad as these fellas, but I understood why y'all wanted to get them back. To tell the truth, I would've done the same. So I let you kids go. I had no idea that it would lead to what eventually happened." Mr. Phillips stared at his callused hands. A group of sparrows chirped playfully in a tree behind us. "Maybe if I had stopped you, things would be different. Maybe nothing would've changed. I don't know the answer, but I do know that y'all don't owe me an apology. You hear me?"

We said we did.

"We also came here to work on the fence," Mikey added.

Mr. Phillips's head shot back. "You boys are far done with that project. You've done plenty of work on it. You don't need to continue now."

"We have to, sir," Randy jumped in. "We must finish it. It's the only way to make things right again, if that's possible."

Mr. Phillips glanced at Randy, and then thought for a long moment. He finally nodded. "I'll have to get dressed, of course. Can you boys give me ten minutes?"

We said that we could. Just before Mr. Phillips shut the front door, Tommy stuck his foot in the doorframe.

"Wait! We forgot to give you something." Tommy showed him the box.

"What's this?"

"Consider it a present. We know you lost yours in the fire."

He frowned in curiosity, opened the box, and smiled at the beautiful straw hat inside. He put it on and gave us a smile that ran from ear to ear.

"Perfect fit. I like it."

"We got lucky. We weren't sure about your size, so we just got the largest hat we saw."

"Thank you, I'll make sure I bring it out with me."

He closed the door and we made our way back to the fence. The eastern sun had risen above the Hillerman Mountains and played behind a patch of white clouds. The air was humid and sticky and the wind was a steady, comforting breeze. We gathered around the broken rails and posts, and stared at the work ahead of us.

To see if we could make things right again.

***

Mr. Phillips had bought eight new rails and two posts. Only two of the rails that had been knocked out of the fence were still salvageable. He had all the materials neatly piled in their respective places. We had twenty-five rails to hammer and two posts to cement. It was a lot of work to finish in one day. It would have taken us weeks if we were just working afternoons, but we did have *all day* and we were determined to complete the job.

Mikey, Randy, and Mr. Phillips took the posts; Tommy, Jason, and I tackled the hammering. We attacked the fence like possessed men. We stripped, hammered, and cemented as fast as our hands could move. The sounds of our work echoed through the Vineyard, and the sweat from our foreheads poured like warm engine oil. The humidity soon hit us and we were forced to lose our shirts. The sun, higher now, beamed through the passing clouds and transformed our backs into a rosy, reddish hue that was certain to remind us that night of what we had been doing during the day.

"Steady, now," Tommy yelled at Jason.

"I got it," Jason replied. "You got it, Davy?"

"Yeah," I said.

Tommy hammered the left end of the rail while I took the right end. Jason, grimacing from the weight of the board on his shoulder, kept our alignment balanced from the middle of the two posts. After a dozen sharp cracks, we set the rail to the posts.

"Good on this end," Tommy said. "How 'bout yours?"

"Ain't moving anywhere," I replied, shaking the board with my hand.

Tommy spit, nodded, and grabbed the next rail. A whistle pierced the air.

"Time for lunch!" Mr. Phillips yelled. The two posts he, Randy, and Mikey were working on were now cemented in the same spots that they had been before the Jerks uprooted them. "I'll bring some sandwiches and drinks. Meet me by the tree."

He pointed to the oak and we nodded. We marched to the spot, our legs feeling ten times their weight. A refreshing, yet short gust of wind flew past us. Beyond the oak's shade, a good twenty yards to the east, a ten-foot dirt devil twisted in the open field. Dead leaves, newspapers, and other assorted trash that had happened to find their way to the Vineyard spiraled around the mini-twister's funnel. It eventually spun itself out and dissolved away, scattering the trapped items to the dirt floor.

"Man I'm tired," Jason said, collapsing by the tree.

"Same here," Randy added, "and hungry, too."

We gathered around Jason and felt our legs give out. We dropped to the ground in four hard thuds.

"Fifteen rails," I said, looking at the clouds inch across the blue dome, shaking my head at the thought. "I've never hammered so many nails in my life."

"Me neither," Tommy said, looking at the blisters in his hand. He had a nasty one in the middle of his right palm. It was a bubble an inch tall and two inches wide. "I don't know if I can stand another hour of it."

"Same here," Randy said. "I thought we could do it all today, but I'm not so sure now. It's more work than I thought it was."

"I thought we'd finish today, too," I said glumly. "I just wanted to get it finally done, you know?"

The Gang nodded solemnly. Mr. Phillips returned with the food minutes later. He had made us each a peanut butter and jelly sandwich and had brought out a cooler of Cokes.

"You're the best," Mikey said.

"It's the least I could do for this fine hat you boys gave me," Mr. Phillips said, winking at us.

We inhaled the sandwiches, guzzled the drinks, and chomped on a giant-sized bag of potato chips that had been stashed inside the cooler. Unlike our lunches at Roosevelt, we ate in silence. There were no disgusting jokes, or lame ghost stories, or bets about which team would win the World Series. Although we didn't know it at the time, Lucy's death had hardened us. Tony had not only stolen Lucy's life; he had also taken our innocence. Our perspective of the Vineyard and

Huckleberry would be forever altered because of it. For the first time in our young lives, we felt vulnerable and mortal.

"Crap," Mikey said, breaking the silence as a gust of wind snatched our near-empty potato bag out and blew it toward the ditch. Mikey sprinted after it. He eventually caught the bag at the foot of the ditch embankment. He bent over and stared at the flowing water.

"What's he doing?" Tommy asked.

We shrugged our shoulders. Heck if we knew.

"GUYS! GUYS!" Mikey screamed, jumping up and down as if he had spiders on his legs.

"What is it?" Mr. Phillips asked, alarmed.

"Come over here! Look!"

We ran over, ignoring the painful protests from our sore thighs and hamstrings. We stopped beside him and stared at the water.

"No way!" Tommy said.

"I'll be damned!" Mr. Phillips added.

I'd given him a one percent chance of surviving. *Only one percent.* Had I better understood the spirit of that little toad, I would have placed the odds in his favor. It was old Mr. Hops, in all his glory and magnificence. No, he hadn't died. Far from it. The little brown amphibian had found himself a missus: another American toad, by God. And there, floating in the water like miniature buoys, were eggs—hundreds of them...perhaps thousands. The classy toad had not met a dark end as I had once thought, but rather, had multiplied beyond my imagination. A whole new generation was waiting to see the new land to which their father had brought them.

"The sapo!" Jason said, his metal teeth practically jumping out of his mouth. "It's really him! I can tell from the markings on his back!"

And then, for the first time and only time, Jason grabbed Mikey and danced. They sang and jumped and laughed. We laughed with them and shook our heads at the wondrous find.

"Mr. Hops and family..." Mr. Phillips said, removing the new straw hat from his head. "I don't believe it."

***

Mr. Hops gave us the lift we needed. We returned to the fence, took up our hammers, and pounded away in the afternoon. Mikey and Randy joined us with the rails, while Mr. Phillips painted over the defaced post with a can of leftover paint he had found inside his house. We fixed rail after rail, ignoring the blisters in our hands and the throbbing in our muscles.

"Got it?" Tommy yelled out.

"You bet," I said, making a circle with my forefinger and thumb.

The scattered clouds rolled over Huckleberry. The wind blew, then settled, then started again. The cracks of our hammers filled the air. Five rails became four. Four turned into three. Three into two. Mr. Phillips finished painting the post. The swastika was gone and so was the nasty message the Jerks had left behind.

"I'll be right back," Mr. Phillips told us, running toward his house.

Jason hammered the left end of the second-to-last rail and Mikey took the right end. Once it was finished, Randy grabbed the last rail.

"Wait," Tommy said, putting his hand on Randy's shoulder. "Wait until he gets back."

"Oh...yeah," Randy said.

Mr. Phillips returned to the area, carrying a long stick in his right hand. We soon realized it was an American flag, and he unrolled it in front of us, showing us its bright colors.

"It's a little early for July 4th, but so what, right?"

We smiled at him and told him we were on the last one.

"Everyone should get to hammer this rail," Tommy said.

We agreed and took turns. Mikey, Randy, and Jason hammered the left side; Tommy, Mr. Phillips, and I fixed the right end.

"I guess that's it," Mr. Phillips said, taking the last nail.

"Hold on!" I said, pointing behind us. "We've gotta see it from the ditch hill."

I ran toward the ditch bridge, and the others followed me. Mr. Phillips stayed behind; he had one last thing to add to the defaced post.

I reached the hill, excited and winded. Tommy arrived next, then Jason, Randy, and Mikey, respectively. We looked down at our work. It lay before us in a beautiful half square—a mighty three-rail ranch fence...sixty-one posts and one hundred and eighty rails. Some might say it was just a stupid bunch of nailed boards, but to us it was something more. A lot more. In our minds that simple fence might as well have been Old Faithful at Yellowstone. It was something so beautiful that we were afraid to blink in fear that it would disappear when we reopened our eyelids. We were scared that it wasn't real, that it was just an image like the picture we had envisioned while looking at Mr. Phillips's blueprints for the first time. But it *was* real. We *did* finish.

The clouds parted and a surprising golden ray of sun spilt over the Vineyard. Mr. Phillips waved the American flag at us, then hammered it to its post.

"She would have loved it," I said to my friends.

"She does," Tommy corrected me, putting his arm around my left shoulder. "She does, Davy."

I smiled and tossed my arm around Tommy's right side and Mikey threw his around my right shoulder. Randy locked his around Tommy's left side; Jason joined in with his arm on Randy's shoulder.

And there we stood...just the guys now...arm in arm, forming our own human fence. We stood proudly and triumphantly, and stared at the work we had created.

Men of the American Vineyard.

Chapter 38

A Return Home

JOURNAL DATE: 8/31/01

Nick and I drove into Huckleberry this morning. After spending the night in Flagstaff, we took the I-40 highway west through Gallup and Grants and into Albuquerque. We then exited I-25 and drove south for roughly an hour. We hit the *Welcome to Huckleberry* sign at a quarter till nine. It was the first time I had driven into my hometown from California, and there was a surreal feeling of déjà vu as I saw the old landmarks from my youth: the Hillerman Mountains; the four-lane Kyser overpass; the town square statue of Mark Twain's mischievous Huckleberry Finn, standing in overalls rolled up to his knees; and the extinct western volcanoes. It seemed like I had made the trip before...not during the years when I lived here, but recently, maybe last week, or the week before it. It seemed smaller, too. When I was thirteen, everything had been magnified through the eyes of a child. Back then I had no comparisons to make between larger cities like Los Angeles, San Francisco, or Chicago.

So we drove into town, and now, with a pen in one hand and the remains of this journal in the other, I'm back in the Vineyard, sitting at the scarred oak. Nick is playing in the ditch behind me, looking for crawdads and grasshoppers in the tall embankment grass. It's late afternoon. I'm trying to finish out the rest of this journal, but I'm feeling the aftereffects of visiting Lewis. It's worth noting that my brother is doing well, and so are his wife and three-year-old daughter. He's still working as a cash register clerk at the Hearty Grocery Store, and his wife, Patricia, who also has Down's syndrome, is kept busy as a part-time prep cook at a small Mexican restaurant named Fajitas 'n Spices. Their healthy blonde-haired daughter, Jennifer, who isn't even in preschool yet, is already doing first grade-math and spelling out her alphabet. Nick and I played with her for two hours this morning, and it's because of her, and her energetic little legs, that I feel like I've hiked Mt. Everest.

It was good to see Lewis and his family. It turned out my mother was right after all. He *could* support himself. All that attention she gave him finally paid off. It still saddens me to think she never got the chance to see it.

Both my parents perished in a car accident six years ago. It happened at an intersection in a little city named Espanola. They were driving in my father's Suburban for a three-day hiking trip. They stopped at a red light, waited until it turned green, then accelerated. Had they looked to their right, they would have seen the '86 Mustang barreling toward the intersection with no intention of stopping. But they didn't do that, and before they moved ten feet, that Mustang slammed into them doing close to seventy. Seth and Nancy Blake died instantly. The drunk driver in the other car was rushed off to a hospital, where he eventually succumbed to severe brain damage. Ironically, my father had stayed off the bottle for fourteen years only to be killed by a drunk.

That was two years before Lewis' engagement, and I received that dreaded phone call from Uncle Larry, the same uncle that enjoyed making his annual ski trips to New Mexico. I was in a heated argument with my wife about whether we would go to her friend's wedding for the weekend or make a trip to Yosemite National Park as I had been planning for the past three weeks. It was a dumb quarrel, and we soon realized how foolish it was when I picked up that phone and heard Larry's mournful voice more than a thousand miles away. I listened, dropped the receiver to the ground, went outside, and cried. Two days later, I flew to Huckleberry to arrange their funeral. I even visited the intersection during that same trip—why I did this exactly I'm still not sure...maybe just morbid curiosity. All that remained of the accident was a few jagged tire marks on the pavement and some shards of glass strewn on the shoulder. The lights still changed from red to green and the stream of cars still flowed up and down the street. Business as usual. For the outside world, nothing had changed.

And that was the last time I was in Huckleberry. I didn't stay long. I wasn't in the mood and was busy at the law firm. Lewis already had the job at the grocery store at that point, and he was able to afford a house with the insurance money from the accident. I helped him with the paperwork and negotiated the best mortgage loan I could bargain. It was then that he, Lewis, my brother and pal, became independent after my mother's death. The same tragic irony that had hit my father had also struck my mother.

But that was six years ago, and the family wounds have healed since then. Not entirely, perhaps. There are scars, but they aren't ugly enough to bite. Huckleberry is now what it was when I grew up here: beautiful and serene. It's that *peaceful easy feeling* that the Eagles so brilliantly sing about in their music. It's the feeling that I'm home again.

I must admit home has changed. The house I grew up in is no longer there. A new, more modern structure has taken its place. The same is true for our neighbors' houses. Some, like ours, have been replaced entirely; others have undergone renovations—a new room here, a two-car garage there.

Even the Vineyard is different. New classrooms have been added around Grant Elementary School, and a sturdy, metal bridge with handrails has knocked out the shabby wooden boards that we had once braved on our bikes while riding over the ditch. While the open fields of the Vineyard are still there, and so is the scarred oak I'm currently using as a backrest, Mr. Phillips's house is no longer the place I once knew. In the spring of 1987, Mr. Phillips remarried and moved to Roswell. The new owner of the house was a retired businessman from Dallas, Texas. His name was Samuel Bogs, and he had ambitions to start his own chili farm and sell the crops to the local Mexican restaurants. That dream never materialized. He lost his money in a bunch of shady stocks his broker had claimed would "shoot through the roof." The stocks tanked, and the only thing that probably shot through the roof was Sammy's temper when he heard the news. He abandoned the house a year later, and the place has remained deserted ever since. It now has broken windows, missing shingles on the roof, and graffiti on the northern wall.

And what about my friends? The Gang? I'll tell what I can, which sadly enough is surprisingly little.

For the first two years of high school, I remained good friends with Jason and Randy. We hung out after classes in the school parking lot and went to all the critical football games where we'd drool over the cheerleaders we wanted to sleep with. Things fell apart during junior year. Jason made the varsity soccer team and got deeply involved with a girl who was a little more than he could handle—one of those damned cheerleaders. I barely cut the list for the baseball team and made my own friends while traveling with the players around Huckleberry. I was a poor hitter—probably because of all that time I spent building rather than practicing in the Vineyard—and a mediocre catcher. Randy found his clique with the Student Government. We soon went to those critical games without each other, and the school parking lot became a social gathering spot to talk to our new friends. Once we graduated, our friendship became even more distant.

Jason went to New Mexico State University and graduated with a degree in International Business Administration. He eventually took over his dad's position at the shipping company and married a slender Spanish woman named Rebecca Villanueva. Last I heard, he had moved with the company to Arizona and was raising three daughters.

Randy Sachs took a year off after high school and worked at odd jobs around Huckleberry—waiting tables, bar backing, book-keeping. He called me during the summer while I was back in town after completing my first year at UCLA. We grabbed a bite together at Dave's Ice Cream Palace, and talked and laughed about the old times at Roosevelt and the Vineyard. He told me how much he had hated the jobs during the last twelve months and how he had figured it best to get a college degree so he wouldn't spend the rest of his days asking customers whether they wanted hot or mild sauce on their burritos. "Hungry people can be meanies," he told me. And that's exactly how he said it, too: "meanies", not "assholes" or "buttheads." I guess that honorable, non-swearing Boy Scout will never be knocked out of him. Randy also told me during that summer visit that he had been accepted to the University of New Mexico and thought about pursuing a major in math. That was the last time I saw him. He married, divorced, and married again. He has one kid with the first wife and two with the other. I heard from many different sources that he had moved to Colorado and was teaching in Denver. Whether or not his second marriage lasted is unknown to me.

I know less about Mikey and Tommy. Since they went to a different high school, I never saw them around, and thus our friendship weakened. I do know that Mikey McNeil dropped out in his junior year (another victim of Gregory's notorious reputation) and joined the army. He put in his four years of service and signed on for another four. It's only guesswork beyond that. I don't know if he's married or has kids.

Tommy Smith graduated from Gregory High with honors and went to Tulane University on a full-ride baseball scholarship where he finished with a double major in finance and economics. He then moved to New York and landed a financial analyst job with Goldman Sachs. He quickly made his way up the company ladder and was soon managing large hedge funds. Tommy, always a natural leader, had decided that the tire business in Huckleberry just didn't suit him. I'm not sure if he's still living in New York, but he *did* eventually marry. He has one son and as far as I know hasn't laid one finger on the kid.

I still think about the days when Tommy and I used to shoot in the Vineyard. It happens while buying the groceries for my wife and son, or while waiting in a traffic jam, or while sitting in a dentist's chair, listening to that bone-chilling drill. I sometimes wish I could give him a call and ask if he could set up a poker game for the Gang at the fort. We could maybe play two-hand-touch in Randy's backyard, or grab our mitts and Jason's Hardhitters bat and slug out that baseball game against Kevin's team we never got to play. Maybe we could eat lunch at our old table at Roosevelt—pass the time together while swapping jokes about Pinner and horror tales about Coach Barr.

It happens at odd times...

And what about the Jerks? Unlike Tommy, Dan ended up working next to his father at the tire factory. Mr. Smith eventually passed away from a stroke inside his house, and a year after his death, in the fall of 1986, the business flopped belly-up. Unemployment hit Dan hard. He became a regular at the Angels and Devils bar, got too drunk one night and knocked up some stripper. He ended up marrying the girl in a small church about a mile from our neighborhood. She filed for divorce eight years later when she caught him threatening their five-year-old kid with a fire poker. He now lives with his mother.

I know literally nothing about Ricky Adams except that he worked two years as a used car salesman in a dealership named Jackie's Autos. I had heard a rumor that he had spent time in the slammer in New Mexico and Colorado for armed robbery, but those rumors have never been confirmed.

Unlike the others, Bruce Brown actually made something of his life. I always thought Bruce was as dumb as a turd (you callin' me stupid, ass munch?), but I guess he had a few more marbles than Dan or Ricky because he graduated from high school and college, and then from Pepperdine University, where he obtained his MBA. He secured a job with a large financial firm and bought a house in Orange County with a pretty little wife that is ten years his junior—whether or not she knows about Bruce's fling with Ricky is something I've asked myself a few times. It freaks me out to think he only lives two hours from me in California, and I sometimes wonder if we would even notice each other if we happened to cross paths in a shopping mall or in a movie line. And what exactly would we say to each other if we did recognize our older selves? *Hey, are you—? What's going on? Got a family?* Simply thinking about it is enough to make my skin crawl.

Speaking of the disturbing, Anthony Sanders just celebrated his 19-year anniversary at the New Mexico State Penitentiary. He was tried as an adult, convicted of first-degree murder, and sentenced to life with the possibility of parole in 2032. It's currently 2001, which makes Tony thirty-five now—he went in when he was sixteen—and he'll be sixty-six when he finally gets out. I suppose the prospect of his release during my lifetime should petrify me, as I'm sure it frightens many others, but I'm really not that scared by it. Fifty years is a long, long time. I seriously doubt old Loony will have the mental stamina or the physical strength to carry out another murder when they unlock his steel door. And anyway, I'm not sure Tony's going to get a get-out-of-jail-free card when he serves his fifty years. If he's anything like he was when he went in, they'd sooner let old Loony sit out that life sentence than release him on the streets.

So...that's all I know about the kids from Huckleberry. It's pathetically limited, I'm afraid. I should have kept better track of the Gang, and I regret not doing so, but what can I say? Woulda-coulda-shoulda. I've got a long list of regrets and I could spend the next five pages talking about them, but I'm dead tired and it's getting close to Nick's bedtime. We've got a lot more to do on this vacation.

The afternoon sun is now low on the western horizon and I can feel the cool September breezes setting in. I can tell it's going to be a chilly autumn and a bitter winter. The dark seasons will pass, though. It's a part of change, that's all. When I first walked across the metal bridge, I half expected one of Mr. Hops's great, great grandkids to jump out and greet me—or scare the life out of me like Mr. Hops would have done. I searched the water, but those sapos, much like everyone else, have moved on. I guess the only thing that hasn't changed around here is that fence we built. It's crazy, but that thing looks exactly the same as it did when we first constructed it. There's not a single trace of wear on it—the woodgrain is unblemished and the rails and posts are still in perfect form. And the

American flag Mr. Phillips attached is in exactly the same spot. Sure, its edges are frayed and the stick that holds it sags more than it used to, but its colors are just as bright. And so is the white paint that lies beneath it. The initials are still there—*TS, DB, MM, JS, RS, BP*—and the dedication remains untarnished: *In united memory of Lady Lucy. Your light shines on.*

It continues to shine on, too. That horrible fire that took her life could never snuff out her spirit. What men like Tony don't understand is that it's what you create, not destroy. I once said that Lucy had the ability to take me to her own little island, a welcoming paradise with no borders or divisions where her light stood out above the rest. She created that place. And after all these years, I still believe in it. Maybe I'm foolish, but I believe she's still around, in some form. I believe in those golden streets she told me about. I like to think they are wider than the Mississippi and more brilliant than the sunsets that set on the ocean outside my San Diego home. And those eternal towers of pearl that comprise the gate? Yeah...I believe in them, too. I like to think they're taller than I ever imagined them, scraping the heavens like pillars supporting a vast and timeless kingdom. I like to think that when you stand next to those white towers, their height and stunning beauty make you feel an overwhelming sense of the triumphant creativity that has taken form, creativity that makes you buckle at the knees and stare in reverence.

The geese are back now, flying in a large V, heading south for another long winter. I can hear their mesmerizing chants over the Vineyard. I can see them soaring in the same blue sky my father once showed me many years ago.

Soaring.

Soaring far, far above.

In Memory

of

David Christian Preston

~

1977-2005

Acknowledgements

A SPECIAL THANKS TO:

Ellie Kay Bockert Augsburger, my cover designer and long-time publishing friend. Thank you for your talent, advice, and generosity.

Carl Augsburger, my editor. Thank you for catching my errors and inconsistencies. You do what I cannot.

My family and friends from New Mexico, California, and New York, especially Mom, Dad, Conner, Sonaleena, Steven, and Alyssa. Thank you for your suggestions, love, and support through the years. I am blessed to have you in my life.

My readers, including those who reviewed this novel during its long prepublication phase. You keep my books alive and inspire me to write. I hope my stories always find a place in your heart.

www.ingramcontent.com/pod-product-compliance
Lightning Source LLC
Chambersburg PA
CBHW021832010726
47493CB00005B/1364
* 9 7 8 0 6 9 2 8 4 5 8 4 4 *